PRAISE FOR THE NOVELS OF

Maya Banks

"[Maya Banks's books] are always full of emotional situations, lovable characters and kick-butt story lines that will leave you desperate for more." —*Romance Junkies*

"Maya Banks blew us away with the erotic *Colters' Woman*. Now comes this scintillating new anthology with three connected novellas and one sexy twist. Nice setup." —*Rendezvous*

"Definitely a recommended read . . . filled with friendship, passion and, most of all, a love that grows beyond just being friends." —*Fallen Angel Reviews*

"Grabbed me from page one and refused to let go until I read the last word . . . When a book still affects me hours after reading it, I can't help but joyfully recommend it!" —*JoyfullyReviewed.com*

"I guarantee I will reread this book many times over and will derive as much pleasure as I did in the first reading each and every subsequent time." —*Novelspot*

"An excellent read that I simply did not put down . . . a fantastic adventure . . . covers all the emotional ranges." —*The Road to Romance*

"This is one of the best books I have ever read and I will be reading it over and over again. I hope Ms. Banks will continue to write intense story lines with strong men and determined women for a long time."   —Erotic-Escapades

"Totally intoxicating, *For Her Pleasure* is one of those reads that you won't be forgetting anytime soon."   —*The Road to Romance*

"I did really enjoy this wonderful and loving story about a woman's quest for love and how she finds it in her home and with the two men who make her complete."   —*Romance Reviews Today*

"This author's accomplishments in the writing arena grow with every new release, and this reviewer never ceases to be impressed with Ms. Banks's imagination and skill."   —*CK²S Kwips and Kritiques*

"I am continually amazed at the depth of emotions Maya Banks pours into her books . . . The scenes of passion in the story are spellbinding and erotic."   —*TwoLips Reviews*

"I look forward to whatever this amazing author has in store for us next. She never disappoints and is a must have for all fans of the erotic romance genre."   —*Sensual*

be with me

MAYA BANKS

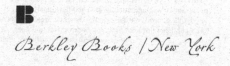

Berkley Books / New York

THE BERKLEY PUBLISHING GROUP
Published by the Penguin Group
Penguin Group (USA) Inc.
375 Hudson Street, New York, New York 10014, USA

USA | Canada | UK | Ireland | Australia | New Zealand | India | South Africa | China

Penguin Books Ltd., Registered Offices: 80 Strand, London WC2R 0RL, England
For more information about the Penguin Group, visit penguin.com.

This book is an original publication of The Berkley Publishing Group.

Library of Congress Cataloging-in-Publication Data

Banks, Maya.
Be with me / Maya Banks.—1st ed.
p.   cm.
ISBN 978-0-425-22404-5 (trade pbk.)
1. Policewomen—Fiction.   2. Group sex—Fiction.   I. Title.
PS3602.A643B3   2008
813'.6—dc22
2008025440

PUBLISHING HISTORY
Heat trade paperback edition / November 2008
Berkley trade paperback edition / March 2013

PRINTED IN THE UNITED STATES OF AMERICA

20   19   18   17   16   15   14   13   12

Cover design by Rita Frangie.
Cover photo by Cindy Xiao/Shutterstock Images.
Text design by Kristin del Rosario.

To Jennifer M: You were the impetus for this book in so many ways. Thanks for everything!

To the Writeminded Readers Group: You guys are the best. Truly the best readers in the world.

To every reader who has ever taken the time to e-mail me after reading one of my books: I appreciate it more than I can ever say.

To Amy, Steph, Larissa and Jaci: This wouldn't be nearly as much fun without you ladies.

CHAPTER I

*R*egina pulled her police cruiser to a halt outside the dilapidated old farmhouse and radioed her twenty. The house was draped in darkness despite someone reporting lights in the abandoned place. Her gaze swept the area, but she detected no movement.

She opened the door and stepped into the night. An uneasy sensation gripped her stomach, and not questioning her instincts, she requested backup. She stood in the open door, one hand resting on the top of the car, the other resting on the stock of her gun. Jeremy was just five minutes away and was already en route to her location.

A high-pitched scream shattered the stillness. Regina grabbed her weapon and broke into a run. She stopped at the front door, gun held high, and pressed her ear to the wood, straining to hear what she could. Only the buzz of locusts and the cacophony of tree frogs echoed through the night.

Gritting her teeth, she stepped back, gripped the stock in one hand and threw open the door with her other.

She swept the room with her pistol but saw no sign of the woman who had screamed. Her heart racing, she slid along the wall, her ears and eyes straining for noise, movement.

She almost tripped over the body.

Keeping her gaze up, she slowly knelt, reaching down with her left hand to feel for a pulse. The body was still warm, but there was no pulse. Her hand came away sticky with blood. Son of a bitch. She had moved her hand to her radio to call it in when she sensed another presence. Before she could react, her head exploded in pain.

Her gun went flying in one direction, and she sailed in the other. She landed in a heap several feet away, sucking air into her bruised lungs like a fish out of water. Holy hell, what had hit her?

She scrambled to her knees and lunged for her gun. A large boot connected with her jaw, and she did a complete roll in the air, landing again on her side.

Fighting unconsciousness, she shook out the cobwebs and lashed out with her foot. She heard a soft grunt and knew she'd connected with his kneecap.

Fire swept over her scalp when a beefy hand grabbed her hair and yanked her up. Fingers wrapped around her left wrist and twisted cruelly. She cried out and once again found herself flying through the air. She hit the wall and slid down like a deflated balloon.

Where the fuck are you, Jeremy?

Another blow to her head made the world go hazy around her. She opened her eyes to see the blurred face of a man leering close. His hand closed around her neck, squeezing slowly, drawing out the moment of her death.

"I've been waiting for you, Reggie love. It's time to make him pay."

The voice sounded like a hiss in her ear. Sinister. Full of dark promise.

"Make who pay?" she croaked.

He laughed softly, and spots filled her vision. In the distance she heard a car. The fingers tightened around her neck. He was too late. Jeremy hadn't gotten there in time. Goddamn it, she didn't want to die.

Drawing on the short adrenaline burst, she jabbed her fingers into her attacker's eyes and rammed her knee into his balls. He grunted, and his hold loosened just as she heard Jeremy's shout.

Suddenly she was free, but she was fighting to remain conscious. She slumped to the floor. A moment later, Jeremy was over her, shouting into his radio and running his hands over her body all at the same time.

"Regina, damn it, don't you dare die on me."

"Get him," she rasped. "Out the back. He went out the back."

"I'm not leaving you," he said grimly.

"Don't let him fucking get away. I'm okay. He killed her. Go get him."

Jeremy swore and got to his feet. She heard the pounding of his footsteps as he ran out the back door, and she lay there, fear, relief and pain rushing through her veins.

Soon, the pain took over, and the room further dimmed around her, causing her a moment of panic. She fought, but couldn't manage to keep the veil of darkness from falling.

This shit wasn't supposed to happen in her pissant town, damn it.

Cam Douglas studied the building plans in front of him with the niggling feeling that something was off. He frowned in irritation as the television grew louder, and Sawyer and Hutch gave a whoop when Houston scored.

He dropped his pencil and glared at his two partners. "Don't you have TVs in your offices? Is there a reason you're watching the game in mine when I'm trying to work?"

Neither paid much attention. They were glued to the game. Cam cleared his throat. Hutch held up a placating hand.

"You have the flat screen. Looks much better in hi-def too."

Cam shook his head. "Does the word *deadline* have any meaning? If I don't get these plans completed by tomorrow, we're going to lose this deal."

Sawyer turned around with a frown. "They giving you a problem, Cam?" He walked toward the desk then leaned over Cam's shoulder. "Looks okay to me."

Cam shook his head. "Something's off. It just doesn't look right."

Hutch sidled over, a Coke in his hand, and Cam stared pointedly at it. He remembered all too well what had happened the last time Hutch got close to his desk with a drink. Hutch ignored him and concentrated on the house plans.

"It's the windows in front," Hutch said. He paused and took a long swallow from the can. Then he pointed to the row of windows on the left side of the front door. Cam's gaze followed Hutch's finger, and even before Hutch spoke, Cam saw what he was getting at.

"The symmetry is off. You've got the left side loaded down with nothing to balance the right. Looks lopsided."

"Freak," Sawyer muttered.

"The freak is right," Cam allowed with a sigh. "Goddamn, Hutch. How do you do that every time? I sit here poring over this shit and then you come along and nail it in two seconds."

Hutch shrugged. "I don't obsess like you do?"

"Someone has to," Cam pointed out.

Sawyer rolled his eyes. "Don't get Mr. Perfectionist started, Hutch. He'll never shut the fuck up."

Cam had opened his mouth to retort when the phone rang. He flipped his middle finger at Sawyer as he picked up the receiver.

"Douglas," he said shortly.

"Cam, is that you?"

Birdie's voice bled over the line. It sounded shaky. Not at all like her usual perky self.

"Yes, Birdie, it's me. What's wrong?" he demanded as he waved frantically at the others to turn down the TV so he could hear.

Sawyer and Hutch snapped to attention when he said Birdie's name. Hutch aimed the remote at the TV to turn it off, and Cam punched the speaker button so they could all hear.

"It's Regina," Birdie said. "She's been hurt."

"Reggie? What's wrong with Reggie?" Sawyer broke in.

There was a pause. "Sawyer? Is Hutch there too?"

"Yes, Birdie. We're all here. Cam has you on speakerphone," Hutch replied. "Tell us about Reggie. What's happened?"

"She's in the hospital," Birdie said in a tired voice. "That's where I am now."

Fear flooded through Cam. He glanced up at Sawyer and Hutch to see a similar reaction in them. "We'll be there in an hour," he said shortly. "Hang tight. We're on our way."

"You be careful, young man," Birdie said, her voice sounding stronger as she admonished her brood. "It takes longer than an hour to get here from Houston, and don't think I won't be timing you. The last thing I need is for you boys to end up in the hospital with Regina."

"We'll be careful," Hutch said. "Birdie? Is she all right?" Cam could hear the worry in his voice, almost as though he'd been afraid to ask.

"She's fine." Birdie's voice softened. "Or she will be. She was pretty beat up when they brought her in, but she'll be okay in a few days."

"Beat up?" There was an edge of steel to Sawyer's voice. "Who the hell beat her up?"

"I've got to go," Birdie said hurriedly. "She's waking up." There was a long pause. "She doesn't know I'm calling you."

The line went dead.

Cam curled his fingers into tight fists and sat back in his chair.

"Let's go," Hutch said shortly.

Sawyer's face was set in stone. "She didn't want Birdie to call us."

Hutch gave him an *I don't give a fuck* look.

Sawyer turned to Cam even as he stood to go. "How long are we going to wait? How long are we going to let her get away with pushing us as far away as she can manage?"

Hutch crossed his arms over his chest, and Cam eyed both him and Sawyer. "We don't. Not anymore."

Hutch grinned, and Sawyer nodded in satisfaction.

"Let's go get our girl, then," Hutch said.

CHAPTER 2

When Regina opened her eyes, she groaned and slammed them shut again. There wasn't an inch of her body that wasn't screaming like a girl. She heard the murmur of voices and cracked open an eyelid to see who was there.

Birdie. Regina smiled then winced. Damn, even smiling hurt. Her gaze skirted over to where Jeremy stood with his wife, Michelle.

"Where's the kiddo?" she croaked out.

Relief echoed in Jeremy's expression. "Jake and Ellie have him. How do you feel, Regina?"

He and Michelle moved closer to the bed, and Michelle gave her a sympathetic smile.

"Do I look that bad?" Regina asked.

Before Michelle could answer, a cool hand fluttered across Regina's forehead.

"Birdie," Regina whispered. "I'm sorry to have worried you, but I'm so glad you're here."

The older woman smiled and bent down to kiss Regina's cheek. "As if I'd be anywhere else."

"You've been here all night, haven't you?" Regina frowned. "For that matter, how long have I been here?" She looked up at Jeremy as more of what happened came back. "Did you get him? And damn, why does it sound like I've got a horde of frogs in my throat?"

Jeremy grimaced. "One thing at a time, okay, girl? No, I didn't get him. But we will. And you sound like shit because he tried to choke you after beating the hell out of you." His eyes glittered with anger.

His wife put a reassuring hand on his arm and squeezed.

Another thought hit her, and panic gripped her throat. "My gun, Jeremy. He knocked it out of my hand."

"It's all right. We recovered it on scene. It's being processed, so you'll have to do without it for a few days. Not like you'll be coming back to work tomorrow anyway."

She grimaced. No, she wouldn't be back tomorrow, but if she had anything to say about it, she wouldn't be laid up for very long. She glanced up at Jeremy and his wife. He looked haggard, and he probably had better things to do than sit here and babysit her ass.

"I'm fine now, so you two should go home. I appreciate you coming, though," Regina said.

"Are you sure you don't want us to stay?" Michelle asked.

"You two go on," Birdie interjected. "I'll be staying with her no matter how much she fusses about it."

Jeremy nodded then stared hard at Regina. "We'll get him."

Regina nodded and regretted moving her head when the room swam in her vision. A few moments later, she heard the door shut, and she slowly turned her head so that Birdie was in her sight.

"How bad is it?" she asked.

Birdie let out a soft hmmpph. "It's not good, but you'll live.

Half the department has been by to see you. The other half has phoned. I finally had to turn the ringer off so it wouldn't disturb you."

"What happened? I don't remember much."

Birdie sighed. "I think your department is hoping you can fill them in on what happened. Jeremy said he responded to your request for backup and found you inside the house with a man's fingers wrapped around your throat."

Regina raised her hand to her neck and rubbed lightly as she remembered the hand that had squeezed.

"Do you hurt?" Birdie asked. Her face softened in sympathy. "I can call the nurse and get you something for pain. The doctor said you're pretty banged up."

Regina looked down and, for the first time, registered that she had a brace on her left wrist. She grimaced as she raised it to view the damage. "Is it broken?" she asked, hoping to hell it wasn't.

Birdie shook her head. "The ligaments in your wrist are strained, and the doctor wants you to nurse it properly until it heals. They were concerned you'd broken some ribs so they took X-rays."

"So when can I get out?"

"You'll stay put, young lady. Don't get any ideas about moving too quick."

Regina sagged onto her pillow. Another day or so in bed sounded pretty good, not that she'd admit that to Birdie. A sudden thought occurred to her, and she turned her head to look at Birdie. "You didn't call my parents, did you?"

Birdie sighed. "No, of course not. I know you wouldn't want that."

She didn't quite meet Regina's gaze, though, and that worried Regina. She eyed Birdie suspiciously, and then her face tightened in alarm. "Birdie, you didn't."

Birdie frowned. "I didn't what?"

"You didn't call *them*. You wouldn't."

Birdie sighed in exasperation. "What are you talking about, Regina?"

Regina groaned. "You did, didn't you? You called them."

Birdie pursed her lips and leaned forward in her chair. "When are you going to stop running from them, Regina? From yourself?"

"That's a damn good question, Birdie."

The low drawl sent a flutter of excitement through Regina's stomach. She ventured a look at the doorway to see Cam, Hutch and Sawyer standing there in various poses. Cam had his arms crossed over his chest, Hutch had his hands shoved into his jeans pocket and Sawyer leaned indolently against the door, watching her.

Hutch was the first to move. He strolled over to the bed, raised one brow when he looked her over, then dragged a chair to the bedside and slouched down.

"You look like hell."

Regina laughed and promptly regretted it as pain wracked her body. God, she'd missed him. She'd never admit it in a million years, but she was glad to see them all. Too glad.

Cam moved closer to the bed, his dark eyes glittering with anger and concern. He put a hand on Birdie's shoulder then leaned down to kiss her.

"You should go home now, Birdie. Get some rest. We'll take care of her from here."

Birdie flashed a guilty look in Regina's direction then smiled and patted Cam's cheek. "Someone has to take care of this one. She won't do it herself."

Regina growled under her breath.

Sawyer chuckled and elbowed his way by Cam. Regina turned

her cheek as he leaned down to kiss her, but he nudged her chin with his fingers and kissed her lingeringly on the lips. His goatee tickled her skin and sent a shiver down her body. He slid his palm down her jaw to the bruises around her neck.

"I'm going to kill him," he muttered.

Regina shoved at him in irritation then fixed her glare on all three of them. "See, this is why I didn't want Birdie to call you. I knew you'd come barging in, swimming in testosterone, beating your chests and muttering threats against humanity."

Sawyer laughed. "You wouldn't exaggerate, now would you, Reggie?"

She shot him a quelling look, but he only grinned in response.

Cam sat down on the edge of the bed and laid a hand over her leg. "Whether you wanted us here or not, we're here. We've been here all night, and I have to say, you're a lot easier to get along with when you're sleeping."

Damn it, she would not smile.

"Furthermore, you're coming home with us when you're released."

She opened her mouth to protest, but Sawyer touched her arm, Hutch put a hand on her shoulder, and Cam's grip tightened on her leg, and she forgot all about saying anything. How did they do that?

"I've already spoken to the doctor," Cam continued. "He wants to keep you one more night for observation. He'll release you in the morning as long as you have a place to stay. Your house alone doesn't count." He stared pointedly at her.

She sighed. "I have a job to do. I have a killer to catch. I don't have time for you guys to fuss over me, and I seriously doubt you have the time either."

"We'll make the time," Hutch said.

She turned to him and frowned. He was the one she could

usually count on not to treat her like an invalid. She'd been so grateful when he walked in and said she looked like hell, because it meant he wasn't going to start posturing like the other two and make a big deal over what had happened.

"I'm a pushover, Reggie, but not when it comes to what's best for you," he said as if he'd reached right into her mind and plucked out her thoughts. Damn the man.

"I agree with them, Regina," Birdie spoke up. "You shouldn't be alone right now. There's no way you can go back to your job until you've properly healed."

"Traitor," she muttered.

"Birdie, you sound tired," Sawyer said. "If you like, I'll drive you home. We're here now. We'll take good care of Reggie."

Birdie smiled even as Regina scowled. "I can drive myself. You boys came a long way to see Regina. I'll leave you to it." She leaned down to kiss Regina's cheek. "I'll be back later. Is there anything I can bring you?"

Regina shook her head. "Thank you, Birdie."

Birdie squeezed her hand. "No need to thank me. You feel like one of mine. Just like these boys do."

Regina smiled and watched the guys momentarily forget about her as they gathered around Birdie to give her hugs and kisses. Birdie did love those boys. She'd given them a home and love when no one else wanted them. And they loved her every bit as much as she did them.

There had been times growing up that Regina had envied Cam, Hutch and Sawyer. It sounded silly. She'd had a privileged childhood in that she'd never gone without food or clothing. But the one thing she'd missed was love, the one thing that the guys had never lacked for once they'd come to live with Birdie.

She'd envied them that. They would have laughed at the idea that she, the daughter of one of the wealthiest men in the state, had envied dirt-poor boys who had been in and out of foster homes and juvenile detention. But in a lot of ways, they had had more freedom than she'd ever dreamed of. And they had Birdie.

It wasn't until junior high that the bond had formed between her and Hutch, Cam, and Sawyer. They had lived with Birdie a few years, Hutch being the last to arrive. It was Hutch who ultimately brought the four together.

He had stumbled across Regina's "pretend place," what amounted to a little hollow in the creek bed a mile from Birdie's house and across the pasture from Regina's own home.

Regina hadn't appreciated the interruption any more than Hutch had liked coming across a *girl*. But with no place else to go and nothing else to do, they'd formed a grudging truce and agreed to share the space.

When Cam and Sawyer had discovered Hutch's new *friend*, they'd teased him relentlessly. That is until Regina bloodied both their noses. While Hutch was a little mortified to be defended by a girl, the three developed a healthy respect for the tiny little spitfire.

By the time they reached high school, the friendship between the four of them was solid. Labeled as hellraisers and not given a spitting chance at ever amounting to much (by the townspeople), the three boys hadn't cared much about fitting in. But no one bad-mouthed them around Regina. Even her father had learned the futility of that.

She sighed. She'd give a lot to go back to those days. Things had been simple. They'd had so much fun. They'd been inseparable.

A warm hand closed over hers, and she jerked her attention back to the present. Birdie had disappeared, and now Regina faced three surly looking men. Hell.

Cam, ever one to take the bull by the horns, didn't bandy

words. She usually liked that about him except when it was her he wanted to be blunt about.

"It's time we talked, Reggie," he said firmly.

She glanced to Hutch and Sawyer in a silent plea for mercy. The determined looks on both their faces told her she wasn't getting any.

"Captive audience, darlin'," Hutch murmured. "You won't be running like a scalded cat this time."

She closed her eyes and clutched the sheet with bloodless fingers. They wouldn't really bring up *that*, would they?

"You pretending we didn't have sex won't change a damn thing," Cam said.

Yeah, they would.

Embarrassment heated her cheeks but she worked, at great pain to herself, to keep the humiliation from her expression.

Sawyer leaned down, tucked one finger under her chin and tapped upward until she met his gaze. "It would be one thing if you didn't enjoy it, Reggie, but we all know that isn't the truth. It would be different if you didn't have feelings for us or we didn't have feelings for you, but we also know that isn't true."

She pressed her lips into a mutinous line and glared up at him.

"We have all the time in the world," Hutch said casually. "You won't be getting away from us this time. You ran hard, Reggie, and we let you. That's on us. But it won't happen again. That's also on us."

Helpless rage tightened her chest. She hated how they made her feel. She loved the way they made her feel. She hated how out of control they made her feel.

She swallowed and winced at the pain in her throat. Sawyer stroked his hand over her forehead and gazed tenderly down at her. "We'll get you something for pain, Reggie. You need rest.

We'll be here when you wake up. We're not going anywhere. You count on that. You also need to know that we're going to talk about this. Us."

He lowered his head and once again kissed her. Hot tears pricked her eyelids, and she blinked furiously, pissed that she'd allow him to affect her so deeply.

"It was just sex," she whispered.

His blue eyes flashed and narrowed. "You keep telling yourself that, Reggie, and one day, you might actually believe it."

"I don't need you here." The words caught in her throat, and she immediately regretted them. Weak. She was weak. But her rejection didn't anger the guys.

Cam just smiled at her, while Hutch stroked her arm above the line of the brace.

"You may not want us here, but you *do* need us," Cam said with confidence that grated on her nerves.

"And we need you," Hutch said simply.

She turned to look at him and felt her stance weaken. What they wanted, no, what they *demanded*, she couldn't give them. How could anyone? It wasn't normal. It wasn't done. It wasn't possible. Not in her world. Not in any world.

Sawyer ran his hand through her hair again, and she instinctively moved closer. He tucked the short, curly strands behind her ears and ran his finger down the sensitive skin behind her ear.

They were doing it again. Lulling her, numbing her senses with their touch, their presence. Hutch stroked her arm, rubbing lightly while Sawyer continued to finger the strands of her hair. Cam laid his big hand over her knee, and she could feel the heat of his fingers through the sheet.

She felt safe. More than that, she felt comforted, as if for this one moment, everything was all right.

She jumped when the door opened and the nurse walked in. She scowled at the interruption even as she realized she should be grateful for the reprieve.

Somehow, Sawyer had maneuvered himself onto the bed beside her, all while stroking her neck. Smooth bastard. He sat with one leg hanging over the side, her head nestled in the crook of his arm.

She realized how cozy, how intimate, they all looked, Hutch on her other side, his hand resting possessively on her arm, Cam sitting at her feet, absently rubbing her knee, and her all hugged up to Sawyer.

The nurse raised an eyebrow but didn't say much as she navigated around the males to get to Regina's IV. The line had been disconnected but the saline lock was still in place to administer medication. Sawyer gently pulled her arm up and rested it on his lap but made no effort to move for the nurse. She shrugged and reached for Regina's hand.

"My best oblivion cocktail coming right up," the nurse said as she uncapped the syringe. She swabbed the port and deftly inserted the needle.

In seconds, Regina felt the slight burn as the medication hit her veins. It swept up her arm, and when it got to her shoulder, she relaxed and sagged further into Sawyer's embrace.

She drowsily registered his lips nuzzling into her hair and him murmuring softly. As the nurse moved away, he pulled her even closer. She raised her other hand, blindly reaching for Hutch. The action contradicted her every word, but as much as she said she didn't need them, didn't want them there, for the last year she'd felt like a huge part of herself was missing.

Hutch caught her hand and lowered it back to the bed, his fingers cautiously laced with hers.

She struggled to open her eyes one more time, and her gaze connected with Cam's.

"I missed you," she whispered, too foggy to call back the words before they slipped from her mouth.

Cam's brown eyes softened. "We missed you too, sweetheart. Now rest and get better."

"Don't go," she murmured as she fought against the lethargy slogging through her body and brain.

"We're not going anywhere, Reggie," Sawyer said close to her ear. "I promise."

She drifted off with the comfort of that promise echoing in her mind.

CHAPTER 3

$\mathcal{T}$he sun hadn't yet peeked over the horizon, and the pale glow of predawn had only just begun to lighten the sky when Sawyer climbed out of the truck and met Cam around the front.

Together they stared at the large two-story house situated on one of the rolling hills of the hundred-acre spread they'd purchased a couple years earlier.

Sawyer's chest tightened with pride. This was theirs. A piece of land. A home. When he was a child, the idea of home and family had been a fantasy. A dream that was for other kids. Not him. Never him.

When Birdie had taken him in, Cam had been there a week already and was not appreciative of the competition for Birdie's affection. He'd been resentful of Sawyer's presence even as he had pushed Birdie away. He hadn't wanted her and hadn't trusted her, but he didn't want Sawyer to have her either.

He hadn't really understood until Hutch had arrived a few months later. Fear and insecurity, two things Sawyer had been well accustomed to back then, had made a terrible comeback.

What if Birdie liked Hutch better? Hutch was quieter. He wasn't as much trouble. What if she decided three boys were too much? Surely she'd keep whoever caused her the least amount of strife.

"Let's go," Cam said, shaking Sawyer from his reverie. "I want to make sure everything's ready for her to come home."

They walked to the front porch and Cam inserted the key into the lock. Though they'd visited the house often when it was in the building stages—(Cam had been more than obsessed with making sure every single detail was perfect and exactly according to the plans he'd drawn up)—Sawyer couldn't help the sense of wonder that slipped over him when he stepped into the foyer.

No expense had been spared in the construction. While it looked and felt masculine, it hadn't been built or decorated with their tastes solely in mind. No, it had been built for Reggie. It was her dream house.

He meandered to the stone fireplace and ran his fingers lightly over the mahogany mantel. Then he walked over to the French doors leading to the deck and stared out. She'd like it. Several trees shaded the sprawling terrace, including one large oak that they'd built around. It was intended to mimic the banks of the creek where she and Hutch had spent so much time nestled among the tree roots.

The deck overlooked a three-acre pond down a gentle incline from the back of the house. They'd stocked it with bass and catfish, and Sawyer was looking forward to challenging Reggie to see who could land the biggest.

"You think this will work?"

Sawyer turned in surprise to see Cam standing next to him at the doors. More surprising was the worry in his voice. Cam . . . he was the steadfast one. He'd been the one from the start to tell him and Hutch when they had doubts that it would work out. It had to. They loved Reggie.

Now Sawyer realized that Cam needed that reassurance too.

"Yeah, man. It's going to work. It's not us she's running from. It's herself. She's afraid. Of what, I'm not sure."

Cam nodded. "It's just that sometimes I think we made a mistake. That maybe we pushed too hard."

Sawyer eyed him before turning his gaze to the outside. "We didn't push, Cam. It just . . . happened. I wouldn't have let you or Hutch force her into anything, just like you wouldn't have let me. We wanted her. But we've wanted her a long damn time."

"I turned on the air and made sure her room was all set. We can head back to the hospital now if you want."

Sawyer turned, accepting the abrupt change in subject. Yeah, he was anxious to return even though he knew Reggie was going to fight them tooth and nail about coming home with them, especially when she learned that home was here and not in Houston.

Hutch listened to Reggie's quiet breathing and gently rubbed his fingers up and down her shoulder. She lay sleeping, her head against his chest, her body nestled into his. His arm was numb and had been for the better part of an hour, but he didn't want to move it and disturb her.

With his other hand, he ran his finger up her slender neck where the vivid bruises marred her skin. The idea that she'd come so close to death scared the hell out of him. He knew her job as a cop put her in danger every day, but this just brought that fact home with a punch to the gut.

He didn't want her putting herself out there like that. He wanted her at home, in his bed, where he could take care of her. If she had any clue of the direction of his thoughts, she'd kick him in the balls. Of the three guys, she considered him her ally.

If she only knew that he wasn't nearly as tolerant as Cam or

Sawyer. She'd been his for longer than she'd ever been theirs. There were times when he had no desire to follow through with the agreement he'd made with Cam and Sawyer. He knew they loved her. Like he loved her. But he was tired of waiting. One of them didn't scare her, but the three of them did.

He sighed. She wouldn't choose between them. They all knew it too, which was why they didn't have any desire to make her. None of them wanted to lose her, and so they were willing to take the biggest gamble of their lives. Convince her that she belonged with all three of them. And hope to hell jealousy didn't eat them all alive.

She stirred and let out a small groan. He kissed the top of her head, and she went still.

"Hutch?"

He smiled. She knew him even coming out of a drug-induced fog.

"Yeah, baby. I'm here."

He felt her smile against his chest, but her words contradicted that action.

"You shouldn't have come. I'm okay. No need for you to all come running over when you have work to do. Birdie said this is a really busy time for you."

He shifted, careful not to bump any of her injuries. His arm was screaming for mercy, and so he slid it out from underneath her and turned on his side.

"We're busy, Reggie. But never too busy for you, and you should damn well know that by now."

"I didn't mean it that way," she said softly. "I just meant that there wasn't a need for you to come. I'm fine. I don't need . . ."

He put a finger to her lips, and she went quiet. Her blue eyes were cloudy from the remnants of pain and drugs, but he could also see anxiety brewing there. He slid his hand over her face down below her ear and beyond to the back of her neck. His thumb stroked over her cheekbone as he simply stared at her.

She was beautiful, and he doubted she knew just how much. Or that as beautiful as she was to everyone else, she was that much more to him. And to Cam and Sawyer.

"Don't say it." He ran his finger lightly over the seam of her lips. "You need us, Reggie. You're fighting that, and for now that's okay. But at some point you'll have to admit to us and to yourself that you need us as much as we need you."

She made a sound of frustration, and he leaned in to kiss her. She went soft against him, and a little feminine sigh escaped her lips as he nibbled gently at them. She'd made those contented sounds when they'd made love to her, and he wanted to hear them again.

A sound at the door made her stiffen, and she lurched away from him, promptly groaning in pain when she jarred her body.

"That was stupid, Reggie," he said grimly as he settled her body against him again.

He looked up to see the doctor walk in, but he made no effort to get up from his position on the bed. The doctor ignored Hutch, but gave Reggie's wrist a cursory exam. After a moment, he eyed Reggie.

"Are you ready to go home, Miss Fallon?"

"Yeah, I am," Reggie replied. "How long will I be out? When can I go back to work?"

Hutch stiffened. He didn't want Reggie back on the job. Not in her condition, or any other for that matter.

"Work is out of the question for the next several days at least. I'd suggest a minimum of two weeks with light duty after that. The good news is you don't have any broken ribs. Your X-rays came back negative. But you have a lot of bruising, and you're going to be tender for a few days."

"The swelling is starting to lessen in your throat, and I don't think there will be any permanent damage to your vocal cords. You also need to take good care of your wrist and make sure you don't strain it.

"I'm writing you a prescription for some painkillers, and I want you to take the anti-inflammatory medicine I'm giving you as well."

Reggie nodded, but Hutch wasn't fooled. She'd agree to anything to get out of the hospital, and then she'd balk at taking the medicine. That was okay because Hutch would force it down her throat if he had to.

"All right then, young lady. I'll give the discharge instructions to the nurse, and she'll have you ready to go around noon or so. Until then, hang tight and take it easy."

"Thanks," Reggie murmured.

As the doctor walked out, Cam and Sawyer shouldered their way in. Reggie tensed against Hutch, and he pressed his lips to her hair in a gesture of reassurance.

Regina swallowed some of her nervousness and was happy to note that today her throat didn't quite feel like she was drinking shards of glass. Her gaze skittered up to Cam and Sawyer, and Sawyer strode over to the side of the bed.

He lightly ran his fingers over the brace on her arm and then bent to kiss her. This time she didn't try to turn away—not that he would have let her—and the warm fullness of his lips pressed to hers.

Her mouth parted, and he took full advantage, deepening the kiss as his tongue brushed over hers. She could feel herself sliding away, giving in. Panic kicked in, and she withdrew, seeking refuge in Hutch.

Hurt flashed in Sawyer's eyes, and she nearly moaned aloud. God, this is why she couldn't do this. She'd never do anything to hurt any of them. Never turn away from one to another. Tears swam in her eyes, and she closed them, unwilling to fall apart in front of them.

"I didn't mean it like that," she whispered.

Awkward silence fell on the room, and Regina wished that she could leave, walk out, go back to her own home and ignore what was staring her in the face.

She opened her eyes and glanced over at Cam, who stood against the window, his hands shoved into his jeans pockets. She always thought his hair was his one rebellion. While Sawyer kept his head shaved, and Hutch wore his in a short spiky do, Cam let his go. For a guy who was as organized and uptight as Cam could be, the long, messed-up hair just didn't fit. But she had to admit she found the combination of his serious, glasses-wearing look and the unkempt, tousled hair extremely sexy.

"Birdie said you had a project due today. How are you supposed to get it done if you're here?"

She was proud of how steady she sounded. After that brief moment of meltdown, she was back in control. The strange thing was, they seemed to be as relieved as she was that she wasn't tearing up anymore.

One corner of Cam's mouth quirked into a half smile. "You let me worry about my job, Reggie darling. You've got enough to keep you busy for quite a while."

She frowned. "That's not an answer, damn it." She looked up at Hutch then back at Sawyer who had sunk into a chair by her bed. "Are you two going to let him run your business into the ground?"

Hutch chuckled. "Nice try. We're on his side in this. You come first."

She sighed then snuck another glance at Sawyer, guilt giving her a big dose of unhappiness.

His expression softened. "Will you quit looking at me like

that, baby doll? I'm a big boy. You don't have to worry about hurting my little feelers. I shouldn't have barged in like I did, but damn if you don't have the most kissable lips I've ever tasted."

Her cheeks tightened. Damn if he hadn't turned that apology right back on her.

When the door opened again, she was grateful for the interruption. When she saw Jeremy and the chief, she tried to straighten, and then she glared at Hutch, who refused to move his carcass from the bed.

"How are you doing, Regina?" the chief asked as he and Jeremy walked over to the bed.

"Good, sir. I'll be going home in a couple of hours."

The chief nodded. "Good. That's good to hear. I want you to take it easy and not try to come back too soon."

She glanced between Jeremy and the chief. "Anything on our killer?"

"We're working on it. We'll need to take your statement as soon as you're up to it. Wondered if you'd be up for some questions now."

Regina looked nervously at Hutch and then at Sawyer and Cam. She didn't want to go over the details of the attack in front of them. They'd just freak out on her some more.

"I could come by the station on my way home," she offered.

Hutch tensed beside her, and Sawyer's lips compressed into a thin line. She ignored their displeasure.

The chief frowned, and Jeremy looked at her in question.

"You sure you're up to that?" Jeremy asked.

"No," Cam interjected.

"Yes," Regina said just as quickly. "I can't think here. I hate hospitals. They make me feel more of an invalid than I am. I'll be better able to answer questions at the station. Whether I'm sitting there or lying here, I fail to see the difference."

She stared hard at Cam, daring him to disagree again.

"I'll ask Birdie to drive me over when I'm discharged," she said to Jeremy and the chief.

"There's no need," Sawyer said smoothly. "We'll be happy to drive you where you need to go. And afterwards, you're going home with us."

The chief nodded his approval. "That's a good idea. I don't think Regina should stay alone right now. Not until we've got this nutjob behind bars. Who the hell knows what he was thinking? I don't want to take chances with the safety of my police officers."

Regina's mouth gaped open, but she held the protest dying to fly off her tongue. The last thing she needed was to make an ass of herself in front of the chief.

"We'll go now," the chief said. "We'll see you in a little while, Regina." As he turned to go, he cracked a smile. "It was nice to see you boys again. It's been a while. Glad you're giving an old man a break these days."

Sawyer grinned while Cam nodded at the chief. "It was nice to see you too, sir," Cam said. "We'll bring Reggie over later."

Jeremy paused for a moment and laid his hand over Regina's leg. "You sure you're doing okay?"

She smiled. "Yeah, feeling much better today. Just stiff and sore as hell, but as soon as I can get up and move around, that'll help."

He nodded then turned to follow the chief out. "See you in a bit."

She braced herself as the door closed. She still stared straight ahead, but her eyes darted sideways to take in the frowns of Cam and Sawyer. She wouldn't even bother looking up at Hutch, because she knew he wasn't happy.

Not willing to give them the chance to flex their muscles, she drew back the sheet with her hand and slid her legs toward the side of the bed.

"Whoa, baby, where do you think you're going?" Hutch asked even as Sawyer moved from the chair to the side of the bed, his hand out to push her back.

"I'm getting out of bed," she said calmly. "I want a shower. I want some clean clothes. I want out of the goddamn hospital."

Sawyer looked guiltily over at Cam. "Did you bring her any clothes?"

Cam shook his head. "I thought Hutch was getting them."

"So which one of you is going to go get them?" Hutch asked.

Sawyer turned to glare at Hutch. "I'm thinking you can go get them. Cam and I have done enough running around this morning."

He swore as soon as he said it, and he looked up at Regina. "That did *not* come out right."

She shrugged. "I'm not the moron sitting around here when I need to be working. I could get a ride to the station, and Birdie could drive me home. There is no reason for you guys to hang around here. I'm okay."

Hutch uncurled his body from the bed and stood with a stretch. "I'm going to get you some clothes. You can stay here and argue with the other two boneheads."

She inched her feet toward the floor again, and this time, Sawyer reached for her arm to help. As annoyed as she was, when her feet hit the floor, she was grateful for his support. She weaved and bobbed like a newborn calf, and a groan worked from deep in her chest.

"Jesus," she muttered.

"I told you that you looked like shit," Hutch offered on his way out the door.

"Tell me again why I put up with him?" she asked wearily.

"I don't know. That's a good question," Sawyer said as he pulled her against his side to steady her.

"Move," Cam said simply as he appeared in front of Regina.

Sawyer stepped back in surprise, and Regina found herself enfolded in Cam's arms. He was careful not to crush her, but she could feel the tension rolling off his big body.

"Cam, I'm okay," she whispered.

His hands ran up and down her back, and he kissed the top of her head.

"You scared me, Reggie," he said. "Don't do that again."

The corner of her mouth lifted as he pulled away from her. "Believe me, I won't make a habit of it if I can help it. Now can I take my shower?"

CHAPTER 4

*R*egina stood in the small bathroom staring at her reflection in horror. Dark bruises marred her entire neck. In fact, there wasn't much skin that wasn't discolored.

She glanced down at the brace on her wrist, the IV lock in her other hand and then the shower. How she was going to manage this she wasn't sure, but she had an unholy compulsion to be clean again, to remove the taint of the killer from her flesh.

With her good hand, she reached in to turn on the water and then started shrugging out of her hospital gown. The IV would just have to get wet. Leaving the material in a wad on the floor, she stepped beyond the curtain and extended her left arm out of the shower to keep it dry.

Water pelted her chest, and she winced as it struck her tender ribs. She turned her face into the spray for a moment then wiped her eyes and looked around for the soap. Too late she realized that wasn't something the hospital supplied.

With an aggravated sigh, she backed out of the shower, dripping water all over the floor. How the hell she was going to manage soaping her hair one-handed while keeping the other dry was a mystery anyway.

She bumped against the toilet and lost her footing, falling with a thump onto the toilet seat. A hiss of pain escaped her when she automatically put out both hands to catch herself.

The bathroom door burst open, and Cam and Sawyer stood in the doorway staring at her in concern. Before she could protest, blush or succumb to embarrassment, Cam rushed forward and cupped his hands around her shoulders.

"Are you all right? What the hell happened?"

"I told you she shouldn't be doing this alone," Sawyer said tersely.

She held up a hand. "I'm fine. Damn it, guys, get the hell out of here." She reached for a towel and tried to cover herself.

"We've seen you naked, Reggie," Cam said patiently.

She glared up at him.

He shrugged. "Just sayin'."

She closed her eyes and sighed. "I need soap. Shampoo would be nice. Only I don't know how the hell I'm going to wash my hair," she muttered.

Sawyer backed out of the bathroom and returned with a small bottle of shampoo. Then he eyed Cam.

"You gonna do it, or am I?"

Cam's gaze flickered briefly to Regina then back to Sawyer. "I'll help her. When Hutch gets back with her clothes, lay them on the counter."

Sawyer nodded, and then his stare found Regina again. She clutched the towel to her chest, but she still felt frighteningly naked and vulnerable under the force of his scrutiny.

"I'll be outside if you need anything," he said softly.

He retreated from the bathroom and closed the door.

"Cam, I don't need your help," she said as soon as he turned to her.

"Reggie, shut up," he said mildly. "You're going to end up falling and hurting yourself. Now get your ass in the shower so I can wash your hair. If it makes you feel any better to have a towel around you then knock yourself out, but I've seen you naked, and I'm certainly not going to jump your bones in a hospital bathroom. If you can control yourself, I guarantee you that I can too."

She laughed then groaned as she took his hand and pulled herself upright. Just as she stepped into the shower, she hesitated then slowly pulled the towel away and handed it back to him.

He tossed it aside then slipped in behind her and retrieved the shower head from its perch above her head.

"I'm going to get you all wet," she muttered.

"I'll survive."

A gentle hand gathered her hair while the other directed the spray over the tresses. He was careful to keep the nozzle pointed away from her injured hand.

"This would be easier if you turn around," he said.

She closed her eyes but did as he suggested. When she opened them again, she found herself staring up into his eyes.

"Put your arm up on my shoulder."

She carefully raised the brace and rested it on his right shoulder.

He poured some of the shampoo over her head then carefully set the shower head back on its mount, pointing the spray away from them both. Then he delved his fingers into her hair, working the soap into a lather.

She closed her eyes and swayed a little unsteadily as his fingers worked their magic.

"Want me to get the rest?" he asked.

She wanted to die of mortification. How could she possibly let him touch her when they both knew she'd react like an adolescent crushing on her first boyfriend?

Her nipples were already tight and aching, her breasts heavy with need. He'd had the decency not to comment on that little tidbit, but he knew. He damn well knew.

"Reggie, you're hurt and you're tired," he said gently. "For once let me take care of you without worrying about what comes next, okay?"

Without waiting for her to respond, he took a washcloth, lathered it with soap and began a slow sweep of her body. Each brush across her nipples yielded needle-like twinges. He worked slowly and with great care across her rib cage, barely touching the bruised area.

His hand slid around back and up and down her spine then over the swell of her buttocks. He knelt and did a quick swipe of both legs before straightening back up again.

He frowned as he tilted her chin upward to expose her neck. Anger glinted hard, like diamonds in his eyes. He ran a single finger over the bruised expanse of her throat. The washcloth followed behind, leaving a soapy trail in its wake.

"Okay, turn around so I can rinse," he directed.

He cupped her elbow to steady her as she swiveled around. He made quick work of rinsing the soap from her hair and body then reached up to turn the water off.

"Stay right there. Let me get you a towel. I don't want you stepping out onto this wet floor. It's slippery."

A moment later, he wrapped her in a towel then curled his arm around her and helped her out of the shower. The door opened, and Sawyer stuck his head in. He extended his hand with a folded pair of sweatpants and a T-shirt.

Cam took the clothes and tossed them near the sink.

"I think I can manage now," she said in a low voice.

He touched her lightly on the arm. "I'll be right outside. Don't be stubborn, Reggie. If you need help, ask for it. I don't want to have to come in here and pick your ass up off the floor after you've taken a nosedive."

She smiled and clutched the towel a little tighter around her. Her chest felt all fluttery, tight, like she couldn't breathe around the little squeeze.

He opened the door and walked out, shutting it behind him. She sank onto the toilet seat and closed her eyes. Her hands shook as she peeled away the towel. She felt dangerously close to crying, and for the life of her she couldn't figure out why.

Maybe because you nearly got your ass killed. Maybe because the three men who mean the world to you have decided to launch a full-frontal assault?

She reached for the clothes, knowing they wouldn't give her long before they came in after her. As she pulled on the sweats, she grimaced. She hated the idea of showing up to an interview with her chief in sweats and a T-shirt, but at the same time she knew that Hutch had chosen the only thing she could possibly be comfortable in. Loose and not confining, the sweats and the T-shirt wouldn't irritate her bruised ribs. Then there was the whole issue of going into the police station without a bra. God help her.

Hutch's leather jacket. The one he was never without no matter how damn hot it got. She could use it.

Feeling marginally better about the situation, she ran her fingers through her hair after toweling more of the moisture from it. The curls spilled around her head in disarray, and with a resigned sigh, she gave up on trying to make herself presentable. No one would give a shit what she looked like anyway.

She hesitated a fraction of a second before opening the bathroom door. Sawyer was there, as though he'd been waiting, and he probably had been. He wrapped an arm around her shoulder and hugged her up close to his side as he helped her toward the bed.

Knowing she would be talking to a brick wall, she didn't even bother offering a protest. She gave a disgruntled sigh and let him put her where he wanted her.

As he helped her back onto the bed, she looked over at Hutch.

"Thanks for the clothes."

He smiled. "Anytime, baby."

She was just about to lean back against the pillows on her bed and indulge in some much-needed rest when the door flew open, startling her.

She tensed, causing a rush of pain to course through her body. As she viewed the man standing in the doorway, an ache began in her head that was absent before.

Her father.

"Regina," he said with a frown as he strode in. "Care to tell me why I had to hear about the incident you got yourself involved in from the media? Damage control. How many times do I have to impress upon you the need for damage control?"

Her hand fluttered to her forehead. God, not now. What she wouldn't give to make him go away.

Sawyer eased closer to the bed. It dipped, and she found herself securely resting against his muscled body. For once she had no desire to make him go away.

Peter Fallon looked around the room as if for the first time seeing that Regina wasn't alone. His scowl grew.

"What is the meaning of this?" he asked, flinging his hand toward Hutch and Cam and then pointing toward her and Sawyer.

Cam stepped forward. "Mr. Fallon, I don't think this is a good time. Reggie is tired and in a lot of pain."

Her father's eyes flashed, and he rounded on Cam. "Her name is Regina, and what the hell are you doing here? What are any of you doing here?" He directed his ire back at Regina. "Do you have any idea how this appears? You're a public figure, Regina. For God's sake, it's time to start acting like one."

She eyed him dully, the pounding in her head vicious and unrelenting. "You're the public figure, Dad."

Power. It was all about power to him. He wanted it, craved it, and it pissed him off that he'd never been able to establish power over his only child.

He ignored her and began pacing back and forth while Cam and Hutch stared at him, their gazes narrow and angry.

"We'll hold a press conference when you're released. I'll need to issue a statement."

Press conference? She wanted to laugh. Who the hell cared about what went on in their little town? He might be able to pony up a one-man crew from Beaumont if it was a really slow news day.

She closed her eyes and leaned into Sawyer. Why had he come? Why was he here? Of course. He was worried how what had happened to her would affect *his* public image, and then he walked in to see three men he loathed all standing around his daughter. Three men he'd never approved of, had done everything in his power to keep Regina away from when she was younger.

"I'm going to have to ask you to leave, Mr. Fallon," Hutch said evenly. "You're upsetting Reggie."

She opened her eyes to see her father bristle with rage and then compose himself. He straightened his suit and then his tie.

"I'll arrange for the statement to be issued outside the hospital," he said. "Surely you can manage that much, Regina. We can't let it get out that our police department is ineffective. It would compromise the community's faith in the department's ability to keep them safe. All you'll have to do is stand there and smile. I'll do all the talking."

She clenched her teeth and trembled in rage. Sawyer's hand smoothed up and down her arm, and his other hand rested on her thigh. He gave her a comforting squeeze. Then he leaned over and kissed the side of her head.

Her father's neck was mottled with anger. He made a show of checking his watch. "I'll be out front waiting. The doctor said you'd be discharged within the hour."

He turned and stalked out of the room, the door closing with a bang behind him.

"Pompous, self-important windbag," Hutch said through clenched teeth. "I swear to God, one of these days I'm going to lay his ass out."

"Reggie, honey, are you okay?" Sawyer's concerned voice sounded in her ear.

"I'm fine," she said quietly.

She looked at each of them, saw the sympathy and the anger in their expressions. And guilt. They knew that the three of them were a serious bone of contention between her and her father.

"What I need to know is who's going to pull the truck around back so I can avoid the bullshit out front?"

Cam grinned. "Leave that to me, Reggie darling. Hutch and Sawyer can hustle you to the ER entrance, and I'll be waiting there."

CHAPTER 5

The nurse, bless her heart, had Regina discharged in half an hour. While she listened to the nurse rattle off her spiel about aftercare instructions, Hutch bent down and slipped Regina's shoes on her feet. A few seconds later, a second nurse appeared at the door with a wheelchair.

"For God's sake," Regina muttered. "I don't need a wheelchair."

The nurse folded a sheaf of papers and handed them to Sawyer. "Hospital policy," she said with a smile.

"Come on," Hutch said as he helped her get up. "It won't be so bad. It'll be quicker anyway."

There was that. Regina had no guilt whatsoever about having Hutch or Sawyer break into a run with the wheelchair if they were spotted by her father.

Press conference, my ass.

Elections were right around the corner, and Peter Fallon would use any means necessary to thrust himself into the spotlight. Positively, of course.

It probably suited him well to have a poor, pitiful daughter injured in the line of duty so he could take his tough-on-crime message to the public. She was only surprised he hadn't dragged her mother along to play up the concerned maternal angle.

But that would require Lydia to cancel her massage or hair appointment or whatever the hell it was she did every day.

"You need to relax, baby," Hutch murmured as he settled her into the wheelchair.

She glanced down at her hands balled into fists in her lap. Hutch reached down and gently uncurled her fingers and laced them with his while Sawyer listened to the last of the nurse's instructions.

Sawyer turned around as the nurse exited the room. "You ready?"

Regina nodded. She was ready to have this day over with. Ready to be done giving her statement. Ready to be at home in her own bed, where she could sleep for about twelve hours.

Sawyer wheeled her around, but Hutch kept hold of one of her hands as he walked beside the wheelchair.

"I wonder if you could pop a wheelie in one of these things," Sawyer mused.

Regina grinned. If she didn't ache so bad, she'd tell him to go for it.

They hustled her down the corridor, and then Sawyer pulled up short when they reached the end.

"Look left, Hutch. Make sure the coast is clear."

Hutch ambled forward and glanced left, then right toward the emergency room.

"All clear."

"Then let's move," Sawyer said as he pushed her into motion again.

He jogged behind the chair as he rolled her through the ER

lobby and to the automatic doors where the ambulances unloaded.

Cam was waiting in the Tahoe.

Without waiting for her to get up, Hutch simply reached down, plucked her up and deposited her into the backseat after Sawyer opened the door. Sawyer climbed into the front, and Hutch hurried around to the other side. As Hutch slid in, Cam took off.

Hutch reached over and secured Regina's seat belt, careful not to catch the tender part of her ribs.

Regina grinned. Their getaway reminded her of old times. Sneaking out during high school, jumping into Cam's beat-up Camaro and hauling ass down dirt country roads.

When Cam pulled up to the police station a few minutes later, Jeremy was standing in the parking lot—if you could call a three-space piece of pavement a parking lot—waiting for them.

Cam got out and Sawyer hopped out to open the door for Regina.

Regina looked over at Hutch as he walked around to her side. "Can I borrow your jacket?"

He glanced down her body then simply reached into the back and pulled out the worn leather jacket. He slipped it over her shoulders, and she gingerly put her arms into the sleeves. She felt a ton better. Not as exposed or vulnerable as she faced walking into the station.

"Your father called, breathing fire," Jeremy said dryly.

Cam stopped cold and glared at him. "You keep his goddamn ass away from here."

Regina blinked in surprise. Even Sawyer drew up short and stared at Cam with a raised eyebrow.

Jeremy held up his hands. "The chief told her father not to butt into an ongoing investigation. Whether he'll heed that is anyone's guess."

"Let's get Reggie inside where she's more comfortable," Hutch said pointedly as he walked to where Regina stood next to Sawyer.

Regina put her hand on Hutch's wrist. "I'll be fine. You can wait out here if you want. There's not a whole lot of room inside."

He looked as though he'd protest, but Regina turned and walked gingerly toward the entrance. Jeremy fell into step beside her after a quick look back at Cam and the others.

"You sure you're up to this?" Jeremy asked as he held the door open for her.

"It doesn't matter," she said shortly. "We have a job to do."

Greta, the dispatcher, looked up from the PBX system, slid her earphones off and smiled broadly at Regina. "How are you feeling?"

Regina smiled back. "I'm good. Sore, but nothing about twelve hours of sleep won't cure."

Greta nodded. "Try some lemon tea. It'll make that throat of yours feel better. You look awful, honey."

Regina laughed, and it came out as a croak. "Thanks, Greta. I can always depend on you to be honest."

Greta thumbed in the direction of a nearby office door. "Chief's waiting on you. Go on in."

Regina walked with as much confidence in her stride as she could muster and stuck her head inside the chief's office.

He looked up and motioned her and Jeremy in. As she went forward, she saw Carl Perkins push off the wall where he'd been leaning. Regina frowned. What was he doing here? He wasn't a day-shifter.

"Sit down, Regina. Get comfortable. No need for you to be standing," Chief Witherspoon said as he gestured to the leather chair in front of his desk.

Trying not to show how grateful she was to be issued that particular order, she perched gingerly on the edge and then relaxed, leaning back into the soft chair.

The chief glanced up at Carl. "Carl is going to head up the investigation into the murder. Jeremy will be working with him and cooperating with the state police and the sheriff's department."

Regina sat forward. "Sir, I want this case."

The chief shook his head. "You're not even coming in for a while, Regina. I don't want to see you for at least a week and even then you'll be pushing paper."

She blew out her breath in frustration. "He killed that woman. He tried to kill me. I want to nail him."

"And we will," the chief said patiently. "Right now I need you to tell us everything you can remember about what happened that night."

"Who was she?" Regina asked softly.

"Misty Thompson."

Regina's brow furrowed in concentration.

"Did you know her?" Carl asked.

"Yeah. I mean, not well. I remember her from high school. She dated Hutch Bishop for a short time."

"Well, we need to determine how she came to be in that farmhouse. She lived in town with her husband and three children."

Regina winced and sighed. Her head ached a little more as she imagined three children who'd never see their mother again.

Carl leaned forward, putting his hands on the desk and staring at Regina. "What can you remember, Reggie?"

Her head jerked and she frowned hard. "Regina. Not Reggie." Then her mouth remained open as a hazy memory filtered back.

I've been waiting for you, Reggie love.

"What is it?" Jeremy demanded.

"Reggie. He called me Reggie."

"Sorry," Carl offered in a confused voice. "Didn't mean to offend you."

She shook her head. "Not you. Him. The guy who killed Misty and attacked me."

"Okay, back up," the chief said. "Start from the beginning and tell us everything."

She drew in a deep breath. "I responded to the call. When I got there, I didn't see any lights as were reported. Place is supposed to be deserted. But it didn't feel right so I called for backup. Jeremy radioed that he was en route. So I waited."

The chief nodded.

"Then I heard a scream. I drew my weapon, ran to the house, listened at the door for any activity. Hearing nothing, I gained access to the residence. I was clearing the living room when I found the body. When I bent to check her pulse and didn't find one, I started to call it in, and that's when he hit me."

"With what? Did he have a weapon?" Carl asked.

"I don't know. Honestly it felt like he hit me with a baseball bat, but I think it was just his fist. I went one direction, my gun went the other. I went for my weapon. He kicked me. Big feet. He had really large feet.

"He picked me up by the throat and held me against the wall. It was then that he spoke."

"And what did he say?" the chief asked.

She frowned. "'I've been waiting for you, Reggie love. It's time to make him pay.'" She looked up at the chief. "No one calls me Reggie, sir. Only Cam Douglas, Hutch Bishop and Sawyer Pritchard call me Reggie."

"Make who pay?" Jeremy murmured.

"Reggie could have been a guess," Carl offered. "A common enough nickname for Regina."

"But how did he know my name at all?" Regina pointed out. "He said he'd been waiting for me. He knew I'd be there. How?"

The chief frowned and sat back in his seat. "Is that all you can remember? Did you get a look at him at all?"

Regina shook her head regretfully. "It all happened so fast, and it was dark. I know he was big. Really big. He picked me up like I was nothing. I'd taken multiple blows to the head, and my vision was blurry. Then Jeremy got there, and the guy took off."

"I don't like it," the chief muttered. "Seems personal. Like it was a setup."

"Think it could be someone with a grudge against her father?" Jeremy offered. "Politicians attract a lot of crackpots with wack agendas. Beyond the fact that he's just a small town mayor, he's extremely wealthy and has wielded a lot of influence for years."

"Could be," Carl said. "It's certainly a possibility. I can't imagine why else he would have targeted Regina. And the bit about making him pay. How better to make a father pay than to kill his daughter?"

Regina remained silent. She wasn't going to dive into her father's motivation for anything. Way too messy.

"I'll have to tell him, Regina," the chief said apologetically. "If this nutjob is targeting you, and him indirectly, he'll need to know, as will his security team."

She swallowed her snort. Security team. Could her father get more pompous? Small town mayors didn't run around with a security team. His wealth had long since gone to his head, though. He, more than anyone, was convinced of his own importance. Hell, he'd probably be secretly smug if there was some sort of vendetta against him.

"I understand," she said quietly.

"I don't want you staying by yourself."

She frowned harder.

"Sawyer Pritchard mentioned you were going home with them," the chief said as he eyed her sternly. "I think that's a good idea for now. Keep your eyes peeled and stay on your toes. Hopefully we'll have caught this asshole before you report back for duty."

She gritted her teeth as she was summarily dismissed. With a sideways glance at Carl, she rose unsteadily to her feet but shrugged off Jeremy's arm when he reached out to help her.

"Keep me posted at least?" she said to the chief as she started for the door.

"Of course. And Regina?"

She stopped and turned back to look at him.

"Get some rest. You look like hell."

The corner of her lip quirked upward. "Thanks."

She stepped into the hallway to see Cam, Hutch and Sawyer lounging against the opposite wall. They straightened when they saw her, and Hutch dug into a small white paper sack.

"Didn't I tell you to wait outside?" she asked in exasperation.

Sawyer shrugged. "Yeah, so?"

Hutch thrust his curled up fist to her. "Here. Take this."

She held her hand out, and he dropped a small pill into her palm. She pushed it back at him, but he caught her hand, took the pill out and held it up to her mouth. Cam handed her a bottle of water.

"Take it," Hutch growled.

"You might as well give in gracefully," Cam said calmly. "It's not going to look good for your chief to come out and see you on the floor, us shoving a pill down your throat."

She glared at him. They wouldn't.

Sawyer stroked the back of her neck. "We'll do it, Reggie," he murmured. "And suffer absolutely no guilt over it either."

Her shoulders thrust up then shot down as she snatched the pill from Hutch's hand. She took the water from Cam and downed the pill on one swallow.

"There. Happy?"

Hutch grinned. "That wasn't so bad, now, was it?"

She shot him a quelling look and started to walk toward the front door. Heat rushed to her cheeks when she saw Greta sitting there, headphones off, a big grin on her face. She'd overheard the entire exchange, and Regina wanted to crawl under the nearest piece of furniture.

The guys spilled out of the police station behind her and they headed for Cam's SUV. She stood beside the truck, weariness assailing her. She couldn't muster the energy to open the door and get in.

Sawyer reached by her, his arm brushing against her shoulder as he took the handle and opened the door. His other hand settled at the back of her neck, and he rubbed the slight indention at the base of her head with his thumb.

His lips pressed to her hair, and she closed her eyes for a moment.

"Let's get you home," he murmured as he eased her into the truck.

He made sure she was inside then shut the door behind her. Hutch climbed into the front seat with Cam, and Sawyer walked around to the other side and slid in beside her.

As Cam started out of the parking lot, Regina frowned. "I didn't give you guys my prescription card. How did you get my stuff filled?"

Cam glanced in the rearview mirror, smiled and shook his head. "We paid for them, Reggie. How else would we have gotten them filled?"

"But you didn't have to do that," she protested. "I have insurance. Did you at least save the receipt so I can file for reimbursement and pay you back? That shit's expensive."

Sawyer reached over and took her hand. He raised it to his lips and kissed her fingers. She opened her mouth to say something else but forgot what it was.

"What it cost wasn't important," Sawyer said as he lowered her hand. "What was important was that we got you what you needed. You're in pain, honey. You can't hide that from us."

She stared over at him. She couldn't formulate an argument. She was just too damn tired.

"Come here," he said as he gently pulled her toward him. He guided her down until she was lying on the seat, her head pillowed on his lap.

She closed her eyes as his fingers stroked lightly through her hair. It felt so good. His touch. Their presence. All of it.

"Tell Cam to take me home," she murmured.

Sawyer's hand stilled for just a moment. "He *is* taking you home, honey."

She nodded in satisfaction and nuzzled a little further into Sawyer's lap. Home. Her own bed. A reprieve from the onslaught of all three men.

The drug Hutch had forced on her was already working its magic. It had taken the edge off her pain and replaced it with a warm, hazy glow. She'd close her eyes and enjoy it until she got home. She wanted to savor these few minutes next to Sawyer.

CHAPTER 6

"*R*eggie is not going to be happy with us," Sawyer murmured as Cam drove up the winding driveway to the house.

He continued to stroke her head then stopped to twirl a curl around his finger. She never stirred. Not even when the truck ground to a halt.

Hutch turned in the seat and glanced back at Reggie. He smiled faintly, but Sawyer could see the glimmer of . . . what in his eyes? It was a mixture of hope and sadness. And need.

As Hutch's gaze flitted across her neck, cold anger froze his features.

Cam opened his door. "Come on, guys. Let's get her inside and comfortable."

Sawyer shifted and carefully opened his door. Supporting her head with his hand, he eased out from underneath her. He grimaced as he stared down at her. There was no way to get her out with minimal disturbance.

"Want me to get her?" Cam asked from beside him.

Sawyer glanced over at Cam, who stood with his hands

shoved into his pockets. "No, I got it. Go open the door, if you would."

The rattle of keys sounded as Cam walked away. Sawyer reached in and gently pulled up on Reggie's shoulders. As he slid her toward him, she stirred. Before she became fully aware, he caught her up in his arms and cradled her against his chest.

Her eyes fluttered open when he took his first step toward the house.

"Sawyer?"

"Shhh, honey. Relax."

Her brow crinkled as she stared around her. "Where the hell are we?"

"Home," Hutch said.

"Put me down, Sawyer," she said quietly.

With a sigh, he slid her body down his until her feet hit the ground, but he kept a firm arm around her. He exchanged glances with Cam and Hutch and saw the uncertainty in their eyes.

Regina stared in awe at the house in front of her. It was beautiful. A two-story with a wraparound porch. Cedar swings lazily spread around the perimeter, inviting and cozy. Flower boxes adorned the windows and ferns hung from hooks in the overhang.

She glanced at Cam and then Hutch in confusion. Finally she looked up at Sawyer.

"I don't understand."

Cam walked forward and reached for her hand. "Come inside, Reggie. We'll talk when you're comfortable."

She took a shaky step. Whatever the hell Hutch had shoved down her throat had kicked her ass. Cam caught her elbow and then put his arm around her shoulders as he guided her up the three steps of the porch to the front entrance.

Hutch cut around them and opened the door. When Regina

stepped inside, her breath caught and held in her chest. She stopped at the entrance to the living room and just stared.

She knew this house. God, she should. It was *her* house. The fireplace. The mantel. The grandfather clock above the mantel, with the gently swaying pendulum.

She couldn't breathe. She swung her gaze over the wooden floors to the French doors leading to a deck out back. She swallowed hard and rubbed the back of her hand over her eyes then blinked furiously so that no moisture betrayed her.

Cam stood there, silent. Hutch and Sawyer stood just behind them, watching.

"What have you done?" she whispered. "What is this? I can't—"

Cam laid a gentle finger over her lips. "Not now, Reggie. We'll talk later. Right now we're putting you to bed. And you're going to stay there."

She opened her mouth to protest, but Sawyer and Hutch moved closer to her and put their hands on her shoulders.

"Stop doing that," she said in frustration.

Hutch raised a brow.

"Touching me. Stop touching me. You know damn well you're manipulating me." She stepped back, desperate to put space between them.

Sawyer stared intently at her, his blue eyes boring holes through her. "You can't run from us anymore," he said quietly, his voice steady, the thread of a vow laced in the words. "And you're going to stop running from yourself."

She hugged her arms around her waist, hating the panic that hit her at the determination in his voice, in the others' expressions.

Hutch stepped between her and Sawyer. "I'm going to take you upstairs. To your room. You're going to get undressed and get into bed. Unless you'd rather lay on the couch down here?"

"Here," she blurted. *Her room.* Just the fact that she had a room in this house scared the holy hell out of her. How long had they planned this? No way she was going up there, to a place they'd prepared for her, made for her.

"I'll go up and get pillows and a blanket," Sawyer said shortly.

Before she could utter a word, he turned and walked out of the living room. Her shoulders sagged. Was she determined to make a mess of everything? She couldn't be around any of them without doing her best to piss at least one of them off.

"You could at least pretend not to be scared shitless," Cam said dryly. "Our egos are taking a beating, Reggie darling."

She whirled back to him and promptly regretted that action. The room dipped and swayed. Hutch caught her arm.

"Whoops," he said as he righted her. "Why don't you get your ass to the couch before you fall over."

She yanked out of his grasp and refocused on Cam. "I am *not* scared shitless," she gritted out. "And if your ego is taking a beating, I'd say it's about damn time."

Hutch cupped her chin and nudged until she turned her gaze on him. "Yes, Reggie, you are. You can pretend all you want. But I know you. *We* know you," he added. "You've been running hard for a year now, and it's time you stopped. One way or another, we're going to face what happened between us."

She shook her head, causing his hand to slide down her neck.

Cam sighed. "Sit down so I can take your shoes off."

"Cam, I'm not helpless. I can take them off."

Cam put his hands on her shoulders and guided her backward until she bumped into the couch. Then he pushed her down until she sat on the cushion. He knelt in front of her and began removing her shoes.

"I'm well aware that you can take off your own shoes," Cam said. "You could also take a shower by yourself. You could also go home from the hospital, alone, and take care of yourself. But we like taking care of you, Reggie. There's no reason for you to be alone."

She stared into his warm brown eyes. A lock of dark hair fell over his forehead, and she reached up to push it back behind his ear.

"Kind of like you've always taken care of us," he murmured. He leaned into her touch, and her fingers slid across his cheek and to the slight stubble at his jaw.

"You need a shave."

He grinned. "And I'll get one, along with a shower, just as soon as you settle down and get comfortable. Unless you want to come help me?"

Her lips twitched as she battled the smile. "In your dreams."

Sawyer walked into the living room carrying two pillows and a down comforter. Cam rocked back and then stood so that Sawyer could arrange the pillows for Regina.

When he finished placing the pillows, he patted one of them and looked pointedly at Regina.

"Assume the position," Sawyer said.

Regina carefully reclined, settling against the plush cushions of the couch. Her head sank into the feather pillows, and she groaned in pleasure. They did know her. Too well. Her likes and dislikes. The things she loved. No one else knew her so well. Certainly not her parents. She almost laughed. No, she was a mystery to her parents. A puzzle they'd never tried to unravel.

But Cam, Sawyer and Hutch? They *got* her. And while it should have comforted her that she had people who cared about her, all she could focus on was the thought of losing one or all of them through her own stupidity.

Sleeping with them, making love with them . . . that had been stupid.

She closed her eyes, unwilling to let the memory of that night intrude on her thoughts. Not now.

The down comforter surrounded her, embracing her in a cloud of softness as Sawyer arranged it around her body. She felt his lips on her forehead, heard him whisper next to her ear.

Hutch's hand tangled in her hair as he stroked the unruly curls. Then Cam touched her arm, above the brace, light and comforting. Even with her eyes closed, she knew each one, the differences.

And then lips against hers, loving and gentle. Cam.

"We'll talk later, Reggie darling. That I promise. But for now, get some sleep."

"Stay with me," she whispered. Had she said that? Was she forever contradicting herself? Her mind was a muddled mass of confusion. She thought one thing and another came out of her mouth.

"I'll stay, Reggie. Now sleep."

His hand crept around hers, laced her fingers with his. She gripped his hand tight and surrendered to the shadows.

CHAPTER 7

The three men sat at the breakfast table just a few feet away from the couch where Reggie slept. Cam stole a glance every once in a while, but she hadn't moved since she'd gone to sleep an hour earlier.

There was a fragility to her that bothered him. Reggie? She was usually tough as nails, full of sass and an attitude to rival a pit bull. Her brush with death had scared her. Hell, it had scared the shit out of *him*. But he knew that wasn't the only thing that had put that vulnerability in her eyes.

With a resigned sigh, he faced Sawyer and Hutch.

"All things considered, I think she took it well," Sawyer said with a shrug.

Hutch laughed. "She took it well because we drugged her ass and she was in shock. We won't get off so lightly when she wakes up and the drugs wear off."

"No one said it would be easy," Cam offered.

Hutch put his hands behind his head and leaned back in his chair. There was frustration and an edge of fear reflected in his expression. Cam could understand that. He felt the two conflict-ing emotions, had felt them for a damn long time.

"Are we kidding ourselves?" Hutch asked. "I mean really? Who the hell has the kind of relationship we're proposing? I wake some mornings and wonder if I haven't lost my damn mind."

Sawyer leaned forward, his beefy arms resting on the table. His fists were clenched tight. "We've been over this, Hutch. How much more do you want to rehash it? What do you want to hear? That in a perfect world, you and Cam would disappear from the picture, and Reggie would only be with me?"

Hutch looked away, his jaw tight.

"This isn't helping," Cam said.

"Oh shut up," Hutch muttered. "You can't tell me you haven't had those thoughts."

Cam raised an eyebrow. "No, Hutch, I can't tell you that. But what good does it do me? We've had this conversation. We agreed that we all love her and that we wouldn't make her choose."

"No, we agreed that she *wouldn't* choose," Sawyer said quietly. "Our *solution* is our only way to have a part of her. Are you hav-ing second thoughts, Hutch?"

Hutch pressed his lips together and finally shook his head. "No. But I'm not going to bullshit you either. Standing back while you and Cam touch her, comfort her, is hard. I've loved Reggie since we were children. I've always felt as though she were mine. That's a hard notion to let go of."

"No one's trying to take her away," Cam said.

Hutch rubbed his hand over his face. "I know that, Cam. I do. But I can't help the way I feel watching another man touch her. Don't you think I realize that jealousy is the quickest way to make this fail? And that as fucked up and twisted as this is, the three of us sharing her, it represents my only shot at having a life with her?"

"I hear you," Sawyer muttered.

Cam nodded. "I understand, man. It's going to take a lot of sacrifice from all three of us. Not to mention patience. Because Reggie . . . she's going to fight this. Not because she doesn't love us. I believe she does, and that's the problem."

"She's stubborn and ornery as hell," Sawyer said wryly. "But she would also cut off her right arm before ever hurting any of us. And in her eyes, this can only lead to inevitable hurt, and so she avoids us, which hurts her."

"Stubborn is right," Hutch grumbled.

"In her mind, she's protecting us," Cam spoke up. "She's been protecting us since we were kids. It's time for that shit to stop. She's going to balk at any notion that we're taking care of or protecting her, but after what happened, I'm no longer willing to sit back and wait for the right time."

Hutch and Sawyer both nodded.

"And look, this probably doesn't need saying, but I'm going to say it anyway," Cam added.

Sawyer rolled his eyes. "Is this the big brother lecture?"

Cam ignored him. "I understand we all have our reservations. We have concerns and fears and maybe even resentment. But we've got to be careful to present a united front to Reggie, otherwise this will never work. If we have a problem, then we're going to have to hash it out privately. We don't want to give her yet another reason to keep running."

"You're right. It doesn't need saying," Hutch said.

"Yeah, it does," Sawyer said. "We can't afford to screw this up with stupid bullshit. We're not a bunch of girls. Reggie means a lot to us all. I'm having to put my trust in the two of you not to screw up *my* chances with her. That's pretty messed up. So yeah, I'd say we need that reminder often."

Cam studied the other two men and saw a calmness to their demeanor he hadn't seen since Birdie had called them about Reggie. Yeah, they'd needed this talk, and maybe they needed it more often just to reinforce what was at stake.

"Okay, now that all that's out of the way, we have other arrangements to make," Cam said.

"Yeah? Like what?" Hutch asked.

"We need to drive back to Houston to get your vehicle and Sawyer's, plus we need to transfer our office here for now, which means moving everything."

"Did you get with the Robertsons about their project?" Sawyer asked.

Cam nodded. "Yeah, they were okay with the delay when I explained the circumstances. Even so, I need to finish up those drawings so we can go ahead with the building."

"What about Reggie?" Hutch asked. "One of us needs to stay here with her."

"I can call Birdie and ask her to come over and stay with Reggie. You two can ride back to Houston with me, and one of you can head right back in your truck. The other can help me get everything together from the office to take back here."

"Hutch can come back in his truck," Sawyer said. "I'll hang out and help you clean out the office. Hutch can arrange to have our calls forwarded to the number here. He needs to grocery shop anyway."

A soft moan from the couch silenced the men. Cam swiveled in his chair to see Reggie stir.

Hutch stood and pushed his chair back. "I'll go see about making some supper," he said in a low voice. "She's going to be hungry."

"Chicken," Sawyer muttered.

Hutch grinned and sauntered toward the kitchen, leaving Cam and Sawyer at the table.

Regina opened her eyes and blinked to try and clear the cobwebs. She felt like someone's personal punching bag. And then she remembered that for all practical purposes she *had* been someone's punching bag.

She tried to sit up, but every muscle in her body protested the movement. With a groan, she sank back against the pillows. Cam and Sawyer appeared in front of her and looked down, concern in their eyes.

"How are you feeling?" Sawyer asked.

"Like someone beat the hell out of me?"

Cam's lips came together in a thin line.

"Bad choice of words," she mumbled.

She tried to sit up again, and this time, Sawyer reached down and helped her. Her stomach rolled, and a hot flash of nausea made her momentarily weak.

"I'm starving," she said. "I don't think taking that painkiller on an empty stomach was the smartest idea."

"Hutch is making supper now," Cam said.

She stared up at the two men towering over her. "What am I doing here?" she asked. "What are you doing here? And where is here exactly?"

Cam and Sawyer exchanged glances. One of those looks that told her they were ganging up on her. She glared up at them, silently daring one of them to pull that touching stunt. They kept their distance, so maybe the subtle threat worked.

Or not.

Cam sat down on one side while Sawyer took the other. Their body heat reached out and enveloped her, wrapped her in a comforting blanket. Forgotten was the down comforter bunched in her lap.

"This is our house," Cam said simply. "We just finished construction a few weeks ago."

She shook her head in confusion. "I don't understand. You live in Houston. Your business is in Houston. We didn't drive that far from the hospital, did we? I wasn't that out of it, surely."

"We bought a hundred acres about twenty minutes out of Cypress," Sawyer said.

"But why? What about your business?"

"You know why," Cam said evenly. "You're here. This is where we grew up. We've always had plans to come back once our business was established."

She raised a shaky hand and ran it through her hair. "I didn't even know you were building."

Sawyer stared levelly at her. "You'd know it if you weren't so intent on avoiding us."

She flushed guiltily.

"Dinner's ready," Hutch called from across the room.

"Hutch to the rescue," Cam said in an amused voice. "It's coming, though, Reggie darling. We're going to have a long overdue conversation. You can't avoid it forever."

She sucked in a deep breath through her nose and locked gazes with him. "I know," she said quietly.

Surprise flickered in his eyes at her acceptance. Sawyer lifted one eyebrow but didn't respond. Instead, he stood and bent to help her from the couch.

She reached up with her good hand to grab Cam's as Sawyer grasped her shoulders and lifted.

"Take it slow," Cam cautioned. "Don't try to move too fast."

Though she still ached from head to toe, she moved with more steadiness than she had before. Her legs seemed to be cooperating better, and her knees didn't feel so shaky.

Sawyer guided her toward a table in front of the French doors and settled her into a chair. He took the seat across from her, and Cam pulled out the chair beside her. A few moments later, Hutch walked in carrying two bowls. He set one in front of her and another in front of Cam.

"Figured this would feel good on your throat," Hutch said as he handed her a spoon.

She looked up at him and went soft. She smiled gratefully and took the spoon, her fingers brushing across his. "Thank you," she said huskily.

He winked at her and returned to the kitchen. She ladled some of the steaming liquid into the spoon and gently blew on it as she raised it to her lips.

She sipped cautiously and made a sound of contentment when the warm broth slid down her throat.

"Good?" Hutch asked as he returned with bowls for himself and Sawyer.

"Excellent," she said. "I was starving."

Hutch took the seat next to her. His knee bumped her leg, and he muttered an apology as he repositioned himself.

She continued to spoon the soup into her mouth, savoring the rich taste. She glanced cautiously up at the others, but they were concentrating on their own food. Sawyer looked up and caught her gaze. Amusement flickered in his eyes.

"Eat, Reggie. We're not staging an ambush."

She dropped her gaze to her soup, her cheeks warm. An ambush was exactly what she'd expected. She frowned unhappily as she stirred the contents of her bowl in slow circles. She hated the loss of their closeness. She missed it. Craved it.

It used to be enough that she could just be around them. Enjoy their company and the friendship between the four of them. Now she viewed their every action with fear and suspicion. Oh, they wouldn't hurt her, and the awkwardness wasn't their fault.

It was hers. Her weakness was to blame. She'd ruined everything.

"It's not going to eat itself," Cam said dryly.

She looked up to see all three of them looking at her. She put her spoon down, knowing she wasn't going to be able to eat until they got the elephant out of the room.

"What happened a year ago . . . shouldn't have happened," she said in a low voice.

CHAPTER 8

Cam, Sawyer and Hutch all stopped eating and stared at her. Hard. The intensity of their gazes unnerved her. Made her feel as though she'd committed some unpardonable sin.

"Why?" Sawyer asked bluntly. "Why shouldn't it have happened, Reggie?"

She blinked in surprise and shifted uncomfortably in her chair. She hadn't expected to be asked why. And it was apparent in Cam and Hutch's expressions that they too wanted an answer.

God. Why should she have to explain it? Shouldn't it be obvious? What sort of person had sex with *three* men? At the same time! Three men who were her best friends. People she trusted. These weren't people to trifle with—to play with their emotions or make promises with her body she couldn't keep.

"It shouldn't have happened," she said stubbornly.

"And we want to know why," Hutch said calmly.

She made a sound of frustration. She scooted her seat back, ready to escape. Cam reached over and wrapped his fingers around her wrist to prevent her flight.

"No more running," he said. "We're going to talk about this, Reggie."

She closed her eyes. "What do you want from me? Do you want me to admit what a twisted, screwed up person I am to have had sex with three men? My God, it equated to a gang bang. You're my friends—"

She was interrupted as Sawyer stood so forcefully that he knocked over his chair.

"Sawyer," Hutch said in a warning voice.

Sawyer ignored him and leaned over the table, his hands flat against the wood.

"Gang bang? You want to reduce what we had to some shoddy porn flick?"

She flinched at the fierceness in his voice. He was pissed.

"Do you honestly think that we'd ever disrespect you like that, Reggie? Because if you do, then we have bigger problems than the fact we had sex. I understand that what happened threw you for a loop. Don't you think it did the same to us? But to relegate it to some cheap thrill with you playing the starring role as a porn bunny pisses me the fuck off, and I don't mind telling you that."

"Sawyer, sit down," Cam said calmly.

"No, Cam. I won't fucking sit down." He stared Regina down, his eyes never moving from her face. "I don't know what that night meant to you, Reggie. I don't know because you won't talk about it. But you want to know what it meant to me? To them?" he asked as he gestured at Cam and Hutch.

"What?" she whispered.

"It was the best night of my life. I waited a long damn time to make love to you. Did I plan it? No. In a perfect world we would have eased you into a situation where making love with us all wouldn't have unsettled you so damn much. But it just happened,

Reggie. We didn't plan it. But I don't regret it either. Can you look me in the eye and tell me you regret it? Really?"

Her mouth went dry. She felt cornered. Not by them, but by her own damning emotions. She'd never lied to them before. She'd never kept anything from them. And yet for the last year, she'd withdrawn, essentially lying by omission, by her refusal to acknowledge what had happened between them.

She got to her feet and turned away in an effort to collect herself. She didn't want to crumble in front of them, and she felt dangerously close to doing so.

She clutched her arms and rubbed up and down, and then she turned back to them.

"I don't know," she whispered. "I don't know. I've struggled so hard to forget, to put it out of my mind. I don't want things to change between us. God, I couldn't bear it. You're my only friends. The only people who matter to me. How could I have let that night happen?"

Hutch started to speak, but she silenced him with a raised hand. She didn't want to tell them what was burning a hole in her gut. Didn't want to bare her soul so painfully. But it was clawing at her chest, straining to get out. And maybe it would be the last straw in their already struggling relationship.

"After that night . . . a few months after it happened, I went out with another guy. I was determined to put that night out of my mind. I had . . . sex with him." She closed her eyes as tears threatened to spill over the rims. And she couldn't bear to see the condemnation in their expressions. She heard a swift intake of breath. More than one.

When she worked up the courage to reopen her eyes, the room was blurry through a sheen of tears. She continued on, determined to rid herself of the guilt and self-condemnation. Or maybe embrace it.

"I had sex with him . . . and the next morning I just wanted to die. I felt . . . I felt like I had *betrayed* you. All of you. I couldn't even look you in the eye. I couldn't face *myself* in the mirror. How fucked up is that?"

Cam stood and started to make his way over to where she was, but she stepped back and held out a hand. He stopped, his expression pained, his eyes haunted. Her gaze skittered to Hutch and Sawyer's faces and saw mirroring pain there. Her heart seized.

"I've had sex before. I mean, you know that. But I never felt like I was betraying you. You've had relationships. I've had men in my life. That never interfered with our friendship. But after that night, I couldn't even think about being intimate with another man because all I could see were your reactions if you knew. And yet I couldn't face you anyway because of what happened. So either way I *lose*," she whispered. "And God, I can't stand the thought of that."

Hutch got up and walked toward her, ignoring her outstretched hand. He grasped her wrist, tucked his arm around her waist as he moved in quick. He slid his hand behind her head and tilted her neck to meet his kiss.

She'd hungered for this. Lain awake so many nights reliving each and every moment of the three men making love to her.

He swallowed her protest and deepened the kiss. His lips moved ravenously over hers as if he'd hungered for it every bit as much as she had.

He pulled slightly away but continued to press light kisses against her lips.

"You aren't going to lose us, Reggie. Not unless you keep running. You keep saying you can't stand the thought of things changing, but they didn't change when we made love, baby. They changed when you bolted like a scared jackrabbit. This last year? We've only seen bits and snatches of you because every time we get close, you find an excuse to be somewhere else. You say you don't want to hurt us, but damn it, Reggie, that hurts us."

"He's right," Sawyer interjected.

Hutch moved to the side, and she stared over at Sawyer who still stood by the table, his eyes glittering with intensity.

"You're angry with me," she said softly. But for some reason she didn't think he was angry because she'd admitted to sleeping with another man. Yeah, it had hurt them, but they seemed to push it aside.

"Yes. No. Yes, damn it, I am," Sawyer said in frustration. "I'm angry at the situation. I'm angry because I don't know what to do to fix this, to make things right between us. I don't know how to make you not afraid."

Cam finally rose to his feet. He took a long, measured stare first at Sawyer and then Hutch. They were doing that whole silent communication thing again, and it unnerved her. Made her feel like she didn't stand a chance in hell against them.

Cam walked over to where she stood with Hutch, and he reached out for her hand. He didn't take it. He just held his out and waited for her to take it.

She eyed him nervously for a minute before relenting and sliding her fingers into his. He squeezed gently and rubbed his thumb across the top of her knuckles.

"We're going to take this slow, Reggie. There's a lot riding on this. We don't want to pressure you, but we aren't going to be dishonest with you either."

Fear tightened her chest, expanding until she could hardly breathe. "What is it you want?"

"You, Reggie. We want you."

"I don't understand."

He nodded. "You understand. If you didn't, you wouldn't be so damn scared. You wouldn't be avoiding us."

"Do we have to spell it out, Reggie?" Hutch asked.

Sawyer closed in on her from the front.

"We want you," he said simply. "With us. Look around, honey." He gestured around the room. "We didn't build this just for us. We built it for you." He moved closer and gathered her other hand in his, raising it and placing it over his heart. "Be with me, Reggie. Be with *us.*"

Her brain shut down. What they proposed . . . even though she knew, knew it before, and feared it, hearing it out loud . . . it was shocking. A jolt to her system. She couldn't wrap her mind around it.

She licked her lips trying to formulate words, some kind of response. What did you say to something like that? How could you possibly respond?

She closed her eyes as fatigue crept over her, clawing at her. Weariness that had little to do with her injuries and everything to do with the emotional drain sucking at her, descended over her like a dark, suffocating blanket.

She swayed, steadied herself against Sawyer and tried to step back. He wouldn't let her go. Instead he pulled her into his arms and wrapped himself around her. His hand caressed her cheek as he pressed her against his chest, and he kissed the top of her head.

"Get her another pill," she heard him say. She started to shake her head, but he stilled her motion.

"This was a lot to dump on you, honey," he murmured into her hair. "We don't expect you to give us an answer today or even tomorrow. All we ask is that you don't run from us anymore. Stay and face this thing between us. Give us a chance. Whether you like it or not, things have changed between us. Where we go from here is up to us. We can let it destroy us, or we can face it head-on. You're no coward, Reggie. It's time to stop acting like one."

He pulled her away and stared down at her, his blue eyes blazing with sincerity . . . and determination. She didn't answer, but then he didn't seem to expect her to.

Her gaze flitted over to where Cam stood solemnly watching her. She stared questioningly at him. He stared back, his dark eyes reflecting the same sincerity she'd seen in Sawyer's. They were serious.

Hutch walked back up and thrust a mug of hot chocolate at her. Sawyer took the mug when she reached for it, and Hutch caught her hand, uncurled her fingers as he'd done before and dropped a pill into it.

"Bully," she muttered.

"When it comes to you, baby, I don't mind being labeled a bully. Now take the damn pill, and I want you to drink your hot chocolate so there's something more in your stomach. You didn't eat much of your soup."

He held up his hand when she would have spoken.

"I'm not finished. And when you're done with the hot chocolate, you're going to carry your ass up the stairs, and you're going to get into your bed."

"Yes, sir."

Hutch's stern expression faltered, and a half grin cracked his lips. "I'd watch that smart mouth of yours."

They all watched as she downed the pill, and then Cam guided her over to the couch. Sawyer handed her the mug, being careful that she didn't spill it.

Hutch went back to clear the table while Cam took a seat beside her.

"We're going to run back to Houston tomorrow morning first thing. I'm going to call Birdie to come over and stay with you."

"But—"

"No buts," he said firmly. "Birdie will stay with you until we return. Hutch is going to start back as soon as he picks up his ride, while Sawyer and I pack up the office and get the things we need to bring back here."

"You're such a pain in the ass," she grumbled.

He smiled and cupped her cheek. He stared at her mouth for a long moment before he finally lowered his head to hers.

She lost herself momentarily in the sensation of his touch. His kiss was warm and gentle. Undemanding. Soft and coaxing. An invitation to respond.

Her hand tangled in his hair, pulling him closer even as she fought the notion that what she was doing was wrong.

Finally she pulled away and rested her forehead against his. She closed her eyes as her breath came rapidly.

Cam's hand came up to touch her cheek, his forehead pressed to hers.

"Don't you dare regret it," he said. "I don't want to see self-condemnation in those eyes when you open them. Just let it happen, Reggie. Stop overthinking it."

She rested her hands on his shoulders then slid her uninjured hand over to curl around his neck.

"I'm so scared, Cam," she whispered. It nearly killed her to say it, to admit it, but there it was.

He cupped the back of her neck and dug his fingers into her hair. "You don't have to be afraid, Reggie. Never with us. Don't you know we'd never hurt you?"

She pressed closer to him, hugging him. She rested her cheek against his chest and held on tight. "I don't want to lose any of you," she choked out. "And I'm so afraid of what will happen. I just want things to go back to the way they were."

Cam wrapped his arms around her. "We can't go back, Reggie. Only forward. But there's no reason why forward has to be a bad thing."

Her eyes drooped as the drugs seeped through her system. She held on to Cam, for now not wanting to let go. It had been so long since she let them close.

"I missed you," she said again.

Cam took a deep breath against her, and some of the tension escaped him. "I missed you too, Reggie darling. I'm not sure you realize how much. You're important to me. More important than I think you'll ever know."

When he moved as though to pull away, she clung to him. "Don't go. Not yet."

"You need to be in bed. It's been a hell of a day for you."

She drew away just enough that she could see into his eyes. "Hold me for just a bit, Cam. I'm so tired of feeling lonely."

He leaned back against the couch and took her with him, cuddling her close against his body. The painkillers were pulling her under, tugging her into sweet oblivion. But she wasn't ready to escape yet. She wanted to live just a little longer in the moment. Feel Cam's arms around her where she felt loved and cherished.

She struggled to stay awake, but his hand stroking over her head lulled her. As her eyes fluttered, she saw Hutch and Sawyer standing a few feet away, watching her. She wanted to say something, to make sure they didn't feel left out. She anxiously searched their expressions for anger or resentment, but all she found was warmth.

She kept her unfocused stare on the two of them until the edges of her periphery started to fade and blacken. She blinked once more and then surrendered to the dark.

CHAPTER 9

S awyer opened the front door and ushered Birdie inside. He hugged her and gave her a sloppy kiss on the cheek.

"Thanks for coming, Birdie. Reggie is still asleep, and we're going to go ahead and take off so we can get back as soon as possible."

Birdie smiled and patted his arm. He grinned at the gesture. It was so reminiscent of when he was much younger, just a boy with an attitude, confused by Birdie's quiet acceptance.

She had befuddled him from the start. Unlike other foster parents who couldn't wait to lay down the law and rein him in, Birdie had smiled at him. Not just any smile but one full of love and understanding. She managed to get her way by using that smile, because who could look at her and not feel guilty?

Sawyer wrapped an arm around Birdie and urged her toward the living room. She felt fragile and slight against him. A curl of panic circled his stomach. He didn't like to think of Birdie getting older. She was too important to all of them.

"Are you getting enough rest, Birdie? Have you seen your doctor lately?"

She smiled as she sat down in the chair and actually rolled her eyes when Sawyer fussed around her, pulling the ottoman over to prop her feet up.

"I'm right as rain, Sawyer. Even Doc Stevens says so."

Sawyer frowned. "Do you think maybe you should consider seeing a doctor in Houston? Maybe a specialist? I mean Doc Stevens is older than dirt. He was practicing medicine in the stone age. Maybe he's not up to date on the latest medical developments."

Her eyes twinkled with merriment. "I'm two years older than Doc Stevens, Sawyer."

His cheeks tightened, and he ducked his head. "I guess that didn't come out too well," he mumbled.

She laughed and put her wrinkled hand on his wrist. "I'm fine. Really. Doc says I'll live another thirty years."

"Good," he said gruffly.

Cam and Hutch walked into the living room, their eyes lighting up when they saw Birdie. Sawyer stepped back as they both enfolded Birdie in hugs. She smiled and preened under their compliments and patted each of them on the cheek as though they were ten years old again. And both of them beamed from ear to ear under her attentions.

Sawyer shook his head. They were all kids when it came to Birdie. She had a way of making them feel important. And loved. They had no defense against her, and none of them had a problem admitting that at all.

"You'll be okay here with Reggie?" Cam asked in a serious tone.

Birdie waved her hand at him. "You boys get on out of here. Regina and I will be fine. I'll make sure she takes her pill just like you wanted. She'll probably sleep until you get back."

"Okay, well you have our cell numbers. Call us if you have any problem at all."

She made shooing motions with her hands. They each kissed her again, and she got up to go see them out. She stood at the door waving as they drove away, and Sawyer stared at her image in the side-view mirror until they turned onto the highway.

"Maybe we should offer to move her out to the house," Sawyer said as he leaned back in the seat.

Cam glanced sideways at him, and Hutch leaned forward from the backseat to rest his arms over the middle divider.

"Who, Birdie?" Hutch asked.

Sawyer nodded. "Yeah. I mean she's getting older. We should think about taking care of her better. She lives alone in that same old house she's always lived in."

"That's home," Cam said. "I don't want her to get rid of the house."

Hutch nodded.

"She doesn't have to get rid of it," Sawyer said patiently. "I just thought we could keep a better eye on her if she was staying with us in the new house."

"One, she'd never go for it," Cam said. "She's too independent, and the fact is, she's healthy as a horse. She'll outlive us all. Two, think about what you're saying." He eyed Sawyer for a moment before returning his gaze to the road. "You'd be putting her in the middle of an already awkward situation with Reggie. It's going to be hard enough to convince Reggie to stay with us. Add Birdie to the mix, and it wouldn't be fair to either of them."

Sawyer grimaced. "Yeah, good point. It's just that . . . having our family there. It sounded nice."

He shifted a little uncomfortably as he felt the other two staring at him. He should've just kept his mouth shut, because he sounded like a damn moron.

"I know what you mean," Hutch said. "But Birdie is close, and now that we're moving back, we'll be able to check in on her more often."

"The more important issue is whether we're going to be able to convince Reggie to stay," Cam said.

Sawyer's eyes narrowed, and he jerked his head in Cam's direction. It was the second time in as many days that he'd heard Cam express doubts. *Fuck it all.* If Cam was unsure, what the fuck was Sawyer supposed to think?

"You don't sound so certain, Cam," Hutch said in a low voice.

Sawyer glanced back at Hutch to see the same confusion registered in Hutch's expression. He exchanged a quick glance with Hutch and offered a shrug in return.

Cam ran a hand through his hair and gave an agitated-sounding sigh.

"I don't know," he muttered. "I'm worried. That's all. This is too important. If we don't handle it just right, we could fuck things up permanently."

"Are you trying to make a point here, Cam?" Sawyer demanded. "If you have something to say, just say it."

Cam frowned and looked his way again. "No man, I wasn't making any point other than exactly what I said."

"Well, your inference was that one of us is screwing things up, and if that's the case, you need to just get it out now."

"Hold up," Hutch said. "You need to back off, Sawyer. Your in-the-face approach ain't going to cut it with us or with Reggie."

Sawyer turned in his seat and pinned Hutch with his stare. "What are you saying, man? You got a problem with me?"

"I've got a problem with you getting in Reggie's face and pushing too hard," Hutch said unflinchingly.

Sawyer felt a prickle of guilt creep up his neck. But he also resented the implication that he was to blame for Reggie's resistance.

He wasn't good at the lovey dovey shit. He wasn't gentle like Cam or laid back like Hutch. He couldn't seem to curb the edge of desperation when it came to Reggie, and as a result he came across too forceful. Yeah, he knew that, but he didn't need Cam or Hutch shoving it into his face.

"I'm not you, and I'm not Cam," he said as calmly as he was able. "Besides, Reggie's not a wuss. She can take it."

Regina lay in bed staring up at the ceiling. She heard footsteps on the stairs and waited as they sounded down the hall and nearer to her bedroom.

She looked over when the door eased open. Birdie stuck her head in and then smiled when she saw that Regina was awake.

"Hello, dear," she said as she walked toward the bed. "I was just coming up to check on you. How are you feeling?"

Regina stretched slightly, testing the soreness of her ribs, and was pleased to find there wasn't as much pain as the previous day. She sat up and returned Birdie's smile.

"I'm feeling better actually."

She raised her hand to touch her bruised throat and probed tentatively. Her voice didn't sound quite as raspy.

"Almost human again," she added.

Birdie sat on the edge of the bed and laid her hand over Regina's. "The boys left medication for you to take. Do you want it?"

Regina lifted an eyebrow. "You're giving me a choice? They all but shoved the pills down my throat yesterday."

Birdie smiled, and the soft wrinkles around her eyes gathered. "They mean well. They love you," she said simply. "Sometimes men go a little overboard when expressing their feelings. Are you in any pain?"

Regina shook her head and avoided Birdie's stare. She wasn't in any physical pain, but the memory of last night's confrontation was sharp. And now Birdie speaking of love. This conversation could only veer into very uncomfortable territory.

Birdie's hand tightened around Regina's fingers. "I see the worry, the fear in your eyes, Regina. I hope you aren't afraid of me."

Regina's shoulders slumped. She chanced a glimpse into the older woman's eyes but only found kindness in them.

"Do you . . . do you know what they want?" she asked tentatively.

Birdie sighed. "I love those boys. You know that. I also know how stubborn they are. Just like another person I know." She glanced teasingly at Regina as she spoke. "If you're asking if I know they love you and they built this house for you and they want you to live here . . . with them, then yes, I know what they want. They were quite honest with me about it."

"And what did you say?" Regina asked softly.

Birdie's mouth twisted a little. "What could I say?" She shifted forward on the bed. "I have the same concerns any mother has. I want my boys happy. I asked them if they'd lost their minds."

Regina laughed. She couldn't help it. "That about covers my reaction," she mumbled.

"Regina, I'm not here to lecture you. I'm not here to tell you what to do with your life. All I want to make clear is that no matter what happens between you and those boys it won't change how I feel about you."

Relief swept over her. She squeezed Birdie's hand. "Thank you, Birdie. That means a lot to me."

"Do you feel up to going downstairs?" Birdie asked. "I've fixed some chicken and dumplings and a big pitcher of tea just the way you like it."

"Oh, that sounds wonderful. I'm starving."

Birdie smiled. "Come on then, and I'll fix you a plate."

Regina threw back the covers and eased her legs over the edge as Birdie stood and moved away from the bed. Birdie reached for her arm when Regina put her feet down and stood.

She really did feel a lot better. Her head wasn't so damn fuzzy, a fact she was grateful for. Maybe now she could face the guys lucidly instead of like a blathering, weepy idiot.

With Birdie at her side, she slowly made her way out the door and toward the stairs. When they reached the top, the sound of a door shutting halted Regina in her tracks.

She glanced at Birdie. "Are they back so soon?"

Birdie frowned. "They only left an hour ago. They would've called if they'd forgotten something."

Regina heard footsteps. They sounded like they came from the back of the house, not the front. Her pulse ratcheted up, and she put a hand on Birdie's arm.

"Get back in the bedroom and shut the door. Lock it. Don't come out until I come for you. If I'm not back in a few minutes, you call the police."

Birdie's frightened gaze met hers, but she nodded and quickly backtracked into the bedroom. Regina ducked into one of the other bedrooms in search of a weapon. She'd obviously stumbled into Sawyer's room, judging by all the baseball paraphernalia. She grabbed a wooden baseball bat from the wall display and curled her hands around the handle. Her injured wrist protested the action, and her brace made her grip clumsy, but she ignored the discomfort and gripped the bat tighter.

Crap. It was an autographed bat. She didn't want to know by whom. Sawyer would kick her ass if she cracked his bat on someone's head.

Ignoring the twinge in her ribs, she hurried to the stairs and silently crept down. When she reached the bottom, she flattened herself against the wall and peered around to the living room.

She strained to hear any sounds, but silence lay heavy over the house. Only the hum of the refrigerator could be heard.

The sound had come from the back. Not the French doors. Was there a door into the kitchen from the back? She honestly couldn't remember.

She whipped around the corner and strode into the kitchen, bat up and ready to swing. She froze when she saw the wide-open door. Damn it all to hell. She was here without her gun in an unfamiliar house.

Her gaze fell on the cordless phone lying on the counter by the sink. She inched her way over, still listening for any sound within the house. Birdie. She'd left Birdie alone upstairs. Christ.

She snatched up the phone and raced back to the stairs. "Birdie, it's me, let me in," she said outside the door.

Birdie opened the door immediately, and Regina strode in. She shut the door and locked it again, then motioned Birdie to move away.

As she started to punch in Jeremy's number, she glanced up at Birdie. "Jesus. I don't even know where we are, Birdie. Can you tell Jeremy how to get out here?"

At Birdie's nod, Regina put the phone to her ear and silently urged Jeremy to answer.

"Miller here."

"Jeremy, thank God."

"Regina, is that you? What's wrong?"

"I need a unit out here. There's an intruder on the premises."

"Where are you?" he demanded.

"I'm going to give the phone to Birdie. I have no idea where the hell I am."

She thrust the phone at Birdie before he could respond.

"It's off county road 126," Birdie said in a steady voice. "A quarter mile past Cypress Creek. It's the second left after the creek. Go up the drive and you'll see the house when you top the hill."

She handed the phone back to Regina.

"Regina? You there?" Jeremy said.

"Yeah, I'm here."

"Okay, hang tight. I'm on my way. I've called in one of the county units. They'll probably be on scene before I will. Stay where you are and keep the phone on you."

Regina hung the phone up and looked over at Birdie. "Someone's in the house, or at least they were. The back door is open." She glanced around the room, her gaze lighting on the large walk-in closet. "In the closet," she directed Birdie.

She was across the room, pushing Birdie toward the door before Birdie could even react. She opened the closet and helped Birdie to the back. She quickly arranged some of the empty boxes in front of her. "Get down and stay down," Regina said in a quiet voice.

"What about you?" Birdie asked. Her voice trembled, and she looked at Regina fearfully.

"I'll be in the bedroom," Regina said calmly. "Jeremy's on his way. He's sending another unit. If someone comes into the bedroom, I'll take his head off with the baseball bat. But no matter what you hear, you do not come out of this closet until either I or Jeremy or another police officer comes in for you. Okay?"

Birdie nodded.

Regina backed out of the closet and closed the door. She readjusted her grip on the bat and scoped the best spot to lie in ambush for anyone coming through the door.

Once again, she found herself waiting an eternity for Jeremy to arrive. She edged toward the window and looked out to see if there was a vehicle or if she could see the intruder on foot.

Nothing.

She returned to the door, put her ear against it and listened. Her breath caught, and sweat rolled down her neck when she heard the creak of the bottom step. The sound halted.

She pressed forward, straining to hear if the intruder was moving up the stairs.

Several long minutes passed. Tension coiled and built in her chest. A painful knot centered between her shoulder blades, and her muscles quivered as she continued to hold the bat up, her hands locked around it.

Her heart leapt, and she nearly dropped the bat when the shrill ring of the phone burst through the air. She eyed the receiver she'd left on the bed. If she let it ring, the intruder might assume no one was in the house. If she answered it, he'd know for sure he wasn't alone.

Despite the fact that it might be Jeremy or Dispatch or even one of the guys, she let it ring. But she couldn't hear what was going on outside the bedroom door over the sound.

She raised the bat higher, ready to strike. Then the ringing stopped, and she heard the scrape of a shoe outside the door of the bedroom.

Anger bubbled up, replacing fear.

Bastard had picked the wrong house to break into. She was tired, grumpy and in pain. She was dying to kick some ass, and at this point she wasn't particular about whose ass it was.

A sudden noise sounded and then the thump of feet on stairs. In a hurry. No care was taken.

She bolted from the bedroom in pursuit. The intruder was fleeing. She hit the stairs at a dead run and took them two at a time. Pain jolted through her chest, but she ignored it and kept going.

The slam of a door directed her to the kitchen. The front door flew open, and she yanked her head around to see a sheriff's deputy burst into the house, gun raised.

"Around back," she yelled. "He went out the back."

The deputy ran out the front, and Regina bolted for the back door. She yanked open the door and stepped out, her head moving rapidly as she scanned the area.

Where the hell could he have gone? There was a pond down the hill from the house, and beyond was a wooded area, but the man couldn't have run that fast.

The deputy appeared around the side of the house, and Regina motioned to her left.

"He had to have gone this way," she said.

"Get back inside. You're not armed."

Regina clenched her jaw in frustration but knew he was right. She'd be a distraction if he had to worry about covering not only himself but her. And there was Birdie to consider, still sitting in the closet, probably terrified.

As she reentered the house, she saw Jeremy's patrol car tear up the front drive, and he and another officer got out and headed toward the side of the house where the deputy had gone.

Regina mounted the stairs and hurried to the bedroom. She threw the bat onto the bed and opened the closet door.

"Birdie, it's okay. You can come out now."

"Thank goodness," Birdie said, her voice trembling as she stood.

Regina reached out to steady her and took her arm to help her around the boxes.

"What's going on, Regina?"

She shook her head. "I'm not sure. The intruder escaped out the back, and Jeremy and the others are in pursuit. We'll wait here until we know something."

She eased Birdie over to the bed and then sat down beside her.

Birdie laid her hand on Regina's arm. "Are you okay? How are your ribs?"

Regina touched her chest experimentally and grimaced. "I'll feel it later."

"We should call the boys," Birdie said. "They'll want to get back as soon as they can."

Regina shook her head. "There's no point. There's nothing they can do. They'd just worry." Freak out, hover some more. It was the last thing she needed right now.

The two women sat in silence, their hands joined as they waited for Jeremy and the others to return. Finally she heard Jeremy call from the bottom of the stairs.

"We're coming up, Regina."

Regina stood and walked to the door. Jeremy appeared a moment later, Carl behind him.

"Did you get him?" Regina asked, even though she could tell by their expressions that they hadn't.

Jeremy shook his head. She stood back and let them into the bedroom. Jeremy walked over to where Birdie sat.

"Are you okay, Mrs. Michaels?"

She smiled. "Yes, thank you for asking. I'm more concerned about Regina. She went after him with a baseball bat."

Jeremy and Carl both pinned her with a questioning stare.

"I didn't have my weapon," she muttered.

"Are you okay? Do we need to take you back to the hospital?" Jeremy asked.

"Did you engage the intruder?" Carl asked.

She shook her head. "No, I didn't actually see him. I went downstairs after we heard a noise. I saw the back door was open. I worried about Birdie so I came back upstairs to call it in. While we waited, I heard him on the stairs and then right outside the bedroom door. He must have heard the sheriff's deputy drive up, because he ran down the stairs. I gave chase. I heard him go out the back. The deputy came in, and I directed him around back. When I exited the house, I didn't see any sign of him."

"We found footprints outside. No way to know if they were his." Carl paused. "But they were big. We'll take a mold, but it looks a hell of a lot like the footprints at our last crime scene."

Regina froze. "Are you saying it's the same guy?"

Carl shook his head. "No, but the coincidences are a little staggering. I'll get more guys out here to comb the area for any evidence. He had to have driven in at some point. Maybe we'll get lucky and find tire tracks. I'll have the house dusted for prints."

Regina looked over at Birdie. "Can you drive me home?"

Birdie frowned. "I don't think that's a good idea, Regina. The boys won't like it. You're supposed to be staying here so you aren't alone."

"I don't plan to stay at my house," she said calmly. "But I want my backup weapon. Chief still has my service gun. I don't want to be without protection while I'm waiting to get it back."

"Probably a good idea," Jeremy said. "Where are the guys anyway?"

"Houston," Regina said shortly. "They had to tie up some things with their job. They'll be back later today."

"We'll try to be out of the way by then," Carl said. "Jeremy and I will stay out here and process the scene. I want the sheriff's deputy to follow you and Mrs. Michaels to your place and then escort you back here. There's no reason to take unnecessary risks."

Regina nodded. "Do you mind, Birdie?"

"Of course not, dear. We can leave whenever you're ready."

CHAPTER 10

$\mathcal{H}$utch turned into the driveway and accelerated up the dirt road leading to the house. The trip to Houston had annoyed him. He hadn't wanted to spend the day away from Reggie. Not when she was just out of the hospital.

When he topped the hill and saw four police cars parked outside the house and Birdie's car gone, his stomach knotted. Maybe it was nothing. Probably just Reggie's coworkers out to check on her.

Still, he gunned the engine and raced toward the house, a cloud of dust billowing in his wake. He skidded to a stop beside one of the patrol cars and hopped out.

Jeremy met him at the door with an upraised hand.

"I need you stay outside," Jeremy said.

Definitely not a social call.

"What the fuck is going on?" Hutch demanded. "Where are Birdie and Reggie?"

"They're fine," Jeremy said quickly. "Birdie drove Reggie home to pick up a few things. They'll be back later."

"What happened?" Hutch gritted out.

"Someone broke in."

Hutch tensed, his jaw ticking. He curled and uncurled his fingers.

"Regina played it right," Jeremy said, as if sensing Hutch's turmoil. "She made sure Birdie was safe. She called it in and waited for backup."

"Did you get him?"

Jeremy shook his head. "We're dusting for prints now. We suspect . . . we suspect it's the same guy from the other night."

"*What?*" Hutch stared at Jeremy in disbelief.

Jeremy shoved his hands into his pockets and walked farther out onto the porch. He glanced at Hutch as if weighing whether or not he wanted to say what it was he wanted to say. Finally he turned back to Hutch, giving him a long, measuring look.

"How much did Regina tell you about what happened the other night?"

Hutch snorted. "Nothing. We hadn't gotten around to that yet."

Jeremy grimaced. "The guy knew who she was. We suspect the attack was premeditated, and Regina was his target."

"What the fuck?"

Jeremy nodded. "He called her Reggie. Regina said only you, Sawyer and Cam call her that. It may or may not have any bearing on the matter, but he also made a veiled threat. He told her it was 'time to make him pay.' "

"What the hell does that mean?"

"I wish we knew," Jeremy said grimly. "Could have to do with her father. I just thought you should know because I don't think Regina should be alone after what happened today. It could be that the two incidences are unrelated, but I doubt it."

"I'm going to get over to Reggie's then. You said she and Birdie headed that way?"

"A deputy followed them so they wouldn't be alone," Jeremy said.

"Good. Thanks, Jeremy. I really appreciate it."

Jeremy nodded. "She's a cop. A damn good one. We look after our own."

Hutch shook Jeremy's hand then hurried back to his truck. He peeled away, anxious to get to Reggie's house as soon as possible.

They'd made a huge mistake in not pressing Reggie for answers after she'd given her report at the station. What he and the others had considered an unfortunate result of her job, of her being in the wrong place at the wrong time, had in fact been a calculated attack on her. They'd taken the incident too lightly. They'd left her and Birdie unprotected.

He swallowed the gnawing fear in his throat. They were obviously going to have to have a come-to-Jesus moment with Reggie. It wouldn't be pretty. But if there was some asshole out to get her, he was damn well going to have to come through him, Sawyer and Cam to get to her.

It took a good twenty minutes to get back into town. Reggie lived in a small two-bedroom house just half a mile from the police station. When Hutch pulled up, he had to park on the street because of the three vehicles parked in the drive. Reggie's RAV4, Birdie's Camry and the sheriff's deputy's car.

He strode up to the door and was met by the deputy. He identified himself, and the deputy let him pass.

The house looked and even smelled like Reggie. Her imprint was everywhere, from the eclectic décor to the clutter piles that looked unorganized but were in fact arranged in a precise manner.

He stopped at her computer desk and picked up a framed photo of him, Reggie, Cam and Sawyer. He smiled, remembering the day it was taken. They'd gone out to the lake after graduation and spent the day in the sun, laughing and enjoying life.

He set the frame in its place and walked back to where he heard Reggie and Birdie's voices. He stuck his head into Reggie's bedroom to see her insert a clip into her pistol, flick the safety on and then shove it into the holster at her waist.

Birdie looked up and saw him.

"Hutch! What are you doing here?"

Reggie looked up, her expression unreadable.

"I was worried," he said as he walked into the bedroom.

He stopped and brushed a kiss across Birdie's cheek. "Are you okay?" he asked.

Birdie smiled. "I'm fine. Regina took good care of me."

Hutch turned to Reggie, and they stood staring at each other for a long moment. He reached out and cupped her shoulder with one hand before finally pulling her into his arms.

She didn't resist.

"Are you all right?" he asked against her hair.

"I'm fine," she said, her voice muffled against his chest.

He pulled her away and cupped her chin. "Are you sure?"

She nodded.

"Good, because when we get back to the house we have a lot to talk about," he said evenly.

She blew her breath upward, sending the curl lying over her brow flying sideways.

"Are you about done here?" he asked. "What exactly did you need that couldn't wait until we got home?"

She lifted one dark eyebrow. "My gun. The only thing I had to defend Birdie and me was one of Sawyer's baseball bats, and I probably would have ruined it after one hit."

"It was stupid of us to have left you and Birdie alone," Hutch said in a low voice. "It won't happen again."

He expected her to argue, but she simply turned away and threw a change of clothes into a gym bag.

He and Birdie exchanged glances, and then he motioned with his head for her to follow him into the next room. She nodded, and he walked back into the living room, where the deputy stood waiting on the women.

"Level with me, Birdie. What the hell happened, and are you and Reggie both really okay?"

Birdie smiled. "We're fine. I expect Reggie is going to feel the results of her little adventure when she's settled down and comes off the adrenaline rush."

"What happened exactly? Jeremy said there was an intruder, but I didn't wait around for details. I wanted to get over here and make sure you two were all right."

Birdie raised a shaky hand to her forehead. "I honestly don't know, Hutch. It all happened so fast. Thank goodness for Regina's instincts. I was helping her down the stairs when she heard a noise. She made me go back into the bedroom and lock the door. She went to investigate."

"She damn well should have gone into the bedroom with you," he growled.

"She came back up quickly with the phone and called Jeremy. She made me get into the closet. Next thing I knew, she told me it was okay to come out and we waited for Jeremy." A smile twitched at the corners of her mouth. "Regina had a baseball bat. I think she fully intended to use it."

"She wouldn't have had to if I'd been there," he muttered.

Birdie laid her hand on his arm and squeezed. "If you and Regina no longer need me, I think I'd like to be getting home. This is all the excitement I can take in a day."

Hutch frowned. "I don't want you going back to your house alone. Maybe it would be better if you came back to the house with us."

She smiled. "This nice young man has already offered to see

me home and come in with me to make sure everything's as it should be. I have the alarm system Sawyer insisted on installing for me." She shook her head in exasperation. "My house resembles a fortress thanks to you boys."

"Someone will be patrolling the area." The deputy spoke up. "I'll make sure a car drives by her house every hour, and we'll call periodically to check in on her."

Hutch nodded. "I appreciate it."

The deputy smiled. "I know Birdie's special to you, but she's also special to this community. She's done a lot for many of us. As soon as the rest of the department heard what happened, they were lining up to volunteer to run patrols by her house. She'll have county and local police protection."

"Let me just go say good-bye to Regina, and then I'll be on my way," Birdie said. "You need to get her home so she can get some rest. It's been a difficult day. She looks like she's about to fall over."

Birdie walked back to Reggie's bedroom and returned a few moments later. Hutch kissed her forehead.

"Call me if you need anything."

"Oh, I will, and you be sure and let me know if you boys or Regina need anything. I'll be happy to come out."

He watched Birdie leave under the watchful eye of the sheriff's deputy then turned to go back in search of Reggie. He found her standing by her bed, her shoulders drooping with fatigue.

"You finished getting what you need?" he asked.

She immediately straightened. "Yeah, I'm ready to go if you are."

He reached over to zip up her bag then picked up the strap. He stopped in front of her and wrapped his free hand around the back of her neck, pulling her close. For a long moment, he simply stood there, face buried in her dark curls.

She trembled against him, and her arms crept around his waist.

"Let's go home," he murmured against her head. "I think you've had enough excitement for one day."

"I won't argue that," she said ruefully as she pulled away.

He put a finger underneath her chin and nudged upward until she stared him in the eye. Slowly, he lowered his mouth to hers in a tender kiss. It wasn't intended to overwhelm her with passion. Rather it was a soft gesture, one for comfort.

To his surprise, she took an active part in the kiss. The arm with the brace slid up his back while she pulled her uninjured arm from his waist and moved it up his chest and over his shoulder and around to his neck. Her fingers slid into his hair, glancing over his scalp as she returned his kiss.

Her tongue met his in a delicate duel. She caught his lower lip between her teeth and nibbled. Then she sucked it further into her mouth.

He was hers. He relinquished every part of himself to her in that moment. Time seemed to stop, and he wanted it to. He wanted to remain in this moment, shutting everything else out around them. For just this minute, only the two of them existed.

He loved her taste, the feel of her all soft and warm against him. He ached. His chest ached. His groin was heavy with warm, fluid arousal. Desire whispered through his veins. He wanted her. Needed her as he'd never needed another woman. There had never been anyone else like her in his life.

She pulled away, her eyes glazed with the same passion that burned inside him. Her mouth was swollen, a temptation that beckoned to him.

He cupped her cheek and ran his thumb over her lips. She opened her mouth and sucked the tip inside the warm, moist haven. He groaned, whisper-soft, at the image of her sucking at his finger. It was too easy to imagine her lips surrounding his cock, coaxing him deeper.

"We should go," he said hoarsely.

She slowly let go of his thumb, and he let his hand drop to his side. She turned and he put his hand at her back to guide her from the bedroom.

CHAPTER II

Dusk was falling when Cam pulled up to the house and parked. Sawyer drove in beside him, and they both got out.

Cam looked over to see Hutch's truck parked and Birdie's car gone. He reached into the back of his SUV for a suitcase then slammed the door shut.

"Let's get all the office shit tomorrow," Cam said as he walked around the front to where Sawyer stood.

"Yeah, good idea. I'm looking forward to a cold beer."

They mounted the steps, and Cam reached for the doorknob, only to find the door locked. He frowned and reached for the keys he'd shoved into his pocket.

"Hutch getting paranoid on us?" Sawyer said dryly.

Cam inserted the key and turned it. He opened the door, shoved his suitcase inside and set it down in the foyer. As he and Sawyer walked in, he glanced into the living room to see Hutch sitting on the couch. The television was on, but the sound was way down.

He walked farther in, and it was then that he saw Reggie lying on the couch, her head on Hutch's lap. Hutch's hand was resting in Reggie's curls, and she was fast asleep.

"Drugged her again?" Sawyer asked in an amused voice.

Hutch didn't smile. There was a darkness to his expression that Cam didn't like. Sawyer caught it too. Hutch held up a finger to his lips then nodded to the chairs beside the couch.

Sawyer slouched into the first armchair, and Cam settled on the couch at Reggie's feet. He slid his hand up the leg of her sweats to rest just below her knee.

"What's going on, Hutch?" he asked.

Sawyer leaned forward in his chair, his elbows propped on his legs, his fingers forming a vee at his mouth.

"Someone broke into the house while we were gone," Hutch said in a low voice.

"What the fuck?" Sawyer immediately turned his head away to staunch the outburst then turned back again. "What?" he asked in a quieter voice.

"Reggie stashed Birdie in the upstairs closet and went after him with one of your baseball bats."

"Christ," Cam muttered.

"It's worse," Hutch said. He looked at both Cam and Sawyer. "They think it might be the same guy who attacked her the other night."

"Who is they, and why would they think that?" Sawyer demanded.

Hutch scowled. "I spoke to Jeremy after Birdie took Reggie home to get her gun."

Cam shook his head then dug his fingers into his hair. He could feel the beginnings of a headache plaguing him.

"Start over. I'm confused. Someone broke in. Cops show up and think it's the guy who attacked Reggie the other night, and she went home to get her gun?"

Hutch nodded. "In a nutshell."

Sawyer gave Hutch a look of understanding. "She held out on us, didn't she?"

"Yeah. She did."

"You going to fill us in then?" Cam asked.

"Jeremy said they think it's personal, that Reggie was the intended target, not the woman the attacker killed. Apparently he called her Reggie, which is something no one but us calls her. While he had his hands wrapped around her neck intending to strangle her, he told her that it was 'time to make him pay.'"

"Son of a bitch," Sawyer growled.

"Do they know anything else?" Cam asked.

"All Jeremy said was that they think it's possible it could have something to do with her father. Politicians attract nutjobs with agendas. Maybe he doesn't agree with Peter Fallon's politics. Who the fuck knows. But they think he was the one who broke in today. No fingerprints. Just shoe prints outside that match the ones at the murder scene from the other night."

"And we left her here with only Birdie for protection," Cam said in disgust.

"Where is Birdie now?" Sawyer demanded.

Hutch turned to look at Sawyer. "She's at home. Reggie's department and the county guys are alternating patrols by her house. She lives just a block from the chief, so he'll be looking in on her too. I wanted her to come out here, but she insisted on going home."

"I'll call her in a little while to check in on her," Sawyer said. "And I'll run by there tomorrow morning to make sure her security system is working properly."

Cam nodded. "That's a good idea. We need to think about beefing things up around here. Obviously we can't leave Reggie alone again. Not if this asshole is stalking her."

He glanced down at Reggie again then frowned when he noticed the brace around her wrist was gone. Hutch followed the line of his gaze.

"She irritated it wielding that bat," Hutch explained. "It swelled, and the brace was bothering her. I took it off and iced it down for a while and made her take a pain pill."

Frustration beat at Cam. He wanted Reggie where she belonged. With them. But not like this. He wanted her to choose to be with them, not forced to remain because they insisted on protecting her.

He rubbed the back of his neck and stared up at the ceiling.

"What's got you worried, Cam?" Sawyer asked. "You seem to be stressing a lot lately, when you were the most confident going in."

Cam looked at Sawyer and then at Hutch and found the same worry reflected in Hutch's eyes. Yeah, he supposed to them he had appeared confident. He was always the one telling them it would work out. He was a goddamn fraud. The truth was, he was scared shitless.

"I'm worried that we won't be able to make her happy. And now I'm worried that we can't keep her safe. I'm worried that I'll lose her," he said truthfully.

"I think we all have those same concerns," Hutch said. "But at some point we have to stop worrying about the what-ifs and focus on only the things we can control."

"And what would those things be?" Sawyer asked dryly.

Hutch turned to Sawyer with a dark stare. "We can't control how Reggie feels about us. We can't control her fears. All we can control is how we react to the situation. And we can damn well make sure we present a united front. This will never work if Reggie senses we're divided in any way."

"He's right," Cam said quietly. "We can't convince her this will work if we can't even convince ourselves."

Sawyer's hand skimmed over his bald head in agitation. Damn good thing he kept it shaved or he'd probably yank his hair out anyway.

"We've been over this." Frustration leaked from Sawyer's voice. "Why do we have to *keep* going over it? I understand that we have to work together, but I won't spend every goddamn minute of my time with her in a group setting."

Reggie stirred beneath Hutch's hand. Cam shot Sawyer a warning stare and held a finger up to his lips. Then his gaze dropped back to Reggie as her eyes fluttered open.

"Cam?" she whispered.

He smiled. "Heard you had some excitement while I was gone, Reggie darling."

She made a face and tried to sit up, but she put her injured hand down to press against the couch. It folded beneath her, and she emitted a gasp. Hutch caught her and pushed her weight off her wrist.

As Hutch helped her sit up, Cam reached for her wrist. He turned it over in his hand and examined the swelling.

"That's what happens when you try to play baseball with an injured wrist," he murmured.

"It wasn't baseball. I was planning to play T-ball with his head."

Sawyer chuckled. "I wouldn't have appreciated blood on my stuff, Reggie. Which one did you use anyway? Tell me my Biggio bat isn't now in police custody being logged as evidence."

She glanced over and smiled at Sawyer, and Cam felt a pang of jealousy. As stupid as it was, as much as they'd all lectured about presenting a united front, he was sitting here resentful of the way

Sawyer could draw a reaction from Reggie. It wasn't always a good one. Sawyer could piss her off in one breath and have her laughing in the next. But she wasn't the least bit indifferent to him. Sparks flew between the two of them anytime they were in the same room.

Hutch reached up and tucked a curl behind Reggie's ear.

"Why didn't you tell us the man was after you?" he asked.

Her lips twisted in annoyance. "Because there's no way to tell if he was. And there still isn't."

"Jeremy didn't seem to think it was too much of a stretch that this guy was targeting you. Neither did your chief."

She stared at Hutch, her lips drawn into a tight line.

"If there wasn't enough evidence to support the idea before, there certainly is now," Cam said. "He followed you here, Reggie. He broke into our home while we were gone. Which tells me he was watching. And waiting for his opportunity."

Her gaze fell to her lap, where she held her injured wrist with her other hand. Tension boiled off her body. Cam wanted to touch her, but even Hutch pulled his hand away from her hair.

"I can't stay here," she said. She kept her head down, refusing to meet any of their gazes. When she finally looked up at Cam, there was steely determination in her eyes.

Ice blue. It was a comparison he'd made often when staring into Reggie's eyes when she was being a hard-ass.

Cam glanced at Hutch and Sawyer. Neither seemed inclined to ask the obvious question. Or maybe they were simply ignoring it, telling her precisely what they thought of that particular statement.

While he could understand their frustration, it wasn't the way to handle Reggie. There were times when he wished he could go all he-man on her and she'd comply, but then she wouldn't be the Reggie he loved so much.

"Why can't you stay?" he finally asked.

As expected, Sawyer gave him a look that suggested he was a dumbass. Cam ignored him and focused his attention on Reggie.

"I would think it's obvious," she said in her oh-so-patient tone that suggested she didn't have any patience at all. "There is someone who has a beef with me. Therefore anyone around me is also in danger."

She cradled her injured wrist in her hand and rubbed her thumb lightly over the swelling. "Birdie could have been hurt or killed," she said quietly. She glanced back up at Cam and then slowly turned to look at Sawyer and finally Hutch. "He broke into your house. Any one of you could have been here. He's already killed one person. What's another?"

"How did I know you'd say something like that?" Sawyer muttered.

"So you think a better alternative is for you to hole up in your house alone?" Hutch demanded. "You're smarter than that, Reggie. Start acting like it for God's sake. This martyr bullshit isn't like you."

She bolted to her feet and whirled around, her eyes flashing with anger. And to think, Cam had been thinking about how Sawyer could always elicit a reaction from Reggie. Cam looked at Hutch in a new light. The usually laid back, calm Hutch was teetering on the edge.

"No one said I was going to stay at my house alone, asshole," she said in a near growl. "Just because I'd prefer not to put the people I care most about in danger doesn't make me a fucking martyr."

Hutch stood, shoved his hands in his pockets and hovered over her, staring down into her eyes. Anger rolled off him in waves.

Reggie didn't back down an inch, and Cam wondered if he was going to have to get between them. Hell, what was up Hutch's ass? It was usually Hutch getting between Reggie and Sawyer.

The irony wasn't lost on Sawyer either. He regarded the two with undisguised amusement.

"Maybe," Hutch said behind clenched teeth, "the people who care about *you* don't like the idea of some asshole trying to kill you."

He inched forward until there was no space between him and Reggie.

Cam sighed. "Come on, you two. I swear you're acting like a pair of pit bulls."

Reggie and Hutch both rounded on him. Reggie glared, and Hutch's brows drew together in an angry line.

"Nobody asked you," Reggie snarled.

She turned back to Hutch and poked him in the chest with a finger. "I can damn well take care of myself. I don't need you and the others hovering over me like nursemaids. Yeah, I got hurt. It happens in my line of work. But I'm not going to let it turn me into some goddamn girl."

Sawyer broke into laughter. "Reggie, honey, I hate to tell you this, but you *are* a girl."

"Shut up, Sawyer."

Hutch shifted, and Reggie dug her finger back into his chest. "And so help me, if you kiss me or do something else to distract me, I'm going to hurt you."

A slow smile worked at the corners of Hutch's mouth. "Are you saying my kisses distract you, baby?"

She backed away and bumped into Cam. Cam reached up to steady her then pulled her down into his lap. She started to reach down and shove away, but he held tight.

"Damn it, Cam," she hissed.

"Stop running," he said calmly. "You tell us you aren't afraid but every time we get close, you make tracks in the opposite direction."

She trembled against him. There was a multitude of emotions in her body language. Fear. Anger. Confusion.

He caught her wrist in his hand, careful not to press too hard.

"This needs to be iced again, and then the brace needs to go back on."

"Why do I feel the sudden urge to go beat my head against a wall?" Reggie muttered.

Cam smiled and stroked a hand through her unruly curls. "You're stubborn, Reggie darling. However, I'm not sure you realize how stubborn I can be as well. Maybe I've given you the impression that I'm a pushover, but you're about to find out that when it comes to you, I'm anything but."

She turned to stare at him, her eyes bright with confusion. "Cam, I've never thought you were a pushover. When did I ever give you that idea?"

He cupped her cheek and rubbed his thumb over her lips. "I said I *might* have given you that impression. I do tend to weaken when you turn those blue eyes on me. In any other matter, I have no doubt you'd get your way. But this has to do with your safety, and I can be more of a hard-ass than you when it comes to that."

Her lips turned down into a frown. He smoothed a corner with his thumb, coaxing it upward again. "I much prefer you smiling."

She sighed. "You're absolutely no fun to fight with. You're supposed to keep pissing me off so I can stay mad at you."

Cam chuckled. "If I kiss you, will that piss you off?"

Her breath caught then expelled in a jerky rush. A spark ignited in her eyes, and she ran her tongue nervously over her bottom lip.

"Or you could kiss me," he said in a low voice.

Her hand came up to his cheek. He closed his eyes and leaned into her touch. When he opened them again, her lips were hovering just inches above his. Uncertainty glittered in her beautiful eyes, but to his satisfaction, there was no fear.

He itched to move to her, to complete the kiss, but he waited instead. He wanted her to come to him. It seemed like forever until she softly pressed her lips to his.

It was a gentle kiss, sweet, so incredibly sweet. The tip of her tongue feathered over the seam of his lips, and he opened for her, wanting her deeper inside so he could taste her, absorb her.

She pulled away, and it was all he could do not to groan his protest.

"I shouldn't want this," she whispered. She glanced over her shoulder to where Hutch still stood, and Sawyer sat just a few feet away. Then she turned her gaze back to Cam, and he could see the guilt in her eyes.

"Reggie, stop," Cam said. "Enough with the guilt. Why are you tearing yourself up over this? We've been straight with you. Do you think Hutch and Sawyer are going to beat the shit out of me because I kissed you? Or does it bother you that they aren't?"

He let the last question hang heavy in the air. Her eyes widened a fraction.

"No. I mean, no, that's not what bothers me."

"Then what is it?" Cam pressed.

Sawyer moved from his chair to the couch, where he could see Reggie and where she could see him. He reached over to take the hand that was resting on Cam's lap.

"Honey, we know what we're asking is a lot. God knows it won't be easy for you. But we're willing to do whatever is necessary, whatever it takes to make you happy, to prove to you that this can work. None of us wants to be without you."

"We've laid it out on our end," Hutch said quietly.

Reggie turned to look at Hutch, and he stared back, his expression intense.

"What we haven't talked about is how you feel about us, baby. We can sit here and tell you how we feel and what we want all day long, but it won't mean shit if we don't know what's going on in your head."

"What about it, Reggie?" Cam asked softly as he touched the curve of her neck. "Have you got the balls to look us in the eye and tell us what you want?"

CHAPTER 12

*R*egina's pulse quickened and raced so hard, she could feel the steady thump at her temple. They wanted answers that she couldn't give. God, she had no idea what to say or how to articulate the mass of confusion that had taken up steady residence in her brain ever since that night a year ago when the three of them had made love to her.

Just thinking about it made her panic.

How did she feel about them? Were there even words to describe such a thing?

She'd spent a year beating herself over the head for something that Cam, Sawyer and Hutch had accepted readily. While she'd been busy trying to shove the incident from her mind, they'd pressed in closer.

But now those memories came storming back. Their mouths and hands on her body. Touching her, loving her, *completing* her.

Suddenly she felt ashamed. Not because of what she'd let happen but because she'd likened it to a smutty porn experience when clearly it had meant more to the guys than just a romp in the sheets.

"What are you thinking?" Cam asked softly. He nudged her chin until she looked into his eyes.

"About that night," she said in a low voice.

Sawyer's grip tightened around her hand and he laced his fingers through hers.

"Was it that bad, Reggie? Did we hurt you? Did we scare you? Do something you didn't want? Talk to us, honey. The not knowing is making us crazy."

She stared down at their entwined hands. She felt small and self-absorbed. So much of the last year she'd spent focusing on how she felt, and she'd never considered how her distance had made *them* feel.

"You didn't hurt me," she said honestly. "I wanted . . . I wanted it. It scared me. I scared me. Not you. But I shouldn't have let it happen. Don't you see? It changed everything. I miss . . . I miss the way things were. I miss you. All of you."

"Ahh, honey, we've missed you too," Sawyer said. He brought her hand to his mouth and pressed a kiss into her upturned palm.

"We can't go back, Reggie," Hutch said quietly. "We can't pretend it never happened. I wanted what happened. I know Cam and Sawyer did too. It was inevitable. We have to deal with it, be straight with each other and go on. Dodging the issue and ignoring what's between us doesn't do any of us any good."

She bowed her head and stared down at her lap. "I know." And she did. If only she knew what to do. So much was riding on how she handled this, on what she decided and how she acted. What if she chose wrong and screwed up her relationship with the three people she loved most in the world?

It terrified her.

Cam sighed. She knew that sound. It was him running out of patience, a sound of resignation. She glanced guiltily up at him and silently begged him to understand.

He touched her lips with a finger, and his brown eyes softened.

"Sooner or later you're going to have to face this, Reggie darling. The only reason I'm not leaning on your harder is because you're hurt and you're tired, and you've had a hell of a day. I'm going to get some ice for that hand, and Hutch is going to get you another painkiller. Then I'm going to carry your ass up to bed. And just so you don't get any crazy ideas, you're not going anywhere. You're stuck here. With us. That's not open for negotiation."

She gaped at the steel she heard in his voice. The entire world had gone mad. Hutch was acting like a bulldog, Cam was going all alpha on her, and Sawyer . . . well he was acting like the damn fool he always acted like, but at least he wasn't acting out of character yet. She expected him to be all forceful and laced with testosterone. Cam and Hutch? Not so much. Especially not Hutch.

Cam patted her on the ass then plucked her off his lap and plopped her onto Sawyer's. He rose from the couch and walked away, Hutch following behind.

"They've lost their freaking minds," she grumbled.

Sawyer snickered. "Maybe you don't have them twisted around your little finger as much as you thought, baby doll."

She glared at him. "You act as though I manipulate them."

Sawyer regarded her solemnly. "Manipulate? No, that isn't your style. But you have to admit, you're not used to them standing up to you and telling you no. You know and I know they'd damn well cut off their right arms for you."

She leaned into his chest and closed her eyes.

"Why did things have to change, Sawyer?" she whispered. "I don't like what's happened to us."

His arms came around her, hugging her tight against him.

"Nothing ever stays the same, honey. And here's something to consider. What you view as changing everything, something you regret, is something that me and Cam and Sawyer have looked forward to. Longed for. Wanted for a damn long time."

She drew away and stared into his eyes. He looked so serious. So somber. "How long?" she asked softly.

He touched her cheek then cupped the back of her neck and pulled her down to meet his lips. There was an urgency to his kiss. His mouth worked hot over hers, molding her to him.

"Forever?" he rasped. "It sure seems like it. If you want a specific date, I'm afraid I can't give that to you. But in a lot of ways, you've been ours since the day you blacked mine and Cam's eyes when we teased Hutch about him having a friend who was a girl."

Her chest tingled, and she felt curiously lightheaded. Ours. Just the way he said it sent a ridiculous thrill through her system. Belonging to someone, being loved by someone, was scary enough, but needed and wanted by three men?

It felt edgy, exciting and terrifying all in one fell swoop.

"Okay baby, open up," Hutch said.

She looked up to see him and Cam standing by the couch in front of Sawyer. Hutch was holding a glass of water in one hand and a pill in the other while Cam held a small Ziploc bag of ice.

Sawyer eased her from his lap to sit beside him. Cam sat down on the other side of her and picked up her wrist. He carefully strapped the brace back on and then placed the bag of ice over it.

Hutch dropped the pill into her free hand and waited as she put it into her mouth. Then he handed her the glass, and she gulped down the pill in one swallow.

"You're starting to scare me with all this compliance," Hutch said with a grin.

She shot him a nasty look and his grin got bigger.

"Don't smile at me," she muttered.

He laughed. "So I can't kiss you or touch you and now I can't smile at you either?"

"No."

"We'll see about that," he said with a smirk.

Regina sighed. Incorrigible. She leaned against Sawyer's side as weariness assailed her. His hand tangled in her hair as he massaged her scalp.

"Mmmm, that feels really good."

When she opened her eyes again, Cam was checking his watch. Sawyer continued to stroke her hair in gentle up-and-down motions as Cam held the ice pack on her wrist.

"You've got two minutes, Reggie darling. And then I'm taking you up to bed."

"Bossy," she muttered. "It doesn't look good on you."

Cam smiled. "*You* look good on me, though."

Her eyes widened. "Cam!"

Hutch chuckled then leaned over the couch to kiss her forehead. "I'll take my good-night kiss now," he murmured.

He touched her cheek as he drew away.

"Be a good girl and stay out of trouble, and I'll cook you breakfast in the morning."

"Ham and pancakes?" she asked hopefully.

He smiled. "Whatever you want, baby."

Sawyer buried his face in her hair and kissed the back of her head. "Sleep tight, honey."

"I'm beginning to get a complex," she complained. "You guys keep trying to get rid of me."

Cam reached down and scooped her up. He frowned and glanced over at Hutch. "Better double up on the pancakes. I swear she's gotten lighter, and she could already be blown over by a stiff wind."

"You'd rather I weigh a ton?" she asked. "At least then you couldn't haul me around like a sack of potatoes."

"Hush," he said. "I just worry about you. You've lost weight."

"I can still kick your ass," she muttered.

He laughed as he started up the stairs. "I don't doubt it, but I'd prefer you wait until you're a hundred percent before you try it."

"You know this is ridiculous, don't you," she said as he entered her room. "I'm perfectly capable of getting myself to bed."

"Aren't there laws about navigating stairs under the influence?"

She rolled her eyes as he placed her on the bed. He proceeded to pull the covers back then moved her up onto the pillows so he could tuck her in. He arranged the ice pack back over her wrist, angled it a few times, and then, apparently satisfied that it would stay in place, he left it alone.

"Good night," he said. He dropped a kiss on her forehead, and she was vaguely disappointed that he hadn't kissed her lips.

She was hungry for him.

"Good night," she whispered.

"I'll be across the hall if you need me," he said softly as he moved away from the bed.

He paused at the door and flipped the light off. She burrowed deeper into the cool sheets and embraced the warm glow of the painkiller.

An hour later she was staring at the ceiling wondering why she hadn't entered the fuzzy, narcotic coma. She was, instead, wide awake. And feeling oddly alone. The ice had melted, and she removed the soggy bag from her wrist.

She turned on her side and stared at her closed door. Were they asleep? Were they even in bed yet? Or were they downstairs hanging out in the living room?

The distance between them sucked. Before, she wouldn't

have given any thought to joining them, hanging out and enjoying their company. Now she worried that she'd give them the wrong idea, not that she was even sure what that was exactly.

How could she give them the wrong idea when they were already rooted in their expectations?

Despite the presence of the medication, her wrist throbbed. She flexed it experimentally and cradled it in her other hand. She flopped onto her back again and resumed staring at the ceiling.

After counting the dots in the textured paint a dozen times, she gave up on the idea of sleep and glanced over at the bedside clock. Midnight.

With a disgusted sigh, she threw off the covers and swung her legs over the side of the bed. She held her wrist to her chest and put her other hand on the edge to push herself up. Despite her state of wakefulness, when she stood, the room spun.

Careful to keep her footing, she shuffled over to the door and opened it. When she stepped into the hall, it was dark. No light filtered up the stairs from the living room.

She glanced left toward Hutch's bedroom and then across the hall to Cam's. Both doors were closed with no light on. Her gaze wandered right to Sawyer's room, and she saw a faint beam shining underneath the door.

She took a hesitant step forward, putting her hand on the wall to brace herself. Her fingers slid over the surface as she slowly made her way to Sawyer's door.

She stopped when her hand brushed over the knob. Her teeth grazed her lower lip as she vacillated about whether to go in or not. Silly. She was being ridiculous. In the past, she wouldn't have thought twice about approaching Sawyer. As much as she preached not wanting things to change, it was she who was changing everything.

With a sigh, she squared her shoulders and quietly turned the knob. She eased open the door and peered inside. Her breath caught in her throat when she saw Sawyer, naked, rubbing a towel over his head. The muscles rippled in his back, and his arms bulged as he worked them over his head.

He tossed the towel aside and turned slightly. That was when he caught sight of her. He jerked around, and then as if realizing his nudity, he swiveled back just as quickly and yanked up the towel.

"I'm sorry," she stammered out. "I'll go. I didn't mean to barge in on you like this."

"No, Reggie, don't go." Sawyer held his hand out while using his other to hold the towel tightly around his hips. "Just give me a second." He looked rapidly around. "Here, sit down on the bed. I'll be right back."

He walked over and touched her tentatively, curled his fingers around her shoulder and guided her toward the bed. He held up a finger as she sank onto the mattress.

"I'll be just a minute. Stay right there."

He hurried into the adjoining bathroom then came right back out, a grimace on his face. He yanked up a pair of shorts and a T-shirt then returned to the bathroom again.

She sat there in awkward silence until a few minutes later, when he appeared in the doorway, now dressed. He walked toward her and then settled on the bed beside her. He pulled one leg up and angled himself so that he faced her.

"You okay?" he asked.

The concern in his voice made her smile. "I'm fine. I just couldn't sleep. I wondered if anyone was still up."

"The painkiller not working? Do I need to get you another?"

She shook her head. "I'm fine. A little woozy even. I guess I just had a lot on my mind, and I wanted some company."

"I'm glad you came looking for me then," he said. "Want to crawl up in bed and watch a movie? Or we can watch the replay of the last UFC fight."

She frowned. "What kind of movies you got? They aren't Cam's or Hutch's, are they?"

Sawyer laughed then cleared his throat and lowered his voice. "You know better. All I have are the action flicks where they blow shit up all over the place."

"Rock on. You choose. I'm gonna go steal your pillow."

He grinned. "I've missed you, sweetness."

She pulled a face. "Don't ruin it by calling me sweet."

He brushed a hand across her cheek. "I have an insatiable sweet tooth, but then you know that."

For once she didn't back away. She didn't tuck tail and run. She met his gaze and truly looked into his eyes. Breathing was hard when she saw the intensity simmering in his blue eyes.

Then she looked down. Despite her best effort, she couldn't prevent the guilt from creeping up her spine.

"What is it?" he asked. "What's going on in your head, Reggie?"

She fiddled with her brace. "Am I supposed to feel guilty for being in here with you while Hutch and Cam are asleep a few doors down?"

Sawyer put a finger under her chin and pushed upward until she reluctantly met his gaze again.

"No."

She cocked her head. "No? Just like that?"

He sighed. "Reggie, no one's keeping score except you. No one expects it. It's not what we want."

"What do you want?" she pleaded. "I think I know. I tell myself I know, but then I tell myself that it's crazy. What sane person would even contemplate it?"

"I never claimed to be sane."

She punched him in the gut with her good hand. He grunted and caught her fist. He carefully uncurled her fingers and kissed each tip.

His gaze met hers again as he kissed her pinky. "Why don't you crawl up and get comfortable, and I'll find us a loud, obnoxious movie. I'm looking forward to spending the time with you, and I'd rather not waste it analyzing my sanity or lack thereof."

Call her nuts, or crazy, or maybe as insane as he was, but she leaned forward and kissed him. Maybe she needed to prove to herself that she wasn't running, or maybe she just wanted to make the move for once. Whatever the case, she found her lips pressed to his, inhaling his sexy male scent.

He stilled against her, and then she heard his sharp intake of breath. She slid her hand over his chest and up the column of his neck. His goatee brushed against her chin, prickling, eliciting a shiver from her.

His lips were warm and pliant against hers. Soft, but not too soft. A hint of firmness.

She sank her teeth into his bottom lip, and he groaned.

Slowly, she pulled away. Her breath came erratically. His eyes were half-lidded as he stared at her, desire clouding the blue eyes, darkening them to midnight.

As if he sensed the moment was over, he turned away and got off the bed. He walked to the TV and knelt to dig in the cabinet where the movies were stored.

Regina crawled up and settled among his pillows. She sucked in several steadying breaths. Wild. Hungry. Those were words that came to mind after kissing Sawyer. She knew he wasn't the type for frilly lovemaking. She knew it long before that night a year ago.

He wasn't the soft, sensitive kind who could murmur just the right words and take all night to make love to a woman. He liked it hard, edgy, the rock-your-world kind of sex. And yet, when he touched her, she still felt . . . cherished.

There was an edge of steel to him, like having sex with him would be akin to chasing a storm. He'd held back the one time they'd made love. She knew it.

Part of her wanted to tap that wildness. The other part of her was scared shitless.

It was also why she was convinced that this thing . . . what they wanted . . . would never work. How could it when each of them held back, reserved that part of himself that made him uniquely *him*?

The mattress dipped as Sawyer eased onto the bed beside her. He pointed the remote at the television then turned back to her.

"You ready?"

She nodded, and he patted the pillow he was resting on. She moved over, and he raised his arm so she could nestle in the crook of his shoulder.

"Put that hand on my chest so it doesn't get bumped or smushed," he said.

She smiled and settled her brace across his body. His arm tightened around her, and his fingers brushed up and down her arm from her shoulder to her elbow.

"This is nice," he murmured. "Been a long time since we did this."

Yeah, it had. And she was to blame. She'd missed it too, though.

Despite the action and noise of the movie, she settled into a comfortable haze. Sawyer's body heat seeped into her and lulled her closer to sleep.

"Sawyer, for God's sake, turn the damn TV down. You're going to wake—"

Regina turned to see Cam standing in the doorway in just his shorts. His hair hung to his shoulders with just enough muss to make him look damn sexy.

"You were saying?" Sawyer said dryly.

Cam walked into the bedroom. "Sorry. Didn't know you were up, Reggie. I could hear the TV all the way in my bedroom, and I worried it would wake you."

She smiled. "I couldn't sleep, and Sawyer was the only one up."

"You could have wakened me. I wouldn't have minded." He turned his attention to the TV. "What are you guys watching?"

"*Rush Hour*," Sawyer replied.

Regina lifted her hand off of Sawyer's chest and carefully patted the space beside her. "Want to watch?"

Cam climbed onto the bed and lay down beside Regina, his shoulder touching her back as she turned toward Sawyer once more.

"Are you all right? Having any pain?" Cam asked.

"I'm good," she replied. She yawned even as she said it.

Sawyer looked down and smiled. "Getting sleepy?"

She frowned. "No. I'm comfortable. Let's watch the movie. I don't want to go back to my room yet."

"Honey, no one said you had to move. Stay as long as you like."

She burrowed deeper into the pillows and nestled between the two men, and it suddenly occurred to her how right it felt. Her brow furrowed as she contemplated that notion.

No, not tonight. She wasn't going to rehash it all. It made her head hurt. For now she just wanted things to be like they used to be. When they were all friends and comfortable around one another. Before sex had screwed up everything.

CHAPTER 13

*H*utch pulled on a pair of jeans and a T-shirt and stepped barefooted into the hallway. He paused at Reggie's door to look in, only to find her bed empty. He walked on to Cam's room, where the door was also open, and found it empty as well.

Everyone was up early this morning.

He headed for the stairs but stopped at Sawyer's door when he glanced in and saw Sawyer, Reggie and Cam all in Sawyer's bed asleep. He leaned in, his arm resting against the door frame, and grinned at the sight.

Reggie was cuddled up close to Sawyer, who was laid out in an uncomfortable-looking position with one arm above his head and the other tucked under Reggie. Cam was relegated to the sliver of bed left by Reggie and Sawyer and was spooned up against Reggie. Part of his ass hung off the bed, and if he so much as moved, he'd probably land on the floor.

Hutch shook his head. No telling how this had all come about, but if he had to guess, he'd lay odds on Reggie seeking out company in the middle of the night.

He stood there staring for a long time, waiting for jealousy to come. Waiting to feel resentment toward Sawyer and Cam. But it never came.

Instead he felt the prickle of anticipation, as if they were one step closer to achieving their goal. And he supposed therein lay the reason for his acceptance. As ridiculous as it sounded that wooing a woman would be a team effort . . . Hell, it didn't sound ridiculous, it *was* ridiculous.

He needed to have his head examined.

With a shake of his head, he turned and headed back into the hall. He walked down the stairs and rounded the corner to go into the kitchen to start breakfast.

That team effort thing—it bugged him. Even as he knew it was something he and Cam and Sawyer had agreed upon, had talked about for many long hours, it still made him cringe. Maybe he wasn't as accepting as he'd thought. But no. It wasn't the idea of sharing her with two other men—no, not just two other men—people he was closer to than anyone. Guys he trusted. It was the idea in general that the woman he loved would never be completely his.

Was he really okay with that? And if he was now, was there any guarantee he'd be okay with it a year from now? Two years?

Children. Jesus. That was one angle he hadn't discussed with the others, primarily because Reggie had never really expressed a strong desire to have kids. But what if she wanted them? Did they draw straws to see who fathered her baby or did they just leave it to chance, and if they were all living together, did it matter anyway?

He was giving himself a killer headache, and he was talking himself in circles. He dragged out the ingredients for pancakes then took the ham out of the refrigerator.

It had been a lot easier when this was all in theory, an arrangement discussed in the hypothetical. Now that they were actually trying to make it work, he wondered if they weren't the biggest dumbasses in the universe. No wonder Reggie was having such a hard time with it all. No sane person could wrap their brain around the fact that three normal men would consent to sharing the woman they loved with one another.

"Dude, if you don't let up on that batter, there's not going to be much left for pancakes."

Hutch's hand stilled from the vicious rotation, and he looked up to see Sawyer standing there, eyeing him with open curiosity.

"Reggie still asleep?" he asked.

Sawyer sat down on one of the barstools and leaned his arms on the counter. "Yeah, she and Cam are still passed out."

Hutch resumed mixing the batter then stopped to slice the ham into thick breakfast steaks.

"So what's eating you this morning?" Sawyer asked casually.

"Nothing. I'm good."

Sawyer snorted. "You're not pissed because Reggie was in bed with me are you?"

Hutch looked up and met Sawyer's gaze. "No," he said honestly. "I think . . ." Hell, what did he think? But then they'd always been honest and up front with one another. There wasn't a reason to deviate from that now. "I think I'm pissed because I'm not pissed."

Sawyer crooked one eyebrow. "That's some messed up logic."

"Tell me about it," Hutch muttered.

"Care to elaborate?"

"Think about it, Sawyer. What normal guy wouldn't be pissed that the woman he loves is curled up in not one man's arms, but two? His two best friends. I'm beginning to wonder if I haven't lost my damn mind. I stood there in the doorway this morning looking at the three of you, and all I did was grin. How fucked up is that?"

Sawyer pursed his lips thoughtfully. "So you're more messed up over the fact that you've accepted our arrangement than you are over the idea of sharing Reggie with me and Cam."

"Yeah, something like that."

"Well, if I had to guess, I'd say that it's very similar to what Reggie is struggling with. I don't think the idea of being with the three of us freaks her out nearly as much as her *considering* the possibility."

Hutch nodded. "Yeah, I can relate to that." He put the knife aside and turned on the electric skillet. "As much as we've always given less than a damn what other people think about us, as much as we've always gone our own way, I can't help but wonder over the fallout over our . . . relationship."

He pulled out a frying pan and set it on the stove then plunked three slabs of ham into it. Then he returned to the electric skillet and held his hand over the griddle to test the temp.

"So you're worried about what other people will think?" Sawyer asked with a frown.

Hutch shrugged. "Maybe? I mean I don't worry so much about me, but Reggie has a public service job. Can you imagine what the citizens of our esteemed community are going to do when they get wind that she's shacked up with the three of us? And her father. Jesus. There'll be no end to his screaming. She could very well lose her job over this."

"We'll always take care of Reggie," Sawyer said.

"But will she be happy?" Hutch asked softly. "Because I want her to be happy more than I want me to be happy or you or Cam."

Sawyer rubbed a hand over his face. "That's a good question," he murmured. "But all we can do is try, Hutch. We *all* want her to be happy. I'm going to do everything in my power to make that happen, and I know you and Cam will too. And maybe in the end, that's all we *can* do."

Hutch sighed. "I know you're right, man. It's just messed up. I mean even the fact that we're sitting here discussing the pitfalls of sharing the same woman . . . it's twisted."

"I didn't realize this bothered you so much," Sawyer said quietly.

Hutch carefully ladled out the batter into small circles on the skillet. "Most days it doesn't. I won't lie to you and say that like you said, in a perfect world, it would only be me and Reggie. I'm okay with this. I really am. And I think that's what bothers me. That I'm *okay* with it. When the sane part of me is screaming *what the fuck* at me."

"Get over it," Sawyer said. "It doesn't do any good to let your sensibilities scream bloody murder. Yeah, it's unorthodox as hell. No doubt it's going to gain us a few raised eyebrows and public censure. But it's our job to be above that and to protect Reggie from as much of it as possible."

Hutch nodded. "You're right. I know." Then he leveled a stare at Sawyer. "I wasn't jealous this morning. I've been up front with you from the beginning. You know I'd tell you if I was."

"It's okay, man, even if you were jealous. I don't expect this to be some freaky utopia where we never have to work at things." He rubbed a hand over his face. "Christ, I'm starting to sound like freaking Cam. He's the one who usually does all the feather soothing. When did it become my job to babysit your asses?"

Hutch chuckled and relaxed. "Sorry, man. I think I just hit the panic button this morning."

"Yeah well, cut that shit out. We've got other things to worry about."

"What are we worrying about?" Cam asked as he entered the kitchen. "And has anyone seen my glasses? I swear I left them in the living room but hell if I can find them."

Sawyer grinned and picked up the wire frames from the counter and held them out to Cam.

"Thanks, man," Cam mumbled. He slid the glasses on and shoved his hair back from his face. "Now what are we worrying about?"

"Yeah, do tell," Hutch said. He picked up the spatula and flipped the first pancake. Perfect.

"Hello? There's some freak out there stalking Reggie?"

Cam's face darkened.

Hutch flipped another pancake and gripped the spatula a little tighter.

"It would figure that it's some psycho trying to get at Peter Fallon. Why he just doesn't go after the asshole directly is beyond me," Sawyer muttered.

"We couldn't get that lucky. Besides, how's psycho boy supposed to know that Peter Fallon could give a shit about Reggie?" Cam asked.

Hutch grimaced. "Good point."

"Maybe we should hold a press conference and announce to the world that the best way to punish Peter Fallon has nothing to do with his daughter," Reggie said in a bitter tone.

They all looked up to see Reggie standing in the doorway of the kitchen, her face pale and drawn.

"Shit," Sawyer whispered.

Cam stood and crossed to where Reggie was standing and took her hand. "I'm sorry. I shouldn't have opened my big mouth."

She raised an eyebrow. "What are you apologizing for, telling the truth?"

He shook his head. "No, just for being an unfeeling jerk, for blurting it out like that."

"You're not the unfeeling jerk," she said pointedly. "My father holds that title."

She moved past Cam and walked over to where Hutch was plating the first batch of pancakes.

"Smells good. Are those mine?"

He stared balefully at her. "You drag your ass out of bed last and expect to get the first plate of food?"

She grinned. "Umm, yes?"

He dropped a kiss on her lips. "Sit down and I'll slap some ham on the plate and bring it over."

"Don't forget the syrup," she added as she walked around to sit beside Sawyer.

Cam walked back over and slid onto the stool next to her. Hutch forked a piece of ham onto her plate and then set it on the counter in front of her. Then he reached into the drawer for a fork and snagged the syrup sitting by the skillet.

"Eat up," he said as he placed the objects next to her plate.

She turned the bottle down and poured copious amounts of syrup over the stack of pancakes. Hutch tried not to wince, but even Sawyer, Mr. Sweet Tooth, was cringing.

She capped the bottle and then licked her thumb. "Are you guys working today? I thought you said you had a tight deadline or something."

"Well, technically, Cam has the tight deadline. He's the architect. Hutch and I are just the grunts who do the hard labor. I turned over the two job sites that are under construction to our foreman so that we could be here," Sawyer said.

She lowered her fork back to her plate and glanced over at Sawyer. "I'm curious about something. Your office is in Houston. You have a house in Houston. And yet here we are in this brand-new house an hour away. Obviously my little run-in with Mr. Freak Show had nothing to do with your relocating here. What about your business?"

Sawyer glanced at Cam and then at Hutch, and it amused Hutch that there was a light of panic in Sawyer's eyes. No doubt he would love for Cam, Mr. Smooth, to step in and take this one.

Cam cleared his throat, and Hutch had to look away or risk laughing. Yep, he'd nailed that one.

"We've had plans to relocate here for a good while," Cam said.

"Obviously," Reggie said dryly. "This house must have taken eons to build."

"For now we're keeping our office in Houston. We have four crews working under us and two others that we contract with when we're pressed for manpower. I can draw plans anywhere. We'll have some traveling back and forth to do, but it's only an hour."

Her eyebrows drew together. "I had no idea you guys were doing so well. I mean I knew you had a great start, but didn't realize you'd expanded so much."

"If you'd spent more time around us and less time running balls to the wall, you'd know that," Sawyer pointed out.

She flushed and dropped her gaze to her plate. "Yeah, I guess you're right," she mumbled.

She ate a few more bites then glanced back up again. "If one of you isn't too busy later, I hoped you could run me over to my house so I could get my car."

Hutch frowned. "Why do you need your car? You sure as hell don't need to be driving yet."

She blew out her breath impatiently. "I would feel better if I had my vehicle here, just like I feel better that I have my gun."

Sawyer broke in. "If you're worried about being here alone again, that's not going to happen."

She shook her head. "I'm not worried about being alone. My concern is having a means of transportation. I don't want to have to rely on one of you to get around. You're busy. You have jobs. I have a job too."

Cam and Sawyer exchanged uneasy glances, and Hutch spoke up before either of them could.

"I'll take you over after breakfast."

Sawyer shot him a dark glance, but Hutch ignored it. Reggie smiled gratefully at him and resumed eating. Hutch shrugged when both Cam and Sawyer pinned him with their stares.

Both of them should realize by now that trying to pigeonhole Reggie was the fastest way to push her away. And she'd already done way too much damn running. It was time to start pulling her in, not shoving her away.

CHAPTER 14

After breakfast, Regina went upstairs to shower and change. She stripped the brace from her wrist and flexed her hand experimentally. It was still tender, but the swelling had gone down.

She viewed her reflection in the mirror as she waited for the water to warm, and to her satisfaction, the bruising around her neck wasn't nearly as visible. The dark purple had faded to light green and yellow with streaks of darker red. The mark on her face was barely noticeable. In a few more days, she'd be as good as new, and then maybe she could get back to work. Which reminded her that she needed to put in a call to the chief to get an update on the progress of the case.

She stepped into the shower and groaned in pleasure as hot water cascaded over her body. She scrubbed her hair and rinsed quickly before stepping out to dry off. Several minutes later, after dressing, she stepped back into the bathroom to try and tame her hair into some semblance of order. Finally she opted to push the curls back from her face and secure it with barrettes.

Then she set about trying to put the brace back on her wrist.

After cursing and fighting the sticky Velcro, she tossed it aside in disgust. She didn't need it anyway.

She hurried out of the bathroom in search of her shoes and quickly discovered that no amount of contorting allowed her to bend enough to put them on without causing considerable pain to her ribs. She posted a huge mental note to get her slip-ons from the house when she went to get her car.

With a resigned sigh, she collected the shoes and socks and headed downstairs.

"You're moving better today," Cam said when she hit the bottom of the stairs.

She looked up to see him standing a few feet away watching her. "Not exactly," she muttered.

She shoved the shoes at him and walked past him into the living room, where Hutch was waiting for her. Cam followed behind chuckling.

She sat down on the couch and pinned him with a glare. To his credit, he didn't say a word as he dropped to one knee and began putting on her socks.

She glanced up at Hutch, whose eyes twinkled with merriment. She twisted her lips in disgust and looked back down at Cam. He slid the tennis shoes on and quickly laced them up. Then he patted the top of her foot.

"All done."

"Thanks," she mumbled.

"You ready?" Hutch asked.

She nodded and started to push herself off the couch but remembered her wrist at the last minute. With another sigh, she reached up with her good hand to grab Cam's. He pulled her up, a wide grin splitting his face.

"You're enjoying this way too much."

He leaned in and gave her a light peck on the lips. "Yes, I am."

"Neanderthal," she grumbled as she walked by him to follow Hutch out the front door.

The drive was mostly silent, a fact she was grateful for. Part of her wondered if Hutch knew she'd slept sandwiched between Sawyer and Cam, and the other part of her was tired of worrying over imagined jealousies and slights.

It wasn't her responsibility to make sure each of them was soothed. God, she couldn't even imagine the exhaustion in trying. Which was why she thought this whole notion of theirs was a disaster in the making.

It still didn't stop the what-ifs from whispering in her ear, though. *What if it could work? What if she could have a deep and loving relationship with all three of them?*

As soon as the thought inserted itself into her mind, she slammed the door shut. Entertaining those kinds of fantasies was only ensuring that one of them, probably her, would get hurt.

"You're quiet, baby."

She looked over and smiled, but it felt stiff even to her.

"Want to talk about it?"

"No," she said in a low voice.

"Stop brooding," he chided. "It won't help anything."

She leaned forward in her seat as they pulled into her driveway. Her silver RAV4 was still parked outside where she'd left it, and it would be a relief to have it with her at the guys' house. It meant not having to depend on them to go when she wanted and where she wanted.

"You can wait here," she said. "I'm just going to run in and get some different shoes. Or you can go ahead and start back. I'll be along in a minute."

He just stared at her.

"No? Okay. Be back in a minute."

She closed the door and shook her head. Not that she really thought he'd start back without her, but she'd offered at any rate.

She unlocked her door and stepped inside, doing a quick survey. Nothing had changed since the day before, and nothing *felt* out of place. The fact that she even considered that someone might have gone into her house irritated the hell out of her. That some nutjob had targeted her because of her father pissed her off even more.

She made a quick pass through her room, grabbing a few more changes of clothes and clean underwear. As she stuffed everything into her bag, she cringed a bit over the underwear. Stuffy, white and plain. Then she shook her head. She was losing her damn mind. What the hell did it matter if she didn't have dainty, lacy underwear?

With a groan, she shoved the remaining clothes into the overnight bag and yanked it closed.

She walked back outside and gave Hutch a small wave as she climbed into her small SUV. She gingerly wrapped her left hand around the wheel and tested the tenderness of her wrist as she inserted her key into the ignition. She moved it one notch, and her radio nearly blasted her ears off. She slapped at the knob to turn it off. The bag in the passenger seat caught her eye, and she realized she'd forgotten to get her flip-flops. Damn it.

She climbed out and held up one finger in Hutch's direction to indicate she'd just be a minute then hurried toward the front door.

As she reached out for the handle, a loud explosion registered just a nanosecond before she was lifted into the air and slammed against the door. Pain speared her skull as she hit the ground. Heat. So much heat. It blazed over her skin. Her head lolled to the side, and it was then that she saw what used to be her vehicle engulfed in flames.

Hutch.

Oh God, where was Hutch?

She struggled to right herself. Her fingers dug into the sidewalk as she dragged herself along the ground.

"Reggie!"

She nearly fainted with relief when she heard Hutch's frantic cry.

He fell down next to her. His hands ran over her body, seeking. "Reggie, oh my God, Reggie, are you all right?"

She rolled so she could look up at him then squinted against the sun. "I'm going to kill that son of a bitch. I just bought that car."

Hutch pressed his forehead to hers, and his fingers shook against her cheeks. "Sweet Jesus, you scared the hell out of me, Reggie."

"Yeah, well, I think I'm going to have to change my underwear."

"Are you all right? Do you hurt anywhere? Christ you hit the door hard."

"To tell you the truth, I have no idea yet. My head hurts. I think. Not sure about anything else."

"Maybe you should just lay there and not move while I call for an ambulance."

"Oh hell no," she muttered. "I've had enough of ambulances and hospitals. Help me up. If I can stand on my own for at least five seconds, you have to promise to take me home with you."

"Baby, I thought you'd never ask."

"Smart-ass."

He laughed, and she tried to smile. Honestly she did. But hell, it hurt. Her whole face hurt. She grimaced as she reached up to grab Hutch's arm. He wrapped his arms around her and gently helped her up.

Her knees buckled, and Hutch caught her before she fell on her face again. She clung to his shirt and took quick stock of her injuries.

Other than a nagging buzz in her head that wouldn't go away, she didn't think she was any worse for the wear. Well, unless you counted some seriously shot nerves.

"We have to call this in," she rasped. "Evidence."

"Already done, baby. You just stay your ass in one place. In fact, I'm going to take you to the truck so you can sit down. If you so much as look like you're going to sway, I'm hauling your butt to the ER."

"Truck sounds pretty good right now," she said.

Hutch picked her up and strode to his truck. Her fuzzy vision took in a large dent in his hood as they passed.

"Ah, fuck. Your truck."

"I don't give a shit about my truck. Just that you're all right."

He opened the passenger door, then shouldered it open wider before he settled her into the seat. Then he reached down and pulled the lever to recline it. He eased her down until she was nearly flat on her back.

"You're a mess," he murmured as he trailed a finger down her cheek.

"So is your truck," she croaked. "And my SUV." She sighed. "I saved up for forever to buy it. It was cute."

"Cute? You're actually admitting to buying a cute vehicle?"

"Hey, I'm a girl. We're supposed to have cute vehicles," she grumbled.

"Now I know you're suffering a head injury."

She reached a hand blindly up until it collided with his face. She cupped his cheek. "I was so scared," she whispered. "I thought . . ." Her voice cracked as tears suddenly welled in her eyes. "I thought maybe it was you. That the explosion got you."

Hutch leaned down and pressed his lips to her forehead. "No, baby, I'm fine. Don't upset yourself." He stroked a gentle hand through her hair. "God, I was fine. Just a cracked windshield and a dent or two. But you . . . Jesus, I watched you hit the door."

Sirens wailed in the distance, growing closer with each passing second. She struggled to sit up despite Hutch holding her down.

"Let me up," she said.

He hesitated but then relented and helped her sit up. She swung her feet around the seat to dangle close to the step down. After blinking a few times to clear her vision, she saw two fire trucks and three police units tear up her street.

Her car was still a smoking mass of metal, but the flames had died down some. And then she saw what the explosion had done to the front of her house.

"My house," she said faintly. "Look at my house."

The front windows were blown out, all three of them. There was debris on the roof and scattered over the lawn. The flowers that she'd lovingly planted were gone. Even the lone dogwood in the yard was now nothing more than a pitiful, smoldering stick in the ground.

The firefighters jumped out and quickly hosed down her SUV. Jeremy, Carl and the chief hurried over to the truck where Hutch stood.

"Regina, are you all right?" the chief demanded.

"I'm fine. Just shaken up."

She slid off the seat, steadying herself by grabbing Hutch's arm. He put his arm around her shoulders as her feet found solid ground.

"What the hell happened here?" Carl demanded.

Regina sighed and quickly related the sequence of events leading up to the explosion.

"Sounds like a delayed timer," Jeremy said grimly. "Christ, if you hadn't gotten out to go back in, it would have exploded with you in it."

Hutch paled, and he tightened his grip on her shoulder. She worked hard to keep her hands from shaking, finally balling her fingers into fists.

Her yard quickly got a lot more crowded as more police and first responders showed up. The entire frickin' town would be there before the hour was out.

The whole area was cordoned off, and she and Hutch were pushed back into the street. She watched with a sense of detachment. It was just any other crime scene. It wasn't *her* home and vehicle. To admit that would be to admit how close she'd come to death. Again.

It was enough to make her religious.

Hutch kept his arm around her, rubbing his hand up and down her shoulder. Every once in a while he'd glance down, concern burning brightly in his eyes.

She stared dully at the chief as he directed the activity around her vehicle. It had turned into a regular police party—locals, the county guys, state police, even a bomb squad guy from the city south of her podunk town. This had to be a first.

And just when she thought things couldn't get any worse, Peter Fallon drove up in his black Mercedes. On second thought, things could get worse. Her mother climbed out of the passenger seat and scanned the crowd until her eyes alighted on Regina.

"Fuck me," Reggie muttered.

Hutch stiffened beside her then squeezed her arm reassuringly. "I'm here, baby."

To her never-ending shock, and she'd truly thought the days of her parents surprising her had ended, her mother rushed over and threw her arms around Regina, hugging her tightly.

"Regina, thank God you're all right."

Regina pulled away, blinking in confusion. "Mom. What are you doing here?"

Lydia smoothed the tendrils of Regina's hair, pushing them back away from her face in a decidedly *motherly* fashion. Hell, maybe Regina had died, or maybe this was some bizarre dream she hadn't awoken from yet. She liked option number two.

"Your father heard about the explosion on the police scanner, and we rushed right over. Are you hurt? Do you need to go to the hospital?"

Peter Fallon walked up behind his wife and stared at Regina. "Regina," he said gruffly. "Are you okay?"

Option one. Definitely option one. Obviously she had died, and this was some sort of purgatory she was assigned to where her mother and father played the role of parents who gave a damn.

"I'm fine," she said.

"You stay with Regina," Peter said to Lydia. "I'm going to find out what the hell is going on here. Someone's trying to kill my daughter, and I want to know why."

Regina gaped at his retreating back. Then she found herself yanked against her mother once more when Lydia enfolded her in another hug. She glanced up at Hutch in astonished horror.

He looked as confused as she did and lifted his shoulders in a shrug.

For a moment, Regina allowed herself the luxury of indulging in a mother's hug. She couldn't remember the last time her mom had hugged her, said she loved her or acted maternal in any shape or fashion.

It felt . . . good.

"You should come stay with me and your father, Regina. You can hardly stay here now," Lydia said as she pulled away again.

"Uhm, thanks, Mom, but I'll be staying with Hutch for the short term." She glanced up at Hutch as she spoke.

Lydia's brow creased in confusion. "But he doesn't live here."
She glanced apologetically over at Hutch. "I know you've been a
good friend to Regina, but surely she should stay in her own community where she can be close to family?"

"I have a house here, Mrs. Fallon," Hutch said evenly.

"Oh, well all right then, I suppose." She focused her gaze back
at Regina. "Are you sure you wouldn't rather stay with us where
you could be in your old room?"

An uncomfortable prickle started at Regina's neck and worked
its way over her cheeks. Her mother would succumb to hysteria,
and her father would blow a gasket if they knew she was staying
with all three men. Even as the thought crossed her mind, she
drew her shoulders up in irritation.

It didn't matter a whole hell of a lot what they thought.
They'd never been invested in what she did, her choices, her *life*.
And she damn sure wasn't going to start pussyfooting around
them now.

She reached for Hutch's hand and laced her fingers through
his, wanting, *needing* his steady strength.

"No thank you, Mom. I'll be staying temporarily with Hutch,
Cam and Sawyer until I can figure out alternate arrangements."

Lydia's eyes widened, and then her lips thinned with disapproval. Peter Fallon's voice could be heard as it raised above all
the other noise.

"How can you possibly draw the conclusion that someone is
using my daughter to punish me for some imagined infraction?"

The chief put a placating hand on her father's arm, and Regina
couldn't hear his response.

Lydia frowned. "What is he talking about, Regina?"

"There is a possibility that the person targeting me is doing so
because of Dad," she responded quietly.

"Oh, but that's nonsense. Why would anyone do such a thing?"

"Because he's a politician," Regina said patiently. "And besides, we don't have actual proof of that yet. It's merely an angle the department is looking at."

"Why, it could be anyone. Maybe someone you've arrested in the past or someone you gave a ticket to. It seems a stretch to assume it would have anything to do with your father."

No one could fault her mother for being behind her husband, that was for sure. But it would make sense to most normal people that a mother would be equally behind her daughter. Regina frowned unhappily. This was turning into one suckass day.

"It's an angle, Mom," she repeated. "The police have to consider all possibilities."

"Regina, can I speak to you for a moment?" Jeremy asked as he pushed in beside Lydia. He glanced at Lydia and Hutch. "Privately?" he added.

Regina frowned and let go of Hutch's hand. "Excuse me for a moment," she said as she left Hutch's side.

She followed Jeremy a few feet away. "What's up?"

"I just got a call from Dispatch. Birdie's house was broken into."

CHAPTER 15

*R*egina grabbed Jeremy's arm. "What?"

"I'm heading over there now. I thought you'd want to go if you felt up to it."

She nodded. "Of course." She turned to look at Hutch, who was staring intently at her and Jeremy. She glanced back at Jeremy. "Where is Birdie now?"

"Brett was making a pass by her house like the chief asked us to do, and he noticed that her door was open, but her car was gone. When he went in to investigate, he discovered that her house had been vandalized. He called it in then intercepted Birdie, who drove up a few minutes later, and took her back to the station. She's waiting there."

Regina took in a steadying breath and tried to sort her scrambled brain. "Okay, I'm going with you. I'll need to tell Hutch so he can go to the police station to be with Birdie. She's probably upset."

"Make it quick. I'll wait in the car."

Jeremy turned and strode toward his police cruiser. Regina hurried back over to where Hutch stood, a frown on his face.

"What's going on, Reggie?"

She put her hand on his arm. "Birdie's house was broken into this morning. I'm going over with Jeremy now."

"What? Is she all right? I'm coming with you."

She planted her hand on Hutch's chest. "Birdie's at the station. You should go over. She's probably very upset, and I know she'd like for you to be there. You'd only be in the way at the house. This is a police investigation."

He looked as though he'd protest, but she turned and walked away before he could speak. She hurried to where Jeremy had parked his car, her sore muscles whining the entire way.

She slid into the front seat, and Jeremy turned on his lights and backed out.

"Do we know anything yet?" she asked.

"No. I just got the call a few minutes ago. Brett was going back in to do a more thorough look through."

Jeremy reached into the pocket of his door, pulled out a napkin and handed it to Regina.

"What's this for?" she asked.

"You're bleeding," he said and gestured to her forehead.

She yanked down the visor and stared at her reflection in the mirror. A thin rivulet of blood ran down her forehead and into her eyebrow. There was a gash at her hairline from God knows what. She couldn't remember that exact injury when her whole body felt like it had taken a beating.

She dabbed at it and winced when she brushed across the wound.

"At the rate I'm going, I'll be cast in the next Frankenstein movie," she muttered.

"There's some weird shit going on around here, Regina," Jeremy said in a somber voice. "Sometimes we go days without anything more than a few traffic tickets, and suddenly we have a murder, an explosion and breaking and entering? What the fuck is going on?"

"I wish to hell I knew. I have a hard time believing all this is connected to my father's politics. I mean why not just take him out if this guy has such a beef with him? Seems more expedient."

Jeremy shot her a look of surprise.

"I'm not advocating that he kill my father," she said impatiently. "I'm just wondering why he'd go to all this trouble to make a point. If he hates Peter Fallon so much, why not go after *him*?"

"Good question."

Jeremy whipped into Birdie's driveway and parked beside Brett's police car. He and Regina got out as Brett walked out to meet them.

"Glad to see you're all right, Regina," Brett said with a nod in her direction.

"Thanks. What have we got here?"

Brett turned and motioned them inside.

When she followed Brett and Jeremy in, she looked around but didn't find anything out of place in the living room. Birdie's place housed an impressive collection of antiques, yet none of them were disturbed.

"It doesn't get weird until you get back here," Brett said as he motioned them down the hallway to the bedrooms.

As they passed each room, Regina looked in and again saw nothing that seemed to be out of place.

When they reached the end of the hallway, she saw a large red smear on the bedroom door. It looked like *blood*.

When she walked into the room, she gasped. It was in shambles. There was more blood on the walls. And on the bed. Large spatters. Pictures lay in broken frames on the floor. Pictures of Hutch, Cam and Sawyer with Birdie. More pictures of the boys. Hutch's high school prom picture.

A feeling of foreboding settled hard into Regina's chest.

"This isn't about me," she said. "It's about *Hutch*."

"Not sure I follow," Jeremy said.

She blew out a shaky breath as she tried to come up with a more plausible explanation than what had just hit her square in the face. Jeremy and Brett both looked at her with questioning gazes.

"The murder victim. Misty Thompson. Hutch took her to his prom. The killer, when he attacked me, said *it's time to make him pay*. He failed to kill me, hence the bomb in my SUV. Now he's broken into Birdie's home and trashed Hutch's room. This was his room when he lived here with Birdie. These are his things. I don't think this has anything to do with my father at all. This guy is trying to make Hutch suffer by going after the people he cares about. People he's had a connection to. And probably Hutch is his ultimate goal."

Jeremy stared back, his expression stunned. "Shit. You could be right."

"I know I'm right. It's the only thing that makes sense."

Her stomach turned and twisted into knots. Somehow it had been easier to deal with when she thought she was the intended target. But to know that someone was after Hutch? That the killer could go after him next or even Cam and Sawyer?

"But why?" Jeremy asked. "What could Hutch possibly have done to piss off someone this badly? It doesn't make sense. I'm not sure we can rule out your father as a motive yet."

"I'm not saying we have to rule him out, just that we have to consider that none of this is coincidence and that Hutch could be the ultimate goal."

"Has it occurred to you that this could be linked solely to you?" Brett spoke up. "Birdie's important to you, as is Hutch. You're a police officer. It certainly wouldn't be the first time some whack job a cop arrested has gone off the deep end and retaliated."

Regina frowned. "Maybe." She closed her eyes. Jesus. If it *was* about her, Hutch, Sawyer and Cam could still be targets. Either way the thought of losing them terrified her.

"You know the chief is going to put you on leave indefinitely," Jeremy said in a low voice.

She grimaced. "Yeah, I know. He'll have to." And suddenly she didn't mind *quite* so much. Her priorities had shifted in short order. While both Jeremy's and Brett's theories certainly held water, she couldn't discount the nagging idea that this was aimed at Hutch and that he or Cam or Sawyer could be next. And if that was the case, she wanted to make damn sure she stayed close to them at all times.

"I've put in a call so we can get some guys over here to dust for prints. Everyone was tied up over at your place," Brett said to Regina. "Although so far, if it's the same guy, he's been careful not to leave any. I'm hoping like hell that this isn't human blood."

"You and me both," Regina murmured.

"I'm beginning to think they don't pay us enough to work in this town," Jeremy said in a weary voice. "I doubt any of us will ever sit around the station hoping for action again."

"You're telling me."

He cracked a grin. "Yeah, I suppose that was bad of me to whine. I mean look at you. You look like something the cat dragged in." His expression became more serious, and his tone lost the light teasing. "I'm damn glad you're okay, Regina. That was a close call."

She smiled wanly. "Yeah, no shit." She rubbed a hand through her snarled hair then let it fall to her hip with a smack.

"Let me take you over to the station," Jeremy said. "And then

I'll come back over to help Brett out here. I'm pretty sure the chief won't be happy if he shows up and you're on scene."

"Yeah, okay," she said.

She turned and walked slowly back out of the house, furious that Birdie's home would be defiled. This house held so many happy memories for Hutch, Cam and Sawyer. And for her as well. It had been a home when her own home felt more like a house. A cold, sterile house that people inhabited but no one *lived* in.

And the idea of anyone doing Birdie harm made her physically ill.

She climbed into Jeremy's car feeling a hundred years old. She needed a long, hot bath. Preferably one she could soak in for three hours.

He pulled out and headed toward the station, his hands tight around the steering wheel.

"I need you to keep me up-to-date on this case, Jeremy," she said. "Hutch, Cam and Sawyer are very important to me. I'm going to do everything in my power to keep them safe. I'll be staying out at their house until this blows over. If that fucker comes near them, he's dead meat."

"I'll keep you in the loop," Jeremy promised. "As soon as we get the scene processed and I bounce our ideas off the chief and Carl, I'll have a better idea of where the investigation is headed. Until then you need to lay low and make sure Hutch does the same."

"And Birdie," Regina said softly. "Somehow I need to persuade her that she can't stay in that house alone until this guy is caught. Whether I'm right about it being about Hutch, or you're right about it being about me, she's important to us both and is at risk either way."

CHAPTER 16

No sooner had Jeremy pulled up to the police station and Regina gotten out, than she looked up and saw Sawyer striding out of the station, his face as dark as a thunderstorm.

"Uh-oh," Jeremy murmured as he walked ahead of her. "He doesn't look too happy."

Sawyer walked straight past Jeremy, and Regina braced for impact. He didn't say a word. He yanked her into his arms, tilted her head back and kissed her hard and fierce.

Her gasp of surprise was swallowed up as his mouth moved hungrily over hers. His arms were bands of steel around her back, strong and comforting. Her body softened and melted into his as he possessed her with his lips.

Warm, soothing honey flowed through her veins. She forgot where they were, lost all sense of time and place. Tongues met. His delved deep, tasting her as she tasted him.

Finally his arms loosened, and his hands swept up her neck and to her jaw before framing her face in his palms. With halting breaths, he pulled slightly away.

His eyes glittered. Need. Fear. Anger. They were all mixed and swirled in the pale blue irises. His fingers stuttered across the gash at her hairline. She could feel him trembling against her.

"Sawyer, I'm okay," she whispered.

"Reggie, oh my God, Reggie."

His voice broke as the words spilled torturously from his lips. He leaned his forehead against hers and closed his eyes. His chest heaved as he struggled to catch his breath.

"I could have lost you," he said hoarsely.

She tilted her chin up so her lips met his. She kissed him. Lightly. Reassuring.

"Regina, what the hell is going on here?"

She stiffened as her father's strident voice intruded. She turned slowly away from Sawyer to see her father standing a few feet away, his face tight with disapproval. Her mother simply stared agape at her and Sawyer.

"Don't you have any sense of decorum?" he bit out. "The press is going to be crawling all over this place after what happened this morning. If you won't think of yourself and your position as a police officer, at least have a care as to how your behavior reflects on me."

Sawyer bristled and opened his mouth to respond, but Regina gripped his arm in warning. Sawyer was already hanging on by a thread, and any outburst from him wouldn't be pretty.

She pinned her father with all the disdain fueling her anger. "Fuck off," she said before turning away.

Her mother gasped, and her father made a sound of outrage.

"Regina, don't you walk away from me, young lady. I didn't raise you to talk to me like that."

She stopped dead, and despite Sawyer's restraining hand, she broke away and rounded on her father.

"No, you self-righteous prick. You didn't raise me at all. You were too busy ignoring me. Talk to you? When was I ever encouraged to say anything at all? You and *Lydia* were too busy with *your* lives for something as inconsequential as a daughter. Be glad you're my father, because if you weren't, I'd knock the shit out of you like I would anyone else who spoke to me like that."

She turned back around before he could see the tears of fury gathering in her eyes. Damn if he would ever see her cry.

Sawyer put a protective arm around her, and when she would have hurried into the station, he held her still. He turned to pin her father with a cold stare.

"I'll only say this once. Stay the fuck away from Reggie. You're not *my* father, and I have no compunction about laying your ass out."

He gathered Regina closer to him and guided her toward the entrance to the station.

"You can't threaten me like that," Peter blustered.

As Sawyer reached for the door, he turned back one last time. "It wasn't a threat, Mr. Fallon."

He ushered Regina inside and closed the door. Birdie was seated in the small waiting area, flanked by Cam and Hutch. When they looked up and saw her, they all rose.

Cam crossed the room, and Sawyer relinquished his hold on her just as Cam swept her into his arms.

His hand tangled in her hair as he buried her face in his chest. His heart raced beneath her cheek, and his chest rose and fell with harsh breaths.

When he finally pulled away, he ran his hands over her head, her face and then her neck.

"Are you all right? Do you need to go to the hospital?"

She put her hands over his wrists as he cupped her neck. "I'm fine, Cam. I promise. Just a little banged up."

"Regina dear, how are you feeling?" Birdie asked.

Regina looked to see Birdie standing beside Cam. He relinquished her, and Birdie enfolded her in a warm hug. This . . . this is what unconditional love felt like. She held on to Birdie for a long moment in an attempt to banish the image of her mother and father out in the parking lot.

"There, there, you've had quite a fright," Birdie soothed as she rubbed her hand up and down Regina's back. "You should be at home, resting, not here."

Regina drew back and smiled. "I had to see you and make sure you were doing okay."

"Oh yes, dear, I'm fine. The policeman whisked me straight here. Wouldn't even let me go inside the house." Her eyes grew troubled. "Is it bad?"

Regina guided her to the side, back into the hallway leading to the door. The guys frowned at her, but she waved them back. They'd demand answers, but she wasn't going to hash this out in front of them right now.

"How much have they told you?" Regina asked in a low voice.

"Nothing yet." Birdie stared anxiously back at Regina. "What is it, Regina? What has happened?"

"The only room in your house that was disturbed was one of the bedrooms. Hutch's old room."

"But why on earth would someone want to mess up a bedroom? Was nothing stolen?"

Regina shook her head. "Not that I saw right off, but later you'll need to do a full inventory for the police report. For now I think you should come back to the house with me and the guys. You shouldn't stay there alone."

"It's sweet of you to offer, but my friend Virginia is here with me. You saw her. She was in the waiting area with me."

Actually Regina hadn't noticed her. Her attention had been focused on Cam and then on Birdie.

"She's offered to let me stay with her for as long as I need."

Regina chewed the inside of her cheek and wondered how best to broach the subject with Birdie. She didn't want to jump the gun and confide her own suspicions. It would be irresponsible, not to mention premature, given that she hadn't even discussed them with the chief yet.

"I would feel better if you had more protection, Birdie. We don't know yet who broke into your house or why. I'm sure Cam, Sawyer and Hutch would feel much better as well if you came home with us."

"Oh you don't have to worry. Virginia and I have already been over that. She has a shotgun. Plus her son, who is a county sheriff's deputy, has promised to stay until the person responsible for breaking into my home is apprehended."

A smile twitched at the corners of Regina's lips. "Birdie, promise me you won't mess with Virginia's shotgun."

"Oh, she won't."

Regina swung around to see Virginia standing a few feet away. Her purse dangled on her wrist by a gold chain. Regina's brow came up as she took in the rest of Virginia's getup. White gloves adorned her hands. She wore a flowered dress and a wide straw hat at an angle, with a large red bow tied above the brim. And fuchsia lipstick. *Bright* fuchsia lipstick. It hurt Regina's eyes to stare at those lips for too long.

"You see, Miss Fallon, the shotgun is my area of expertise. I'm quite adept with it, if I do say so myself."

"Ah . . . okaaay," Regina said. "Still, Virginia, I would feel much better if you didn't go around wielding a shotgun. If your son is going to stay with you, perhaps you should leave the weapons to him since he's a trained police officer."

Virginia looked down her nose and narrowed her eyes.

"Hmmph, and who do you think taught Kyle his way around a gun?"

Regina pursed her lips and tried to stifle her laughter.

Birdie laid a hand on Regina's arm. "Virginia really is responsible with firearms, and she was such a dear to come down and stay with me at the station."

Regina shook her head, unsure of what one had to do with the other, but then her brain was a complete muddle.

"Birdie, if you like we can go now. I left our ladies' tea, but it lasts another hour if you'd like to join me."

Birdie glanced worriedly at Regina. "Oh, I don't know, Virginia. Regina might need me here. She's had such a trying day. I want to be able to help her any way I can."

Birdie patted Regina's arm then squeezed gently.

Regina smiled at her then gave her a quick hug. "You go on, Birdie. Be sure and leave your contact information with Greta so one of our officers can call you. He'll need to ask questions, and he'll want to take you over to the house so you can make a list of any missing items."

"You take care, dear. And call me if you need anything."

Regina watched as Birdie went back into the waiting room, spoke with Greta for a moment and then went over to where the guys were standing, so she could to hug each one of them.

It was a sight that always made Regina's heart twinge just a little. Birdie with her boys. Now all grown men, but no less her boys.

Birdie walked out with Virginia wrapping a comforting arm around her slight shoulders.

Regina swayed, and her own shoulders slumped forward. Strong, comforting arms surrounded her from behind, and a gentle mouth found the top of her head.

"It's time to take you home, Reggie darling."

She closed her eyes for a moment and curled both hands around Cam's arm.

"Regina, I hate to interrupt, especially as I know how badly you need to go home, but the chief called and specifically asked you to wait for him. He's on his way in now," Greta called from her desk.

She sagged against Cam's chest. She knew what was coming. Understanding it didn't make it any easier. Her job was something uniquely hers. An achievement she was proud of. For so long she'd existed under the shadow of her father, ignored and only brought out when it was opportune for Peter Fallon to play the family man for the media.

And now she was going to be asked to stand down from that job for an indefinite period of time.

"We'll be here with you, Reggie," Cam said against her ear.

"Thanks, Cam," she said as she straightened in his embrace.

Hutch walked forward and took both her hands. He pulled her toward one of the chairs.

"At least sit down while you wait, before you fall over."

She stared at Hutch, and damn if her eyes didn't go all watery again. But when she looked at him, all she saw was the blood on the walls of his bedroom. The malice behind the destruction. And the fact that this maniac could well target him or one of the others.

She couldn't lose them.

"Hey," he said softly. He rubbed his thumb underneath her eye. "What's that for?"

She sucked in a breath and sat down in the chair. Sawyer took the seat beside her and Hutch knelt down in front of her. Cam stood behind Hutch, a frown on his face.

It pissed her off that she was showing such weakness in front of them, but she couldn't seem to stop the tears from leaking down her cheeks.

Hutch picked her hand up and brought it to his lips. He brushed a kiss across her knuckles while he rubbed his other hand over her injured wrist.

"It's nothing," she lied. "Just reaction I guess."

Sawyer reached over and pulled her against his side.

"Quit the brave front shit, Reggie," he growled. "You were almost blown to hell. I'd say that's worth being upset over."

As much as she wanted to burrow into Sawyer's arms and stay there for a year, this wasn't the place to do it. Her chief would be in anytime, and she didn't want him seeing her cuddled up with three men in the police station. Her father? He could go to hell. But the chief she respected.

She slowly straightened then pushed forward out of her seat. "I need to go to the bathroom," she said.

Sawyer and Hutch both reached for her to help her up. As she walked by Greta's desk, the dispatcher gave her a sympathetic look.

"Why don't you go wait in the chief's office," she offered. "It would sure be a lot more comfortable than sitting out here in these hard chairs."

Regina smiled. "Thanks, Greta. I'll do that." She glanced up at the guys. "You'll wait?"

Sawyer frowned darkly. "Of course. We're not going anywhere."

She turned and went into the bathroom, more to compose herself than to use the facilities. At the sink she splashed cold water on her face and tried to wash some of the dried blood from her forehead.

She looked like someone's battering ram.

After drying her hands and her face, she slipped back into the hall and walked into the chief's office to wait. As she settled into the plush leather chair, she closed her eyes in sheer weariness. She was nearly asleep when the door opened.

She jerked upright and made a mad effort to straighten her clothing and hair.

"Take it easy, Regina," the chief said gruffly as he walked around his desk to take a seat. He settled down and stared hard at her. "You look like hell. How are you feeling?"

"I'm good, sir. Just a little shaken and sore."

The chief nodded. "I'll get right to the point so you can go home and get some rest. I've spoken to Jeremy about the break-in at Birdie's. We agree that there are several possibilities, all of which need to be pursued. I've got every man available on it. We're going to nail this bastard."

She nodded. "Yes, sir."

"Now, I'm sure you know this is coming, but you're on leave indefinitely. At least until this mess has been straightened out and we've removed the threat to you."

She nodded again and tried not to grimace.

"I know this is hard for you, Regina. You're a damn good cop. Dedicated. But you need the time off. You've been through a hell of a lot in the past several days. My advice is to take the time off and enjoy it."

"Begging your pardon, sir, but I can't enjoy anything while there is a possible threat to Hutch or to Birdie."

"I understand. Keep your eyes open. We're going to keep a close eye on Birdie, and the county will be sending regular patrols by the house where you're staying."

Regina leaned forward. "About that, sir. I thought you should know. I'll be staying with Hutch Bishop, Sawyer Pritchard and Cam Douglas . . . until this is all settled."

"Okay, we'll make sure we have a regular patrol by to check on you." He eyed her curiously. "Was there something else?"

She shifted uneasily. "Well, my father thinks it's a big deal. Where I'm staying, I mean. I thought you should know. That's all."

He leaned forward. "Regina, what you do in your personal life is your concern. I try to stay out of my officers' business when at all possible. Most folks around here know that you've been friends with those boys since you were kids. I doubt anyone will bat an eyelash over it."

She almost felt guilty. What the chief construed as a deep friendship . . . well if the guys had their way, it would be a lot more. Why she should feel guilty over it went beyond her, but she wasn't kidding herself. If such a relationship as what they proposed ever got out, she'd be crucified.

"Keep your head up, Regina. And be careful. If you spot anything out of the ordinary, you call it in immediately. I'll keep you up-to-date on any developments, and we'll fully investigate all angles. If this is personal to either you or Hutch, we'll find it."

"Thank you, sir."

"Now, why don't you get on home. I'd say you're long overdue for some rest."

She smiled weakly. "I won't argue that."

She stood and braced her hands on his desk before turning to walk out the door. The chief hurried around to open the door for her and put a comforting hand on her shoulder.

She made her way back out front where the guys were waiting. Sawyer, who had been pacing back and forth, stopped and hurried over to her.

"Come on, honey. Let's get you home."

Home. The word sounded incredibly sweet to her. And for once she didn't fight the notion that her home was with them.

CHAPTER 17

$\mathcal{T}$he ride home was tense and silent. When they pulled up to the house, Sawyer got out and reached up to help Regina down.

Hutch parked his battered truck beside them and was out just as quickly.

Sawyer curled his arm around her and ushered her inside the house. He didn't stop in the living room. Instead he half carried, half helped her up the stairs.

A few seconds later, he shoved the door to her bedroom open.

Cam and Hutch followed them in, stopping a few feet from where Sawyer halted.

Before she could so much as blink, Sawyer began tugging her shirt from her jeans. He reached down and unbuttoned her pants and began pulling the denim over her hips.

"Sawyer, what the hell are you doing?

She put her hands down to stop him but drew up short when she caught the fire in his eyes.

"Not a damn word, Reggie," he said through gritted teeth.

Her mouth fell open when he spun her around. She met the

determined gazes of Cam and Hutch, who stood, legs apart, arms crossed.

Sawyer yanked her jeans down then straightened and pulled her shirt over her head. Her pants around her ankles, she sat on the edge of the bed with a thump when he pushed her shoulders.

Cam knelt and took her shoes off then pulled her pants the rest of the way off. Sawyer sat down beside her and nudged her shoulder until she turned, baring her back to him. He fumbled with the clasp of her bra, and suddenly it came loose.

Her arms crept over her chest in a protective gesture when the strap of her bra tumbled down her shoulders. For the moment, she was left to sit in just her panties.

Sawyer stood and started stripping off his clothing. Regina swallowed, and her eyes widened.

"Sawyer, what are you *doing?*"

He paused a mere second before pinning her with glittering eyes, and then he resumed the shucking of his clothes. She glanced nervously down at Cam and then over at Hutch, but neither offered a single word.

When Sawyer was down to his boxers, he held out a hand to her. She eyed him in confusion, not at all understanding what the hell was going on. Surely they weren't . . . not *now*.

With an impatient sigh, Sawyer snagged her hand and pulled her to stand in front of him. Before she could speak or react, he turned her in the direction of the bathroom and planted a firm hand in the middle of her back.

She lurched forward, and he grabbed her arm with his other hand to steady her. He flipped on the lights in the bathroom as they entered. Her bare feet met the cool tile, and she halted to stare at her nearly naked body in the mirror.

The eyes that stared back at her weren't hers. Hers weren't so haunted, her face not so drawn.

Sawyer reached in to turn the shower on. When he turned back to her, he slid his boxers off, giving her an unabashed view of his cock. She averted her eyes as heat singed her cheeks. But she was compelled to look back.

It wasn't the first time or even the second she'd seen him nude, but the sight never ceased to affect her. He had a beautiful body. All hard muscles and smooth planes.

Light hair dotted the upper portion of his chest then tapered into a thin line that led to his navel and below to the dark thatch at his groin.

His cock was semi-erect, and this time she couldn't look away. She remembered all too well how he'd tasted, how he'd felt sliding over her tongue, between her lips. She closed her eyes to banish the images of that night.

"Ditch the underwear, Reggie."

Her eyes flew open again.

"You and I have a date with the shower."

Hesitantly, she hooked her thumbs into the thin band of her panties and began inching them down. They fell to the floor at her feet, and Sawyer again held out his hand to her.

Her legs trembled as she tucked her fingers into his. He pulled her into the shower after him and positioned her under the spray.

She closed her eyes as water coursed over her face. When she opened them again, Sawyer was staring fiercely at her, his eyes glittering like ice chips.

He framed her face in his hands, his thumbs resting on her cheekbones. Then he backed her against the wall of the shower as his lips descended to hers.

His body pressed in against hers, covering her and molding her softness to his hard contours. He didn't simply kiss her. He devoured her. Hot and hungry, with a restless, desperate need that left her aching.

His hands shook against her face. He moved from her lips to her eyes, pressing light kisses against her lids and then her cheeks and to her ears. Then he stopped and buried his face in her neck.

His cock, swollen and hard, butted against her belly. Burning. His heat, combined with that of the water, singed her skin like a firestorm.

"I almost lost you," he whispered so low she almost didn't hear over the water.

No longer willing to play a passive role, she wrapped her arms around his shoulders then slid one hand up the column of his neck to cup the back of his head.

He raised his head, and her hands fell away. Raw emotion bubbled in his eyes. There was so much fear. She felt an uncomfortable twinge in the vicinity of her heart.

"You didn't lose me."

He gathered her hands in his and raised them to his lips, turning one over to press a gentle kiss to her palm.

Water beaded and rolled down his broad chest, and she followed the rivulet with her gaze until it slithered past his protruding cock.

Her fingers tingled with the need to touch him, to reach out and grasp the hard flesh, but to her surprise he simply turned her around and reached for the soap.

He washed every inch of her skin. Every scrape, every bruise, each pinkened spot from the heat of the blast. His hands slid down her body with ease, to her belly, and then he paused and inched them back up to her breasts.

He cupped the mounds and brushed his thumbs across the taut points of her nipples. A small gasp escaped her parted lips. He continued to gently knead the globes, lathering the soap in bubbly circles.

Then he placed both hands flat against her body and smoothed them downward, over her abdomen. He skimmed over the wet curls between her legs to the inner portion of her thighs.

The edges of his fingers brushed ever so softly over her pussy as he worked his way in and then down the inside of her legs.

He knelt on one knee and picked up one small foot, placed it on his other knee and soaped it with infinite care.

As long as she lived, she'd never forget the image of this big man kneeling in the shower, almost humbly as he washed her feet. There was such reverence, such love and concern in his actions, his every touch and caress.

Tears burned the corners of her eyes.

She was a fool for running for so long.

When he'd finished both feet, he rose and reached for the shampoo. He squeezed a generous amount into his hands and gently worked it into her hair, taking care around the gash at her hairline.

There was a slight pinch as he ran his thumb over the cut to wash the dried blood away. She tried to control the wince but her eye twitched.

He leaned forward and pressed his lips to the cut. "I'm sorry, honey. I didn't mean to hurt you."

She smiled and reached up to wipe the soap from his mouth. "It's okay."

"Turn around so I can rinse."

He kept his hands on her shoulders as she slowly rotated. She turned her face up into the spray and let the water fall over her head. Sawyer's fingers threaded through her hair and separated the strands.

He slid one hand over her cheek and underneath her chin. Carefully, he pulled back until her head rested on his chest and she was staring up into his eyes. He lowered his mouth to her forehead and closed his eyes.

She rested comfortably there, content to let his strength surround her. Finally he reached over to turn the water off. He put his hands on her hips and slowly slid them up her body, over her arms and up to her shoulders. He squeezed once and then reached over to open the shower door.

To her surprise, Cam was waiting. He swept her into his arms, wrapping a warm towel around her body as Sawyer dried off and dressed in a pair of shorts. She stared up at Cam as he proceeded to pat the moisture from her skin.

He took one end of the towel and carefully dried the area around the cut on her head then dabbed at the gash itself. As Sawyer had done in the shower, Cam placed a gentle kiss over the wound.

Unable to resist the warmth of his embrace, she snuggled into his chest and wrapped her arms around his waist. He stiffened the slightest bit before she felt him relax again.

The towel was trapped between them, and Sawyer was getting a prime view of her ass, but she didn't care. She burrowed her face into Cam's soft T-shirt and bumped her head underneath his chin.

"Sorry," she mumbled against his chest.

His arms crept around her, and he squeezed tightly. "Never apologize for this, Reggie darling. I've waited a long time for it."

She sighed and rubbed her cheek against him, closing her eyes as contentment invaded her heart.

He kissed the top of her head. "Come on, let's get you back into the bedroom."

He pulled away and carefully wrapped the towel around her, tucking the end between her breasts.

She started back into the bedroom, Cam and Sawyer following. Hutch was standing by the bed, and he motioned her over.

She gave the towel spread out over the bed a puzzled look as she walked toward Hutch's outstretched arm.

"Take the towel off," he murmured.

Her gaze flew to his, and she clutched her arms over the seam of the towel. His stare bored into her, peeling away that towel effortlessly. She felt naked, and she hadn't even relinquished her hold on it.

"Just do it, Reggie," he said patiently.

He was asking her to trust him. To believe that they wouldn't push her to do anything she didn't want. Why he wanted her naked, she wasn't sure, but she would never give him the idea that she didn't trust him. She did.

Slowly, she unwrapped the towel and let it pool at her feet. His gaze held steady with hers, never moving or falling to her body. The soft green of his eyes glowed in the light. Radiated a yearning for something that sex just didn't cover.

"Lay down," he said softly. "On your belly, but only if it doesn't hurt your ribs."

She put a knee on the bed and climbed up, crawling to the center of the towel. She eased down, testing her body for soreness as she settled into the soft mattress.

"Put your arms up, baby. Rest them on the pillow at your head."

Her hands slid over the sheets until they collided with the plump pillows. The bed dipped, first on her left and then on her right and then again at her feet. She was too comfortable to lift her head to investigate.

Warm hands, slick with oil, glided over her skin, sending shivers up her spine to the nape of her neck. The tiny little hairs stood on end as goose bumps threaded their way through her scalp.

Loving, gentle, exquisitely tender, they stroked—petting, rubbing, massaging tired, sore muscles. She knew their touch, each individual, knew by the *way* they touched her.

Sawyer was to her left, his fingers firm, rubbing deeper, blatantly sensual as he skimmed across her back to the globes of her ass. He trailed a finger across the seam to the small of her back and down again. He palmed one cheek, massaging in a slow, circular motion before turning his attention to the other.

Cam was at her feet, attending each leg, kneading her calves, down to her ankles and ultimately to her feet. His touch was seeking, inquisitive, mellow, like him.

She moaned as he dug deep into the arch. He placed his palm against her heel and pressed his thumb into the center of her foot. She existed in a warm haze, a euphoric shimmer that clouded her eyes, blurring her vision.

Hutch was to her right, both hands settled on top of her shoulders, his thumbs pressed against the column of her neck. He worked his fingers higher, into her damp hair, digging into her scalp and working sheer magic.

At this rate she'd be comatose in five minutes.

Lips replaced hands, and a shudder rolled over her body. A gentle kiss to the nape of her neck. One at the back of her knee. One at the small of her back and then lower, just below the cheek of her ass.

Husky breaths blew over her between the featherlight kisses. A warm tongue pressed at the cleft just above her behind and trailed up her spine.

She shivered uncontrollably.

The mouth at her neck opened wider. Teeth grazed the sensitive skin below her ear. One nip. Two.

Lips closed over one small toe, sucking lightly, the tongue warm over her skin.

A ragged groan worked from the depths of her chest. It was the headiest, most pleasurable sensation she'd ever experienced. She felt loved. Cherished. Such simple, loving actions.

She was awash in need. Craving.

Once again their hands moved across her skin. Then they were gone. She whimpered in protest, and the bed moved, dipping and swaying beneath her.

"Turn over, honey," Sawyer whispered in her ear.

She couldn't muster the energy to move.

He tugged at her shoulder, helping her rotate. She saw Hutch holding a glass of water in one hand, and she knew what was coming.

"Take it," Hutch urged.

She didn't want to zone out on a painkiller. She very much wanted to stay in the here and now. Wanted them to continue touching her.

"We aren't going anywhere, Reggie darling. Take it."

Cam's husky voice slid sensuously over her, wrapping her in a comforting blanket. With Sawyer's help, she sat up and took the small pill Hutch held out to her. She downed it in one swallow then handed the glass back to Hutch.

"Do you want a T-shirt to sleep in?" Sawyer asked.

She shook her head. She wanted them against her. Skin on skin. She found Sawyer's gaze and then looked down to Cam and then back to Hutch. "Stay with me?"

"Always," Hutch said evenly.

Sawyer lifted her easily from the bed, and Cam balled the towel up and hurled it across the room toward the bathroom. Hutch pulled back the sheets, and Sawyer set her down again in the center.

Then he climbed in beside her. She turned on her side and snuggled back against his chest. He put an arm around her and spooned up against her, his groin cupped against her bottom.

In front of her, Hutch stood at the side of the bed undressing. He stripped down to his boxers then lifted the sheet and crawled in next to her. Sawyer moved his arm so that it wasn't between her and Hutch and instead rested it down the length of her leg.

She looked for Cam, wondering how he'd fit. She wanted him here. He lay across the end of the bed and put a hand over her blanket-covered foot. He squeezed reassuringly and smiled.

"Go to sleep, Reggie darling. God knows you need it. Tomorrow . . . tomorrow we'll talk about it all and figure things out."

She held his gaze for a long moment, savoring their connection. Then slowly, her gaze drifted back up Hutch's body, and she found him staring back at her.

He moved his hand to cup her cheek and then moved his mouth to cover hers in a gentle kiss.

"Do as Cam says, baby."

He trailed a finger down her cheek and kissed her one last time.

Sawyer's body, molded so tightly to hers . . . Hutch in front of her, barely an inch separating them, and Cam at her feet, his hand reassuringly on her leg . . . she wasn't sure it could be more perfect than this or that anything else would ever feel so right.

CHAPTER 18

*R*egina came awake with a gasp. Sweat dampened her body, and despite the heat emanating from the two men sleeping on either side of her, she shivered.

The nightmare still lurked on the edge of her consciousness, but it wasn't about her. She hadn't seen images of *her* dying in an explosion.

The terror that surrounded her, gripped her throat, was because in her tormented dreams, it had been Hutch, Cam and Sawyer who had been threatened. It was them in the vehicle when it blew up.

Nausea welled in her stomach and she sat up, the covers stretching and pulling as she clutched them to her breasts.

She glanced to one side and then the other to see Sawyer and Hutch sleeping. When she looked to the end of the bed, she noticed that Cam had gotten up.

Her panic wouldn't subside. The dream had been too real.

She released the covers and then carefully climbed over them on her hands and knees to the end of the bed. She eased off and quietly picked up Hutch's shirt from the floor. On quiet feet, she headed for the door, pulling the T-shirt over her head as she went.

Cam's door was open across the hall, but the light wasn't on. She slipped inside, leaving the door wide open in her haste. The bed was empty and wasn't unmade.

She tried to swallow back her panic. She was being completely unreasonable. But locked inside was the compulsion to find Cam, to make sure he was all right.

Her hand slid up her chest to her clammy neck as she reentered the hallway and headed for the stairs. She gripped the railing with her right hand as she descended on shaky feet.

The living room and kitchen were dark. Where was he?

Then she remembered the office located off the formal dining room. Maybe he was there.

She walked through the dining room, across the polished wood floors. Relief rose up, sharp and all-consuming, when she saw the door ajar to the office and light emanating from within.

Her fingers glanced off the surface as she fumbled for the knob. The door swung open, and she looked in to see Cam sitting at his desk going over drawings.

He looked up when she stepped in.

"Reggie, what are you doing up?"

He pulled his glasses off with one hand and set them down in front of him with a frown. When she just stood there, feeling a little stupid but tremendously relieved just to see him and know he was all right, he got up and walked over to her.

"Are you okay? What are you doing down here?" he asked. He reached out and touched her cheek, frowned again and threaded his fingers through her damp hair.

"Bad dream," she croaked.

He drew her into his arms and rested his chin on top of her head. "I'm sorry. Can I get you anything? You want something to eat or drink?"

You. She just wanted him. Wanted to stay this way for a little longer, until the paralyzing aftereffects of the dream faded.

She shook her head against his chest then pulled slightly away despite her desire to stay nestled in his arms. "Am I disturbing you? Weren't you working?"

He smoothed her hair from her cheek. "You're never bothering me, Reggie darling. I was just working on some plans."

"Want company?" she asked hopefully. Even sitting here watching him work seemed preferable to returning to her dreams.

"I've got a better idea. Why don't I make us some hot chocolate, and we'll go curl up on the couch in the living room and watch some TV."

She wrinkled her nose. "What kind of TV?"

He grinned. "I recorded stuff from the Discovery Channel I haven't watched yet."

She was pretty sure her eye twitched, but she kept her expression neutral. "Uhm sure, sounds great."

"Liar."

"I watch educational television. Sometimes."

His eyes glittered with amusement. "Since when does slapstick or watching men with IQs lower than my shoe size beat the crap out of each other constitute educational?"

She grinned up at him. "It's very educational. It's a study in brain cell loss."

He turned back to flip off the lamp over his desk.

"Are you sure you don't need to work?" she asked. "I could make the hot chocolate and sit in here with you. I don't mind."

He slipped an arm around her and herded her out the door. "Nah, my eyes were crossing anyway. I can finish it later."

He stopped in the hall closet and pulled out a blanket and a couple of pillows before directing her into the living room.

He sat her down on the couch, plopped the pillows on either side of her then draped the blanket across her.

"You stay right here, and I'll be back in a minute with the cocoa."

She smiled and burrowed into the covers as he walked toward the kitchen. This suddenly needy side of her bugged the hell out of her. Some part of her wondered if she'd always been needy, and she supposed she had. She'd latched onto the friendship with Cam, Sawyer and Hutch and held on tight through school and into their adult lives.

Because she'd always been secure in that relationship, it hadn't manifested itself in this dark, edgy need that was rearing its head now. Now that she wasn't so secure. Now that things had taken a decidedly different turn.

She had plenty of casual friends and acquaintances. Her fellow police officers and even a few of the wives, Michelle in particular. No, she didn't hang out regularly. She much preferred her status as a loner. It was too ingrained.

Growing up in the solemn, isolated Fallon house had taught her reserve, and only around Cam and Sawyer and Hutch did she allow herself to be openly affectionate and outgoing.

But she'd held a part of herself back. Even from them. She'd sheltered the growing need for more from them, too afraid of losing them. When they had taken that first step, she hadn't known how to react. She still didn't.

She closed her eyes and pulled the covers to her chin. What would happen . . . What if she just let it happen? What if she stopped fighting the inevitable and embraced it instead?

Her stomach twisted. Part in anticipation, excitement, and the other part in nervous fear.

It wasn't as if they hadn't already had sex. One afternoon of playful teasing and conversation had led to a night she'd never forget.

There were so many what-ifs. What if she hadn't tucked tail and run? Would they have spent the last year together, laughing and loving, or would they even now be hopelessly separated, having ruined their friendship with a premature sexual relationship?

And then, in one of those stunning moments of clarity, which she might have already had if she hadn't spent the last several days in a drug-induced fog, she realized that all her angsting was a moot point.

It didn't matter one iota what she thought might or might not happen if they started down the path the guys were nudging her onto. They had already trucked down the street, run the stop sign and reached the fork in the road.

The question was, what was she going to do about it? Continue as before and lose not only their friendship but any hope of *more?*

She shook her head. When had she decided she wanted more? *Crazy. You're crazy.*

Her head was spinning, and she was growing more agitated by the minute. She closed her eyes and sucked in deep, steadying breaths.

For now, she wasn't going anywhere. Not when some lunatic seemed determined to go after everyone she loved most. Whatever happened in the meantime . . . well, it happened, and she wasn't going to fight it. Nor was she going to be a passive participant. It just wasn't her style.

Her pulse ratcheted up about ten notches. Or thirty.

She craved them. It went beyond a need for sex. She'd gotten that after that night a year ago. Her chest tightened and squeezed uncomfortably as she remembered how awful she'd felt after her

one-night stand with a man she couldn't even remember with
any accuracy.

What she wanted, what she needed, was their touch. Their
friendship.

Their love.

Which meant she had to be willing to give it in return.

And hadn't she always? Loved them? Wasn't it there, hadn't it
always been there? She'd just never sat down and analyzed her
feelings. As if. Because who admitted she loved three different
men? What normal person contemplated such a thing?

"I feel like there should be smoke pouring from your ears,"
Cam said.

Her head came up. Cam was standing in front of her with two
mugs. He was staring intently at her, a clear question on his face.

Instead of responding to the unspoken question, she simply
reached up to retrieve one of the mugs. Cam shoved the pillow
over and settled down beside her. He reached over and turned the
lamp on, bathing the area in low light.

Suddenly she had no desire for the cocoa. Her skin prickled
with the urge to feel him against her. To make the connection
she now realized she wanted more than anything.

"What'll it be? A documentary on the rain forests or the mat-
ing habits of the chimpanzee?" he asked in a teasing voice.

No way she was going to watch a bunch of monkeys screw.

She turned her head so she could look at him. "Can we just
leave it off? I kinda like the idea of sitting here with you without
the noise in the background."

He stared back at her, and she felt warmed to her toes by those
eyes. They reminded her a lot of the sweet chocolate he'd
handed her.

"We can do that. It's been a while since we got some time to
catch up."

She smiled and refused to feel guilty over the fact that they hadn't caught up because she'd been too busy running in the other direction. That was all going to stop. Right now.

She brought her other hand up to the mug and cupped it to her lips, blowing on the liquid before allowing it to seep into her mouth. Mmmm. Double sugar, just the way she liked it.

She licked over her upper lip as she pulled the cup away, and she felt Cam still staring at her. She cocked her head to the side and glanced over.

"You're not drinking your chocolate."

"It's not what I want," he said as he set it on the end table next to the couch.

Her breathing sped up.

"What do you want?" she asked softly.

He didn't answer right away. He didn't have to. The answer was there in his eyes. The way he looked at her. Wordlessly, she handed him her cup.

His brow furrowed in confusion as he took it and set it on the table next to his.

Gathering her courage around her, she put her sore arm on his shoulder and gently pushed herself up. Before he could help or say anything, she turned and swung her leg over him and settled onto his lap facing him.

She didn't know what to do first. She was in complete overload. She wanted to dive in, press herself against his chest and hold on tight. She wanted him to hold her. She wanted to snuggle down deep, feel his heartbeat against her cheek.

Tentatively, she put her hands on his chest, and then she slid them around his body, under his armpits, burrowing them between him and the couch.

She leaned in, pressing her cheek against his chest and rubbing lightly over his T-shirt.

He tensed against her. His pulse raced, bumping a steady rhythm against her face. She inhaled deeply, wanting to absorb his scent and the feeling of being in his arms.

Had she not been so reserved this past year, this wouldn't have come as such a surprise to him. She could feel him struggling with her gesture, and it hurt her. Hurt her that she was responsible for the distance between them.

She pulled away and stared at him for a long moment, plucking up her courage before it deserted her completely. It was her move. In this it had to be. They'd made all the moves so far, and she knew they wouldn't push her. She was going to have to come to them.

"Cam, I want to ask you something . . . and I want you to be honest with me."

He regarded her evenly. "I've always been honest with you, Reggie. About everything."

She nodded. "What would happen if I asked you to make love to me? Right here. Right now."

His body drew up as he sucked in his breath. Then he expelled it in a long whisper. A discernible bulge nudged his jeans at his groin, just inches from the juncture of her thighs where she straddled him.

"What are you really asking?" he said in a hoarse voice. "I think what you want to know is what happens afterward. Am I right?"

She closed her eyes for a moment then reopened them and met his steady gaze. "Sawyer says I'm the only one keeping score, and maybe he's right. But I have to ask. What happens if we make love? Will it put you at odds with Sawyer and Hutch? Are they going to resent you? Be angry with me?"

"Are we talking hypothetically, Reggie?"

She didn't look away. Didn't flinch or dodge the issue. "No," she whispered.

His body rippled with power, a brief surge that sent heat racing to her core. He wanted her. He vibrated with it. His muscles coiled and tensed beneath her body, and his chest rose and fell with stuttered breaths.

"I want to make love with you, Reggie," he said softly. "More than anything. But maybe we should get a few things out of the way.

"I'm not competing against Sawyer and Hutch. Will they be jealous? I honestly can't answer that. They want the same things I do. To be with you in every way imaginable.

"Maybe we gave you the wrong impression with the . . . way we made love to you that first time. Together. It wasn't planned, but at the same time, if you'd made love to only one of us, would you have understood what it is we want? Or would it have pushed you even further away when you felt like you had betrayed the other two? Isn't that what worries you now?"

Slowly, she nodded.

"If we make love, Reggie, it's because we want to. We don't owe Sawyer and Hutch an explanation just as they wouldn't owe me one if it was one of them sitting here with you right now."

"But will they be okay with it?" she whispered. "Will they think I'm choosing you over them?"

He reached out and cupped her cheek. "Are you?"

She shook her head.

"Then they won't think that."

He looked away for a brief moment then pinned her again with his intense stare. "You wanted honesty, so I'll be completely up front with you. If I knew you had made love with Sawyer or Hutch, I'd feel relief."

She cocked her head in confusion.

"Think about it. You've spent the last year avoiding us while we've been racking our brains trying to figure out how to make what we're suggesting acceptable to you, even desirable. I'd view you making love with Sawyer or Hutch as a crack in the armor, a sign that maybe we're getting close. I imagine that's how they'd view you making love to me.

"Will they be envious? Of course. Hell, I'd be green at the idea of you being in their arms when I want so much to hold you and touch you. But they'll be content to wait for you, Reggie. Just like we've waited the last year."

Tears shimmered in her vision at his heartfelt words. It was hard to doubt his sincerity when his entire face was so earnest, so serious. Her heart fluttered and turned over, and finally she said the words they'd both been waiting for.

"Make love to me, Cam."

"Are you sure, Reggie?" he asked quietly. "I'd never do anything to hurt you, never push you into a decision you weren't ready to make. As long as I've waited, I'll wait as long as it takes."

A single tear slipped down her cheek, followed quickly by another on the opposite side. Instead of answering—words were cheap except when he spoke, such tender loving words—she eased off his lap to stand in front of him.

He stared up at her, desire and hope lighting the darkness. Slowly, she pulled the T-shirt over her head and let it drop to the floor.

She was bruised and scraped. She knew she didn't look her best. But she'd never *felt* as beautiful as she did in this moment, so intensely wanted and desired.

Even though she'd asked him to make love to her, she was gripped by the need to make love to him. To show him how much he meant to her.

"Stand up," she said in a husky, nervous voice she almost didn't recognize.

He put his hands on the edge of the couch and pushed himself up to stand in front of her.

There were just inches separating them. She ran her hands down his chest, gathered the hem of his shirt then snuck her fingers underneath and began pushing upward, taking the shirt with her.

She paused for a moment and stared up at him. "There's one more thing," she said in a low voice. "We've talked about how Hutch or Sawyer might feel, but I have to know, Cam. If after this . . . if after this I make love to them, how are you going to feel?"

He reached under his shirt and captured her hands against his chest. "I'm not going to be angry. Or hurt. As long as I can be with you, Reggie darling, I don't mind sharing you with them."

She shoved the T-shirt over his head and leaned up on tiptoe to kiss him. "I want you, Cam, but I'm so scared too. I'm so afraid of messing everything up."

He caught her face between his hands and fused his lips to hers in a slow, melting kiss. Heat sizzled down her spine, spreading into her belly.

"You can't mess up, Reggie darling. Don't you know that? You can't mess up something so perfect as your love."

Her fingers slid into the waistband of his jeans and then around to the fly. She was clumsy in her haste, but she managed to undo the snap. With shaking hands, she worked the zipper down over the bulge.

"Take them off," she whispered.

CHAPTER 19

*C*am hurriedly kicked down his jeans, stepping out with one foot then shaking off the pant leg with his other. Unlike Sawyer and Hutch, he wore plain white briefs, stark against his tanned skin.

Regina reached for him, wanting him against her. He enfolded her in his arms, and she slid her hands around his back and down inside the band of his underwear. Her palms curved over his tight buttocks. She pulled her wrists down, taking the briefs with them.

She brought her hands around to the front and felt the shock of his rock-hard erection against her palms. She curled her fingers around his thickness, stroking and caressing his rigid length.

She leaned further into him, sandwiching his cock between their stomachs. His hands skated up her arms and over her shoulders to her neck. He cupped her face, curling his fingers behind her ears, and dipped his head to capture her lips in a hungry kiss.

It was warmth and tenderness wrapped in a sensual package

that left her breathless. His body cupped hers, a safe haven, a shelter from the rest of the world. From reality.

Her hands left his cock and skimmed over his taut abdomen to his chest. She pushed at him, walking him backward until he collided with the couch and went down with a thump. She went with him, straddling his lap again.

She pressed in close, her lips a hairbreadth from his. Her tongue darted out, running along the seam of his mouth and lingering at the corner. His lips parted, and a ragged groan escaped, swallowed up by her intake of air.

The light stubble on his jaw bristled against her mouth as she slid her lips along his skin toward his ear. She found the pulse at his neck, licked over it once then nibbled lightly at it. He flinched, sucked in a breath then trembled as she worked down the cord of his neck to the curve of his shoulder.

He tasted like comfort. Safety. Smelled masculine and strong.

She put her hands on his shoulders and slipped her legs from the sofa to crouch over him. She kissed her way over his chest, savoring the taste, the feel. The light hairs in the center of his chest tickled her nose. She swept her tongue out to circle one flat nipple, teasing the nub.

She worked down, lowering herself to her knees as her mouth pressed to his navel. The tip of his cock brushed the underside of her chin, and she angled her head so that she rubbed her cheek down the length as she settled onto her heels.

She stared up at him as she placed her arms over his knees to lever herself. His hair hung to his shoulders, the strands wild and unkempt. Later she would wind her fingers through it while they made love. Her fingers itched to feel the silky waves.

Her gaze dropped to his cock. It jutted upward and leaned heavily against his belly. She slid her hand over the top of his thigh to his pelvis before she curled her fingers around the base.

His penis jerked as her hand closed around it. Warm and thick in her hand, yet soft as she stroked upward to the tip.

"Reggie, you don't have to do this," he rasped. "Let me make love to you. Like you asked. Please."

She rose again on her knees and placed her other hand in the coarse hair surrounding his cock.

Ignoring his plea, she dipped her head until her mouth hovered precariously close to the blunt head. Then she licked him in one long stroke.

He arched off the couch, and he put his hands down to brace himself.

His warm, musky scent surrounded her as she closed her lips around his cock and eased him deeper. Her hand moved down as her mouth did, engulfing him.

Soft on her tongue, yet so hard, so strong. The plump vein on the underside called her to play, and she pressed her bottom lip to it, enjoying the subtle give as she moved upward again.

She reached lower, moving her fingers over his balls, cupping them in her hand as she sucked him deeper still. She closed her eyes and savored the closeness, the intimacy of her actions.

Silky fluid, just a drop, spilled onto her tongue, and she lapped at the small slit as she drew him nearly out of her mouth.

She looked up as she let the head rest on her tongue, and she saw his head tilted back, eyes closed, his expression one of almost pain. Yet there was a peace about him as well. As though he'd waited a lifetime for this moment. The one where she finally accepted him.

She too closed her eyes and lowered her mouth, taking him all the way, until his crisp hairs tickled her nose. She inhaled, drawing his scent deeper. It surrounded her, danced in the air, filled her.

His hands moved up her arms, gripped her shoulders then tangled in her hair. His fingers dug into her scalp, and he raised his hips, sliding deeper into her mouth, thrusting to meet her motions.

"God, Reggie," he gasped.

She knew he was close, and she certainly wasn't willing to finish things so soon. Not when she ached to take him inside her.

Her pussy tingled. Tiny little heated pulses thrummed through her groin. Her clit swelled and ached with the desire for his touch. His mouth. Oh God, his mouth.

No, not now. Now she wanted to take him. As he'd taken her a year ago.

She released his cock then stared up at him and licked her lips. His eyes glittered, edgy, so close to the breaking point. In that moment, he looked dangerous. Not at all like safe, comfortable Cam.

She stepped over his legs as she moved to straddle him. She bent her knees and slid them onto the couch. One hand curled over his shoulder to steady herself while the other reached down and grasped his cock.

She inched forward and up as she positioned him between her legs. He brushed over her clit, and she nearly came. Sharp darts shot from her pussy, radiating to every nerve ending in her body.

She moved him until he came to rest at her entrance. She was wet and ready, and rather than delay the moment, she lowered herself, sheathing him in a rush of hot, liquid fire.

They both gasped.

Cam gripped her hips with both hands, and she leaned forward to grasp his shoulders. She rose once, allowing him to slide almost free, and then she fell back down.

Her eyes flew open, and she cried out in shock.

Cam jerked beneath her, and he lifted her up, relieving some of the tension.

"Jesus, Reggie, stop. Don't hurt yourself. God, I don't want to hurt you."

She leaned down to kiss him, taking his mouth in a savage, possessive manner. "You didn't hurt me, Cam," she said against his lips. "I want all of you. It's just been a long time."

"Take it slow, Reggie darling. We've got all the time in the world," he murmured.

He slid his fingers underneath her ass and lifted, then allowed her to slide back down. Each thrust was an agonizing brush over highly sensitized flesh. Tiny little sparks ignited as her pussy sucked and clutched at his cock.

She moved closer, wrapping her arms around his neck. The bristle on his jaw scraped over her chest as he nuzzled at her breast. His tongue swept over her nipple, sending shock waves down her spine.

His teeth grazed the puckered point, and then he sucked it hard between his lips.

She cried out and wrapped her hands in his hair, clutching him closer to her breast.

He moved her faster now, with more urgency. His fingers dug into her ass as he lifted and lowered. She moved with him, establishing a rhythm.

Her orgasm built. Tension. Beautiful, exquisite tension grew, blossoming and radiating outward in a steady stream.

Each thrust drew her tighter, closer to the inevitable explosion.

The slap of her ass meeting his thighs filled the room. Wet, sucking sounds mixed in as his cock drove deeper, sliding and driving. Friction. Unbearable friction. It was good. So good.

She closed her eyes, shutting them tightly as her face drew inward in agony. She couldn't bear it. She was going to come apart.

"Oh God, Cam, I can't. I can't!"

"Yes, you can, Reggie darling. I've got you, love. You're so beautiful. I wish you could see yourself in my arms, your head thrown back, your eyes shut so tight. That I can give you that kind of pleasure . . ."

"Cam!"

He tightened. She tightened. She grabbed his shoulders, desperate for something to hold on to. Out of control. She was coming apart at the seams. She flew in a dozen different directions.

She opened her eyes, but the room blurred around her.

He arched spasmodically into her, his hips jerking as he thrust. And then he moved one hand, sliding just his thumb between them, into her soft, damp folds.

His other hand cupped her ass, and his thumb brushed ever so softly over her clit.

Her pelvis rammed into his hand, trapping his fingers between them.

Her cry split the night.

She simply unraveled. Exploded. Burst into flames and then floated free.

She collapsed forward, but he was there to catch her. He held her tight as his hips spasmed with his release. Soft words were murmured lovingly against her ear as he stroked her hair.

Their chests heaved. She wrapped her arms around his neck and hugged him to her. She lowered her head to his shoulder and nuzzled closer to him.

His hand stroked up her arm and over her shoulder. He swept aside the curls at her neck and her face and tucked them behind her ear.

Then he rotated, taking her with him, and laid her gently onto the couch. He slid out of her body in a warm rush. He bent to kiss her, lingering for just a moment as he toyed with her lips with his tongue.

"I'll be right back," he said softly. "Let me get a towel."

She lay there waiting, her body still rippling with the after-effects of her orgasm. He returned in a moment, his hand encased in the towel as he wiped his cock. He pulled it away then put the other end between her legs to carefully clean her.

He tossed aside the towel when he was finished, then sat down with his back to the arm of the couch and motioned for her. "Come here."

As she crawled over him, he extended his legs down the sofa so that he could recline. He gathered her in his arms and positioned her head underneath his chin. When she was settled, he reached for the discarded blanket lying on the floor and pulled it over them both.

"That was incredible," he whispered.

"Mmmm."

He chuckled, and his chest vibrated against her cheek.

"Is that all you can say?"

"Mmm-hmmm."

"How about you get some sleep now, Reggie darling. You've worn me out. Sleep here with me where I can hold you."

His arms tightened around her, and she could feel him tremble ever so slightly, as if he was every bit as overwhelmed as she was.

He teased her response, but it was all she could muster. She didn't have the ability to put into words all she felt, all she wanted to say. Her tongue tangled and swelled at the idea.

How could she possibly explain that she felt whole? Complete? Like she'd come home after being lost for so long? And so she said the only thing that seemed to matter.

"I missed you," she whispered.

"I missed you too," he murmured into her hair. "No more running, Reggie. I couldn't bear it."

A part of her heart loosened and unfurled at his quiet plea. It told her unquestionably that she had the power to hurt him, and that was something *she* couldn't bear.

"No more running," she agreed.

CHAPTER 20

*H*utch woke to see Sawyer in bed a few feet away but no sign of Reggie. He rolled out immediately. Not that he hadn't shared a bed with Sawyer before, but they'd been *ten* for Christ's sake. Without Reggie there between them, it was just damn awkward.

Maybe they should implement a rule that Reggie had to stay where she was put.

His shoulders shook with laughter as he contemplated being kneed in the balls after delivering that particular dictate.

"What the hell are you finding so amusing this early in the morning?" Sawyer said in a sleepy, grumpy voice.

Morning person, Sawyer was not.

"I was contemplating the humor in laying down the law to Reggie about leaving us in bed together," he said.

"No shit," Sawyer grumbled as he rolled out of bed. "But at least I didn't wake up with you draped across me or some shit like that."

Hutch narrowed his eyes at Sawyer. "Very funny."

"I thought it was," he said as he reached down for his shirt.

"Where the hell is Reggie anyway? Do we need to put a bell around the girl's neck?"

Hutch snickered. "No, but I'll tell her you think so."

"Right after you tell her about your bright idea to give her the law as determined by Hutch Bishop?"

Hutch reached for his own clothes and pulled them on. "My guess is she's wherever Cam is. I'm going to head down and start on breakfast."

Sawyer grunted. "I'll be down after a shit, shower and shave."

"Thanks for sharing," Hutch said dryly.

Hutch walked out of Reggie's bedroom, crossed the hallway and peeked into Cam's room. Anal bastard was already up and had his bed made. He'd been Birdie's dream kid. Neat and orderly. Studious in school. He saved his rebellious streak for when he was out of range of Birdie's eagle eye.

He and Sawyer hadn't been as smart.

He backed out of Cam's room and started down the stairs. He wasn't sure how he'd landed the job as designated cook. Oh, wait. Yeah, he remembered. The others sucked at it. Not that he'd win any culinary awards, but at least he could manage a meal without burning it. Sawyer had damn near burned down their house in Houston when he'd left a pot of grease on the stove. After that, they'd banned his ass from the kitchen except to eat. Dipshit probably did it on purpose.

When he hit the bottom of the stairs, he glanced into the living room and froze. Then he blinked, sure he wasn't seeing what he thought he was seeing.

Cam was flat on his back on the couch with Reggie's naked body draped across his chest. The blanket was in a ball at her feet, and Cam's hand was cupped over her smoothly rounded ass.

But she'd been naked last night when they'd gone to bed.

Could be she'd just come down in one of her late night forays and ended up snuggled up with Cam.

His gaze drifted to Cam's clothes lying on the floor, and he quickly disabused himself of that notion.

He was simultaneously bombarded by a whole host of emotions. One part of him wanted to jump and do a fist pump, but then what kind of a moron did that make him? The other part honestly wanted to go drag Reggie off of Cam, wrap her in that blanket and take her upstairs, where he'd lock her in his room for the better part of a week.

The second option sounded better and didn't make him as big of a pussy as the first.

Hope bubbled up in his chest. Was she any closer to accepting them? Obviously Cam had succeeded in getting past her barricades. As relieved as he was, he was also jealous as hell that it hadn't been him. That she hadn't trusted him enough. That she'd chosen Cam over him.

Even as the dark thoughts crept over him, he pushed them aside. He wasn't going to go there. He didn't want to feel the bitterness that licked at him. The hard edge of resentment that had his fingers curled into fists at his side.

He walked into the kitchen and quietly took out the skillet for scrambled eggs.

A few minutes later, Sawyer walked in just as Hutch was pouring the eggs into the pan.

He didn't offer a greeting or smart-ass remark. Instead he flopped down on a bar stool and propped his elbows on the counter. Hutch glanced sideways at him and saw him just about bristling with the need to say something. A vein was about to pop on his forehead, and he rubbed his hand over his freshly shaved head.

But he remained silent. Tension was heavy in the air. So thick it made Hutch uncomfortable.

Was Sawyer having the same thoughts he was? Was his mind traveling down that dark road? It didn't bode well for the future of their arrangement if after the first time Reggie had sex with one of them, the other two wigged out.

With a resigned sigh, he picked up the skillet, carried it over to the trash and scraped the dark brown eggs into the can. So much for not burning shit. He dropped the pan into the sink and went to retrieve another from the cabinet.

He was cracking more eggs into a bowl when Cam sauntered in and sat down on the bar stool next to Sawyer.

Both Hutch and Sawyer stared at Cam. He was wearing the same clothes he'd been wearing the night before, his hair hadn't been combed, and dark stubble dotted his jaw. He looked rode hard and hung up wet.

Cam didn't usually walk out of his bedroom in the morning until he'd showered and shaved, dressed and made his bed. Right now he didn't look like he gave a shit.

There was a contented light in his eyes. He looked . . . happy.

Sawyer looked over at Hutch and raised one eyebrow. Hutch shrugged and turned back to the stove, determined not to burn the eggs again.

Silence continued as he plated the eggs and pulled the biscuits out of the oven. He set the food on the bar then went to the cabinet to get plates.

"Good morning," Reggie said brightly as she walked into the kitchen.

Hutch looked up to see her smiling at him. Her blue eyes shone with lightness he'd missed. The shadows were gone.

Her hair lay damply at her neck and around her ears, forming a curly cap. She moved with ease, as though she experienced no pain or stiffness today.

"Good morning," Hutch returned. "Sleep well?"

As soon as he said it, Sawyer coughed discreetly, and Hutch could have swallowed his tongue. His perfectly innocent question sounded staged. Damn it.

She frowned, and Hutch braced himself to dig his foot out of his mouth.

"I didn't at first. Bad dream. Cam made cocoa though, and I slept great."

The smile returned and she bounced—good grief, she actually bounced—over to Sawyer, stepped on the rung of his stool, hoisted herself up and placed a big kiss on top of his bald head.

"Morning. I see you're as verbose as ever."

He regarded her strangely. Actually he was looking at her like she'd just descended the alien mother ship.

Had the sex been that good? Hutch was starting to think of all the ways he'd never measure up.

He shot Cam a sideways glance, only to see him smiling softly at Reggie. Then Cam turned and met Hutch's gaze. There was hope in Cam's eyes. Hope that Cam hadn't exactly been full of lately.

Hutch's pulse sped up, and he cocked his head in question at Cam. Cam briefly shook his head and put a finger to his lips.

"No good-morning kiss?" she said teasingly to Sawyer.

Sawyer didn't answer. Instead his hand shot out, curved around the back of her neck, and he yanked her to him, slanting his lips over hers in a hard kiss.

Hutch had to look away as anger surged through his veins. He'd never been comfortable with Sawyer's hard edges. It worried him that Sawyer could frighten Reggie.

He shoved a plate across the bar toward her, but when he looked up she wasn't there.

She pounced on him from behind, jumping onto his back. She wrapped her arms around his neck, her legs around his waist, and giggled in his ear like a goon.

Despite his dour mood, he grinned. Man, he'd missed her.

He promptly backed her into the refrigerator and winced when she tugged on his ear in retaliation.

"Hey, watch that shit," Sawyer spoke up. "You're going to hurt her ribs."

Hutch stared at him in shock. Mister He-Man Hard-ass was going to lecture *him* on being careful with Reggie?

"Party pooper," Reggie muttered in his ear. "I thought that was Cam's job."

Hutch snorted with laughter. He clutched the underside of her legs and hoisted her higher on his back. She giggled again and kissed the side of his neck.

He closed his eyes as her lips slid over his skin. How many nights had he lain awake, reliving her touch, how she'd felt underneath him, her smell and her taste.

She wrapped her arms tighter around him, hugging him against her slight form.

Then she relaxed, let her feet fall and started to slide down his back. He caught her and lowered her carefully to the floor. When she had her footing, he pivoted and pulled her into his arms.

He tilted her chin up and kissed her leisurely, enjoying the feel of her soft, full lips against his.

"Good morning, Reggie. You're awfully chipper this morning."

She grinned mischievously. "I feel much better today."

"You'll feel even better when you eat."

She rolled her eyes and bounced back over to the bar, where Sawyer had moved down to give her the seat between him and Cam. She climbed up, moving closer to Cam as she settled onto her seat. They shared an intimate smile, and Cam reached out to touch her cheek.

"Good morning," he murmured.

She looked almost shy. And a little uncertain. That look gave Hutch's chest a little squeeze. It suddenly made perfect sense why she'd come into the kitchen bright and cheerful. She was terrified.

She leaned forward and kissed Cam then ran her hand over his face.

"You need to shave," she said lightly.

She turned to her plate and picked up her fork. Hutch softened all over. She was nervous and trying to cover her awkwardness, and he and Sawyer certainly weren't helping by adding to the tension.

"I've got to go grocery shopping today," he said as he dug into his own plate. "Want to come with?"

Reggie looked up and smiled. Then she cast a sideways glance at Cam. "You're not coming, are you?"

Cam laughed. "Afraid I'll confiscate all your junk food before it makes it to the basket?"

"Hutch lets me buy it," she said defensively.

Cam rolled his eyes. "No, I'm not going. I need to finish up those plans."

She turned back to Hutch and smiled sweetly. "In that case I'll go. Any chance you'd run me into Beaumont so I could pick up a few changes of clothes? I'd rather not . . ." She frowned and took a deep breath. "I'd rather not go back to the house."

Hutch reached across the bar and took her hand. "Of course, baby. We'll go wherever you need. They've opened a new grocery store over by the mall. Supposed to have a kickass meat counter."

"Oh yum. Steaks." She turned to Cam. "You'll grill, won't you?"

Hutch was so happy she was speaking in terms of being here awhile that he'd buy her an entire cow.

"You buy it, I'll burn it," Cam cracked.

She looked over her shoulder at Sawyer, who was still shovel-ing eggs into his mouth. "No, that's Sawyer's job."

"Hey," he said around a mouthful. "Like you cook any better? I'm thinking you make me look like a Food Network guru."

"Don't start, you two," Hutch said with a groan. "Eat up, Reg-gie, so we can go."

As she picked up her fork again, the phone rang. Or *a* phone. It wasn't the main line. All three men looked around for their cell phones. Sawyer reached across the bar and snagged the of-fending phone, opened it and stuck it to his ear.

"Pritchard," he said.

There was a long silence and Sawyer frowned. Then it turned into a dark scowl.

"Fuck. Are you shitting me? No, don't do anything. One of us will be over to take care of it. Just sit on it until we get there."

He closed the phone and dropped it on the bar with a gri-mace.

"We have a problem."

"Obviously," Cam said. "What is it?"

Reggie stared curiously at Sawyer, waiting for his response.

"Job site's been shut down by the city."

"Which one?" Hutch demanded. Plans were Cam's thing. But Hutch and Sawyer oversaw the construction.

"The art gallery."

"Why?" Cam asked.

"That I don't know," Sawyer said in a disgruntled voice. "That was Tom on the phone. Said someone from the city came out and cited three violations. Pulled the permit. Goddamn it. One of us is going to have to go down there."

CHAPTER 21

*R*egina sucked in her breath as panic surged in her chest. She didn't want one of them going off alone. It left the door wide open for whoever had a beef with her, or Hutch, or her father, or whoever the hell it was, to get to them.

"I can go," Hutch said.

Sawyer sighed. "No, I will. It's my project. You and Reggie need to get her shopping done."

Shopping. Her brain worked overtime as she struggled to figure out how she was going to prevent them from splitting up. She couldn't protect them if they were all in different places. Together, they posed a much more serious threat, and after two run-ins with the psycho trying to kill her, she'd had enough. Her body had taken enough punishment, and she had no desire for the wack job to get to her, any more than she wanted the guys in his line of vision.

"We could all go," she blurted.

Three heads turned in her direction. Hutch frowned, and Sawyer stared curiously at her.

Oh boy. She had to make this good. Going from avoiding them all the time to suddenly wanting to be around them twenty-four seven?

"Well, I mean if you wanted to," she finished lamely. "I wouldn't mind getting out of town for a while." She scanned all their faces as she said the last.

Cam's expression was thoughtful. Sawyer's was more calculating, and she could see he liked the idea of removing her from the immediate vicinity of the danger she faced. Hutch looked more undecided.

"And I do have to get some clothes," she added when no one spoke up. "Not that I want to do any hard-core shopping, but surely there's somewhere close to your house where I could pick up some jeans and a few shirts."

She sounded desperate. She sank further down and picked up her fork to shovel the remaining bite of cold eggs into her mouth. They were never going to buy into her sudden change of behavior.

She clutched the empty plate and backed off the stool. "It was just a thought," she said as she rounded the bar to dump her plate into the sink.

"I like the idea," Sawyer finally said. "This might take a couple of days to wrap up, and it gets you away from here. Hopefully by then the police might have a suspect or even make an arrest."

"I could finish up the plans at the office," Cam offered. "Another hour or two isn't going to make a difference."

Regina turned to look at Hutch, who was still regarding her rather curiously. She would have said suspiciously, but she was going to ignore that thought. Besides, she had decided to stay with them regardless of the danger they might be in, hadn't she?

"Are you sure you feel up to this, Reggie?" Hutch asked. "I know you're feeling better, but that's not the same as being ready to run off to Houston and go shopping."

She made a face. "Shopping here or shopping there. It's still shopping. Besides, I can kick back in your house there same as here, right?"

A prickle of discomfort worked up her spine. She'd all but invited herself, and while that would have never bothered her before a year ago, now she felt like she was assuming a lot.

"I, uh, suppose I should have asked if it was okay if I tag along and if you and Cam actually wanted to go back to Houston with Sawyer."

Hutch closed the distance between them and pulled her against his chest. "Don't be ridiculous, baby. You're welcome anywhere we are and that's a fact. You're just going to have to let us catch up here. After a year of trying to pin you down in any one place long enough to exchange more than a few pleasantries, it's a little hard to deal with the fact you're here, and you want to be with us."

Her chest tightened, and guilt blasted her despite the fact that she knew she wasn't using or manipulating them. Okay, maybe she was manipulating them, but it was for their own good, and she did want to be with them. She'd just have to wait until later to sort through her feelings surrounding the idea of having all of them. Preferably when there wasn't someone determined to kill her and possibly them.

She wrapped her arms around his middle and laid her head over his heart. "I'm sorry, Hutch."

He took hold of her shoulders and gently pried her away from him.

"What are you sorry for, baby?"

She glanced over at Cam and Sawyer, who were still sitting at the bar watching with undisguised interest.

"For not having more courage. For being afraid. For not trusting you all."

"Does this mean you'll stay?" he asked softly. "Beyond the immediate future, after the danger to you is past, will you stay? Will you be with me? Us?"

She swallowed hard and again looked to Cam and Sawyer. There was hope . . . and fear in their gazes.

"I'll stay," she whispered. "I can't make any promises—"

"Shhh," he said, putting a finger over her lips. "All we want is a chance, Reggie. Just a chance. Nothing more."

He followed his finger down to her lips and slid it out of the way just in time for his mouth to press gently against hers.

There was a reverence in his touch, such exquisite tenderness, almost as if he were afraid to hope, to believe that she had agreed.

She wrapped her arms around his neck, and for the first time was able to shut out the fact that two other men were in the room, one of whom she'd made love to last night. She didn't feel guilty for pouring her love into this kiss, nor did she worry over the possibility that Cam or Sawyer would feel excluded. There were only so many things she could control, and that wasn't one of them.

So she relaxed and let go. Put all the longing and emotion that had boiled beneath the surface over the last long year into returning his kiss.

He wrapped his arms tighter around her, finally hoisting her up so that their mouths were even. Her feet dangled inches above the floor, and the pressure on her ribs started an ache in her chest, but she didn't care.

"I need you, Reggie," he whispered hoarsely against her lips. "God, I need you."

"I *need* you too," she said in return.

She closed her eyes and rested her forehead against his as their ragged breathing whispered between them.

Finally he eased her down his body until her feet hit the floor again. She winced as the pressure against her chest released, and Hutch swore.

She shook her head before he could say anything. "Stop treating me like I'm breakable, Hutch."

He hooked a finger under her chin and nudged it upward. "Not breakable, baby. Just very precious."

What could she possibly say to that?

Sawyer cleared his throat. "I hate to break this up, but if we're going to go, we need to head out pretty quick."

"I need to call in and let my department know where I'll be," she said as she moved away from Hutch.

There was a lot more she needed to call and arrange before she left, and she needed privacy in order to do it.

"Then let's get our shit together and get on the road," Cam said as he got up from the bar.

One by one, they got up and headed for the stairs. Regina lagged behind and headed for Cam's office. She needed quiet. And she didn't need to be overheard.

She closed the door behind her and walked over to sit behind his desk, reaching for the phone as she did so. She dialed Michael Harvey's number and prayed he'd be in.

A few moments later, he answered, and she breathed a sigh of relief.

"Michael, it's Regina Fallon."

"Regina. Glad to hear from you. I heard you've got a lot of excitement going on up there in Cypress."

"Yeah, no doubt. Look, I need a favor, and I don't have a lot of time to get into the whys and wherefores."

"I'm listening."

"I need a full on surveillance system set up at a residence outside Cypress. There's a grove of trees set off from the house a bit that I'd like some trail cameras put in. And the house, I need all angles covered. If someone so much as sets foot on this property, I want to know about it."

"I see. And when do you need this done?"

She winced. "Today. Tomorrow. No later than tomorrow."

She heard him blow out his breath.

"Man, you know I'd help you out any way I could, Regina, but that's a mighty tall order."

"I know," she said quietly. "But it's important, Michael. These people are important to me. I've got some crazed lunatic trying to kill me and threatening people close to me. I can't let him get close again. I want to shut him down."

"Okay, tell me where. I'll get a couple of men on it. We'll get you squared away."

She sighed in relief. "Thanks, Michael. Be sure and send me the bill."

"Oh, I will, and trust me, sweetheart, it won't be a cheap one."

She tried not to cringe. But whatever amount it cost her, it would be worth it if she could nail this bastard before he harmed Birdie or one of the guys.

As she hung up, another thought occurred to her. One she hadn't considered. She closed her eyes and rubbed her forehead. If the lunatic wasn't targeting her because of her father, and if he wasn't targeting her because of Hutch (that was still her number one scenario), and he was in fact going after her because he was some pissed-off moron she'd arrested in the past, then not only were Birdie and the guys potential targets, but her parents could be as well.

A groan escaped before she could stop it.

Trying not to let the possibilities send her into meltdown, she punched in the number to the station and waited for Greta to answer.

"Greta, is the chief in?" she asked when the other woman's voice came over the line.

"Sure, hon, just a second."

There was blank silence and then the chief's gruff voice sounded in Regina's ear.

"Regina, how are you today?"

"Much better, sir. How is the investigation going?"

"We wrapped up at your house. Still waiting for a report on the explosive used in your vehicle. Preliminary suggests a home-made job, nothing professional. We're in the process of questioning your neighbors and investigating the connection between this guy and you, Birdie, Hutch and Misty Thompson, if there is one."

"Sir, is it possible that my parents could be at risk as well? Whether this guy is targeting me, them or Hutch or someone else entirely, they would be likely victims."

"Already on it. Your father is spitting mad, but he'd already agreed to double the security around him and your mother."

She shook her head and rolled her eyes. "I wanted to let you know that I was leaving town, possibly for a couple of days. I'm going to Houston with Cam, Sawyer and Hutch. They have some work to do, and I thought leaving the area might be a good idea."

The chief made an approving sound. "Let me know when you roll back in. Depending on what we dig up in our investigation, we're going to need to question Hutch and possibly Cam and Sawyer."

"Will do."

"Take care of yourself, Regina."

She hung up and glanced guiltily at the door. Then with a firm shake of her head, she stood and brushed away any lingering doubts. Keeping the people she loved safe wasn't something she'd ever apologize for.

She walked out of the office and hadn't gotten two steps down the hall when she nearly ran into Cam. She froze and stepped back, hoping he hadn't been close enough to overhear her conversation.

"Hey," he said in a soft voice as his hands came to cup her shoulders. "I need to talk to you a second."

Her brows rose, and her pulse sped up as uncertainty gripped her.

He moved one hand to cup her cheek. "Stop looking so worried."

He turned her around and ushered her back into the office, shutting the door behind them.

"You're the one who looks worried," she said. And he did. There was concern in his eyes, an edge of uncertainty grooved into his forehead.

He reached out to touch her again, his hands sliding up her arms to her shoulders.

"We didn't use protection last night, Reggie. I'm such an idiot. Are you on something?"

Relieved, she relaxed under his hands. "I'm on birth control, Cam. I get a shot every three months."

He frowned. "Are those effective? I mean is it as safe as using condoms?" He dragged a hand through his hair. "I could kick my ass over this. I should have done more to protect you, to take care of you."

She smiled and reached out to touch his cheek. "Stop. I honestly didn't think about it either at the time. I mean I didn't go downstairs with the sole intent of seducing you. But if you're asking if I'm safe . . ."

He shook his head sharply. "That's not what I was asking. It's just that this didn't come up before . . . when we had sex before. We all used condoms then."

"Condoms aren't foolproof either, you know," she said dryly.

"I know," he said quietly. "I just didn't want to make you pregnant. I'd never force something on you that you weren't ready for."

She walked into his arms, pressing herself against his chest. "About the condoms, Cam. Is there any reason, any health reason for you . . . any of you to need to wear one?"

He pulled her away to stare down into her eyes. "I suppose this is a conversation we all need to have together."

She nodded. "If we're really going to do this . . ." She sighed and rubbed her face, feeling a little ridiculous. It was hard to shake. "If this is what we're going to do, the relationship that we're going to share . . ."

"Just say it, Reggie. It won't kill you. If you're going to be with the three of us."

"If I'm going to be with the three of you, there has to be trust and openness between all of us, not just between you and me and then between me and Sawyer and me and Hutch."

"I understand. We all do. Believe me when I say discussing my sexual history with two other guys is not something that thrills me, but what each of us do or have done affects the others. All of us. So we have to address it. But, Reggie? It's not going to be a long conversation."

She lifted an eyebrow in question.

"There hasn't been anyone else for me in a long time. Not since I came to terms with my feelings for you. I don't know for certain, but given what I know about the way Hutch and Sawyer feel about you, I can't think it's any different for them."

"Are you trying to say you've all been celibate? That there hasn't been anyone in the last year?"

"Not just the last year. Years."

Shock rounded her mouth. And close on the heels of that surprise came swift and agonizing guilt. Oh God. While she'd been off having her one-night stand and doing her best to prove she didn't need him, he'd been waiting for her.

Cam let go of her shoulders and turned to the side, shoving his hands into his pockets. "I'm not a saint. I can't speak for the others. There were women. Especially in college. One or two afterward. But when I realized I was in love with you, other women ceased to exist for me."

Love. The word sizzled through her brain like a fire fueled with gasoline.

She knew they felt deeply for her. Even loved her in a way. It was hard not to love one another when their friendship had run so deep for so long.

But to hear him say, so matter-of-factly, that he was in love with her weakened her at the knees. It called to a long buried need in her that blossomed and strained to be set free.

She wanted to be loved. Maybe she'd always wanted it. But it was something she'd learned to live without.

"You love me?" she whispered.

He gave her the strangest look. The longer he looked at her, the more complex his expression became.

"You don't know, do you? You really don't know what I feel for you?"

He moved in close, still staring at her with those intense brown eyes, so dark they made her shiver.

"I've always loved you, Reggie darling. Always. But I realized I was *in* love with you two years ago. I watched you being sworn in to your position as a police officer, and I can still remember the panic that hit me right in the chest as I realized the risk you would be taking. I broke into a cold sweat when I realized that this was something I couldn't protect you from. And then I contemplated the possibility of losing you, and that's when it hit me that I didn't just love you, didn't feel some deep affection reserved for a long-standing friendship. I was completely and utterly, hopelessly in love with you."

"I don't even know what to say," she said in a lost and confused voice she couldn't control.

"You don't have to say anything," Cam said in his gentle, understanding way. "That's what's so great about love. It's freely given. It doesn't require understanding or a response. Just know that you have mine."

She buried her face in his chest. She quaked against him, unable to stanch the raw emotion that raged through her heart.

He rained tiny kisses over her hair as his hands smoothed up and down her back.

"I—I love you too, Cam," she said quietly. And in that moment, she knew she meant it. She only hoped to God that it was enough to get them through the difficulties that lay ahead.

His arms tightened around her, and he shook as he slowly pulled her away from him again.

"Tell me . . . tell me you don't regret what happened between us last night," he said.

She gazed intently at him, not holding anything back. "I don't regret it, Cam. I won't run this time."

He laid his hand against her cheek, and she nuzzled into his palm, rubbing her face over his smooth skin.

"No matter what happens . . . with the others . . . it won't ever change the way I feel about you, Reggie. I need you to know that."

"I know," she said softly even as her chest gave a little squeeze. What he didn't say, however, was how they could possibly have a future together at the expense of two people they both loved.

It had to work. It was an all-or-nothing situation. One that frightened the hell out of her.

He leaned forward and kissed her brow, allowing his lips to linger for a moment.

"Come on, love. I'm sure the others are waiting for us."

Chapter 22

It was a little strange to walk into a house she hadn't been in for a year. A place she had been a regular visitor to before that night.

The large home in the upscale Houston suburb doubled as their offices, although they did maintain a smaller office in downtown Houston. Who was manning it now that they had taken up residence in Cypress, and how could they hope to keep the business thriving living an hour away? How much were they giving up to pursue the arrangement they said they wanted?

It didn't make a lot of sense to her. She wasn't even important to her own parents. How could three men feel so deeply for her that they'd risk everything they had worked so hard for?

As she walked into the living room, images from that night a year ago flashed before her, heating her cheeks and her body. A warm flush centered in her abdomen and washed through her veins, bathing her in heady desire.

The four of them on the couch. Then the carpet and finally on the bed in one of the master suites.

The next morning she'd awakened amid a tangle of male bodies, their arms and legs possessively entwined in hers. She'd bolted. Run as fast and as far as she could back home.

She'd ignored their phone calls, and when they finally showed up at her door, she'd used work and anything else she could think of to avoid them.

And then the phone calls stopped. The pleas to talk to them ceased. Silence had stretched between them like a chasm. That was when the true pain had hit her, because that was the moment she'd lost them.

Until a few nights ago, when they'd appeared in her hospital room, determination etched into their features like stone.

All the while she'd thought they'd given up on her they'd been moving quietly in the background. Waiting. For her.

She sat down heavily on the large sectional. Unworthy. She felt completely and utterly unworthy of such love and devotion. It baffled her.

"Reggie, are you okay?" Cam asked.

She looked up to see him standing by the couch, concern in his eyes.

"I'm fine. Just thinking."

He sat down beside her, their legs nearly touching.

"About that night?"

She nodded.

"I think about it too," he said. "All the time."

"We all think about it," Sawyer said from the doorway.

He started across the room and stopped a few feet away from her. She motioned to the place next to her.

"Sit down. You make me nervous standing over me that way."

"That's because he's a big bastard," Cam said in an amused voice.

Sawyer cast him a dark scowl but sat next to Reggie. His hand came to rest on the back of her neck as he leaned back. He rubbed over the knotted muscles, and she teetered backward from her perch on the edge of the couch, seeking more of his touch.

"You're so responsive," Sawyer murmured. "You were that night too. I touched you, and you came alive in my hands. I was so hungry for you. I'm still hungry, Reggie. There's never been another woman like you for me."

She rotated, causing his hand to slide down her back.

"Every time I think I know how I feel or what to say, you manage to say or do something that renders it completely ineffectual," she said raggedly. "What do I say to something like that? That I'll never feel worthy of the devotion the three of you have shown? That I look at you, and I remember that night and know that no one will ever mean as much to me as the three of you do?"

Tears clogged her throat, and she swallowed against the heavy knot, determined not to break in front of them. She clenched her teeth and sucked in air through her nose.

Shocked silence ensued before Sawyer all but imploded. He reached for her, dragging her across his lap and into his arms. There was no gentleness in his actions. She didn't expect any.

He framed her face in his hands and locked his lips to hers. He touched her cheeks, brushed his thumbs across her eyelids, dragged a finger through her curls.

"Don't you know? You're everything to me, Reggie. Everything. Not worthy? Dear God. How can you even think such a thing? You've believed in us, loved us since we were rebellious little snot-nosed brats. You defended us when no one else would. Worthy? We're not worthy of you, honey, but I'm not going to let that prevent me from having you."

"Then take me," she whispered.

A ragged groan worked from his chest. "There's nothing I'd love more than to drag you upstairs and lock you in my bedroom for the next twelve hours."

She smiled at the tortured sound of his voice. "I hear a *but* in there."

"But all I have time for is a quickie, and you deserve more than that."

She frowned, but he shushed her with a finger.

"I have to go out to the job site and find out what the hell is going on. But don't think I won't forget where we left off here. You asked me to take you, and believe me I'm going to take you. Over and over."

She shivered at his sensual words. Her gaze fastened on his lips—hard, yet so inviting. She leaned in to kiss him, the bristle of his goatee skittering over her chin. Warm, soft, wet, their tongues glided together.

"I wish you didn't have to go," she whispered.

He groaned again. "Me too, honey. My dick is so hard, I'm going to have trouble walking."

She giggled. Leave it to Sawyer to ruin a perfectly sensual moment by being a guy. Her gaze slid sideways to where Cam sat a few feet away, and she could see the undisguised interest on his face. The desire. And if she wasn't mistaken, he was as hard as Sawyer reported himself to be.

Interesting. She'd been so worried about showing one of them affection in front of the other. Of kissing or touching for fear of making them jealous, but Cam's reaction was far from jealousy or resentment. He looked as though he wanted to join in.

It wasn't as though they hadn't done it before.

Heat suffused her cheeks. She was going to have to get over

her embarrassment about that night. It was obviously going to happen again. And soon, if she had to guess. The sexual tension between them all was at its boiling point, and something had to give.

"You better go before I tie you to the couch," she said lightly.

His entire body tensed. His muscles contracted and rippled, and a shudder worked across his shoulders.

He lifted her off his lap, set her between him and Cam, then rose abruptly.

"I'll be back later," he said shortly.

Without a backward glance, he strode for the door, nearly colliding with Hutch as Hutch walked into the living room.

Hutch stared curiously after him but shrugged then walked over to where Cam and Regina sat.

"You ready to go shopping, baby?"

She sucked in her breath. Yeah. Shopping. Anything to get her mind off the sizzling tension between her and Sawyer. Or the fact that she was sorely tempted to run after him, tackle him and fuck his brains out.

She reached her hand over to Cam's and squeezed. Then she leaned over to kiss him before she got up from the couch.

"Later," he said in a husky voice. "If Sawyer hasn't carried you off to parts unknown by then."

There was knowing amusement in his voice, but also an easy acceptance that warmed her. God, they might really be okay in all this.

"Love you," she whispered, thrilled at how it sounded coming past her lips.

"Love you, Reggie darling. Have fun with Hutch. I'll be working. Stick your head in when you get back so I'll know you're here."

She smiled and got off the couch to walk over to Hutch. He

reached for her hand when she got close. He laced their fingers together and pulled her toward the front door.

Not one to take on any of the large malls in the Houston area, Regina instead opted for the nearest Super Wal-Mart and bought a couple of pairs of jeans, a few shirts, underwear and socks, and she snagged a pair of flip-flops. Because while she could at least reach down to lace her shoes now, it was still damn uncomfortable.

When she suggested they pick up steaks for Cam to grill as they'd originally planned, Hutch look at her, appalled. She raised her hands, palms up. "What?"

"You're such a barbarian," he muttered. "You and Sawyer, I swear."

"What?" she demanded again.

"You do *not* buy steaks from Wal-Mart. If it's not against the law, it should be. If you want steaks, we'll run by City Market on our way home."

"That's at least forty-five minutes out of the way."

He shrugged. "So? You not feeling adventurous today?"

Her eyes narrowed. "Was that a dare?"

He grinned innocently. "Would I dare you to do anything? I could pick up some good wine and the fixings for cheesecake. I make a mean one."

Her mouth watered. "You had me at sugar."

He pulled his wallet out to pay for her clothes, but she frowned and put her hand out to stop him. He sighed heavily but moved out of her way so she could give the cashier her bank card.

"Any chance you'd make some fudge?" she asked hopefully as they climbed into Cam's SUV.

The corners of his eyes crinkled with amusement. "I could be talked into it."

"Yum," she said enthusiastically. "Overcook it a little so it's hard like I like it."

He stared balefully at her. "I've got something hard for you, little wench."

She burst out laughing. "Hutch!" Then she glanced over at him mischievously. "Make me chocolate, and I'll do something about that something hard of yours."

For a moment she worried she'd gone a little overboard with the seductive tramp talk. It didn't sound like her. Oh, not that she was pure sweetness and light. In fact, before a year ago, she could be just as crude as the guys when they horsed around.

She grimaced. That was the problem. There were a lot of things she used to do when she hadn't been worried about what they thought of her. With a sigh, she turned and looked out the window before he could respond.

They navigated 610 and exited to go to the large gourmet grocery store that was a favorite of Hutch's. She went in with him and watched him analyze every piece of beef behind the glass case before finally choosing four large ribeyes.

While the butcher wrapped them, Hutch meandered down the display, perusing the other selections. Regina reached up for the package just as Hutch returned.

"Let's go over to the seafood. Thought I'd get some shrimp to do one night."

"Beer-battered with hush puppies?" she asked.

"Of course. According to Sawyer, beer is its own food group," he said dryly. "Well, that and ketchup."

That was true, and although Hutch tolerated Sawyer's affinity for beer (and Reggie's), he never once drank alcohol himself. The wine he was holding he got for the rest of them, but he never consumed it either.

It had something to do with his father. That much she knew,

and nothing more. Hutch never talked about his life prior to his arrival at Birdie's.

"You spoil me," she finally said.

He grinned. "I try. I'm not suave like Cam, not as intelligent and refined, and I'm not the great hulking muscle-bound beefcake that Sawyer is, so my plan is to seduce you with food."

She laughed. "Knowing what you do about me, then, should tell you that you'll get a lot further than the other two."

He winked at her. "I know. Your stomach is the door to your soul."

They checked out and walked back to the truck.

"How are you holding up?" he asked as he slid into the driver's seat.

"I'm good," she said as she buckled her seat belt. "Don't worry." She held up her wrist and bent and rotated it for him. "See? Almost completely well. Just a little stiff and twingy."

"Your bruises are almost gone," he said quietly.

Her hand went to her throat reflexively. "Really all that I still feel is the cut on my head. I should be able to go back to work soon." Or maybe not if her department didn't have any luck with their investigation. That thought depressed her.

Hutch scowled as he drove out of the parking lot. "I wish you weren't going back at all," he muttered.

She stared at his profile in surprise. "Why would you say something like that?"

He glanced briefly away from traffic and locked gazes with her. "You want me to lie?"

"No, of course not."

He turned his attention to merging onto 610. "It's dangerous," he said. "It worries me."

She twisted in her seat as much as the belt would allow and faced him. "I can take care of myself, Hutch. I'm a trained police officer. I can fire my weapon with pinpoint accuracy. I qualified first in my department at the range. I'm trained in self-defense, and I've taken numerous classes in martial arts and hand-to-hand combat. I'm not just a skirt and a pretty face behind a badge. I'm damn good at my job."

"All of that training didn't help you the night that bastard attacked you. Qualifying first with your gun doesn't help if it gets taken away from you," he said darkly. "He almost killed you. He *tried* to kill you."

She took deep breaths and struggled not to let anger get the best of her. She knew he worried about her.

"I didn't say I was invincible," she said calmly. "No one is. No one person could have withstood that attack. Sawyer couldn't have taken it, and he's a big guy. This guy was bigger. Much bigger. And crazy as a loon.

"A normal person, I would have taken down and made the arrest."

"But it only takes one not normal person, Reggie," he said quietly. "He could have raped you. He could have beaten you to death. He could have choked you. Any number of things could have happened to you because he was bigger and stronger. I get that the result would have been the same with anyone else. But you're not just anyone else to me, baby."

She gazed steadily at him. "I know all those things, Hutch. I do. I train for the worst. I prepare for the worst. Yes, he could have raped me. I know that. But it didn't happen. I did what I was supposed to do and it paid off. I'm alive because of my training."

He paled at her words. "How can you be so calm about this? So matter-of-fact? You talk about being raped like it's all part of the job. Like him beating the crap out of you was just a hazard of the profession."

"It *is* a hazard of the profession," she said gently. "It's not one that occurs with frequency, but it's always a possibility. I could get shot. I could get beat up. I could get raped. Or run over. There's a million what-ifs. I knew that going in."

His fingers were white around the steering wheel, and his jaw was drawn tight. "You knowing it doesn't make it any easier for me to sit back and worry every time you go to work."

"What are you saying, Hutch? Are you giving me an ultimatum here?" Worry clutched at her belly, and warning bells were clanging with ferocity in her head.

"No, of course not," he muttered. "Damn it, I just worry. That's all I'm saying."

She reached across the seat and put her hand on his shoulder. "I know you worry, Hutch. I wish there was something I could do to make you stop. All I can promise you is that I'll be careful and that I'll do everything in my power to come home to you each and every time."

"Are you?" he asked. "Going to be coming home to me every time?"

She glanced away. Maybe she'd been precipitous in saying that. "I'm willing to see where things take us," she said quietly.

"That's all I can ask, baby."

He picked up her hand and kissed it then lowered it to his lap, where he kept his fingers laced through hers. They drove the rest of the way in silence, but he kept his hand tight around hers.

CHAPTER 23

*R*egina and Hutch took the food into the kitchen, and Hutch unwrapped the steaks and set them to marinating. When he started to put the ingredients for the cheesecake into the fridge, her brows went up.

"Not going to fix it?" she asked.

"Later," he said shortly.

Then he pulled out a pen and paper and scribbled a note. He propped it against the pan the steaks were marinating in then went to the sink to wash his hands.

Regina walked up and leaned over to read the note. Hutch's hand curled around her shoulder, and she jumped.

"Just me telling Cam that the steaks will be ready to grill in an hour," Hutch said easily.

"You going somewhere?" she asked.

"Upstairs. With you."

Her eyes widened, and her heart skipped a beat, giving her that panicky, hiccup feeling in her chest. He pulled her into his arms and stared down at her mouth with half-lidded eyes, as if he wanted nothing more than to kiss her.

Her mouth fell open as she tried to gulp more air into her painfully squeezed lungs. She was nervous, yes. Particularly now, after having made love to Cam. Hutch knew it, he had to. She and Cam hadn't exactly been discreet.

What were Hutch's motives? And did it matter, when she wanted him so badly?

He angled his head and slowly closed the distance between them. His lips pressed gently to hers, taking possession of her mouth.

His tongue glided effortlessly over hers, tasting, offering his taste to her. He was present, inside her, every time she inhaled. His scent filled her. Comfort. Safety. Love.

For all practical purposes, this was the first time they'd make love together. Just the two of them. And suddenly she was scared to death.

Hutch felt her tremble against him, shake underneath his fingertips as he held her close. Her little gasps came raggedly, and when he drew away, her pupils were dilated. She looked frightened.

Pain curled its fist around him, squeezing uncomfortably. She was afraid. Of him.

"Why are you looking at me that way?" she asked.

He must have allowed his feelings to show, not that he'd ever been good at hiding them from her. She had a way of prying him open, flaying him wide for the world to see. Not a comfortable prospect for a man.

"You're afraid of me," he said in a low voice.

Sorrow filled her eyes, and she reached out to cup his face. He couldn't help the reaction that had him turning into her palm to kiss the baby-soft skin.

"Not of you," she whispered. "Never of you, Hutch. But I won't lie to you and say I'm not afraid. Not of you, but of what you think. Of what you feel."

His brows drew together in confusion. He sensed this was an important conversation, and he didn't want to have it down here, no matter that he was supposed to be willing to share Reggie with Cam and Sawyer. No one ever said he couldn't hold some part of her special, away from the others.

"Will you come upstairs with me, baby? We can talk in the bedroom."

She nodded, and he took her hand, holding it tightly in his. They walked to the stairs, side by side, and he curled his arm around her waist as they started up.

He nudged her into his room and shut the door behind them. Without hesitation, he pulled her against his chest, tilting her head back so he could claim her lips.

"I've waited so long to have you like this, Reggie," he whispered as he walked her backward toward the bed. "In my arms, looking at me like you looked at me in the kitchen."

He eased her down onto the bed, coming with her, holding himself above her as he stared intently into her eyes.

"Tell me what you're afraid of, baby."

She gazed up at him and reached to touch his face. She traced the lines of his forehead and feathered down to his jawline. Tentatively, she ran one finger over his firm lips.

He caught the tip between his teeth, nipping ever so slightly as he sucked it into his mouth.

A quiver worked over her body. She wanted that mouth on hers. He would be so exquisitely gentle. He'd always treated her like fine china. Had always been protective of her, always supported her hopes and dreams.

"I'm not afraid of you," she hastened to explain. "Never of you,

Hutch. I'm afraid of seeing the way you look at me changing. Of the way you feel about me changing."

His brow crinkled, and his eyes flared. "Why would any of that change?"

"Because I made love with Cam," she said quietly. "Because . . . I'll make love to Sawyer."

His breath blew slightly over her hair, ruffling it from her forehead.

"Cam said . . ."

"What did Cam say?" he asked, a note of curiosity in his tone.

"He said that if it had been you or Sawyer who made love to me the other night, that while he would have wanted it to be him, he wouldn't have been upset. He said he'd have been relieved."

"Relieved." He frowned a little as he said it, and she held her breath until his expression eased. "I suppose I can understand why he put it that way."

"Can you?" she asked. "Are you angry or hurt that I was with him?"

He shook his head emphatically, even as his expression remained indecisive. He slid his knee between her legs and shifted a little to her right so they rolled to their sides. He pillowed her head on his muscular arm, and he stroked his other hand down her side until it came to rest on her hip.

"I'm not angry or hurt, baby. I knew if this was going to work for us that you would be making love with Cam and Sawyer. I don't expect the times you spend with them to always be in a group setting. I don't expect to share my every moment with you with them, so it isn't fair for me to expect it of them."

"But are you really okay with it?" she asked anxiously. There was still an undercurrent of doubt in his voice, and it pulled at her.

"Define 'okay,'" he said with a wry laugh. "I won't lie to you and say that when I walked downstairs and saw you lying with

Cam on the couch that my chest didn't cave in just a little. But there was also a lightness there, *relief*, as Cam put it. I wanted it to be me, but I also realized that it *would* be me. All I had to do was give you time."

He worked his hand back up to her shoulder and then to the curve of her neck and finally her face. He kissed her again, just a light peck at the corner of her mouth, but she felt the love behind the gesture, felt it to her toes.

"I feel like I've loved you forever, Reggie. Ever since we met in that creek bottom, and if I didn't love you then, I lost my heart when you decked Sawyer and Cam for making fun of me. There are times when I resent the fact that I have to share you with them. In my heart, you were mine first."

She sucked in her breath and trembled as tears welled in her eyes.

"But I also know as much as I love you that they love you too. And then I imagine having to be without you, and it hurts me. It's a physical ache I can't control. I know it's how they'd feel. They're brothers to me, and I know you love them too. I can sit here and talk about the hurt it would cause me and them, but it's nothing to the pain it would cause you if we made you choose. I know you well enough to know it's something you'd never do. It's why you ran so hard. Because you didn't want to hurt us, no matter how much you were hurting yourself."

Tears slid down her cheeks. He gently thumbed them aside as he gazed earnestly into her watery eyes.

"I do love you, Hutch," she whispered. "Thank you for understanding and for not feeling threatened by the fact that I love Cam and Sawyer too."

"We just want you with us," he said so seriously as he stroked her hair. "We know it won't be easy, but we're willing to do whatever it takes to keep you with us always."

"Make love to me, Hutch. I've waited so long."

He rolled over her, planting his knees into the mattress as he looked down at her. With clumsy fingers, he eased her shirt up her body until it gathered around her neck.

Slowly, he moved each arm above her then worked the shirt over her head. He tossed it aside then lowered his head to her belly.

Warm, sweet lips pressed to her rib cage. He feathered kisses over her skin, starting at the edge of her bra and working down to her navel.

His damp tongue brushed over the hollow, swirled around the center, and then his teeth grazed the shivering skin. He fumbled with the button of her fly, finally popping it. The zipper scratched downward, and his fingers tucked into the waistband.

She arched upward to allow him to pull the jeans over her hips. They slid down her legs, gathering at her ankles. She kicked as he pulled, and seconds later she was free.

She lay there in the middle of the bed in her bra and panties. Her plain white, unsexy underwear. He didn't seem to mind her taste in lingerie. He looked too interested in getting her out of it to notice.

He leaned down again and gathered her in his arms. He pressed a kiss in the valley of her breasts as his hands dug between her and the bed. His fingers found the clasp of her bra, and he worked it free.

He moved his hands up and over her shoulders, dragging the straps with his fingers as he lowered them down her body. His eyes glittered with desire as the cups of her bra came away from her breasts.

Her nipples puckered and tightened painfully, and he hadn't even touched her yet. The bra went sailing across the room and then his hands returned to her sides. He wrapped those long, lean fingers around her rib cage, his touch firm and possessive.

A whispered sigh escaped her lips as his dark head bent to her breast. He lapped his tongue over one sensitive point, dragging it slowly over the tip.

She closed her eyes and whimpered as flashes of pleasure centered in her core, tightened her pussy and sent a raw, aching need straight to her heart.

"Please," she whispered. "I need you so much, Hutch."

He raised his head, and their gazes connected. Heat sparked across that connection, enveloped them and sent electricity racing through her veins.

He moved up to claim her mouth again. His fingers found her breasts, plumping the soft flesh against his palms then fingering the nipples.

"You're so beautiful, Reggie. You take my breath away every time I look at you."

Her heart twinged, and she glowed under his words.

"I love you," she whispered. "I've always loved you. You were the first person to truly love *me*."

His mouth grazed down her jaw to her ear and then below, whispering down her neck. His fingers flexed at her breasts, splaying over her body, leaving a trail of fire wherever they touched.

Kisses tickled her skin. She bowed her back when his mouth closed hot around a nipple. He sucked it between his teeth and held it there, nipping lightly at the taut bud.

She pulsed at her center. Hot, aching and needy. She was swollen and ready. Her body was on fire and burning more out of control with each sweep of his tongue, each tender caress of his fingers.

The light rasp of his palms over the curves of her hips elicited light shudders. He hooked his fingers into the band of her panties, and he pulled downward until the small triangle of curls was exposed to his sight . . . and touch.

He rolled away, taking her underwear with him to drop on the floor. He stood hastily by the bed and began pulling at his clothes.

He was shorter than both Sawyer and Cam, but his body was honed into a solid form of muscle and sinew. He and Sawyer both worked alongside their crews, and it was evident in the dark tan and the ripple of muscles across his shoulders and chest.

As he pulled his pants down, her breath caught when his rigid cock bobbed into view. Surrounded by dark, wiry curls, it jutted upward, thick and heavy.

It was a sight that mesmerized her. She imagined his hardness inside her mouth, her body, stroking hard and deep within her.

She twisted and fidgeted on the bed, restless in her edgy desire to have him. All of him.

When he started for the nightstand, she knew he was going after a condom.

"Hutch," she said softly. "Don't."

He glanced up sharply, his gaze questioning.

"Are you sure you don't want a condom, Reggie?"

She shook her head and sighed, knowing that before things went any further they were going to have to have the same conversation she'd had with Cam.

She glanced down and closed her eyes as the bed dipped and he returned to her. He nudged her chin up with his fingers.

"What's wrong?" he asked.

"I just regret that because of me we even need to have this conversation," she said with a sigh.

Genuinely puzzled eyes stared back at her. "Baby, you lost me." Then his gaze sharpened. "Did Cam not wear a condom?" He looked almost angry.

She blew out her breath. She was making a huge mess of this. "No, Cam didn't wear one. We didn't think about it at the time. He was pretty worried about it the next morning, but I assured him I was on birth control."

Hutch frowned. "It's not about you being on birth control. Cam should have protected you better than that."

"If I hadn't had a one-night stand with someone after that night a year ago, we wouldn't be bothering to have these conversations," she said in a low voice.

Hutch blinked. "What? You think . . . Wait a minute. What exactly do you think here?"

She shifted uncomfortably. "I used protection that night. I'm safe. It only happened that once. I was so sick about it the next day that I couldn't stand the thought of anyone other than you or Cam and Sawyer ever touching me."

She glanced down guiltily as she finished.

"Reggie, baby, look at me," Hutch said softly.

She glanced up nervously, worried about what she'd see in his eyes. Disappointment? Disgust? But she saw neither. She saw love.

"I'm not even sure what to say here. I don't want to say the wrong thing. I'll be honest. When you told me that you'd slept with someone else after what happened here, I was gutshot. I wanted to go hunt the bastard down and kick his ass. I wanted to wrap myself around you so far that you'd lose yourself in me and only me.

"But then I saw the look in your eyes. The self-condemnation and the worry that you'd somehow betrayed us. I saw vulnerability and pain, and I was gutshot all over again."

He stroked his fingers over her cheek, up and down, and then rubbed the back of his knuckles across her jaw.

"What happens now is what's important. Not what happened then. Don't get me wrong, if you go crawl into bed with someone other than me . . . or Sawyer or Cam," he added in a strangled voice, "I'll kick not only his ass but yours as well. And then I'll tie you to my bed for the next year."

Her laugh came out shaky and ended on a sob.

"I'm sorry, Hutch. I've never said it but wanted to so many times."

"Don't, baby. We came at you out of nowhere. We blindsided you and scared you out of your mind. No matter what *we* wanted, you hadn't made a commitment to us. You didn't owe us anything."

She shook her head blindly. "I did. I at least owed you an explanation, a conversation before I crawled into someone else's bed." She closed her eyes as tears crept in. "I hate myself for doing it. I don't even know why I did. I was . . . lonely. I wanted you but didn't know how to ask for what I wanted."

"Ahhh, baby," he murmured as he pulled her into his arms. He cradled her against his chest and pressed tiny kisses to the top of her head, her forehead, and over her closed eyes.

He stroked her hair for several minutes as she squeezed tighter against him.

"About the condoms, Reggie. I want you protected."

She pulled away, just enough that she could see him. "Cam said . . . he said there hadn't been another woman since he realized he loved me."

Hutch's eyes flared in surprise.

"He's safe, and I'm safe . . . but if we're going to—"

"If we're going to walk into this kind of relationship, we have to make sure we're all on the same page," Hutch said evenly.

She nodded.

"I've made love with two women," he said solemnly. "A girl I dated my freshman year in college and then . . . you."

She went still against him. "That's all?" she whispered.

"Like Cam, there was never another woman after I realized my feelings for you." Pain twisted his features. "Actually that's not true." He looked down, and it was her turn to force his chin up so he stared back at her.

"What's not true?" she prompted.

"I've always loved you. And I suppose it's why I can't be angry with you for sleeping with another man, because I slept with another woman knowing that I loved you and that I didn't have a prayer of ever not loving you."

Her heart twisted into one huge knot. Then it loosened, took wings and flew. Love bubbled into her chest, filling it until she thought she just might burst.

"I love you," she said simply. "And you were right. What was isn't as important as what is and what will be."

"What will be," he murmured. "What's going to be, baby, is that I'm going to love you and do my damnedest to make this arrangement work."

"Then love me. Make love to me. I need you, Hutch. I've always needed you."

His mouth closed over hers, feeding hungrily, sipping at her lips then devouring. She sucked at his bottom lip, nipping gently with her teeth then soothing with her tongue.

His hardness settled between her legs as he moved his body over hers. She cradled him against her, absorbing his heat, his power. Her hands ran over his body, his shoulders, his back, down to his muscular buttocks. They tightened underneath her fingertips as she explored the rounded globes.

He settled his elbows on either side of her head and dipped to kiss her as he shifted his hips to work further between her thighs.

His cock brushed the curls between her legs then delved deeper as he flexed his hips.

She opened for him, wanting him. Her pussy throbbed, each

little pulse sending a surge of liquid adrenaline rocketing through her pelvis.

The broad head of his penis nudged at her folds, brushing across her clit before settling lower at her entrance. Spasms of delight, centering at the quivering nub of flesh between her legs and radiating outward in all directions, licked at her as he brushed upward again from her entrance through the delicate, damp flesh.

"Hutch, please," she gasped.

Propping himself on one arm, he reached between them with his other hand and grasped his cock, positioning it then sliding forward just an inch.

She sucked in her breath and tensed from head to toe as an explosion of sensation rocked her to her core.

He was so thick, so hard.

She closed her eyes and threw her head back as he eased forward. Her body stretched to accommodate him, giving in to his persistent intrusion.

And then he withdrew, and she moaned in protest. He settled back on his arms on either side of her head, flexed his hips to enter her once more then captured her mouth in a demanding kiss.

She could feel the strain, the fight within him. He was afraid of hurting her. She smiled, slid her mouth down his jaw until she reached his neck and then sank her teeth into his skin.

"Reggie, dear God, stop that!"

She grinned and nibbled up to his ear before sucking the lobe into her mouth. He shuddered against her and surged deeper. She let out a contented sigh. Much, much better.

She wiggled underneath him, adjusting the angle of her hips so she could take him deeper.

"Are you trying to kill me?" he groaned. "Stop moving or it's going to be over in about two seconds flat."

She chuckled then wrapped her arms and legs tightly around him. She planted her heels in his hard ass and hoisted herself higher, seeking to plant him deeper.

"Impatient little wench."

"Demanding too," she murmured against his ear, and then she licked him again, rolling her tongue over the inner shell.

His big body shuddered against her, and it was as if the last string holding his control snapped right in two. He rose on his knees, drew his hands back between her legs, shoved them underneath her thighs and pushed forward.

Spread wide beneath him, she cried out when he thrust and planted himself deep into her body.

He worked her legs higher, and he leaned into her. And then his hips met her pelvis as he slid all the way in.

She gasped at the incredible sense of fullness. Her pussy quivered, stretched around him, every nerve ending pulsing and throbbing against his cock.

He dropped her legs and lowered his body until his chest pressed against her breasts. He burrowed his arms underneath her back, pulling her close. His legs strained as his knees held the bulk of his weight from her.

He flexed his hips, withdrawing and then sinking into her again.

"I've waited so long for this," he said softly. "For it to be just you and me, you wrapped around me like a blanket and me so deep inside you that I get lost."

She dug her nails into his shoulders and lifted her hips to meet his thrust. She was slick around his cock, and he glided easily back and forth.

Delicious friction. He worked faster and harder, his earlier concern of hurting her seemingly gone.

Deep within, the burn began. Small at first but growing larger.

A tiny kernel of pleasure blossomed, rolling tighter and tighter, faster and faster.

She moaned and urged him on. She grabbed at him, her hands slipping. She wrapped her legs around him and came off the bed, straining against him with all her strength.

He buried his face in her neck, kissing and nibbling, his breaths coming in gasps as the sounds of flesh slapping against flesh grew louder.

His body rose and fell against her. They grabbed for each other, holding, grasping, desperate in their attempt to get closer, for no space to be between them.

"Hutch," she whispered. "Oh, please, don't stop."

"Come with me, baby. Come now. I can't last. Oh God, baby."

He raised his head, pressed his forehead to hers, his eyes closed tight. He kissed her, forceful, their tongues clashing.

Her orgasm built, became unbearable in its tension. She reached for it, desperate for release.

He withdrew then thrust into her in one forceful lunge. He cried out, and his every muscle locked against her. Even as his raw power slammed into her, he sheltered her, cradled her tenderly in his arms.

Kisses fell on her lips, her cheeks and down her neck.

Oh God, she was almost there, and he was slowing down. She let out a groan of protest, and he stiffened then looked down at her, regret flashing brightly in his eyes.

She was sorely tempted to fake it, but he'd know. He knew her better than anyone. She wouldn't lie to him this way, and she was so desperate for release, there was no way she could fake the lazy aftermath of a really good orgasm when every nerve ending in her body screamed and begged for mercy.

"Jesus, I'm sorry, Reggie. God, I'm a selfish bastard."

He reached down and slid his fingers between them. He found

her clit and rotated one finger around the quivering mound of flesh.

She moaned and strained upward, reaching for the pleasure he offered. His hips rocked back and forth, slower now but with enough force to give her what she wanted.

"Tell me what you like, baby," he murmured. "Show me what to do."

"That," she gasped. "Your fingers. Touch me, harder."

He complied, applying more pressure, and he thrust deep.

She closed her eyes and clenched her teeth together. She was rising rapidly, nearing her peak with frightening intensity. After being on the edge for so long, she hit the rise with a sharpness that was nearly painful.

He rolled her clit hard, pressing in with his finger, finding that sweet spot. She exploded around his cock, her legs, her body, straining and spasming.

"That's it, baby. Come for me. God you feel so good."

She reached for his hand and pulled it away, no longer able to bear the sharp pulses shooting through her pussy. She pulled him down to her, and he continued to thrust until he slipped out in a warm rush.

He kissed her and pushed her hair away from her face with a gentle hand. Regret shone bright in his eyes, but she put a single finger over his lips.

"I should have taken better care of you, Reggie," he said around her finger. "You weren't with me, and I damn sure should have made sure you were before acting like a randy teenager with his first girl."

She smiled and rubbed her hand over his cheek. "I'm only your second girl, Hutch."

She could swear his cheeks reddened.

"I didn't say that to embarrass you," she said quickly.

He smiled back at her. "I know you didn't, baby. I'm just sorry I didn't make it better for you."

She shook her head. "It was perfect, Hutch. You were perfect. Just perfect."

He eased off her then looked down. "Want to take a shower with me? As much as I'd love to stay in bed with you for the rest of the night, I did promise you cheesecake and fudge."

"Mmmm, can't wait," she said drowsily.

"I'll go turn on the water. Meet me in two minutes."

He stood then leaned over and kissed her brow before turning to walk toward the bathroom. She watched him, enjoying the view of his toned body.

She'd almost give up cheesecake and fudge to spend the rest of the night in bed with him. Almost.

CHAPTER 24

When Regina came downstairs a few minutes after Hutch, Sawyer was sitting on the couch watching television. He looked up when she stopped in the doorway.

Quiet intensity made his pale blue eyes even paler. He stared at her with something more than want or need. It was longing.

She crossed the room, and without waiting for his invitation, she crawled onto the couch next to him and snuggled into the crook of his arm.

He was warm and solid. She burrowed deeper, and he chuckled.

"If you don't quit digging, you're going to be underneath me in a minute."

She grinned and laid her arm across his chest. He caught her hand in his and simply held it, lacing their fingers together.

"Where's Cam?" she asked.

"Out firing up the grill."

"Oh. We'll have to go out in a bit and keep him company."

Sawyer grunted. "I'm comfortable right here."

"Mmmm, me too, but we should go out. Crank up some music. Maybe eat outside. It's not so hot today."

"Sure, if that's what you want," he said easily.

She raised her head to look at him. "Did you get things straightened out at the job site?"

He grunted again, and she smiled and shook her head.

"Your verbosity never ceases to amaze me. Of course you have plenty to say when you're ordering me around," she said dryly.

He laughed, and she watched in fascination as the action lifted away the darkness in his expression. The brooding look faded from his eyes as he gazed back at her.

"I have to go back out in the morning to meet the guy from the city, but it looks like a simple miscommunication. At the worst, we lost two days on the job. We can make it up."

She leaned up and pressed her lips softly to his. "I'm glad you're back. I missed you. Now, let's go outside and find Cam."

Sawyer studied her for a moment and then he touched a finger to her chin, tracing a line to her mouth and around her lips.

"You look . . . happier," he said.

Before she could respond, he pushed himself off the couch. When he reached down to take her hand, she pushed him around so his back was to her. Then she stood up on the couch and hopped onto his back, wrapping her arms around his neck.

He chuckled but reached around to grab the undersides of her legs with his big hands.

"Playful today, I see."

She pressed her cheek to the side of his head as he walked toward the patio doors. "Maybe I'm just finding my way back."

He stopped for a minute, his hand on the handle of the door. "It's about time. We've missed you, baby girl."

Sawyer stepped outside, and Cam looked up from the grill. He grinned when he saw Regina perched on Sawyer's back.

"Where's Hutch?" Cam asked.

"Making me cheesecake and fudge," she said gleefully.

Cam shook his head and rolled his eyes. "Sugar's going to kill you, Reggie darling."

"Yes, but what a way to go."

"I can think of better ways," Sawyer said with a hint of suggestion to his voice.

She squeezed her arms a little tighter around his chest.

Sawyer walked over to the porch railing, turned and bent enough that Regina could rest her bottom on the rail but still hang onto his back.

"When's the meat going on?" Regina asked hopefully.

"In about two minutes," Cam replied. "Hungry?"

"Starving. I want the biggest steak."

Sawyer grunted again, and she poked him.

"Where the hell do you put all that food, Reggie? I swear you have tapeworms."

She grinned and stared at Cam over Sawyer's shoulder. "I need food. And sugar. Red meat and sugar."

"What you need is to start eating healthier or you're going to keel over with a heart attack before you hit thirty."

"That gives me two more years of culinary bliss then."

He eyed her balefully. "Not funny. I want you around a lot longer than that, love."

She softened and went all gooey inside at his tender words. She could endure daily lectures from Cam when he topped them off with statements like that.

"You've got Hutch all wrapped around your little finger," he continued. "That's why he's in there contributing to your bad habits. I on the other hand am not so easily manipulated."

"Which is why you're grilling steaks?" Sawyer asked innocently.

Cam shot him a glare.

"Maybe Sawyer and I should do the cooking," she suggested.

Sawyer choked against her, and Cam looked so horrified, she giggled.

"It was just an idea," she said.

"Yeah, a bad one," Cam muttered.

She moved her arms from Sawyer's neck and burrowed them under his arms and around his waist. She laid her head between his shoulders and sighed contentedly.

Life didn't get much better than this. Nice weather, steaks on the grill, good times and her three best friends on earth. Correction, her three lovers. They were still the best friends she'd ever have, regardless of the fact that she was sleeping with them. And she'd never love anyone else more.

She hugged Sawyer tighter. When would their time come? And would he hold back as he'd done a year ago? There was so much latent power bottled up inside him. He wouldn't make love to her as Hutch had, and it both excited her and made her nervous as hell.

Sawyer was . . . all rough edges and wild, untamed urges. And knowing him as well as she did, she knew he'd try and hide that part of him from her.

She sighed.

Sawyer tensed against her. "What's wrong, Reggie?"

She smiled. "Nothing. Just thinking."

He took her wrists and pulled them away from his chest and slowly turned around in her arms.

"About?"

"You," she said simply.

"Going to share those thoughts?"

She stared up at him as an impish grin took over her face. "Nope. That's for me to know and you to find out."

There. She'd seen it. Flashing in his eyes. One moment of un-restrained power and dark, edgy desire. If she didn't know Sawyer so well, he'd scare the shit out of her right now.

Big, hulking mass of humanity, intense blue eyes boring holes straight through her. His shaved head and trimmed goatee just added to that tough-as-nails exterior. The whole look made him unapproachable by most, and she suspected it was purposely af-fected. Sawyer didn't exactly get up close and personal with any-one outside of her, Cam and Hutch. It was something she and Sawyer had in common.

She reached up and fingered the gold hoop earring in his left ear.

"You know, for someone who looks like such a badass, you sure are a big marshmallow."

He frowned. "What was that for?"

"Just thinking out loud," she said unapologetically.

"Well keep it to yourself," he grumbled.

Cam snickered, and Sawyer turned to give him a ferocious glare.

He turned back to Regina. "Marshmallow? You call me a marsh-mallow and I'm not supposed to be offended?"

She grinned. "But you're my marshmallow and you're only marshmallowy with me."

"*Marshmallowy?* Reggie, have you been sniffing cleaning prod-ucts?"

Instead of answering, she leaned into his chest again and hugged him tight. Soon. She'd have him soon, and she'd make damn sure he didn't treat her like a piece of glass. But for tonight, she was ready to enjoy being near them all again. Laughing and having a good time with the three people who meant everything to her.

CHAPTER 25

*R*egina slid the last bite of cheesecake into her mouth with something that resembled orgasmic bliss. When she opened her eyes, she saw all three guys staring at her. Not just staring at her, but devouring her with their eyes. Like she was the cheesecake she'd just scarfed down.

"What?" she asked.

"I think I've changed my mind about letting you have cheesecake," Cam muttered. "If you eat it like that every time, I'll be glad to let you have it as often as you like."

She slowly drew the fork out of her mouth, letting her tongue linger on the tines as she got every last morsel.

Hutch groaned.

She grinned and set her saucer on the coffee table. "Is that all you guys ever think about?"

"Yes," came the identical response from all three directions.

She leaned back as Hutch collected the saucer then made a pass through the living room to get the other dishes on his way to the kitchen.

The similarity between that night a year ago and tonight wasn't lost on her. Much had been the same. She'd driven over. They'd grilled out then sat around joking and laughing. And somewhere in the middle of all of it, one of them had kissed her. She couldn't remember who had instigated it. At the time she hadn't questioned something she'd wanted for so long.

Tonight there was subtle tension. They were *all* thinking about that night, but they were probably also thinking about the fact she'd hightailed it the next morning.

It would be up to her to make any move. They wouldn't push her. They didn't want her to run again.

Her heart pounded as she gathered the nerve to do what she most wanted. They'd done the seducing the first time around, but tonight she would do it.

She pushed herself off the couch and walked slowly to the center of the room. She turned to see Sawyer and Cam staring curiously at her. Hutch returned from the kitchen and stopped behind the couch, his gaze on her.

She started to raise her hands to her shirt, but they shook too badly. She curled her fingers into tight fists and drew in breaths to regroup.

Nervous? Yes. But she wasn't afraid. Not this time.

Slowly she uncurled her fist and began unbuttoning her shirt. She raised her stare to the three men in front of her as she shrugged out of the shirt and let it fall to the floor.

Hutch stood, hands shoved in his jeans pocket, his gaze riveted to her. Cam sat at the end of the couch, watching her every movement. Sawyer . . . he stared at her, peeling back her skin, digging deep. He simmered. She could feel the tension rolling off his shoulders. Big, powerful . . . hungry.

"Reggie, what the hell are you doing?" Sawyer growled.

"What does it look like I'm doing?" she asked softly.

Cam scooted forward, perching on the edge of the couch, obviously torn between the need to go to her and the need to gauge the reactions of Sawyer and Hutch.

"But *why* are you doing it?" Cam asked in a steady voice. "We don't want this if you don't."

"But I do."

She reached to undo her jeans and shimmied out of the confining denim. She kicked off the flip-flops and stood before them in just her panties and bra. Honestly, she'd prefer they do the rest. She hadn't ever performed a striptease, especially not in front of an audience, but she wasn't a coward either. Not anymore.

Her fingertips glanced over her rib cage as she ran them underneath her bra, around the back to the clasp. One hook, then two, and the bra fell loose around her. She straightened her arms, letting it glide to the floor with her other clothing.

Their gazes burned over her skin, leaving prickly awareness in their wake. Her nipples hardened painfully. When they still didn't move, a twinge of insecurity took hold, and she folded her arms over her chest protectively.

She scraped her teeth over her bottom lip and eyed them with growing nervousness.

Sawyer swore softly then shot to his feet. He closed the distance between them with two strides. His hands closed around her shoulders, and he pulled her against his chest.

His strength, the power resonating from within him enfolded her, surrounded her, captured her in its strong current. She wanted so much to be in his arms, for him to touch her, to unleash that carefully hidden power she felt surging just underneath the surface.

His mouth closed over hers, demanding and lush. The short hairs of his goatee scraped across her chin and at the corners of her lips, and she imagined what it would feel like on the rest of her body as he kissed and nibbled.

A long sigh escaped her as she met his tongue with hers. So much time wasted. But finally she was where she belonged.

Another warm body moved in behind her, and she found herself trapped between two hard chests. Cam. His hands glided down her sides, pausing at her hips then pulling her back until her ass nestled into his groin.

"Are you sure you want this, Reggie?" Cam whispered in her ear. He moved his hands back up, catching her hair and lifting it away from her neck so he could kiss her.

Shivers racked her spine when his teeth grazed the spot where her pulse hammered below her ear.

"I do," she whispered. "So much. Love me. Please."

Sawyer swung her into his arms and headed for the stairs. She looked behind him to see Cam and Hutch following close behind. Their gazes connected, locked together in a bond she hoped tonight strengthened.

Then she looked up at Sawyer, at the determination in his face. Her heart fluttered and did a quiet flip. Would she break down his barriers tonight? Or would he hold himself away from her as he'd done the last time?

He walked into the bedroom. The one at the end that none of the guys used. Cam or Hutch flipped on the light as Sawyer gently deposited her on the huge bed in the center of the room.

"Tell me, Reggie," Sawyer said quietly. "Tell me you want this. That you're sure this is what you want."

Cam and Hutch stood at the end of the bed. They all looked at her, gauging her reaction.

Her mouth went dry. She swallowed and tried to get her tongue to cooperate.

"I want this. More than anything. Show me what to do. What you want me to do."

"Just lay back and let us love you."

Sawyer's words sizzled over her skin, scorching her with a heat trail that felt as though the sun's rays were beating down on her.

She watched as they began to undress. Shirts, jeans, underwear. It all came off, tossed aside with no care.

It was sensory overload. Try as she might, she could only recall bits and images from that night a year ago. It had happened so fast. She'd been in a daze. That wasn't going to happen again.

She viewed the three gorgeous, naked men in front of her. Men that wanted her. Desired her. Thought she was beautiful. They cared for her. Loved her.

It was almost too much to process.

She shivered again when the bed dipped and Sawyer and Cam eased onto it beside her.

"Don't be afraid, Reggie darling," Cam murmured close to her ear. "We'd never do anything to hurt you."

She turned to stare at him, into those warm brown eyes. "I know, Cam. I'm not afraid."

The mattress moved underneath her again as Hutch crawled onto the bed at her feet. His hands slid up her legs, spreading them as he went.

Sawyer lowered his head to her breast, sucking the nipple gently into his mouth. She yanked her hand to his smooth head, holding him in place.

Her legs moved wider apart, and she saw Hutch's head move between her thighs. Every muscle in her body tensed for what she knew was coming.

As his fingers delved into her wetness, Cam's lips found her other breast.

Her vision blurred. It was too much, and they'd only begun. How would she ever hold out under their onslaught?

Hutch pushed her legs upward, and then Sawyer reached down to curl his hand around her knee. Cam reached for her other knee, and they spread her for Hutch, holding her in place. The sheer eroticism of such a pose had her gasping, already on the fringes of orgasm.

And then Hutch's tongue swept through her folds, licking over her entrance and her quivering clitoris. She cried out. Sawyer's mouth crashed over hers, swallowing the sound. Cam ran his tongue in a tight circle around her nipple, lapping as Hutch slowly worked his tongue deep into her wetness.

Hutch nibbled gently, with just enough pressure to drive her mindless.

"You taste so sweet, baby," he murmured, the soft words vibrating over the taut bud.

"You're my sweet tooth, Reggie," Cam whispered. "Who needs sugar when I can taste you?"

Sawyer's tongue delved deep, lapping over hers, exploring her mouth in a sensual pattern. His grip tightened on her knee when her legs began to shake. He pulled upward, bearing her further to Hutch's attentions.

She moaned into Sawyer's mouth.

"That's it, honey," he encouraged. "Take what we're giving you."

Hutch's tongue scraped upward again, then slid downward, tunneling into her pussy, licking and tasting, thrusting inside as he fucked her in sweet strokes.

It was too much. Lightning seized her. Her entire body coiled and drew up in a tight knot. His mouth shot up, and he sucked her clitoris into his mouth.

Tension radiated in rapid streaks through her pussy, clenching every single muscle in a spasming mass. And then she splintered. Came apart in one tumultuous explosion.

She writhed and bucked. Cam nipped sharply at her nipple. Sawyer rained hot kisses on her neck, her shoulder, then down to her other breast. Hutch worked her down from her orgasm with light, long licks until she flinched with each touch.

Hutch pulled away, and Cam left her side. She reached blindly for Cam, but it was Hutch who caught her hand and tucked it gently into his.

Cam moved between her legs, and Hutch reached for her knee as Cam had done, pulling it slowly upward. Cam's hands burrowed under her ass, lifting her slightly as he moved over her.

Her gaze flew to him as he nudged his cock against her still throbbing pussy.

An agonized groan started in her chest and pushed outward as he penetrated her. One long, even thrust and he was seated deep inside her body. She convulsed around him, her tissues still on fire from her release just moments ago.

He clenched his eyes shut and let out a deep breath.

"You feel so good, Reggie darling. So good."

"Love me," she said, her body aching for him.

Hutch bent to lazily work his tongue over her breast. His fingers gripped her leg as he held her for Cam. Then he relaxed his hold and moved his hand underneath her knee to grip the underside of her thigh. He pushed back even further, causing her to tighten more around Cam's cock.

They both groaned.

Sawyer moved his hand as well, pushing her leg further toward her body. Both he and Hutch sucked at her nipples as Cam began to thrust. Slowly at first but then with more speed and power.

"Touch me," she gasped. "Please."

"Where, baby?" Hutch murmured. "Tell us how to please you."

"My clit."

Sawyer looked down hesitantly at where she and Cam were joined, his cock deep in her pussy. He glanced up at Cam and then back at Reggie. And then as if making a decision or coming to terms with the intimacy such an action suggested, he released her leg and slowly slid his hand down to the curls between her legs.

Cam eased back, giving Sawyer room. His finger delved into her soft flesh, finding the little bundle of nerves. He started to stroke just as Cam thrust forward again.

Sawyer tensed but didn't move his hand as Reggie's moans filled the room. Cam put his hand to the leg Sawyer had released and held it in place as he began to move harder and faster.

Each motion rocked Sawyer's hand against her clit. His mouth found hers, hot and breathless. Tongue flashed across tongue.

Cam tightened against her, settled deep and held there for a moment. Full. So full. Hutch's mouth suckled gently at her breast, his tongue darting in and out to lave over the puckered tip. She gasped for breath against Sawyer's mouth, wanting and needing more of him. Of them all.

Slowly, Cam pulled away from her, and she whimpered in protest. She was so close. And then she realized as Cam slipped free of her pussy that he'd already come.

She moved restlessly against Sawyer's hand, wanting her own orgasm, but he too pulled away from her, sliding his hand over her belly, leaving a damp trail over her skin.

"On your knees, baby," Hutch whispered as he moved away from her.

Sawyer helped her sit up and then rolled her until she dug her knees into the mattress. He moved in front of her, on his back and then shimmied underneath her so that her mouth was close to his straining cock. He threaded his hand through her hair, his fingers grasping at her scalp.

There was a shift and a slight jolt, and then Hutch's palms glided over her buttocks and up her back. Then back down again, spreading her as he positioned himself behind her.

As she lowered her head to take Sawyer in her mouth, Hutch slid into her pussy. Gentle. Just one long thrust and he was inside her.

Sawyer groaned, and his hands tightened in her hair as she ran her tongue down the back of his penis. The crown bumped the back of her throat, and she swallowed reflexively.

Hutch stilled for a moment as though giving her time to adjust to Sawyer's demands. She took Sawyer deep, then raised her mouth, allowing his cock to slide nearly free of her lips.

She absorbed his taste, letting it linger on her tongue before swallowing it away. His hips bucked upward, seeking more. And she gave it to him.

Sucking in a deep breath, she took all of him.

Hutch began pumping his hips forward and back, hard thrusts, then shallow ones. He withdrew until he was barely inside the rim of her pussy, paused and then lunged forward again, causing her to gasp around Sawyer's cock.

Sawyer's breath released in a long hiss. She glanced up to see his eyes tightly closed, his head thrown back. He was beautiful. Wild and utterly perfect.

The muscles in his chest and arms rippled as he strained against her, almost as though he were in agony, though his face was lined with the sweetest of pleasures.

She was doing that to him.

In that moment, she realized her power. Not to hurt, but to love. To give what they needed just as she needed what they offered.

She closed her eyes and lowered her mouth again, engulfing him, taking him unreservedly.

The smack of Hutch's flesh against hers filled the room. Wet, sucking noises filled her ears as she took Sawyer with abandon.

Razor-sharp, her orgasm welled, building in her pussy, expanding into her belly, to her legs as they began to shake uncontrollably.

She braced her hands on either side of Sawyer's hips, fighting for the strength to hold on.

She sucked and licked. Tightened her mouth around his thick cock. She wanted to give him as much pleasure as she felt. Was it even possible?

Rising. Higher and higher until she felt light-headed, and yet she still didn't hurtle over the edge.

She couldn't take it. God. It was too much.

Hutch drove deep, angling her hips higher as he rode. His hips ground against her ass. His fingers curled around her hips, holding her as he plunged.

"Reggie. Reggie!"

Sawyer's urgent voice infiltrated the fog surrounding her.

"Honey, I'm going to come. Let go."

She ignored him and sucked him deep, holding him there as she worked her mouth around him.

"Oh God, honey—"

His voice broke off in a strangled gasp.

She squeezed her eyes shut against the pain, the exquisite, unbearable pleasure. Something had to give. She couldn't go any higher.

Faster, harder, Hutch plunged. Relentless. His hips pounded against her ass, the friction of his thrusts sending fire scorching through her pussy.

She screamed around Sawyer's cock then broke off when the

hot splash of his cum filled her mouth. She took him deeper, determined not to deny him anything.

She swallowed then sucked, running her tongue up the back of his cock.

Hutch thrust again, deeper this time, and she whimpered at the dual sensation of him locked in her pussy and Sawyer in her mouth.

She pulsed around Hutch's cock, the sensations almost too raw, too pleasurable to bear.

For a long moment, he remained there while she continued to gently tongue Sawyer's softening erection. And then Hutch eased from her body.

She flinched and moaned as his cock came free.

Finally, she raised her mouth, allowing Sawyer to slip from her lips, and she slumped onto his belly, his cock still pulsing, against the skin of her throat.

Her chest heaved against Sawyer as she tried to catch her breath. Hell, she just wanted to breathe. She was completely and utterly spent.

Sawyer tenderly stroked her hair, smoothing it away from her face.

"Just stay," she whispered. "I can't move. Don't want to move."

"Then stay with me," Sawyer murmured. "As long as you want, honey."

She closed her eyes, content for the moment to remain between Sawyer's legs, her head pillowed on his belly. She felt a gentle kiss on her shoulder and honestly didn't know if it was Cam or Hutch, and she was too tired, too utterly content and sated, to open her eyes and look.

Then a blanket drifted over her body. Sawyer reached down, hooked his hands underneath her arms and dragged her up his body until her head was nestled just under his chin. He tucked the blanket around them both and held her tight against him.

"I love you," she mumbled drowsily.

There was a pause and then right above her ear: "I love you too, honey."

CHAPTER 26

*S*awyer woke with silky curls fluttering across his nose. When he tried to raise his arm to assuage the itch, he brushed across a warm, soft body. Reggie.

Still sprawled across him, limp, sound asleep, her head tucked firmly under his chin.

The sheets were tangled around his feet, and he could still smell the faint scent of sex. He breathed deep, and his dick stirred. Arousal hit him square in the groin. Tightened his balls.

He'd have loved nothing more than to roll her over and have her wake to him balls deep in her pussy. His muscles twitched, and light sweat beaded his forehead.

Instead he gently smoothed down her hair and pressed his lips to her head. He willed himself to calm down. Tried to slake the fierce urge to claim her, raw and urgent.

She was still here. She hadn't run, and he wasn't about to scare her to death and make her bolt again. If it meant he had to temper himself around her, then he could deal.

He looked up when he heard the door open. Hutch stuck his head in. "Good. You're awake. Breakfast in fifteen."

Sawyer grunted in return, and Hutch ducked out.

Reggie stirred against him, sliding sensuously over his body, stretching like a cat and almost purring like one.

Heaven help him. His dick was already stabbing her in the gut, twitching like it was on fire. She rubbed her cheek against his chest, sighed in contentment and then pulled her head up to look at him with sleepy, contented eyes.

They shone a brilliant blue. There was light and sparkle. She looked happy.

When he tried to breathe out, his chest caught and squeezed uncomfortably. He loved Reggie. He didn't mind admitting that. What he didn't love was how damn weak he felt if she so much as looked at him.

He loosened and came apart at the seams. Like a damn puppet cut from his strings. He had no control around her, and he couldn't afford to lose it. Not with her. Never with her.

"What are you thinking?" she asked softly.

He ran a finger from her temple around the curve of her jaw and then to her lips.

"That I'd like to wake up this way every morning."

She smiled. "It does have its appeal, doesn't it?"

She moved her hands down, reaching between them. Her fingers closed around his dick, and he damn near blew a gasket.

Need boiled through his gut. Each fingertip pressed against his erection felt branded on. Ah, fuck it. This wasn't going to work.

He rolled suddenly, his arms around Reggie so he didn't jar her too bad. His cock came to rest between her legs, pressing against the wispy hairs of her pussy.

Instead of spreading her wide and sinking deep into her velvet warmth, he kissed her forehead and pushed himself off her. He didn't look back as he let his feet fall to the floor with a thump. He was afraid he'd find something in her eyes he couldn't resist.

"Sawyer?"

Her voice sounded small and confused. Hell. So much for not looking at her.

He braced himself, making sure he had on his best lazy smile when he turned back to her.

"Hutch popped in a second ago. Said breakfast was about ready. You hungry?"

She frowned slightly. "Sure. I just need to jump in the shower."

He rose, turning so his very obvious hard-on wouldn't be in plain view. She had him so twisted in knots that his dick was reaching for his belly button.

"You take the one in here. I'll grab a shower in the other bathroom," he said, right before he bolted for the door like a man with a pit bull on his ass.

Regina sighed and remained lying on the bed, her gaze fixed on the ceiling. What the hell was running through that man's head was anyone's guess.

He wanted her. There was no doubting that. He'd been the least tactful of the three guys when it came to letting his wants and desires be known. While Cam and Hutch had been somewhat content to back off and give her room, Sawyer had been more in her face, refusing to let her put a barrier between them.

Which was pretty damn ironic when you considered the cement roadblock he'd just constructed.

Twice now she'd made love with all three guys, and twice Sawyer hadn't done more than come in her mouth. Not that she minded, but she wanted him deep inside her body. She wanted her legs wrapped around those muscled thighs as he pumped and strained against her.

A ragged moan escaped as her clit started throbbing in response.

She sighed and rolled over, burying her face in her pillow. This wasn't something that could be addressed between the four of them. This was more personal to her and Sawyer. How the hell did he expect this to work when he spent his time avoiding her during sex?

The tension between them was tangible. She wanted him, and he wanted her. She was no dummy. But she had to crack through whatever moronic thoughts he had in regard to making love to her.

Yeah, he was rough around the edges. He'd always approached most things like a bull in a china closet, but damn it, she knew that. Hell, *everyone* knew that.

There were only a few possibilities for his reluctance. One, he wasn't really into performing in front of two other guys. He'd seemed markedly squeamish about coming into contact with Cam when she'd asked him to touch her. And really, she couldn't blame him for that. It still made her nervous to be making love with more than one guy at a time.

Two, he didn't want her.

Three, he was afraid of hurting her or scaring her.

Since two was obviously not the answer, it had to be one or three. She was betting it was a combination of the two.

She didn't know what to do about one, but she could damn sure do something about three.

With a determined twist to her lips, she rolled out of bed and headed for the shower. Sawyer and Hutch were heading to the job site early, and Cam had phone calls and plans to go over. She had her own agenda, which included checking in with the chief and also with Michael to see if he'd been out to the house to get the security measures she'd asked for in place. She needed it done before they headed back.

The house was quiet. She'd talked to Michael, and his guys were finishing up at the house as they spoke. She'd missed the chief when she called the station but had talked to Jeremy. They wanted Cam, Sawyer and Hutch to come in for questioning as soon as possible, and she didn't relish passing along that information. They'd want to know why, and whether she told them or the chief told them, they'd find out that the case was a lot more complicated.

She curled up on the couch and closed her eyes. A dull ache had inserted itself in her temples.

Once they were questioned, it wouldn't really matter if they knew about the security measures she'd had Michael install at the house. It would probably be easier if she just told them herself rather than let it all come out later.

What she worried about was Hutch's reaction if the finger pointed at some personal vendetta against him. He'd want to take off and put as much distance between him and the others as possible. It was likely what she would do. Hell, she'd tried it herself when it looked as though she might be the focal point of the threat.

She couldn't, wouldn't, let him do that. They had to stay together. Hutch would make himself too easy a target by going off alone. And she wouldn't be able to protect him.

The quiet hum of the ceiling fan lulled her to sleep. The next thing she was aware of was the murmur of voices.

"She's cute all curled up on the couch," Hutch said.

Sawyer made a rude noise. "She'll kick your ass for calling her cute. But yeah, she is kinda sweet looking. You know, when she's asleep and doesn't have her knee in your balls."

She grinned and cracked open one eye. "You two are so full of shit."

Hutch ambled over and dropped a kiss on her forehead. " 'Lo, sleepyhead."

"What time is it?" she asked. A giant yawn nearly cracked her jaw, and she rubbed it as she sat up.

Sawyer glanced at his watch. "Nearly five."

Her eyes popped open wider. "Five in the afternoon? Holy shit, I slept the entire day."

Hutch opened his mouth, but she stilled him with a glare. "Don't say it. Just shut up."

He turned his palms up. "What?"

"He wouldn't dare lecture you about how you need the rest and how it's about time you took it," Sawyer said. Then he grinned. "But I would."

She tossed a small pillow at him, which he caught and lobbed back at her head.

"You guys get everything straightened out at work?"

"Yeah," Hutch said. "Where's Cam anyway? He still holed up in his office?"

She nodded. "Haven't heard a peep out of him all day."

She stretched but didn't get up from the couch. Truth was, she was too damn comfortable to think about moving. But she was hungry. She glanced hopefully up at Hutch.

"Oh, I know that look," he said with a roll of his eyes.

"What?" she asked, mimicking his innocent question.

"You either want food or sugar. I'm guessing, since Cam isn't here giving you the evil eye, that you'll want sugar."

"Mmmm fudge. Or maybe cheesecake." She gave him her best cajoling smile. "Both?"

Sawyer laughed and walked over to plop onto the couch at her feet.

"How about you get *one* while I fix some supper?" Hutch said. "I'm making stir-fry."

"Mmmm." She sighed again. Her stomach growled.

Sawyer frowned. "Didn't Cam feed you anything for lunch?"

"You say that like I'm cattle that has to be fed and watered regularly," she said sourly. "I was asleep all day. If he'd woken me up, you'd be pissed because I need so much rest, remember?"

"You also need to eat." He eyed her speculatively. "You've lost weight, and you didn't have any to spare to begin with."

"Well, I'll be sure to keep my skinny parts from your oh-so-buff ones," she said.

Sawyer blinked in surprise, and she could have killed herself for sounding like a petulant whiney ass moron. God. Was this what sex and emotion turned you into?

Yeah, it bugged her that he was keeping all that lust and desire packaged up, but she wasn't taking it personally. Or was she?

Jesus. She needed to get a grip.

"Reggie . . . ," he began.

Ugh, so not a conversation she was going to have right now. Not with Hutch looking on like he was missing several parts to a puzzle.

She swung her feet over the couch and pushed herself upright. "I'm thirsty," she announced and headed for the kitchen.

The phone rang, but she ignored it. Wasn't her phone. Plus Cam would get it.

She dug around in the fridge and latched onto a beer. Been a while since she'd enjoyed one. But then she frowned and put it back. Hutch wasn't comfortable around alcohol. Then she gritted her teeth and snatched it back up.

It wasn't as though she was going to tie one on, for God's sake.

She closed the fridge, popped the cap on the bottle and took a long drink. Cam walked into the kitchen a second later, phone in hand.

"It's for you," he said, holding it out to her. "Your chief."

"Oh, thanks."

She put her beer down, wiped her hands on her jeans and took the phone.

"Regina, we've made an arrest," the chief said with no preamble.

Her pulse surged. "You have? What happened? Who made the arrest? Did you get a confession?"

"Slow down," the chief said. "One thing at a time. No one made an arrest. Son of a bitch turned himself in. Damnedest thing. Just walked into the station and told Greta that he was who we were looking for. Damn near gave her a heart attack. I wanted to call you so you didn't worry about having the guys in for questioning tomorrow. Looks like we won't need them. At least, not yet."

"Is the evidence solid?" She wanted to ask what the asshole's beef was with her or Hutch, and which one of them he'd been after, but she didn't want to bring it up while the guys were all standing around, hanging on her every word.

"Well, nothing's for certain, but it looks pretty airtight. We got a confession for Misty Thompson's murder. He's been tight-lipped about everything else, but we'll lean on him some more."

"That's great," she murmured. "I can come back to work then, right?"

"I didn't say that," he said dryly. "But yes, when you're feeling better, you can come off leave."

"Sir, I feel just fine."

He made a sound of impatience. "Give it a few more days, Fallon. Let's see how this case shakes out. If everything works out, you can come in on Monday and we'll discuss it."

"That's great. I'll see you on Monday then."

She hung up with a surge of elation. When she glanced up, she saw Cam, Sawyer and Hutch all eyeing her, their postures stiff.

"They made an arrest," she said.

"And?" Cam asked cautiously.

"And what? It means we can breathe easier now." She shrugged even as their scrutiny made her uneasy.

"Don't you think going back Monday is pushing things a bit?" Hutch said.

"I feel fine. Besides, the chief wants me to take it easy, go in on Monday and we'll assess things then. I need to get back anyway. They'll have cleared out the scene at my house, hopefully, and maybe I can start getting cleaned up."

Sawyer's jaw ticked ominously. He bristled and swelled up, his cheeks reddening.

"Tell me you didn't expect that I'd quit my job or hide out forever," she said quietly.

Sawyer stepped forward, his right eye ticking. His lips were pressed so tight together that he looked ready to explode.

"You tell me, Reggie. Are you blowing us off now that you don't need us anymore? Is it going back to the way it's been for the last year where we don't ever see you and you spend all your time hiding behind your job?"

Her mouth fell open. "What's with you? I thought you'd be happy that the freak who's been trying to kill me is behind bars and that maybe we can get on with our lives without worrying that one of us will be blown to hell the next time we get in our car."

Cam moved quickly, ever the calm one, but even he had a hint of anger, of frustration set in the lines around his mouth. He put his hands on her shoulders, and she could feel the tension in his fingers.

"We're very happy that you're safe now, Reggie. You should

know that, if nothing else. I think what Sawyer was trying so delicately to ascertain was whether or not you're going to stay with us."

Her eyes narrowed. "I think that depends on what you're expecting from me. It's not a matter of me *blowing you off now that I no longer need you.* I'll point out that I didn't call you. I didn't ask you to swoop in and play the protector. You did that on your own. So don't make this about me asking for something and then shoving you away when I don't need what I asked for anymore."

Hutch swore rather crudely, and Sawyer turned and stalked away.

Cam released her arm. "What have we asked you for, Reggie? What have we ever asked you for other than to be with us, to stop running from us?"

"I won't quit my job," she said stubbornly. "Not even for you."

Cam relaxed then dragged a hand through his hair. "No one's asked you to quit, love. You're jumping the gun, don't you think?"

She shifted uncomfortably.

"We were focusing on the part where you said you wanted to get back to your house, get back to your job. Now, to us that sounds a lot like you don't need us or want to be with us now that there's no reason to be."

"I—I said I would stay."

"Yes, but for how long?" Hutch spoke up. He moved toward her for the first time, his green eyes sparking like firecrackers.

Shit. She hadn't expected things to be resolved this quickly. She'd wanted time with them to figure out if this was something that would ever work. Now she was faced with a decision she wasn't sure she was ready to make.

"I don't know," she said in frustration. "It's not like you made it sound. I only meant that it was okay for me to go back and pick up the pieces. My house is trashed. I don't have a car. I'm out of a job temporarily. My entire life is falling apart around me, so you'll have to forgive me if I sounded a little eager to get all that back on track. It wasn't personal. I know I made it look like it was all too easy for me to have a one-night stand then go on my merry way, but I'm not that callous. I wouldn't just leave and pretend nothing has happened. Not this time."

She balled up her fingers into fists then shoved her way past both Cam and Hutch.

"Reggie, baby, wait," Hutch called.

She ignored him and kept walking. She heard Cam call him back. Yeah, he'd see the wisdom in giving her space right now before she went postal. It was another way in which she and Sawyer were so much alike. Calm and centered they weren't.

She flung open the door to the patio and stepped outside then slammed it shut behind her.

CHAPTER 27

*C*am watched as Reggie thrust her hand into her hair, pulled it out then dug back in. Her other hand was balled tightly at her side, and she paced back and forth. He could see her lips moving as she muttered to herself.

Yeah, she was agitated.

He wanted to go out there and just hold her, tell her it would be all right, but hell, who was he kidding? He didn't know if it would. That scared him shitless.

"What the fuck are we going to do, Cam?" Hutch asked.

Cam glanced sideways at him then turned away from the door that Reggie had stormed out of.

"Christ, I don't know, Hutch. Give her some space?"

"We tried that. Didn't work."

"Pushing her won't help. We know that."

"I don't want her to go back to that goddamn job," Hutch said tersely.

Cam sighed and went over to the couch. No sign of Sawyer,

but then he'd have to calm down before he reappeared. He'd looked to be close to bursting a blood vessel.

"I don't want her to either, man. But that's not our call. It can't be." He glanced up at Hutch, who'd walked around to flop into the recliner. "Just like we knew we'd never ask her to choose between us, we can't ask her to now choose between us and her job."

"What if she walks away again?"

There was a healthy dose of fear in Hutch's voice. It was the same fear that was close to gutting Cam.

"We can't make her stay with us," Cam said quietly. "All we can do is show her how much we love her and try and convince her that it'll work. We knew it wouldn't be easy."

Hutch threw his head back and stared at the ceiling. "I don't get her wanting to be a cop. Sometimes I think . . . sometimes I think she did it just to get back at her old man, you know? And if that's the case, it's not where she needs to be. How happy could it make her?"

Cam leaned forward. "Are you happy with your life, Hutch? Are you happy with our business? Reggie aside, are you satisfied?"

Hutch rocked his head forward to look at Cam. "You know I am."

"You can't tell me you didn't set out to make something of yourself to piss off all the people who thought we wouldn't amount to shit. Reggie's old man being one of them. Does that make you any less happy with the results because of the motivation behind your actions?"

Hutch screwed his face in annoyance. "Good grief, Cam, cut the analytical bullshit out. I swear you give me a headache with all your philosophizing."

Cam chuckled. "You know I'm right. Regardless of why Reggie chose the profession she did, she's happy. She's tough. She can handle it. Do I like it? Hell no. In a perfect world, she wouldn't work at all. She'd stay home. In our home. And we'd take care of her. But can you honestly ever see Reggie going for that? She'd make eunuchs of us all."

Hutch's face eased into a grin. "Yeah, I hear you." His gaze skirted toward the door. "So what do we do?"

Cam followed his stare to see Reggie still pacing out on the patio. "We chill. Let her work this out herself. And we don't issue ultimatums or even make it look like we're handing her one."

"But she's pissed."

"Yeah, so? How many times have we pissed her off over the years?"

"Yeah, but a lot more is at stake this time," Hutch said.

"I won't argue that, but Hutch, we're not entering utopia here. There's going to be arguments. Hell, with Sawyer and Reggie in the same house? You're talking two bulldogs who don't know the meaning of the words 'back down.' You can't let it get to you."

He leaned further toward Hutch. "And I'll tell you something else. You can't worry about my relationship with Reggie or Sawyer's with Reggie. You can't make it right for the rest of us. We'll fuck up, but you can't go around picking up the pieces of other people's mistakes."

"Yeah, I got you," Hutch said in a low voice. "I just don't want to screw this up, Cam. I don't think we'll get another chance."

Cam swallowed against the panic caused by Hutch's resigned statement. It mirrored his own thoughts too precisely. No, he didn't think they'd get another chance if they screwed this one up. But damn it, Reggie had to be willing to meet them halfway.

Sawyer ran through another repetition of curls before he finally set the weights down. His chest heaved with exertion and sweat soaked his clothing. Work out. Yeah, this was supposed to help burn off the frustration, right?

All he'd gotten for his time was a good case of exhaustion and a need for a shower. Two of them.

He headed for the locker room to scrub the dozen layers of sweat from his body.

He shouldn't have popped off at Reggie like that, but damn, she made it hard. Stubborn as a pack mule. He ought to know. They were two peas in a pod. Which is why they butted heads so damn much.

He rested his arm on the shower wall and laid his forehead against his wrist as the water sluiced over his back. Reggie going back to her job. Her house. Her life. Without them?

What about her promise to stay? To try and work things out? Or had they just been a temporary diversion?

No, Reggie wasn't like that. She might be scared to death, but she wouldn't use them like that. Not intentionally.

He scrubbed his body and rinsed then stepped out of the shower to towel off. His muscles ached like a son of a bitch, but at least he was a little calmer now.

Bolting like that was probably a bad idea, but if he would've stayed, things would have just gotten tenser. They didn't need more tension. There was already enough of that simmering between them all.

He didn't know whether to kiss her senseless or kick her ass. Both options held a certain appeal.

Stubborn, ornery, beautiful woman. Mouthy, sassy, sexy-as-hell wench.

What would he ever do without her?

He didn't want to find out. He'd already spent way too much time away from her. Not by his choice, but at some point, it all had to end. Whether they decided to give it a go or they said to hell with it and went their separate ways.

As much as the latter tore a hole in his gut, he couldn't go on this way, hoping and reaching for something that might never happen.

"Mountain out of a molehill," he muttered as he climbed into his truck.

It was one frickin' argument. Not the end of the world. The day he and Reggie stopped bickering would be the day they buried one of them. Yeah, he'd overreacted, but so had she. Not that it was anything new.

He drove home knowing he'd have to eat some serious crow, but then wasn't that what life with a woman was all about? He grinned. Men humbled themselves all the time at the altar of woman. If they didn't, the population would have died off a long time ago.

When he pulled into the driveway, he noticed the house was mostly dark. Probably all went to bed without him. He tried real hard not to be jealous of the fact that Reggie was probably all tucked in between Cam and Hutch or that they'd probably already screwed her six ways to Sunday.

"Down, boy," he muttered as his dick surged to attention.

But when he walked into the darkened living room, he saw that Reggie wasn't upstairs with Cam and Hutch. She was curled up on the couch asleep. In just a T-shirt. Had she waited up for him?

All smart-ass remarks aside, the idea that his woman had waited up for him sent a bolt of pure pleasure through his veins. Humbling himself at her feet didn't seem quite as bad as it had a few minutes ago.

He dropped his gym bag on the floor and walked over to where she lay.

He knelt beside her and trailed a finger down her arm. Little goose bumps puckered and jumped up on her skin in the wake of his touch.

She stirred and did one of those little sleepy snuggles that he loved so much. Of course he liked it a lot better when she'd done it on top of him. But damn, she looked so darn cute. Sweet even.

Well she damn sure wasn't going to sleep down here, and if Cam and Hutch had been dumb enough to let her sleep alone, that was their problem. He was taking her to bed with him.

He slid his arms underneath her and hoisted her up. She landed against his chest with a soft thud, and he stood there a moment, just enjoying the feel of her warm body all tucked up against his.

Yeah, life was good. Most of the time. At least until she woke up and handed him his ass. Until then he'd get as much enjoyment out of the situation as he could and practice up on his looks of humility.

He mounted the stairs and took her to his room. Shouldering his way in, he gave the door a kick to close it behind him.

He laid her on the bed and pulled the unmade covers over her hips. Then he stepped back and hastily shrugged out of his jeans and shirt.

When he crawled in beside her and cuddled up to her back, she stirred and turned over, snuggling into his arms.

"Sawyer?" she asked sleepily.

"Yeah, honey?"

"I'm sorry for getting all pissy with you."

He smiled. "Me too."

She nuzzled her face into his neck, and he sighed in contentment.

"Reggie?"

"Yeah?"

"Are you going to stay?"

There was a brief pause, and he felt a little hiccup in her breathing. He found himself holding his own breath as he waited for her to answer.

"Yeah, Sawyer. I'm staying."

Relief was so strong that it damn near blurred his vision.

"Good. I'm glad."

He pulled her closer against him and wrapped himself around her tight. He hooked his leg over hers, drawing her further in line with his body.

"You just try keeping those skinny parts away from me," he muttered.

He felt her smile against his chest.

CHAPTER 28

*W*hen Regina woke, the bed was empty. She frowned. So much for waking up in Sawyer's arms. She yawned and stretched then sniffed. Food. She was starving.

She got out of bed and stumbled toward the shower. She hoped to hell Sawyer still wasn't pissed. There was a vague memory of him carrying her up the stairs, and she definitely remembered apologizing and then snuggling into his arms. Everything else was kind of a blur.

Oh well, it wasn't the first time they'd gotten into each other's face, and it wouldn't be the last.

An uncomfortable sensation settled into her stomach. This time, though . . . this time it mattered. Really mattered. It was more than two friends bickering.

She sighed and stepped into the shower. She soaped and rinsed her hair then turned to reach for the body wash.

A warm, naked body melded to her back. One hand slid around her middle, pressed to her stomach. The other circled her throat, ran up to her jaw and turned her face back and upward to meet seeking lips.

"Good morning, Cam," she murmured.

His heavy erection burned the small of her back. The hand at her stomach slid downward, between her legs, dipping into the wet curls, to the throbbing flesh hidden underneath.

Wordlessly, he turned her around to face him then backed her against the shower seat in the corner. She sank onto the wet surface, the spray from the showerhead bouncing off the walls and spritzing her body.

He reached for the showerhead, released it from the mount and then knelt in front of her.

This silent, mysterious side of Cam was seriously sexy stuff. Not that he wasn't always somewhat quiet and serious, but this brooding thing was getting her worked up.

His hair hung wetly down his neck, carelessly strung forward over his shoulders. There was fire in his eyes. And determination.

He nudged her knees apart then hoisted one ankle upward until her heel rested on the ledge she sat on. He picked the other one up and did the same.

She was spread out before him, her pussy open and accessible. She was so damn turned on that she could have come with the slightest touch.

As if reading her thoughts, he reached with one finger and gently rolled it over her clit. Fire ignited and blazed over her. He touched one more time, and her orgasm flared and burst like a short fuse.

She gasped as her pussy pulsed with sharp, agonizing bursts. That had to be a record.

He gripped the shower head tighter in one hand and adjusted

the spray to pulse setting. Her eyes widened when she realized what he was going to do. Oh hell, this was going to be good.

Using two fingers to part her folds, he brought his other hand up and swooshed the thin stream of water over her still quivering clitoris.

She arched up as a spasm worked over her pelvis.

"Cam!" she cried out.

He smiled. Silent bastard. Then he aimed the spray back over the taut bud and worked gently up and down in tiny increments.

Wave after wave of blissful, agonizing tension rolled through her. Tighter and tighter she wound, coiling viciously. Could she have another orgasm so fast?

The answer was yes.

He kept the spray steady, and every muscle in her groin screamed for mercy. She worked higher and higher, nearing the breaking point but never quiet toppling over.

"Cam, please! It hurts!"

He chuckled. "Don't fight it, love. Let it happen."

Her legs shook spasmodically. She braced her hands against the seat, threw back her head and screamed as another orgasm lashed through her body.

He dropped the nozzle. He surged to his feet and yanked her into his arms. He hoisted her up then pressed her back to the shower wall.

"Wrap your legs around me," he rasped.

He reached between them, positioned his cock and thrust upward. He rocked her against the wall as he drove deep.

The spray from the discarded shower head arched upward, bathing Cam's back with warm water. It rolled up and over his shoulders, dripping between them and down to where he was joined with her.

He cupped his hands over her ass, squeezing and spreading as he hammered forward again. He was wild and insatiable. She hung on for dear life, her hands locked behind his neck and her ankles locked at the small of his back.

Each stab was like static electricity. Almost painful as he dragged his cock over swollen, sensitive flesh.

And then he was taking her frantically. Over and over. Desperate. Frenzied.

His lips sucked at her neck, and her breasts were flattened against his heaving chest.

Mine. His every action, his every movement screamed it. He was staking his claim. *Mine.* His.

She closed her eyes, nearly exhausted from the two orgasms she'd already experienced. And yet another called to her, pulled sweetly at her, slower and less intense than the others.

He coaxed her flesh, teasing and intoxicating. Each pull of his cock, each stab forward.

"Yours," she whispered.

"Mine," he agreed.

He strained forward and every muscle in his body stiffened. He yelled hoarsely. Her name spilled from his lips in an agonized groan as he poured himself into her.

Even when he began to soften, he stroked in and out of her, gentle, less demanding. When he finally slipped out of her body, he backed up a step and gathered her in his arms.

Finally he let her slide down his body until her feet met the shower floor. He reached down for the showerhead and quickly rinsed them both off before replacing it above.

"I can't even walk," she said wryly. "I think you've crippled me, Cam."

He smiled and kissed her, his lips lingering over hers in a sensual dance.

"Then I guess I'll just have to carry you out and dry you off. I don't mind taking care of you in the least."

She sighed and let him do his thing. The entire world was a nice sparkly haze after three orgasms. Who needed drugs? This had to be the sweetest high you could experience.

"Does this mean I'm forgiven for last night?" she managed to say as he rubbed her down with a towel.

He straightened and dropped the towel on the counter.

"There's nothing to forgive, Reggie darling."

He kissed her then pulled her out of the bathroom. He swatted her playfully on the behind before heading toward the door. "I'm sure Hutch has breakfast ready by now. Get dressed and come on down. We're planning to leave right after we eat."

She got dressed with a smile, letting contentment . . . and peace . . . roll over her, bathing her with their warm, heady glow.

When she was done, she hurried down the steps, eager to start the day.

Sawyer was sitting at the bar, wolfing down an omelet, and Hutch was standing at the stove. Wanting to be at ease with Hutch, she walked over and wrapped her arms around his waist, burrowing her head into his back.

He turned with a smile and wrapped his arms around her, holding the spatula away from her back with one hand.

"Good morning," he murmured.

She leaned up to kiss him, letting her body melt into his. She loved how they fit, how he accommodated her with such ease.

"Still mad at me?" she murmured against his lips.

He leaned against the oven, pulling her with him.

"I love you," he said simply.

"Then feed me," she said with a grin.

He dropped another kiss on her upturned mouth then shoved her toward the bar. "Sit and I'll dish it up in two minutes."

She headed around to sit by Sawyer just as Cam walked into the kitchen. He strolled over to take his place on her other side with a lazy contentment that she herself felt.

He gave her a loving smile before sliding onto the stool next to her.

"Noisy shower this morning," Sawyer observed, his mouth full of eggs.

She laughed and managed not to blush. But she reached over and squeezed his knee. He grinned and glanced sideways at her.

Yeah, things were okay again. The sense of rightness settled more firmly into her chest. And with it came hope. Fluttering, budding. Like a flower unfurling in the spring.

Hope and acceptance. New, but strong.

CHAPTER 29

*T*hey were up to something. There was an air of expectancy as they turned into the dirt road leading up to the house. That and the smug grin that adorned each of their faces.

Regina viewed them suspiciously from her perch in the backseat of Cam's SUV. They topped the hill, and the three guys looked toward the house. She followed their gaze to the vehicles parked outside the garage.

To her astonishment, there beside Hutch's truck was a shiny, silver RAV4. Her mouth dropped open as the guys' smiles got even broader.

Cam pulled to a stop but she just sat there staring at the brand-new Toyota sparkling in the sun. Dealer tags still on it.

Then she turned to them and gaped.

"Well, get out and look at it," Hutch said beside her.

She scrambled out of the backseat and slammed the door behind her.

"You didn't," she said. "You freaking didn't!"

"We did," Sawyer said smugly.

"Oh my God," she breathed. "Holy hell."

She threw open the driver's door and inhaled the new car smell. The key dangled from the ignition and on the seat was a pile of papers including the manual. She yanked up the top sheet, the title, and saw her name typed in the space for the owner.

She let out a squeal of delight and then turned and promptly pounced. Cam was closest, and she launched herself into his arms.

He laughed as she peppered him with kisses. She wrapped her arms around his neck and squeezed mercilessly. Then she tackled Hutch, who stood there grinning like a loon.

Sawyer was standing away from the other two, and when she started for him, he backed away, hands outstretched to ward her off.

She took a running leap and landed smack in the middle of his chest. He stumbled and then fell, his arms around her. They landed on the ground, her on top, him flat on his back.

He let out a groan about the time she smothered him with a flurry of kisses.

"Are you trying to kill me?" he complained. But his grin told her he didn't mind at all that he was lying in the dirt with her perched atop him like a mad hatter.

"I love it!" she shrieked. "Oh my God, I can't believe you guys."

She kissed him square in the forehead as his hands settled comfortably at her hips, his grip possessive.

Cam and Hutch were laughing in earnest, and Sawyer shot them both glares.

"Felled by a woman half his size," Cam snickered.

"You could get off me and go look at your car," Sawyer complained.

She scrambled off, leaving him to pick himself up. She all but danced around the vehicle, inspecting the trim, the paint job and all the nooks and crannies in between.

"How on earth did you get it here?" she asked.

Hutch rolled his eyes. "Uhm, we called the dealer, told him what we wanted and where we wanted it and voilà."

She sniffed and rubbed her eyes with the back of her hand.

"Ah shit, Reggie, don't start crying for the love of God," Sawyer muttered. "We can take it back."

She shot him a glare. "You don't touch my car. Oh my God, *my* car." She wanted to pounce on them all over again, and they must have seen it coming because they all backed hastily toward the house.

She rolled her eyes then reached in to grab the keys before following them up to the porch.

"So you like it?" Cam asked.

"Like it? I love it! I was so upset that my other one got destroyed. I saved for that car forever." Then she frowned as she realized that unlike her other vehicle, she hadn't paid for this one. They had. They hadn't even waited to see if her insurance covered the old one.

This time Sawyer rolled his eyes. "You're as easy to read as a book, Reggie. Don't even say it. This is a gift. It stays."

"Yeah but this isn't something like flowers or chocolate. It's a freaking car."

Cam threw an arm over her shoulders as he herded her into the living room. "Yeah, but we knew you'd appreciate this more than flowers or chocolate. Besides, you're not a flower kind of girl."

She grinned. "You know me so well." Then she turned to hug him again. "Thank you. I love it."

He hugged her back. "You're quite welcome."

She stood back while Sawyer and Hutch carried in the few bags they'd brought to Houston.

"I'm going to head to the grocery store since we're about out of food, and I never made it the other day. You want to go with?" Hutch asked Regina.

"Uh, no. I think I'll stick around here." All the better to catch Sawyer by himself hopefully. Maybe then she could remove whatever stick he had up his ass when it came to making love to her.

"I'll be back with food later then," he said and dropped a kiss on her cheek as he headed for the door.

Regina gripped her bag and headed for the stairs. She'd unpack, and if she knew Cam, he'd hole up in the office and work for a while. Which left Sawyer to her mercy. An evil grin worked over her face. She rather liked that image.

It was sick that she was so nervous, but the butterflies had been doing cartwheels in her stomach since Hutch left.

Just go down there and seduce him, you weenie.

Yeah, piece of cake. Not.

He wanted her. He vibrated with desire every time she came within a foot of him. But he kept all that need tightly leashed.

Well, she was about to tap into the beast. Set him free and hope he ravished her.

With a grin, she headed for the stairs to look for Sawyer and found him in the kitchen.

He was making a halfhearted attempt to unload the dishwasher. Part of the deal. Hutch cooked. Sawyer and Cam split cleanup duty.

She snuck up behind him, slid her arms around his waist and squeezed. He tensed for a moment then relaxed and cupped his hands over hers.

"You coming to help with the dishes?" he asked.

She snorted. "Ah, no thanks. I had something different in mind."

He rotated in her arms, leaned back against the sink and eyed her curiously. "Do tell."

"I wanted to talk to you," she said.

Amusement centered in his eyes, and the corner of his mouth lifted. "Is this one of those girl talks that make all men quake with fear?"

She shrugged. "Could be."

His face fell. "Ah hell. It is."

"Pick me up," she said.

Surprise flashed in his eyes. "Huh?"

She started to climb up his chest, grabbing at the back of his neck for leverage. "Pick me up."

He slid his hands underneath her legs and boosted her up until she straddled his hips. Her hands hung loosely at his neck, and he eyed her warily.

"Much better. Now I can look down at you," she said mischievously.

"What did I do?" he asked in resignation. "Whatever it is, I apologize. I was wrong. Wrong, wrong, wrong, and you were right, right, right."

Despite the actual gravity of her proposed topic, she laughed. "You're so full of shit. You don't even know what I want to talk about."

"Doesn't matter," he said solemnly. "Men as a species are wrong. We're better off admitting it up front, taking our punishment and then hoping for good makeup sex."

"Hmm, well actually sex is what I want to talk about. Still interested in being wrong?"

He perked up. "Sex? Um, sure. If me being wrong gets me sex, then sign me up."

She frowned. "That's just it, Sawyer. I get the impression you don't want sex . . . with me."

The look of absolute *what the fuck* on his face cheered her considerably. He looked so stunned by her statement that he went slack against her, and she nearly slid down his thighs. She scrambled upward, and he caught her behind again, hoisting her back up.

"Not want sex with you?" he said in a strangled voice. "Jesus, Mary and Joseph, woman, where did you get that dumbass idea?"

She gazed down at him, all attempts at teasing gone. "Why do you hold back with me, Sawyer? Don't you think I'd figure it out? You haven't exactly been subtle. I know you. Maybe better than anyone. The two times you've made love to me, you haven't once actually penetrated me. Well, unless you count a blowjob."

He stiffened at her bluntness. Unease crawled across his face, and this time he actually did let her slide down his legs until she was back on the floor, standing in front of him again.

"You think . . . you think it's because I don't want you?" he asked hoarsely.

She shrugged. "Honestly? No, I don't think that, though it's easy to see why I would. What I really think is that you're holding back out of some misguided fear of hurting me."

There was a flash of acknowledgment in his eyes that told her she was definitely on the right track.

Sawyer sighed and tried to turn away, but she nailed him in the chest with her finger.

"Oh, no you don't. You're not dodging this one, buddy." She grabbed handfuls of his T-shirt and pulled tight. "Talk to me, Sawyer. Please?"

Troubled blue eyes stared back at her. Regret. Fear. Shining like beacons. Her stomach knotted.

"It's not because I don't want you, honey," he said gruffly. "Hell, I'm a walking hard-on around you."

"Then why?" she prompted.

He looked down. "I'm not like the others, Reggie. Not smooth like Cam. He's all cultured and *sensitive*."

"You make him sound like a pussy," she said dryly.

Sawyer ignored her. "And Hutch is all lovey and tender. Shit, I wouldn't be surprised if you were his first and only."

"Second," she corrected.

"I rest my case."

"But Sawyer, what does that have to do with anything? So Hutch hasn't slept around much. So Cam prefers the Learning Channel to sports. We're not all joined at the hip. It's okay to be different."

"Because you deserve better. I've slept with a hell of a lot of women. I'm not proud of it, but I'm not torturing myself over it either."

"You're not?" she asked pointedly.

"Let me finish," he said impatiently. "I like sex. I like sex without commitment. I've had sex with a lot of women who were on the same page as me. But you're different, Reggie. With you . . . it matters."

He cupped his hands over her shoulders and stared earnestly into her eyes.

"You deserve to be made love to." He shifted uncomfortably and relaxed his hold on her shoulders. "I'm not good at that."

"So what are you good at?" she asked calmly. "Are you saying you suck at sex?"

She had to work to suppress the grin when he bristled. There was only so far you could push the fragile male ego.

"I do *not* suck at sex," he growled. "What I suck at is the gentle lovemaking stuff."

"So what are you good at? The hot, sweaty, make-you-scream type sex?"

His eyes glittered. "Yes."

"And if I want hot, sweaty, make-you-scream sex?"

"Hot, sweaty, *kinky*, make-you-scream sex, Reggie. I like it hard and rough."

"And if I want it that way?" she prompted again.

His eyes narrowed with a predatory gleam. "What if I told you that I fantasize about bending you over the couch and taking you from behind. Hard. Fast. That I'm not satisfied with just taking your mouth or your pussy. That I want all of you."

Her breathing shallowed and came in rapid spurts as warmth seared through her body. Her nipples beaded and tightened painfully, spearing the thin T-shirt she wore.

"And what if I told you that what I want is you? Not a watered down version, Sawyer. You. All of you. I don't want you to change. I love you. I don't want a pale imitation of Cam or Hutch."

His mouth crashed down on hers, his tongue plunging deep. His teeth nipped at her full bottom lip, and he sucked it deeper into his mouth.

Wild. God. He felt so wild. Unleashed. All that power simmering, just waiting to boil out.

He tore at her clothes, and she tore at his. Hot, breathless, they went after each other like starving animals. He yanked at her shirt, ripping it over her head. It went sailing across the kitchen.

They made short work of the clothes, and then they were pressed tight together.

He hoisted her up his body again until she straddled him as she had before. He tilted his head back as she claimed his mouth. Savage. It was all she could think as she swooped down like a bird of prey.

He brought out the animal in her. He made her wild, just as she imagined he was. How long she had waited to tap into that tightly held control.

It was a dark, heady sensation. Frightened? She was scared to death. In a thrilling, oh-my-God-I-can't-wait way.

She devoured his mouth. If he thought he was the only one with wild, kinky fantasies, he was *so* in for a surprise.

His hands gripped her hips, hauling her close, cradling her pussy against his rigid erection. Her swollen folds slid up and down the back of his cock. His heat scorched her. Seared her pussy and sent tremors racing through her core.

"I want you," she whispered. "You, Sawyer. The real you. That's the man I love."

He groaned against her lips. "You're going to be the death of me, Reggie."

He pushed off the counter and stalked across the kitchen, his arms around her, holding her tight against his chest. She bounced with each stride, and his cock bumped tantalizing close to her entrance. Just a little bit higher and she could sheathe him. She groaned when, instead, she slid farther down, and the tip of his penis brushed across her lower abdomen.

When they reached the living room, he put her down abruptly, her feet colliding with the floor. He closed in fast, not giving her a chance to breathe. She backed as he stalked. Her breasts brushed against his chest.

A ripple of awareness shuddered through her. Her nipples, already painfully taut, twitched and stabbed forward.

She felt hunted. And dear God, but she'd never been as turned on as she was right now. Sawyer was one big ball of quivering testosterone.

Muscles bulging, his eyes simmering with the promise of exactly what he was going to do to her, he came to a halt when she bumped into the back of the couch.

A slow, predatory smile curved his mouth. His eyes glinted with satisfaction.

"You remember my fantasy," he said in a near growl that sent shivers racing down her spine.

Oh holy hell, she hoped he was serious about bending her over the couch and fucking her senseless.

She gulped and nodded. Her gaze drifted down to his groin. His cock, thick and ruddy, jutted upward from the triangle of coarse hair.

She licked her lips as she remembered the taste and feel of him on her tongue, how he'd spilled into her mouth. Only this time he wasn't going in her mouth.

Sweet Lord she'd waited forever for this.

He plucked her off her feet, twisted her in his hands so she faced away from him, and bent her over the back of the couch. She put her hands out to catch herself on the soft cushions as her feet dangled down the back.

Heaven help her, her ass was stuck in the air.

His hands came down on her back. Heated palms. She flinched as he slid them down her spine to her ass, cupping and kneading each cheek.

There was no buildup, no teasing. He spread her, she felt the bump of his cock against her entrance, and then he thrust into her.

She lurched forward, her eyes flying open, her mouth open in a silent scream. Delicious pleasure ripped through her pussy as she convulsed around him, the tissues grabbing and sucking hungrily at him.

His hard belly pressed against her buttocks as he strained, pushed, rode her. His hands grasped at her hips, pulling her back, meeting his forward thrusts with edgy desperation.

She had no chance to process, to filter the barrage of sensations. His deep penetration, the angle of his cock, her release flashed over her with lightning precision, tightening and squeezing every nerve ending.

His pelvis slapped forcefully against her ass. She was stretched tight around him, and each thrust sent a spasm coursing through her pussy.

"Give it to me, Reggie. Come."

His fingers dug into her skin as he rocked against her. He paused then slowly withdrew, dragging his cock across her engorged flesh. He was nearly out of her, the head of his penis rimming her entrance when he suddenly lunged forward again, sinking deeper than before.

She threw her head back and yelled as she came apart in his hands. He pounded furiously against her, and she went liquid around him. Her vision blurred. Her body pulsed and contracted. Everything went fuzzy and she lost all sense of time and place. All she could do was feel.

Feel.

Sawyer's big body covered her. He heaved against her back, dragging breaths in and out of his mouth. Then his lips moved sensuously up the nape of her neck.

"I'll be right back," he murmured.

Back? Where the hell was he going? She started to push herself upright, but he planted a hand in the middle of her back and held her in place.

"Oh no," he said in a soft voice. "You don't move."

She shuddered but remained where she was.

He reached for her hands, pulling them up and around to the small of her back. Then he leaned over so his mouth was close to her ear.

"Does this hurt you? Your ribs?"

She shook her head vigorously. Ribs? Did she even have ribs? The only thing she was aware of was her pulsing vagina. And the fact that she wanted him again. Now.

He gathered her hands closer together and then he wrapped

something around her wrists. He twisted and rotated the material, and she realized he was tying her hands with her underwear, or rather doing an intricate figure eight to secure her wrists together.

"Hey," she protested. "What the hell are you doing?" She pulled against the material but her hands remained tightly bound together.

His hand skated up her back to her neck and then into her hair. He gathered the strands in his fist and pulled upward with a gentleness that didn't denounce the authority of his grip.

"My way, Reggie. You asked and now you're getting. Just say the word, and we'll quit."

"Kiss my ass," she muttered.

He laughed then bent over and pressed a tender kiss to her left ass cheek. "I'll take that as *I'm shutting up now. Please fuck me, Sawyer.*"

"Bastard."

She closed her eyes and imagined what she looked like. Perched over the back of the couch, her ass in the air, feet dangling off the floor, her wrists bound together with her own panties. She shivered and closed her eyes.

His footsteps retreated, and she heard him go up the stairs. She lay there trying to catch her breath, tried to collect her scattered thoughts. What the hell was he doing?

A few minutes later, she heard the slight sound of his bare feet padding across the wood floor. No preamble. His work-roughened hands slid across her ass, spread her, and he sank inside her again.

Oh damn, he was hard already. And she was still shaking from her orgasm. Each thrust was sensitive to the point of pain as his thick cock pushed and pulled over swollen nerves.

"You feel so damn good," he rasped. "I'm like some two-minute teenager around you, Reggie. I lose it as soon as I touch you."

She smiled and closed her eyes again as he sank gently into her welcoming body. Forward. So slow. Back. With exquisite tenderness. Who said he sucked at the slow, sweet lovemaking?

Then he pulled out of her, and she squirmed in protest. His light chuckle brushed over her ears, and then she heard a squirting sound.

One thumb, slick with gel, rubbed over the seam of her ass. She flinched and gasped as he paused right over the tight entrance and pressed his thumb inward. Her body protested the invasion at first, holding resistance, but he persisted and with a light pop, his thumb sank inside.

Her mind buzzed. Her breaths came in rapid hiccups, and heat raced through her body, bathing it in a warm flush. Her breasts tingled, the nipples beading and straining.

He gently worked his thumb in and out of the tight hole as he smeared lubricant on the outside and the inside. She knew what he wanted, and if she could collect her senses long enough, she'd be begging for him to take her.

A shudder rolled up her spine when he pulled his finger away. There was barely a moment before it was replaced with the blunt head of his cock. Swollen and hard, it pressed against the small ring.

There was a battle as her body fought to keep him out, and he refused to back down. With one hand pressed to the small of her back, holding her in place, he held his cock to her anus with his other hand. His knuckles brushed against her cheek as he pushed forward.

Her body opened around him, stretching with fiery torment. Her stomach clenched, her pussy quivered, and her entire ass was on fire.

And then he slid forward as her body gave way and surrendered.

Her head lurched up and she cried out. Oh dear God it hurt. Just when she was about to tell him to get the pole he'd just thrust up her ass out, the burn gave way to an indescribable sensation.

There weren't words. He withdrew slowly and the relief was overwhelming. But then he thrust forward again, and she bit her lip as the burning returned.

"Relax," he murmured. "Give in, Reggie."

She sucked in air through her nose and clenched her jaw against the urge to scream. Not in pain. No, it hurt but in a good, good way. How twisted was that?

She moaned as he withdrew, allowing the head of his cock to further stretch the entrance. Then he lunged forward, burying himself to the balls in her ass.

His fingers curled around her bound wrists, and he held her as he rode her relentlessly, his balls slapping against her pussy with each pump of his hips.

Just when she thought he would come, he slowed his pace, pulling out and letting the head of his cock rest against her spasming hole.

She felt it quiver and begin to close, regaining its normal shape. And then he tucked his cock against the ring and thrust forward again, reopening her mercilessly.

"Goddamn it, Sawyer!"

He paused, his balls sandwiched against her pussy, his cock as deep as he could work it into her ass.

"Hurt, Reggie?"

"Yes, no, yes, damn it."

He chuckled. "Hurts good, doesn't it?"

"I'll get you for this," she muttered. "I swear I will."

"Just remember you asked for it, honey. I'm only giving you what you demanded."

He slid back and thrust again and she moaned.

"It's damn hard to work with you two making so much noise," Cam said dryly.

Regina's head popped up, and she saw Cam leaning against the doorway to the living room. There was no disguising the bulge between his legs or the fact that his gaze was fastened on Sawyer's cock sliding back and forth into her ass.

"Get off on looking at another man's dick?" she snarled as embarrassment heated her cheeks.

Cam smiled lazily. "I do when it's stuck up your sweet little ass, Reggie darling. I believe it's called dick envy. And right now I envy his."

"You could do something about that mouth of hers," Sawyer offered.

"Mmmm, I think you're right."

Cam pushed off the doorway and sauntered over to the couch. Regina's heart pounded even as Sawyer pounded her ass. The rasp of Cam's zipper echoed through the room.

He didn't bother getting undressed. He merely reached in and pulled his cock out of his jeans. He threaded one hand through her hair and pulled upward so that her mouth was just inches from his erection.

And Sawyer thought Cam was all cultured and sensitive? Right now he resembled a caveman. All he-man and alpha, commanding his woman to pleasure him.

It pissed her off and thrilled the hell out of her all at the same time.

He positioned himself on his knees on the couch, adjusted her head to the proper level and then rubbed his cock over her lips.

"Open up, love," he ordered.

"I ought to bite it off," she said sullenly.

Sawyer smacked her ass with the palm of his hand. The sound ricocheted like gunfire through the room. She jumped and let out a cry of surprise as heat raced across her ass.

"Be nice, baby doll. Men don't like to have their dicks threatened."

Holy hell in a bucket. She was so close to coming. She should turn around and kick his ass for spanking her. Spanking! But she was too close to something truly incredible to even launch a faint protest.

"Be a good girl and suck his dick, Reggie. Do it or you don't get to come."

"What the fuck?" she growled.

But she was prevented from saying more when Cam took advantage of her open mouth and thrust inside.

She was suspended between the two men, buffeted from two sides. Cam thrust into her mouth while Sawyer continued his relentless assault on her ass.

Sawyer rammed deep and stopped, his thighs pressed against her ass. He just stood there, and she realized he was probably watching Cam fuck her mouth. It should have dawned on her that Sawyer was the voyeuristic type. Hell, she guessed they all had to be somewhat turned on by watching if they could all get it on with her at the same time.

"Had to tie her up, Sawyer?" Cam asked with amusement. "Did she threaten to kick your ass?"

She grunted around a mouthful of his cock, but he only thrust deeper to quiet her.

Sawyer's hands skimmed over her ass, touching and petting as he remained buried and unmoving in her bowels.

"I think she looks cute when she's helpless. She couldn't hurt a flea in her position. How many times do you get to see that?" Sawyer asked, and she could hear the smile in his voice.

She nipped downward with her teeth, forcing Cam's penis to scrape as he withdrew.

"Hey, watch it now," Cam warned.

Sawyer admonished her with another smack on the ass, and she tightened all over.

"You know, Sawyer, I think she likes that," Cam said. He reached under to cup her breast, running his thumb over the achingly hard nipple.

"Fhhuck wu," she growled around his cock.

In response, he sent his dick sliding even deeper into her mouth, until it nudged the back of her throat.

Whatever happened to treating her like a piece of glass? To wrapping her up in cotton because they were afraid she would break? Right now she was being treated more like a damn sex slave.

And hell if she didn't abso-freaking-lutely love it.

"Think we should let her come?" Sawyer asked in a nonchalant voice.

"Mmmm, maybe."

She rolled her tongue over Cam's cock and sucked as he slid back into her mouth. He groaned.

"Oh yeah, Reggie, you definitely know how to get what you want."

She smiled. They weren't the only ones with evil weapons in their arsenals. Two could play this vicious seduction game.

Sawyer hoisted her hips so that her belly no longer rested over the back of the couch. He slid fingers underneath, sliding through her wetness, and God, she was soaked. As soon as he touched her clit, she nearly exploded, but he retreated immediately, leaving her hanging on the edge of an orgasm she already knew was going to be shattering.

"You'll come with us, Reggie," he said silkily. "So I advise you to play nice with Cam. I can last as long as I need to, so really, it's up to you. Make him come, and we all come."

Cam's hand tightened in her hair just as she tightened her mouth around his cock. He trembled in her mouth, and with a smile, she realized he was close.

He began to move back and forth with quick, forceful thrusts. She relaxed and opened fully to him, allowing him use her mouth as he wanted.

Sawyer withdrew, agonizingly slow, scraping his cock across her stretched opening. Then he rammed forward and began fucking her in earnest.

All that could be heard in the room was the slap of Sawyer's hips against her ass, the wet sucking sounds of her mouth around Cam's cock and the groans of the two men.

Sawyer found her clit again, and he rolled it between his fingers. She shuddered violently and jerked between him and Cam as she lurked so close to her release.

It frightened her. This wasn't going to be a nice, warm, fuzzy orgasm. This one threatened to tear her in two. She both dreaded it and craved it.

"Ah shit," Cam gasped. "Make her come, Sawyer. I'm almost there. I want her to come while I'm fucking her mouth."

His words spurred her forward. Sawyer pinched and manipulated her clit, and he rode her without mercy. Savage.

She was no longer aware of anything but the two cocks working her body. The rest of the world slipped away into a hazy veil.

"Yours," she whispered as Cam's cock slipped free only to thrust back into her throat.

"Ours," Cam agreed. "Only ours, love."

And she came apart. Completely and utterly shattered. She screamed as Cam exploded in her mouth. Streaks of throbbing pleasure erupted, pouring over her, tearing through her like a vicious wind.

She twisted violently, her body writhing helplessly. Sawyer gripped her hips in an attempt to steady her while Cam grabbed her shoulders.

She couldn't stay still, couldn't bear it.

She swallowed or risked choking as Cam poured himself into her mouth. Behind her, Sawyer thrust in a mad frenzy. He spilled into her, hot and scorching but still he continued to pump.

Then he yanked himself out of her ass, and she felt his hand bump against her behind as he jerked his cock. Hot splatter hit her skin, slithered inside her wide-open ass and ran down her leg.

The tip of his cock bumped against her as more liquid hit her back. And then he slid back into her ass, rocking deep and holding there, pressed tight against her behind.

Cam held her jaw, the other hand still buried in her hair. He slid over her lips, the last of his cum filling her mouth.

"What the *fuck* is going on?"

Hutch's furious voice doused her body in ice.

Cam slipped free of her mouth, Sawyer retreated from her ass in a warm rush, and she yanked her head up to see Hutch standing in the doorway, his face pale, fury sparking in his eyes.

He stalked over, doubled his fist and punched Sawyer in the jaw.

"Hutch, no!" she cried as she struggled to right herself.

Goddamn hands were still tangled in her panties. All she managed to do was tumble forward on the couch and then finally to the floor at Cam's feet.

Cam put his arms around her and pulled her up. He freed her hands and tossed the underwear aside. But she was focused solely on the scene in front of her.

Sawyer stumbled back, his eyes like ice.

"You son of a bitch!" Hutch yelled. "How could you do that to her? She's not one of your whores, Sawyer." He turned and whipped his gaze over Cam. "And you. I never thought you'd treat Reggie like this."

He turned back, ready to hit Sawyer again, and Sawyer just stood there, his eyes dead, waiting for whatever punishment Hutch decided to inflict.

Hutch punched him again, and Sawyer staggered back, but he made no move to defend himself. She could see it in his eyes. Resignation. Guilt. Standing there like he deserved it.

When Hutch started for him again, Regina screamed.

"Hutch! Stop! Goddamn you, stop!"

Her fingers balled into fists at her sides. Cam touched her arm reassuringly, but she shrugged him off.

She glanced between Hutch and Sawyer, both furious but for different reasons. There was fear, anger and concern in Hutch's face. All wrapped up in one giant ball of emotion.

Sawyer was pissed, but hurt also lurked in his eyes. And rejection.

And this was it. That moment she'd refused to entertain. The entire reason she had fought against this whole arrangement they wanted. Because it was now they expected her to choose sides. If she went to Sawyer, Hutch would see it as a betrayal, whereas if she went to Hutch to figure out what the fuck his problem was, Sawyer would see it as a rejection of him.

"You swore," she said in an unsteady voice. "You swore it would never come down to this, to me choosing, and goddamn you it has. I won't do it. I *won't*."

She yanked herself from Cam's grip, tears burning her eyes. She stumbled away, ignoring Cam's worried call.

No. Never. This wasn't going to happen. She wasn't going down this road.

She ran past Sawyer, into the kitchen to collect her clothes, minus her underwear.

In the distance, she heard a door slam with such force it shook the house. Sawyer.

She closed her eyes to hold back the tears of frustration and pain.

She finished yanking on her clothes, grabbed her keys and bolted out the back door, no clear idea of where she was going other than away.

CHAPTER 30

Cam drove through town keeping a sharp eye out for Reggie's new RAV4. His hands curled tighter around the steering wheel as he fought the rising tide of panic.

Things had gone to hell fast, and this time . . . this time he wasn't sure the rift could be mended. Hutch had gone all postal on Sawyer. Sawyer and Reggie had both left the house, and Hutch was barricaded in his room.

And he was out searching for Reggie. Hoping like hell she hadn't run far. Her house was out. It was still in shambles. He'd swung by Birdie's place, but she was still staying with Virginia. A stop by her house hadn't netted him any results.

He drove by Jeremy Miller's house but didn't see Reggie's car. He hit her other haunts, but again, nothing.

"Where are you, Reggie?" he murmured as he drove back toward Birdie's place. There was only one other spot he could think of, and it was a bitch to get to.

He pulled behind Birdie's house and set out across the pasture that led to the back boundary of the Fallon spread. When he topped the next hill, his lights caught the back reflectors of Reggie's RAV4.

Relief made him shaky. But on the heels of his relief came fear of the impending confrontation with Reggie.

It had happened. What she'd feared. What he'd feared. They had all feared. Meltdown.

Cam had no idea what had caused Hutch to wig out. It didn't really matter now since the damage had been done. Maybe they'd all been fooling themselves. Maybe this hadn't ever had a snowball's chance in hell of working.

He parked beside Reggie's truck and prepared to make the trek down to the creek bed. But when he got out and glanced over at the RAV4, he saw Reggie curled up in the front seat.

He opened the passenger door and blinked when the overhead light came on. She didn't move or acknowledge him as he slid in and shut the door again.

His heart clutched as he looked down at her slight form. She looked vulnerable. Lost. He swallowed the knot lodged in his throat and struggled with what to say. How to say it.

Finally he opted to say nothing at all. He reached down, hooked his hands underneath her arms and gently tugged her upward until he could pull her into his arms and against his chest.

Her body shook as a sob escaped her.

He hugged her tightly and buried his face in her curls.

"I'm sorry, love," he whispered.

For the longest time, she huddled against him and didn't say anything. The longer she took to speak, the more worried he became.

"I knew this would happen," she finally whispered. "It's not fair, Cam. I can't choose sides. How could I?"

"No one wants you to choose sides, Reggie darling." God, he

hoped he hadn't just lied out his ass. He would have never thought Hutch would pull the stunt he had, and now he was stuck here speaking for both Hutch and Sawyer.

"Not in so many words."

Her voice was muffled by his chest, and he adjusted her position, sliding her head back so he could hear her better.

"What was I supposed to do, Cam?"

The ache in her voice made him ache. She sounded small. Tired. Utterly defeated, as though she'd spent the last several hours beating herself up for something she couldn't control.

"It's not up to you to fix this," he said softly. "This is Hutch's problem. He crossed the line. He has to make things right with you and with Sawyer."

She sighed and wilted further into his arms. "I was fooling myself. This couldn't ever work," she said sadly.

He halted the protest, the denial that wanted to burst out of his mouth, his heart. Instead he drew in a steadying breath and prepared to try and fight.

"It will work, Reggie."

She pushed away to stare at him in the dark. "I shouldn't even be talking to you. It's not fair to run to you when I have problems with Hutch or Sawyer. It wouldn't be fair to go to them if I had a problem with you."

He reached out to touch her face. He needed to touch her. To make that connection. His fingers were trembling so bad that he curled them into his palm and simply rested his knuckles against her cheek.

"Why? Reggie, you're being too hard on yourself. It's not up to you to be all things to us. How can you expect to be the rock with no one to ever confide in? Talking to me about a problem you have with Hutch or Sawyer isn't a betrayal."

"It's not fair," she said stubbornly.

"Why isn't it? We talk about you. We're a unit. A fucked-up, twisted kind of unit, but we're a unit nonetheless."

"What the hell do you say about me?" she demanded.

He smiled in the darkness at the irritation in her voice.

"Oh, just about how stubborn you are. How infuriating you can be. That we worry about you. And that we miss you."

She leaned back into his arms. "I don't know what happened tonight, Cam. I thought I'd finally gotten through to Sawyer."

She broke off and went silent.

"And?" he prompted.

"I shouldn't discuss him with you."

Cam sighed. "See? Stubborn. That characteristic weighs heavily in our conversations about you, Reggie darling."

She huffed against him.

He rubbed his hand up and down her shoulder. "What did you mean about getting through to Sawyer?"

She lay there for a long time, and he could feel the battle raging inside her. Loyalty was strong in her, and she'd always been loyal to him, Hutch and Sawyer. In her mind, confiding in him about one of the other two was a betrayal. It was choosing him over them.

They had been right in realizing that she'd never choose between them and that their only chance of a life with her was convincing her to belong to all of them. Only now Hutch was doing his best to fuck everything up.

Despite his best effort, anger swelled within Cam. It was irrational. It didn't serve anything, but it still pissed him off that with one fit of temper, Hutch had risked everything. Not only his relationship with Reggie but Cam's and Sawyer's as well.

"He held back," she finally said. "A year ago he held back, and then when we made love again the other night, he wouldn't . . ."

She seemed to struggle with the right words, and Cam thought back to those encounters to try and see what she was seeing. In both instances, Hutch and Cam had been the only ones to actually take her. He frowned. Both times Sawyer had used her mouth and nothing more. Until today.

"He didn't penetrate you . . . vaginally," Cam offered, stumbling over the damn word like a moron.

"He's afraid of hurting me," she said quietly. "Sawyer's rough around the edges. No secret there. And I think he feels guilty because he's had frequent sexual encounters with other women."

Cam frowned again. It made sense in a twisted Sawyer kind of way. To be honest, he'd never evaluated Sawyer's performance during sex. Just wasn't high on his list of priorities, but now that Reggie had brought it up, he could see her point.

"So you threatened to rape him this morning?" Cam asked with only a thread of amusement.

"Something like that," she mumbled. "I sorta jumped him in the kitchen and made it very clear what I wanted from him."

"Hell, I think I'm jealous," Cam murmured.

She dug her fist into his gut, and he grinned.

"Things were going great. Well, except his need to tie me up," she said darkly. "And the whole spanking thing."

Cam chuckled. "You loved it."

"Yeah, well, that's not the point. But then Hutch flipped out. I mean what the fuck was he thinking? Does he really think you or Sawyer would ever hurt me? If he doesn't trust you and Sawyer, how on earth does he think this could ever work? I mean I guess I can understand his protective streak when it comes to other people or dangers I might face, but protecting me against you and Sawyer?"

Cam didn't have an answer to that, because it was something he wanted to know as well.

"Did you see the look in Sawyer's eyes, Cam?"

Emotion squeezed her voice, and she sounded near tears.

"He just stood there while Hutch hit him like he deserved it, like he deserved all the accusations Hutch hurled at him. And I couldn't even go to him because then it would look like I was taking his side against Hutch."

She leaned away again and stared up at Cam.

"What was I supposed to do, Cam?"

"What did you want to do?" he asked gently.

Her shoulders sagged. "I wanted to knock Hutch on his ass, and then I wanted to wrap my arms around Sawyer and tell him that I love him, that I know he'd never hurt me."

"Then that's what you should have done."

"You make it sound so simple," she grumbled. "How is me doing that not choosing between you?"

"Because Hutch was being a horse's ass, and if it had been over anything else you would have immediately called him on it and set him straight."

"There is that."

He shifted and adjusted his long legs to get the cramp out of one of them. Then he picked her up and moved her to his other knee before curling her back into his arms.

"You need to cut yourself some slack, love. You cannot be all things to everyone. Moreover, we don't expect you to. If one of us is being a dickhead, we don't expect you to suck it up and take it because it might look like you're picking one over the other."

"But what if . . . what if this can't be fixed, Cam? What then?"

The fear in her voice echoed his own fears. But damn it, fights in a relationship were inevitable. Granted they usually occurred between the man and the woman and not two other men. What a fucking mess.

"You're not a damn piece of meat to fight over," he said, allowing the first shard of anger to bleed through in his words.

She went still against him. "You're angry too."

He sighed. "Yeah, I'm pissed. I don't know what set Hutch off, but he didn't handle it worth a damn. He knows that me and Sawyer would never hurt you. Damn it, he *knows*."

"So what do I do?" she asked again.

"Only you can answer that," he said, though he wanted to tell her to go kick Hutch's ass and then make things right with Sawyer. But he couldn't make that choice for her, not matter how badly he wanted to do whatever it took to keep her.

"I just wish I knew what the hell he was thinking."

"You and me both," Cam murmured.

Hutch had always been defensive when it came to Reggie, though Cam wasn't going to volunteer that information. No sense building her case that this wouldn't work.

He rubbed her arm again then kissed the top of her head. "Why don't you come back to the house? I'm betting you haven't eaten all day. You can kick Hutch's ass and Sawyer's too if you want. I'll even clean up the blood when you're done."

He forced lightness into his voice, hoping that if he didn't make a big deal out of it then neither would she.

"You go on ahead," she said in a low voice. "I need to think about things for a while."

His breath caught and held. "But you're coming back, right?"

Silence stretched between them, and he tensed as he waited for her response.

"I won't run anymore. Whatever happens I'll face it head-on."

Her answer didn't make him feel any better. But he also heard the resolve in her voice. This is where he was going to have to trust her and hope like hell that another man hadn't fucked up any chance of a future *he* had with the woman he loved.

CHAPTER 31

*R*eggie pulled up to the house and cut the engine. Sawyer's truck was gone. With a sigh, she got out and wearily headed for the door.

She and Sawyer were a lot alike. Both hotheads, prone to blowing up, and taking off was their way of dealing with it.

This time, however, she'd promised Cam that she'd deal with it rationally. Her and her big mouth. What she really wanted to do was tuck tail and run. Just like she'd done a year ago. Only it hadn't helped.

As soon as she mounted the steps, the front door flew open, and Hutch yanked her into his arms.

"Reggie, thank God. I was worried."

She stiffened then pulled away and slugged him right in the gut.

He doubled over with a grunt but managed to keep hold of her elbow as he dragged her inside the house.

She twisted free from his grasp and shut the door behind him. He stood in the foyer, his hand beneath his T-shirt rubbing his gut.

"I deserved that," he said in a low voice.

She glared at him. "Yeah, you did."

A long sigh spilled from his lips, and she softened when she saw the misery etched on his face. He didn't have to know she'd gone all gooey though.

She fixed him with a frown, and he returned her stare bleakly. "Can we talk?" he asked as he gestured toward the living room.

"Where's Sawyer?" she asked as she walked in front of him.

"I don't know," he admitted. "He hasn't been back yet."

A twinge of fear rippled through her chest. She rounded on Hutch and used her anger to block out that fear.

"What the fuck were you thinking, Hutch? What was that all about?"

He flopped onto the couch, dug his elbows into his knees and buried his face in his hands.

"I'm an asshole," he muttered.

She sank down in the chair across from him. "Yeah, well that's been established. Care to tell me what prompted this particular assholic venture?"

He stared up at her with such pain in his eyes that she recoiled. A prickle of unease skirted down her spine, and her anger was replaced by concern.

"What's wrong, Hutch?" she asked softly. "What would cause you to think that Sawyer or Cam would ever hurt me? Did it look like I was protesting?"

Hutch took in a deep breath, and she could see the battle he fought, could see the muscles twitching and the nerves jumping in his taut body.

"I didn't see how you could possibly have a chance to say no with your hands tied behind your back, your mouth full of Cam's dick and Sawyer's shoved up your ass," he said bluntly.

She flushed, and her lips tightened. "Look at me, Hutch."

He turned dull eyes on her. They had the same haunted look of Sawyer's.

"What's going on? You know they wouldn't hurt me. You have to know that. Do you honestly think I'd just lie there like a moron and take it if they were doing something I didn't want?"

His protest was swift. "You're smaller than them, Reggie. Especially Sawyer. It wouldn't be hard for him to overpower you, and there isn't a damn thing you could do to stop him."

There was fear in his voice and a thread of anger, but it went beyond what had happened on the couch. His gaze was unfocused, as if he was lost in some other place. Another time.

"Do you honestly think Sawyer would ever hurt me, Hutch? Look me in the eye and tell me you think something so bad of a man who's been your brother since you were ten years old."

A dull flush crept up Hutch's neck. "No," he muttered. "He loves you. He'd die before hurting you."

"Then what the fuck were you thinking today?" she demanded. "You hurt him, Hutch. Did you see the look in his eyes? How the hell am I supposed to ever get him to even look at me now?"

She curled her fingers into fists and willed herself not to lose the tenuous grip she had on her temper. Hutch was hurting too. She didn't have a clue why, but something else was going on here.

Hutch looked away. His shoulders shook, and he dragged a trembling hand through his short hair.

"I know, Reggie. I know. I'm sorry."

"It's not me you need to apologize to," she pointed out.

"Yeah, it is. I embarrassed you. I decked my brother. I put you in a difficult position, and for that I'm sorry."

"But why?" she asked softly. "What happened, Hutch? It's not like you to go off like that. Is it the situation? Are you jealous? Is this something you can't deal with?"

"No," he said sharply as he snapped his head around.

He shot to his feet and began to pace restlessly. His body language screamed agitation. Tension rolled off him like a heat wave.

She waited and watched as he grappled with whatever demon held him in its grip.

He stopped and turned to her, one hand on the back of his neck. "It just hit me wrong, baby. I walked in the door, and I see you bent over the couch, hands tied behind your back, Sawyer's handprint on your ass. What was I supposed to think?"

He blew out his breath, but she could see he wasn't angry any longer. He seemed confused. And *sad*.

"My dad used to beat up on my mom," he confessed in an ashamed whisper.

Her heart lurched and squeezed, but she remained quiet, wanting to hear what he had to say. He never talked about his family. Never talked about his life before he arrived at Birdie's. As close as they were and had been for years, everything she knew about him came forward from that point.

"He was a bastard. An alcoholic who was almost as mean when he was sober as he was drunk. When he got tired of knocking my mom around, he'd come after me and my brother."

She gasped. She didn't even know he had a brother.

"I remember how helpless I felt and how angry it made me because I couldn't help her. I couldn't help my brother. I was completely and utterly powerless."

"Hutch, you were just a boy," she said gently.

"Yeah, just a kid," he said derisively. "I haven't thought about those times in years, Reggie, but when I came home and saw that, it was like seeing my dad and my mom all over again. I know what I did was wrong, but it sickened me to think of anyone ever hurting you like that."

He looked away guiltily. "And maybe I've just been waiting

for Sawyer to screw up. I've never liked how rough he was with you, but I've sat on my hands and held my tongue because I knew it would only cause an argument, and I guess deep down, I know I'm being an ass."

She opened her mouth to speak, but he began pacing again.

"He killed her, Reggie. And the bastard got away with it. Her death was ruled an accident. Ironically she was drunk. She never drank, but I guess that night it was just too much for her. He pushed her down the stairs and then played the grieving husband. I couldn't stay there anymore so I ran, and I never went back."

The ache in her heart grew as she saw the raw pain grooved into his face. He looked as lost as Sawyer had looked when Hutch had condemned him.

"I thought your parents were dead . . . like Cam's and Sawyer's," she said quietly. "I never realized . . . I mean you never talked about them."

"What's to tell?" he said derisively. "My old man wasn't exactly something to write home about, and I was always afraid that I'd get sent back to him. It was easier to pretend he didn't exist."

She rose falteringly, her feet unsteady beneath her. And then she went to him, sliding her arms around his waist and burying her face in his chest.

"I'm sorry, Hutch."

He gripped her tightly to him, his chest heaving with unspent emotion. "You have nothing to apologize for, Reggie. I was a complete and utter jerk. I jeopardized everything. Not only for me but for Sawyer and Cam. Can you ever forgive me for that?"

She closed her eyes, hoping it was as simple as forgiveness. For all of them.

"You have to make this right with Sawyer," she said quietly.

"I know. But first I had to make it right with you. What I did was unforgivable. I did exactly what we swore we wouldn't. Put you between us. I love you, Reggie. And I'm sorry."

She squeezed him tighter. "I'm going to go up and wait for Sawyer, okay?"

Hutch rubbed his hands up and down her back. "I'm so glad you came home, baby. I was so worried. Don't leave like that again please. Next time stay and kick my ass or make *me* leave, but don't walk out. This is your home. You belong with us even though I don't deserve you."

She smiled and then tilted her head back so she could lean up to kiss him. "I'm tired and it's been a long day. I'm gonna head up and crawl into Sawyer's bed. I just hope to hell he comes home so I can talk some sense into his head."

Guilt flashed again across Hutch's face. He started to speak, but she held a finger over his lips.

"Save it for Sawyer," she said gently.

He nodded and loosened his hold on her. She let her hands slide down his arms to his wrists, and then she squeezed his hands once before turning to head up the stairs.

She hadn't meant to fall asleep, but when she heard the door creak open and saw the time, she realized she had.

The light flipped on, and she threw an arm over her eyes as her eyeballs all but exploded.

"Fuck! Sorry, Reggie," Sawyer muttered before slapping at the light switch to plunge the room back into darkness.

"It's okay," she said groggily. "Turn it back on."

Instead he walked over and switched on the bedside lamp. Cautiously, she removed her arm from her face and stared up at him.

He looked . . . rough. Like he'd been a few rounds with a guy much bigger than him, though she wasn't sure there were many of those around.

"What the hell happened to you?" she demanded. "And where've you been?"

The corner of his mouth cracked up in what looked suspiciously like a half grin.

"Went and had a few," he said with a shrug.

Her eyes narrowed. "And you drove home? Damn it, Sawyer, why didn't you call me? Are you just trying to kill yourself or get arrested?"

He plopped down on the bed, leaned forward then turned his head to look at her. "You stayed up just to give me a lecture?"

"No, dumbass, I stayed up because I wanted to see you. Because I wanted to talk some sense into your thick head."

"I can see why I came home for such abuse." His voice was thick with amusement, but shadows still haunted his eyes.

She crawled across the bed, grabbed handfuls of his shirt and yanked him forward. His mouth fell open in surprise about the time she swooped in to kiss him.

She slid around his body like she was a pole dancer on the make. Then before he could so much as blink, she shoved forward, knocking him flat on his back.

She went with him and they both landed with a thump.

Her lips found his again. She kissed him then released then kissed him again. "Don't." *Kiss.* "Ever." *Kiss.* "Run." *Kiss.* "Off." *Kiss.* "Likethatagain!"

His hands slid up her back to cup her shoulders as she peppered his mouth with hers.

"So says the woman who took off like a bat out of hell," he said dryly.

She raised her head and glared down at him. "And how would you know what I did?"

"Oh, let's see. A, you're just like me. And B, Cam left a somewhat frantic message on my cell phone saying you'd run off like a scalded cat again."

"I came back," she mumbled.

He moved his hand to her front and tucked a curl behind her ear. His expression grew serious. "Yeah, you did. Dare I read anything into that?"

"I don't want to talk about me," she said softly. "I want to talk about you. And Hutch."

His eyes flickered and became blank. He shoved at her, and she fell to the side as he rolled away from her.

"Nothing to talk about," he said tonelessly.

"That's where you're wrong."

He turned back to face her, his eyes swarming with intensity. If she didn't know him so darn well, she'd be pretty afraid right now. He bristled with power. It boiled off him like water from a hot radiator.

But she eyed him calmly, refusing to let him intimidate her.

"It won't work. You're going to sit here and listen to me or so help me I'll tie your ass to the bed. Then we'll see how much you like being at *my* mercy."

His lips lifted in a smirk. "I hate to break it to you, honey, but if that's a threat? Color me not afraid. I can think of worse things than being at your mercy."

A warm buzz blew through her veins, and she trembled despite her determination to kick his ass into submission.

She moved forward again, getting into his face until they were nose to nose. "You're going to listen to me, Sawyer. We're going to talk about this. If you refuse, I'm gone."

He blinked, and then his eyes narrowed to dangerous slits. "I don't do ultimatums, Reggie."

Never make a threat you're not willing to carry out. It was a concept solidly ingrained from years of living with a father who was more bluster and hot air than flesh and blood.

Without a word, she backed off the bed, turned around and stalked out the door. Her hands shook, but this was too important. It wasn't a bluff. How the hell could she stay here and try to make this work if he wasn't willing to let down his guard around her?

She wasn't taking this kind of shit from Hutch, and she sure as hell wouldn't take it from Sawyer. Dramatic? Yeah and she almost felt guilty because this so wasn't her style. Well, apart from the stomping off. But making idle threats or playing stupid mind games wasn't her deal.

But Sawyer wasn't someone you could calmly approach. He took drastic measures because he was every bit as pigheaded as she was. Probably more so.

She stalked into her room, threw the few changes of clothes into a duffel bag and started for the door. Still no sign of Sawyer. With a sigh, she thumped down the stairs. She was more than willing to leave and let Sawyer try and explain to Cam and Hutch why she wasn't there.

She gripped the front door handle, and Sawyer still hadn't left his room. She knew because the house hadn't shook yet with the force of a slamming door. Maybe that could be her exit, but then she didn't want to wake Hutch and Cam.

She walked outside and down the steps toward her RAV4. Her hand was on the door handle when she heard something that sounded remarkably like a bellowing bull. She barely had time to suppress her grin when she was lifted into the air and thrown over one bulky shoulder.

Sawyer stomped up the steps with her swinging behind him, her nose bumping his ass the whole way. He slammed the door behind him, and she winced. So much for not waking the guys up.

He looped an arm over her ass and then tossed her onto the couch. She landed with a thump, momentarily winded. Sawyer stood over her, a dark scowl on his face.

"What the fuck, Reggie? Since when do you pull shit like this?"

She raised her left eyebrow. "Excuse me? I'm not the one acting like an ass here. You haul me around like that again and I'll arrest you for assaulting a police officer."

He bent down, placed his hands on either side of her legs and got into her face.

"Arrest me then," he snarled.

She glared at him, and he glared back. Then she smacked her hands against his face with a little more force than necessary and yanked him to meet her kiss.

Hot and hungry. She was so hungry for him.

He kissed her back just as hard, just as forcefully. He leaned her back until she hit the cushion, and he pressed her against the back of the couch.

Then he pulled away and stared at her with fierce determination. "You're not going anywhere."

No, she wasn't, but he didn't have to know that.

"If you don't talk to me, Sawyer, I'm going. I won't stay here with you putting a foot of distance between us at every turn."

He ducked his head away from her and swore. Crude words even for him. She raised her eyebrows.

"Goddamn, Reggie. What do you want from me?" he said after his cursing streak was over.

"Everything," she said with no hesitation. She didn't wait for him to put her off again. She cupped his face with her hand and rubbed her thumb over the stiff bristle of his goatee. "He was wrong, Sawyer. Hutch was way out of line. He had no right to say the things he said. You know it, and I know it. He knows it."

Uncertainty flickered in his eyes. "He wasn't wrong," he said quietly. "I had no right to treat you like that, Reggie. Like some cheap lay out for kinky thrills."

She dropped her hand from his face, crossed her arms over her chest and adopted a look of outrage. "Did you just fucking call me a cheap lay?"

He swore again. His jaw was wound so tight he was going to break his teeth. "You know goddamn well that's not what I was saying!"

She smirked up at him, knowing she was about to push him right over the edge. Something had to give. Might as well be his tight ass.

"So you're saying that me wanting kinky thrills doesn't make me a cheap lay?"

He growled and threw his hands up. "I swear to God, if I didn't already shave my head, I'd be a bald motherfucker. You're going to drive me to drink."

"The feeling is entirely mutual," she said sweetly.

"Are you just trying to piss me off?" he asked.

"Yes."

He gaped at her.

"Talk to me, Sawyer," she said, dropping the sneer, the arguing and everything else. "I won't let you run from this. Sound familiar? You had no qualms about pinning my ass down. The tables are turned now. I quit running, and now you're damn sure not going to tuck tail on me."

He stared at her for a long moment, his blue eyes burning holes through her. "God save me from stubborn women," he muttered. "There's nothing to talk about, Reggie. It's over with."

She shook her head. "I saw you, Sawyer. I saw that look on your face. I know you better than anyone. Don't tell me I don't."

"Yeah, you do," he said softly. "Better than anyone. You love me better than anyone, and that's why I don't ever want to hurt you."

A low scream of frustration tore from her lips. He flinched away and looked at her in surprise.

"How is you having sex with me hurting me? *How?* God, that doesn't even make sense. You think I don't have kinky fantasies? Granted they've never really centered around you tying me up and smacking my ass, but you know, I just might come around on those points. What's so terrible about you? That you don't murmur little sweet lovey words while you're stuffing that big cock into my ass?"

His eyes widened in shock at her crudity. He opened his mouth but nothing came out, and she plunged ahead, unwilling to let him interrupt her tirade. Not when she was just getting warmed up.

"Or maybe it's that you fucked my ass? Do you think you're the first to do that, Sawyer? Here's a clue. You weren't. I've been around the block a time or two. Certainly more than Cam or Hutch, it would appear. Now according to your self-imposed criteria, that fact makes me completely unsuitable. In fact, I should lock myself away from the three of you and live the rest of my life in celibacy."

"Jesus Christ. Shut the hell up, Reggie."

"Sounds stupid when I say it, doesn't it?"

"I don't give a shit how many guys you've been with in the past," he said. "All I care about is how many it's going to be from now on."

"And I don't care about the women in your past," she said gently. "I don't care that you're rough and unpolished or that you don't whisper sweet nothings in my ear while you're fucking me. If it makes you feel any better, I'll have Cam do the whispering while you fuck me."

A low growl rippled out of his throat. "I don't need Cam to do my talking for me."

"Good. That's settled then. You and I can make love without anyone else's help. I feel so much better now."

"You are such a miserable smart-ass," he said, sending his eyes rolling upward.

"But you love me anyway."

He sighed morosely and gave her a forlorn look, the look of a man solidly defeated. "I do love you, Reggie. More than you'll ever know. More than I've ever loved anyone else."

"And I love you," she said softly. "Now take me upstairs and fuck me, you big goof."

CHAPTER 32

*R*egina looked up at Sawyer as she waited for him to react. After a brief flicker of indecision crossed his face, he seemed to come to grips with his uncertainty and another gleam lightened his eyes. A pure predatory gleam. One that made her shiver.

"I kinda like that he-man act of you throwing me over your shoulder," she said casually.

"Is that an invitation?" he asked huskily. The deep timbre of his voice washed over her skin, warm and mellow.

She grinned cheekily up at him. "I'd say it was a demand, but you might refuse on principle."

"Feel free to make those kinds of demands anytime you want."

Before she could say another word, he lifted her and tossed her over his shoulder as easily as if she were a five-pound bag of sugar.

She giggled like an idiot the entire way up the stairs, which earned her a smack on the ass and an admonishment not to wake the rest of the house. As if they could have slept through one of her and Sawyer's rows.

He carried her into his bedroom and tossed her on the bed. He reached down to pull his shirt off and tossed it across the room. The sheer sexiness of watching a stacked man undress wasn't lost on her. Her eyes were glued to his physique.

His muscles rippled beautifully. He looked almost graceful despite his size.

He popped the button of his fly, hooked his thumbs in the waistband and yanked downward. The blue boxers he wore came with the jeans, baring his engorged cock to her view. It bobbed free of confinement and stood erect.

He caught her staring and stood there, legs apart, completely unabashed. "Like what you see?"

She swallowed and nodded.

"Take off your clothes," he ordered.

"And if I want you to take them off?" she said lightly.

"Now."

Alrighty then. His tone brooked no argument, and she was close to panting.

She hurriedly yanked at her jeans, but he stopped her with a look.

"Slow," he said. "Nice and slow."

A sultry smile curved her lips upward. So he wanted a show, did he? She crawled up to her knees then stood up on the bed so that now she looked down at him.

With a seductive sway to her hips, she began inching her jeans over her hips, being careful to keep her underwear in place. When they fell down around her ankles, she picked up one foot and shook it free of the denim and then picked her other foot up and kicked the jeans toward the doorway.

Placing her palms at her hips, she smoothed her hands up her body, underneath her shirt and higher, working the material up her chest.

She pulled the shirt over her head and sent it flying after the jeans. Still swaying back and forth, she snaked her hands behind her back to unclasp her bra. The straps came loose and tumbled down her arms. She yanked her hands back around to hold the cups in place, and then she slowly let the lacy bra slide down her body, freeing her breasts to his avid gaze.

Unable to resist the temptation to make him a little crazy, she swallowed her inhibitions and let her fingers dance across her breasts. She cupped each small mound then worked the nipples between her fingers.

She let out a small moan that mixed with his sudden intake of air.

Keeping one hand caressing the puckered tip, she trailed the fingers of her other hand down her midline, traced a line around her navel and then dipped lower to the band of her panties.

Soft as a whisper, her fingers delved underneath the filmy material, through the crisp curls between her legs, deeper into the damp flesh between her folds.

Her middle finger rolled over her clitoris, inciting a delicate shudder that began in her groin and ended at her shoulders. Her nipples tightened in response, and she plucked at one with her fingers, enjoying the sharp tingles that erupted.

She locked eyes with Sawyer as she manipulated the tiny nub of flesh between her legs. When she was sure he was solely focused on her, she threw back her head, closed her eyes and undulated her hips in rhythm with her fingers.

She didn't have long to wait.

He grabbed her wrists and yanked her forward until she fell to her knees on the bed, her body just inches from his broad chest. His fingers still wrapped tightly around her wrists, he leaned in and devoured her mouth in a ravenous kiss.

"You make me crazy," he muttered against her lips.

"Good," she murmured back.

He pulled her arms apart and leaned her backward, falling forward onto her as her back hit the mattress. He hovered just inches over her, his body pressed firmly against hers.

He was a man who might scare a lot of women. There was no softness to him. Big and mean. That's what he looked like. But when he smiled at her, when he looked at her, there was such a gentleness to him, that it made her chest ache.

Hers. He was all hers, and she reveled in that fact. He may have been with a lot of women, but she knew none of them had ever owned his heart the way she did. It wasn't something he had to say either. His actions proved it.

His goatee brushed across her chin as he rolled his mouth over hers, drinking deeply of her. He tasted, licked and nibbled at first her lips and then her tongue.

His body arched over hers as he drew in his hips to position himself between her legs. He nudged the underside of her thigh with a knee so that she was more open to his advances.

Curling his fingers around her wrists again, he drew her arms over her head then collected both of her hands in the firm grip of one of his.

Then he let his free hand trail over her face, exploring the lines of her jaw and feathering over her swollen lips. His fingertips danced down her neck, around her collarbone, until little goose bumps rose in his wake.

He traced the slight indention between her breasts and circled each nipple in turn until it puckered and strained under his attentions.

He dipped his head and tugged on one of the tight little nubs with his teeth. She cried out as lightning chased through her veins. Her breasts swelled and plumped, begging for more, wanting his touch, his mouth.

She begged. She wasn't ashamed of her need. She wanted more. Demanded more.

"Please," she whispered. "I want you so much. I need you, Sawyer."

"Ah, Reggie," he groaned. "You make me feel as though I'm the only man in the world."

His cock brushed over her slick flesh as he arched his hips forward. Two more adjustments, and he slid into her in one long push.

She bowed her back and strained against him, wanting closer, wanting more. He was so thick. Every nerve ending in her pussy was stretched tight, on fire as he rubbed back and forth over her swollen flesh.

He continued to hold her hands with his while his free hand teased and pleasured her nipples. His hips rocked forward gently, setting an easy pace. It reminded her of the gentle waves on the Texas coast. Warm, soothing, lapping to the shore and spreading along the sun-scorched sand.

She sighed in contentment as he rocked between her legs. He'd lied when he said he knew nothing about slow, sensual lovemaking. She'd never felt more loved or cherished than in this moment. The idea that this warrior, this big-ass man with bulging muscles and hands larger than her head could love her so tenderly brought tears to her eyes.

Yes, he'd lied. He knew exactly how to give her sweet lovemaking.

He rested inside her, his eyes closed as shudders rolled over his body. There was peace on his face. Pleasure and contentment.

Then he began to move again, rolling forward like the tide. Deeper he sank. With each thrust, he reached further into her body. And her soul.

"Wrap your legs around me, honey. Hold me tight."

She slid her heels up the back of his legs before crossing them at the small of his back. She pulled her lower body upward to meet his every thrust.

A small pinch settled deep in her pussy, one that grew bigger, tighter, expanding until she writhed with edgy need. That need grew, larger with each passing second. It pooled in her groin and radiated outward in a hundred different directions.

He finally let go of her wrists and slid both of his hands down her body to cup her ass. His fingers splayed out over the cheeks as he palmed her behind. Cupping her to him, he rode her, his body meshing with hers like the missing piece to a puzzle.

Faster, harder. Higher they flew. Soft then hard. Gentle then strong. Slow then quick.

She took a running leap, diving for the edge of the cliff. Over she fell, spreading her arms wide as she entered her free fall. Arms outstretched, eyes closed, the wind in her face. And then she flew. Soaring and dipping, she chased the wind.

And through it all, he held her. Those words he swore he didn't know were whispered in her ear. His love. It wrapped around every part of her body, filling her, surrounding her.

Love.

"I love you," she whispered as he shuddered against her.

"I love *you*," he answered hoarsely. "I'm so sorry, Reggie. I never meant to make you feel like you didn't mean the world to me."

She smiled as he came to rest on top of her. "I've never doubted that I mean a lot to you."

His head rested on her shoulder, his face pressed against her neck. She curled her arms around him, holding him there. They were still joined, and the intimacy of their embrace was something Regina would carry with her forever.

CHAPTER 33

Sawyer eased out of bed the next morning, careful not to wake Reggie. She was all curled up, dead to the world, and he couldn't help the smile that eased the strain at his forehead.

He reached down to touch the curls that spilled across her cheek. Beautiful. She was so beautiful. His need for her went far beyond the physical. He'd found physical release in a lot of places over the years, but he'd never found anyone who soothed the ache in his chest like Reggie. He never would.

No, he wasn't good enough for her. Never would be. But for some reason, that didn't matter to her. For all his faults, she still claimed to love him. And want him.

Something happened when he was around her. She always managed to find his cracks, slip inside him and worm her way into his heart. She'd inserted herself so deep that he had no desire for her to ever find her way out again.

Despite the fact that he had to share her with two other men, men who loved her, she still managed to make him feel like he was the only man in the world.

Discomfort settled into his chest when he thought of Hutch. He turned away, knowing that what had happened would have to be settled. It wasn't a confrontation he relished, but for Reggie, he'd do anything.

Reluctantly he left her sleeping. He took a quick shower and headed downstairs. Hutch was in the kitchen as he'd expected.

When he walked in, Hutch looked up, and Sawyer could see the guarded look in his eyes. The silence made Sawyer uncomfortable, and he slid onto a bar stool and tried to act casual.

For a while, only the bang of pots and pans echoed through the kitchen. Hutch set out the ingredients for pancakes without looking back at Sawyer.

"Look man, let's just forget it happened," Sawyer finally said.

Hutch stopped stirring the batter but didn't look up right away. He slowly let the spoon fall against the bowl, and when he finally did look at Sawyer, there was a lot of regret in his expression.

"I was wrong," Hutch said simply. "I was an asshole, and neither you nor Reggie deserved it."

"Okay, we're good then," Sawyer said, eager to get on to other things.

Hutch sighed and frowned. "No, this needs to be said. What happened had nothing to do with you and everything to do with me. You pushed some buttons, but it has to do with issues I had with my old man. I freaked out on you, and the thing is, I know you'd never hurt Reggie. I know that. And I need for you to know that. I owe you an apology, but more than that, I owe you more respect than I gave you."

Sawyer shifted uncomfortably on the stool. "I got you. We're cool."

Hutch relaxed and resumed stirring the batter. "You iron everything out with Reggie, or did I fuck things up between you?"

"She set me straight," Sawyer muttered. "We're fine."

Hutch grinned. "Yeah, she decked me."

Sawyer jerked his head up. "For real?"

Hutch rubbed his gut with his free hand. "Yeah. The heifer packs a mean punch."

Sawyer laughed, and he was astonished at the lightness he felt. Relief. Hope.

Hutch caught his gaze and stared him in the eye. "I'm sorry."

Sawyer shook his head. "We're good."

Cam walked in carrying a handful of electronic equipment, a frown smeared across his face. He dumped the stuff on the bar with a clatter.

"Been out shopping?" Sawyer asked with an arched eyebrow.

The frown didn't ease from Cam's face.

"Either of you two know what the hell this stuff is?" he asked.

Hutch leaned over and perused the collection. "Looks like surveillance equipment."

"Yeah, my thoughts too," Cam replied.

"Where'd you get it?" Sawyer asked.

"Good morning," Reggie said as she entered the kitchen. She offered the three of them a smile, and only Cam didn't return it.

She slid up next to Hutch first, snuggling against his side. Then she looked down at the stuff on the counter and froze. A peculiar expression crossed her face, followed quickly by a spark of guilt.

Sawyer frowned. This didn't bode well.

"I found it here," Cam said darkly. "Cameras. Recording equipment. It was surrounding the house."

Sawyer continued to stare at Reggie. "Got any ideas where it came from?" he asked her.

She stepped away from Hutch as Cam turned his surprised stare on her.

"Uh, it's mine," she said in a low voice.

"Yours?" Cam's frown got deeper. "What the hell is going on, Reggie?"

She wiped her hands down the legs of her jeans and bit absently at her bottom lip.

"I had it installed. While we were in Houston," she added.

The lightbulb came on. Sawyer saw the unease in her body language and knew that whatever explanation she came up with, he wasn't going to like it. The others were quickly catching on as well.

"Is that why you were so keen to get us all to Houston?" Sawyer asked.

Regina tried to quell the panic knotting her throat. This wasn't the way she wanted to explain things to them. She'd wanted to come clean with them, not be found out like she was sneaking around behind their backs. Which was in fact what she'd done.

She sighed and flopped onto a stool.

"Reggie?" Hutch prompted.

"A friend of mine owns a security company. High-tech stuff. Does a lot of police surveillance contract work. I asked him to wire the place while we were gone."

"Okay, why?" Cam asked. "I mean I understand why since the place was broken into, but why did you think you needed to keep it a secret from us?"

"Because you didn't know the whole story," she said in a low voice. "I didn't want you to know the whole story."

"Well, by all means, do share," Sawyer drawled.

They were annoyed. But she knew they'd be more pissed before the end of it.

"I was trying to protect you," she said. "All of you. I have reason to believe that the murder, the attack on me, the break-ins here and at Birdie's . . . and the car bomb were personal to Hutch."

"*What?*" Hutch exclaimed.

Sawyer and Cam looked equally stunned.

"I don't know that for sure," she said mildly. "Misty Thompson was someone Hutch dated. The rest of the connections are self-explanatory. And the night she was murdered, the man called me Reggie and told me it was 'time to make him pay.'" She glanced at Hutch, wincing as he paled even further. It wasn't the way she would have wanted to break the news to him. The victim's name was public knowledge, but Hutch wasn't very tuned in to the local news.

"My department followed the reasoning that it had to do with my father since he's high-profile, wealthy and a politician. But when Birdie's place was broken into, the only room disturbed was Hutch's."

"Goddamn it, Reggie, why didn't you tell me any of this?" Hutch demanded. "Don't you think I had a right to know if someone was trying to kill people close to me? That someone had already *died* because of me?"

"It wasn't my decision to make. My department wasn't convinced, and they were investigating every angle. They wanted to question all three of you . . . today. But they made an arrest and got a confession for the murder, so it wasn't necessary after all."

"That's bullshit," Sawyer said bluntly. "Tell me something, Reggie. Why did you decide to stay? Why the sudden about-face? I'd bet an awful lot that it had nothing to do with us protecting you, or that you even suddenly decided to quit fighting the attraction."

The blood drained from her face. This was what she was afraid of. Them making the connection. It hadn't been like that, damn it, but she knew how it looked. How on earth was she supposed to convince them otherwise?

"He's right, isn't he?" Cam asked in a voice that sounded dead. "You were protecting us, weren't you? You moved in so you could keep an eye on us. Hell, you even set up an elaborate surveillance system to monitor the house. You never had any intention of giving us a chance."

"That's not true," she blurted. "Goddamn it, Cam. That's not fair. It wasn't like that."

Hutch was pale, and he looked decidedly unsteady. "Fair? You want to talk about fair, Reggie? You *lied* to us. When have you ever lied to us?"

She couldn't bear to look at the hurt in their faces. They looked completely and utterly betrayed.

"I didn't lie," she said quietly. "Not about us."

"You look me in the eye and tell me you didn't stay because you were protecting us," Cam bit out.

She stared back at him unblinkingly. "I can't tell you that, Cam. I did stay to protect you, but that wasn't the only reason. Haven't you figured out yet that I'd do anything for you? All of you?"

Sawyer swore and turned away from her. A crack ricocheted through her chest, nearly splitting her in two.

"How hard?" Cam bit out. "How hard did you have to look for an excuse to stay with us? At least be honest now, Reggie. Would you have ever stayed with us if you weren't worried about our safety?"

She froze, unsure of what to say, of how to say it. Yeah, in the beginning, she'd needed all the prompting in the world to agree to something so outlandish. That didn't make her an evil bitch, for God's sake. What mattered, what should matter, were the conclusions she'd come to since. But maybe she'd been wrong, because they didn't appear to trust her very much after all.

"I'll take your silence as all the answer I need," Cam said in disgust.

The phone rang, and Cam yanked it up, his face dark with anger.

"Hello," he barked.

He paused for a moment then thrust the receiver toward her.

"Your chief," he said shortly.

She took the phone, damning the timing. She didn't have time for work shit. She had to make this right with the guys. But Cam wasn't waiting around. He turned abruptly and stalked away. Fear took hold. A knot formed in her throat. Cam never walked away.

With trembling hands, she raised the phone to her ear.

"Yes, sir," she said by way of greeting.

"I need you to come in," he said, cutting straight to the point. "DA wants to meet with you. There are some holes in this case we're trying to sew up."

"Sir, this really isn't a good time," she began.

"I'm sorry, Regina. I need you here. This is too important. Can I expect you within the hour?"

She sighed and closed her eyes. Damn, damn, damn!

"Yes, sir. I'll be right there."

She punched the Off button and slowly put the phone down on the counter.

"I've got to go. I can't put this off," she said in a low voice. "We'll talk about this when I get back."

"Will you be back?" Hutch asked coolly.

Her gaze flickered up to his, and she couldn't hide the hurt in her expression.

"Do you want me to come back?"

"We only want you back if this is where you want to be," Sawyer interjected. "But maybe you ought to be thinking about *why* you'd come back. Because you being here out of some fucked up sense of obligation or you wanting to protect us from the big bad wolf? I don't want you here for that. This isn't about some stupid ass equipment, Reggie. It's about you and us and the fact that maybe we're tired of putting our lives on hold when you have no intention of giving us what we want. And hey, maybe it's not what you want. That's cool. Just say it. But quit jerking us around."

Panic rolled through her like a locomotive. Had they finally reached the end of their patience with her? Numb. She was numb from head to toe. And then she looked up and saw the dead look in Hutch's eyes.

She turned and walked out of the kitchen. It was either go now or break down in front of them.

She heard the crack of a fist meeting a wall, and she flinched, but she didn't go back. She couldn't go back until she had the time to convince them that she loved them and that she wanted to be with them. Always.

She only hoped to hell they'd listen to her this time and that she hadn't used up her allotment of second chances.

CHAPTER 34

*R*egina drove into town with her chest so tight she thought she was going to split open. All she wanted to do was wrap up with the chief and get the hell back home.

"You're looking much better, Regina," Greta said when Regina entered the reception area of the police station.

She didn't feel any better. Not now. "Chief still in? I'm supposed to meet with him and David Conley."

"Let me buzz you in. He's with the DA now." Greta picked up the phone. "Regina's here, Chief. Want me to have her go back?"

Greta gestured to the hallway and nodded at Regina.

Regina walked to the chief's office and tapped at the door. When his call came to enter, she pushed open the door and ducked in.

David Conley rose from his seat and turned to acknowledge Regina. He was a younger DA, but he was a hard-ass in court, where it counted. He'd won reelection in a landslide.

"Regina, you're looking better," the chief said as he gestured for her to take a seat next to David.

"I'm feeling much better, sir," she lied. "I hope to be back at work on Monday as we discussed." But for the first time, returning to the job didn't hold the appeal it had even a day ago.

The chief nodded.

"You've got the right guy in custody?" she asked, cutting quickly to the point. She didn't have time to spend exchanging pleasantries. Not when her entire future was dangling by a thin thread.

Both the chief and David nodded.

"We have his confession," David said. "We're still collecting evidence, but it's formalities. I read your statement, so I know you didn't get a good look at him and couldn't provide a description, but do you think you'd recognize him if you saw him again?"

She frowned. "I just don't know. Sorry. It all happened so fast. I might be able to ID his voice, but he didn't say much. Just the one line about him waiting for me and making 'him' pay."

David grimaced. "That's the only angle we haven't been able to shore up."

Her eyebrows lifted. "What do you mean?"

"His connection to you and who he meant to make pay. He's admitted to the murder, and he provided cursory details about the crime. Location, motive, et cetera. But there was no mention of you, why he attacked you or what his motive was for doing so. We were hoping you'd remember something else about that night that might help us."

She flashed an uncertain look at the chief. "So you don't know if you have the right guy?"

"That's not what we're saying," the chief responded evenly.

"Everything adds up," David broke in. "Except his connection to you. He's admitted to the murder; however, he hasn't said a word about the break-ins or tampering with your vehicle."

"You think he's copped to a murder he didn't commit," she said.

"I didn't say that either," David replied.

"Then what are you saying?"

"There are two possibilities," David said. "One, that the murder and the attack on you that night have nothing to do with the break-ins or the bomb and we're looking for two different suspects. Or two, that we've got a guy in custody who for whatever reason has confessed to a murder he didn't commit. I'm leaning toward the first possibility."

She shook her head. "But that doesn't make any sense. The coincidence is too staggering, and the guy who murdered Misty Thompson most definitely knew who I was and made specific threats against me."

"We'd like to question the suspect again with you present," David said. "I'd like to get a feel for whether he recognizes you, pick up on his body language and see what else we can get from him when we question him directly about you."

She nodded. "I agree. I'd like to hear him speak. I realize a voice ID is shaky at best, but I don't think I'll forget his voice anytime soon."

"Okay, then let's do it," the chief said. "I'll have the prisoner brought in to one of the interrogation rooms." Then he eyed Regina across his desk. "You're still not acting in an official capacity. You're a witness, nothing more."

"I understand, sir. I'll follow your lead."

She rose from her seat.

"Just a minute, Regina," the chief said. He reached into his desk and pulled out her service piece. He slid it across the desk toward her.

"This was through processing a few days ago, but you were out of town. If the doc clears you, we'd be glad to have you back on Monday as we discussed."

"Thank you, sir," she murmured.

She patted the badge in her jeans pocket, drawing comfort from knowing that with everything else in her life spiraling out of control, she at least had her job back. The chief started for the door, and she quickly arranged the shoulder holster and secured her gun before following him out.

It should have meant more. She should have been more relieved. As she walked down the corridor toward the interrogation room, she tried to shake the foreboding that gripped her. It would be all right. She had her job back, and once she explained everything to the guys, things would be okay there too. They had to be.

She took a seat beside David and waited for the prisoner to be brought in.

Two hours later, Regina headed home, her mind in overdrive. Her gut screamed that the guy in custody wasn't the one. He was a smooth son of a bitch. He said all the right things, and if he hadn't killed Misty Thompson, he'd sure done his homework.

But he hadn't so much as blinked in recognition when he'd walked into the exam room. He'd treated her just as he did all the other cops. With polite disdain and smug assuredness.

And his voice was all wrong.

There was enough doubt that the chief had warned her to keep on her toes, even though things had been remarkably quiet since the car bomb incident. David was groaning over the idea of having the wrong guy, and worse, having the wrong guy cop to a murder he didn't commit.

If this guy wasn't the one, it meant they were back to square one. No leads. No suspects.

She increased her speed, her reasons for wanting to get back home in a hurry twofold. Not only was she desperate to make things right with the guys, but now she had to worry that a killer was still on the loose. Someone she knew in her gut was after Hutch.

Then she had to bring them all back in for questioning. Whether they were still speaking to her or not. And now, once again, she was going to be faced with their skepticism over her motives. She sighed. How was she ever going to be able to make them see that she loved them and wanted to be with them, damn the consequences?

When she was a mile from the turnoff to the house, she saw a familiar truck pulled to the side of the road. She leaned forward and frowned as she got closer. It was Hutch's truck.

She pulled up behind it but could see that no one was inside. Dread crept up her spine, and she reached for her gun. Prickles of unease danced across her skin as she slowly got out, her gun in front of her.

As she walked toward the driver's side door, she saw the scrape of red paint on the white exterior. Sideswiped. Someone had sideswiped him and forced him onto the shoulder.

The door was slightly ajar, but what stopped her cold in her tracks was the splatter of blood on the ground. Her gaze traveled upward to see a smear of blood on the window.

She peered inside but found it empty. She whirled around to look on the ground and found a flurry of footprints, crossing over one another, some pressed deep into the dirt of the shoulder.

A struggle.

Her hands shook and panic swelled in her chest. He had Hutch. The son of a bitch had Hutch. She *knew* they had the wrong guy.

She took in the black tire marks leading from the far right of the road toward the middle and then back into the right-hand lane. Traveling north.

She ran for her car and yanked open her cell phone to call it in.

Please, Hutch. Be all right.

And then she prayed they'd find him in time.

CHAPTER 35

*H*utch's eyes flicked open, and pain stabbed him in the temple. He winced and closed his eyes again as he tried to figure out what the hell had happened.

A surge of adrenaline rocketed through his veins when he recalled the van slamming into his truck and forcing him to the shoulder.

Before he'd been able to get out and bitch at the driver, he'd been hauled from his truck by a man over a head taller and about a hundred pounds heavier.

Hutch had fought back, but a crowbar to the head had ended the fight in two seconds.

He tried to raise his fingers to his head to see how badly he was hurt but quickly figured out that he was trussed tighter than a Christmas turkey.

Goddamn it.

He wiggled his fingers experimentally and tried to restore some feeling to them. His hands were tied behind his back and his ankles were bound together.

Fear washed over him. Not for himself but for Reggie. Was this the same asshole who'd attacked her? What was it she'd said? That this whole thing was some sort of payback against him?

He didn't have any fucking enemies that he knew of. His only close friends were Reggie, Sawyer and Cam. He'd fired a few construction workers, but come on. That happened a lot and they didn't go around killing people over it.

The pounding in his head viciously increased, and he had to pant against the nausea curling in his stomach. He had to get the hell out of here. He had to find Reggie.

"I see you're awake."

The sneer echoed across the dimly lit room and startled him into stillness. He lay there unmoving, uncertain of where the man's voice had originated from.

He didn't have to wait long. Light from a kerosene lamp flooded the room as it bobbed closer to him.

A large figure loomed over him. Christ, the man was big. Fear tightened his gut. Was this the asshole who attacked Reggie? Rage replaced his fear.

"Look at me," the man said angrily.

Hutch stared back at the man. "Do I know you?"

Rage simmered across the other man's face. Hatred. Hatred directed at Hutch.

"You don't recognize your brother, Hutch?" he snarled.

Hutch blinked in shock. Brother? Daniel?

"Yeah, that's right. Your little brother in the flesh. Although," he said, "you're looking more like the little brother right about now, don't you think?"

God, it was like looking at his father. They were nearly identical in size and personality. Bile rose in his throat as memories of the night his mother died came crashing back.

"Why do you hate me so much?" Hutch asked faintly. "Why

are you trying to destroy the people I love? What have I ever done to you? If you want to hate someone, hate our father."

Daniel's eyes went cold. "Why do I hate you? Because you left me, you son of a bitch. You left me with that bastard. I endured years of his beatings, his drinking and his mood swings while you were off getting a new life, replacing me with other brothers. You had everything and you never once gave a damn about me."

The words, so harshly spoken yet with such an edge of pain, took Hutch's breath away. His chest swelled until he had a hard time breathing.

"I was just a kid," he said hoarsely. "You can't hold it against me that I had to get away from that monster."

"You left me with him," Daniel choked out. "I'll never forgive you for that. I'm going to take away everything you replaced me with. Your foster mother. Birdie's her name, isn't it? Sweet lady. She could have been my mother too, but you didn't give a damn what happened to me."

"Christ," Hutch said, the words he wanted to say nearly strangling him. "Daniel, listen to me. Birdie isn't to blame. All she did was take in boys who didn't have a home. She would have taken you too if she'd known about you. Don't blame her. Blame me."

"And your cop girlfriend," Daniel continued on as if Hutch hadn't spoken. "I would have killed her but the bitch fought back."

That's my girl. Thank God she was so damn ornery. Now that he'd seen Daniel, he didn't know how the hell Reggie had managed to escape with her life.

"And your business partners. Do you call them your brothers? You were all raised together."

"They're my best friends," Hutch said quietly. "They didn't know about you either, Daniel. They had a rough childhood just like you. It's me you're angry with. Deal with me. I'm the only one to blame for leaving you."

"Yes, you are," he said simply. "But if I kill you first, you won't suffer. I want you to live long enough to suffer the knowledge that the people most important to you are dead."

Helpless rage boiled over him, bubbling up and threatening to explode. He was completely helpless. Unable to do a goddamn thing but lie there and listen to his own brother plot to kill the people he loved most.

"Daniel, what can I do to make this up to you, to make things right?" Hutch said as calmly as he knew how. His only chance was to reason with him, though God only knew how he was supposed to reason with someone who'd obviously lost his grip on sanity a long time ago.

"Where is our father now?" he asked, trying a different tack and subject.

An eerie calm settled over Daniel. His eyes lost some of their wildness, and an element of peace seemed to cloak him. It was chilling.

"I killed the son of a bitch."

Just like he'd killed Misty Thompson, whose only sin had been going to Hutch's senior prom. His throat ached when he imagined her husband and children, alone now, all because of a mistake he'd made when he was just a boy. Just a kid. Scared out of his mind and no longer able to take the brutality of his father. He'd barely been able to take care of himself. How could he have been expected to take care of a younger brother?

You should have tried.

He closed his eyes. It was too late. All the guilt in the world, all the coulda shoulda wouldas in the world wouldn't change the fact that his brother hated him with enough passion to take someone else's life.

"I'll help you, Daniel," he said gently. "We can be a family again. Just promise me you won't hurt anyone else. I have money.

We can buy a house. Just you and me. Go fishing. I remember how much you liked that."

Daniel put his hands over his ears like a child and shook his head vigorously. After a moment, he dropped his hands and moved closer to Hutch. His face was drawn in anger. Dark menace lurked in the brown eyes so much like Hutch's own.

Hutch twisted his wrists, trying to loosen the ropes. They cut into his skin, but he didn't care. He had to try something, anything to escape. There were too many people at risk.

Daniel curled his fingers and reached menacingly toward Hutch. "Back away or I'll shoot!"

Reggie. Jesus Christ, what the hell was she doing here? His gaze flew to the door where she stood, legs apart, her gun aimed at Daniel.

Daniel leapt toward Hutch and, true to her word, she shot. Daniel grunted as he landed on Hutch, knocking the breath out of him. They rolled with Daniel's momentum, and Hutch landed on top of his brother.

Daniel scrambled to his feet, and Hutch felt the warm smear of blood. Reggie had hit Daniel.

A cold blade pressed to Hutch's neck, and he held his breath for fear any movement would send the knife slicing through his skin.

"Put the gun down or he dies," Daniel snarled.

Hutch's gaze found Reggie across the room. Her gun was trained on Daniel, or maybe it was him. They were meshed so close together, Daniel's arm wrapped tight around Hutch, that for all practical purposes she was aiming at both of them.

Her eyes narrowed in intense concentration as she walked forward.

"Put the knife down," she said in a voice that would intimidate even the biggest guy. For the first time, Hutch appreciated what a badass she was when she was in cop mode.

"In a few minutes this place will be swarming with cops. You won't get out alive," she said coldly.

"As long as he dies, it doesn't matter," Daniel said with an edge of desperation to his voice.

Reggie stalked sideways now, adjusting her grip on the gun, trying to get a better angle to take Daniel out. As much as Hutch wanted out of his current predicament, his heart sank at the idea of his brother dying. Such a goddamn waste.

The knife cut into his skin and a trickle of blood slithered down his neck. Reggie stopped in her tracks and held the gun in unwavering hands.

"What have you got against Hutch?" she asked in a calm voice. "I mean I know he can be a pain in the ass, but surely that isn't worth the death penalty."

Gee thanks, Reggie. He glared at her, but she didn't so much as look at him. All her attention was focused on Daniel.

"Tell her who you are, Daniel," Hutch rasped, careful not to send the blade any deeper into his neck. "She'll want to meet you."

"Daniel. Nice name," Reggie commented. "Got a last?"

"It's Bishop," Daniel snarled.

Hutch saw Reggie's eyes widen as she made the connection.

"Well you obviously aren't his father. I'm gonna guess you're his younger brother. You know he used to talk about you all the time."

Daniel stiffened and Hutch almost groaned. What the hell was she doing? He'd never mentioned his brother. Hell, she hadn't known he had one until the other night.

"What did he say?" Daniel demanded, and Hutch marveled at how childlike he sounded.

"Just that you two used to have some good times," she said in a calm, measured voice. Damn she was good. "What a sorry bas-

tard your father was to both of you and how he regretted that you
didn't get out with him."

Somehow, she'd managed to get a grasp on the situation. Either that or she was a damn good guesser. But she'd plunged right
into the heart of the matter.

"Yeah, right," Daniel spat. "He felt real bad. He got everything. A mother. New brothers. You. He got you. I want him to
watch all of you die. I want him to know what it feels like to lose
people he loves."

The knife dug deeper into his skin and more blood slid down
his neck. Christ. This wasn't good.

Reggie raised the gun and leveled it with an ice-cold look.
"Put the knife down, Daniel. You don't want to do this."

"Back off!" Daniel screamed. "I'll kill him right now. It won't
matter if you shoot me or not. I'll slice his neck before I die."

Reggie hesitated, and her eyes narrowed in concentration.
Obviously she was judging his determination. She relaxed and
lowered her gun. Maybe she realized he wasn't bluffing.

"All right," she said soothingly. "Let's do this your way. I'll put
my gun down. You let Hutch go. It's me you want, right? You
want Hutch to watch me die. He can't do that if he dies first,
Daniel."

"Reggie, no!" Hutch bellowed. "What the fuck are you thinking? Shoot him. Do it now."

She ignored him and crouched down, hunkering on the floor.
She laid the gun on the carpet and slowly stood again. She kicked
the gun away and it went spiraling across the floor.

"There. Gun is gone. Now show me some faith here. Let Hutch
go. You'll have me. I'm who you want. He loves me, you know. You
kill me and he'll suffer."

"Reggie. Goddamn it. *No!*" He wouldn't let her sacrifice herself for him.

But the choice wasn't his. He found himself shoved forward, falling to the floor with a thump. He rolled, desperate to see what was happening around him.

Reggie crouched in a defensive position as Daniel closed in on her. Hutch yanked at the ropes around his wrists, uncaring of the fact they were shredding his skin. He couldn't let her face Daniel alone. She didn't stand a chance against the big son of a bitch, no matter how good she was.

Daniel lunged, and she ducked then launched herself across the floor toward her gun. She hit the carpet with a thump when Daniel snagged her ankle.

"Bitch," he snarled. "You'll pay for this. He'll watch you die all right. And it won't be quick. I'm going to enjoy taking you apart, piece by piece."

She whipped her other foot out and connected with his jaw. He grunted but held on to her ankle and slowly dragged her toward him.

Hutch yanked frantically, trying desperately to loosen the ropes. He wouldn't watch her die. Damn it, where were the cops she promised were showing up?

Daniel let go of her ankle, but grasped her shirt in his beefy hand and yanked her to her feet. He held her up so that her feet dangled from the floor. And then he backhanded her, sending her reeling.

Son of a bitch! Fury ignited like a brushfire. One of the ropes gave way and he had his hand free. He tore at the ropes that were slick with his blood.

Reggie recovered quickly and backed away, keeping space between her and Daniel. Her gun was behind Daniel.

Good, keep him away from you, baby. Please.

The final piece of rope fell free, and he reached for the bonds circling his ankles.

Keep him busy. Just a few more seconds. I won't let you die for me, Reggie.

Daniel grunted in pain, and Hutch looked up to see Reggie on bended knee, her fist buried in Daniel's balls. *Good girl.*

But then she went sprawling when Daniel clipped her with one of those big-as-a-brick fists.

Her cry of pain split the air. Hutch cursed his numb fingers as they fumbled with the ropes.

There was a flurry of action when Daniel went after Reggie and she came up fighting. She connected with a roundhouse kick that managed to knock Daniel back a step. She pressed her momentary advantage by throwing a barrage of punches to his midsection, and then she clipped him with an uppercut.

She was a blur of elbows, fists and feet as she continued to back Daniel across the floor. If Hutch hadn't been so damn scared for her, he'd have admired the way she totally kicked ass.

Blood poured from her nose, but she didn't even stop to wipe it as she continued her relentless assault. She executed a mean jab and must have found the bullet wound, because Daniel's muffled cry of pain echoed across the room.

Finally the rope came free, and Hutch scrambled to his feet. He launched himself at Daniel, and they went down in a heap. His brother was built like a damn cement block. It was like hitting a brick wall going sixty miles per hour.

Hutch played dirty. He rammed his fist into the shoulder that had taken the bullet. Daniel grunted but threw a punch of his own, knocking Hutch off him.

As Hutch struggled to his feet, Daniel charged him, bellowing like an angry bull.

Reggie stepped in front of him and went down under Daniel's assault. Rage blinded Hutch. Fury that Reggie had placed herself in front of him, fury that Daniel had hurt her.

Reggie reared back with her head and butted Daniel right in the nose. Blood spurted as Daniel howled in pain. Hutch leapt for him, knocking him off Reggie as they rolled in a mass of twisted arms and legs.

Hutch slugged him in the shoulder again then followed it up with one to his nose. The combined force of him and Reggie was getting to Daniel. His attack was weakening. Hutch felt a surge of hope. He and Reggie might get out of this yet.

Daniel connected with a fist to Hutch's chin, and Hutch fell back. Daniel turned on Reggie again as she dragged herself to her feet. The gun was just a few feet from her, and she lunged for it, landing on her stomach as she reached.

Daniel reached down, grabbed Reggie by the back of her neck and pulled her up with one hand. He tossed her back, and she landed with a thump several feet away. Hutch lunged for the gun, but Daniel got to it first.

It was one of those moments when according to books and movies, things were supposed to move in slow motion. But Hutch barely processed the next few seconds.

Daniel raised the gun and pointed it directly at Reggie.

"Noooo!" Hutch yelled.

The shot echoed like a cannon in the small room. Hutch looked at Reggie in horror, but it was Daniel who faltered and then sank like a sagging puppet to the floor. The gun fell from his hand, and he clutched at his chest, sucking air like a friggin' guppy.

Hutch yanked his head around to see Jeremy standing in the doorway, gun drawn. Behind him, a half dozen cops poured into the room. The entire world had gone to hell.

Reggie.

He whirled around again, searching for her. She sank to her knees, but she was alive. Sweet relief burst over him. Never had he seen such a beautiful sight as Reggie kneeling on the carpet as her fellow cops surrounded her.

He dragged himself to his feet and stumbled over to her. He threw one cop out of the way and yanked her into his arms.

"Don't you *ever* scare me like that again, baby."

"Me?" she sputtered. "You're the one who disappeared on me. I find your empty truck on the side of the road, your blood, and you nowhere to be found. If anyone was scared it was me."

He held her close, stroking his hand over her hair.

"Can we get out of here?" he said.

They pushed themselves to their feet, unsteady as a couple of toddlers learning to walk. She looked like hell, and God only knew how bad he looked. But he needed air. He needed to be away from the sight of his brother lying on the floor as the paramedics tended to him. As much as he wanted to feel hatred for Daniel, all he could summon was deep sadness.

Reggie hooked his arm over her shoulder, and began helping him toward the door. Oh hell no.

He dropped his arm and tucked her against his side, determined to help *her*.

She dragged his arm back up to her shoulders and held it there in her firm grip as they both staggered out the door into the night.

"How the hell did you find me?" he muttered. "I don't even know where the fuck we are."

"It wasn't easy. I had to comb the entire countryside after I found your truck. I had the whole department looking."

"I feel like I got run over by a damn Mack truck," he said with a groan.

"You look like it too," she said.

"Well you don't look much better."

She grinned, and he felt the heaviness in his chest ease.

"Aww, fuck," she muttered.

He followed her gaze to see Sawyer and Cam standing by one of the police cars. They both looked worried as hell, but when they recognized him and Reggie staggering toward them, he could see relief lighten their features, drawn harsh by the glare of flashing lights.

He glanced back down at Reggie and saw the haunted look in her eyes, the fear and strain crowding her features. He tightened his arm around her.

"You two look like shit," Sawyer said.

"Aren't you observant," Reggie said snidely.

Cam heaved an exaggerated sigh. "They probably think they deserve special attention. I'm not doing all the cooking."

Reggie glared at both Cam and Sawyer while Hutch did all he could to hold in his laughter. God, this was what he needed. For a moment he could forget that he'd almost lost everything that was important to him to someone who had once meant everything to him.

Reggie trembled against him and started to sag. He made a grab for her, but his own knees buckled, and they went down in a heap on the ground.

He groaned and looked up to see Cam and Sawyer staring down at them, both shaking their heads.

Sawyer made a tsking sound. "Pathetic." He reached down to haul Hutch up while Cam reached for Reggie, cradling her in his arms.

"Be careful with her," Hutch rasped. "She took a beating in there."

"Yes, I see," Cam said quietly.

Two medics from the second ambulance on scene hurried over, jump bags in hand. One of them reached for Reggie, only to be halted by Cam's steely glare.

"Let us check her out," the paramedic said.

Sawyer was holding Hutch up, which was a good damn thing, because he'd lost all the feeling in both feet.

"I'll carry her," Cam said. "Where do you want her?"

"Over by the truck." The medic gestured toward the flashing ambulance twenty yards over. "Can you walk?" he asked Hutch.

"I'll make sure he gets there," Sawyer said grimly.

"Thanks man, I owe you," Hutch said as Sawyer half dragged, half carried him toward the ambulance.

"No offense dude, but I think I'll wait to collect until you're looking a little better."

Hutch snorted. "Big of you."

There was silence as he and Sawyer followed behind Cam. Then in a low voice, Sawyer asked, "How bad is she, Hutch? What happened in there?"

They got to the ambulance, and Cam laid Reggie on a stretcher while Sawyer leaned Hutch against the back of the ambulance.

"She stuck up for me," Hutch said quietly. "The little fool gave herself up for me and taunted Daniel into letting me go in exchange for killing her. Then she tried to beat the hell out of him. Succeeded for the most part."

Sawyer shook his head. "It doesn't surprise me in the least." He chanced a glance at Reggie, who was being checked over by the paramedic. "You think she'll be okay?"

"Yeah, I do," Hutch replied. "She took a beating but she gave as good as she got. We'll both feel like shit in the morning, but I don't think it's anything serious." He hoped. God, he hoped.

His gaze found Sawyer's. "I understand why she did it," he said quietly.

Sawyer cocked his head. "Did what?"

Hutch took a deep breath. "When I was in there, and Daniel was whaling on Reggie, when I thought for sure he'd kill her and

I'd lose her forever, I realized why she deceived us, because in that moment? I'd have done anything to protect her. I'd lie, cheat, steal. I would kill a man and I wouldn't give a shit about the consequences. But you know what? It doesn't mean I don't love her. It just means I'd do anything to keep her safe. If she loves us half as much then I understand why she lied to us."

Sawyer heaved a sigh, looked away then glanced back at Hutch, his eyes a little wild in the headlights and flashing blue and red. "Yeah, I hear you, man. I feel the same way. But in the end, she has to want to stay, you know? We can't force her, and I wouldn't want to."

Hutch nodded, but he felt a little lighter and not as panicky as he had earlier. She loved them. She had to. He wouldn't believe that it had all been an act. No one was that good.

Hutch waved off the medic as he walked over to check him over.

"I'm fine," he said.

"Are you sure?" the medic asked.

Hutch nodded. "Yeah, I'm good. Just check Reggie out. Make sure she's okay. Make sure she hasn't broken her damn wrist. It was already injured."

The medic chuckled. "I think she'll be just fine. She's steadily cursing my partner over there. I left before she started threatening me as well."

Sawyer laughed, and Hutch could hear the relief in his voice. If Reggie was making threats, she was just fine.

CHAPTER 36

*R*egina lay curled in a ball on the ambulance stretcher, scowling as one of the medics poked and prodded at her. Cam's fingers were laced with hers, a gesture she drew comfort from. He couldn't hate her too much, right? He was here. He and Sawyer both were here. Only she'd lost track of both Sawyer and Hutch in the confusion.

"Sawyer? Hutch? Where the hell are they?" she demanded. Where the hell were they? Surely they wouldn't leave. They couldn't be that angry with her, could they?

The grip around her fingers tightened. "Calm down, Reggie. They're here."

What wasn't Cam telling her? Had Hutch been hurt worse than she thought? Panic tightened its grip around her, squeezing mercilessly.

She struggled against the hands holding her down, fought to sit up. "Hutch!"

"I'm here, baby."

She saw him push his way through the people surrounding her, and she went weak with relief. "Where's Sawyer?"

Her gaze scanned the faces. They all swam in the cascade of flashing lights, and she blinked to try and make sense of it all.

A strong hand gripped her shoulder and shoved her back down on the stretcher. Relief caved her chest inward. Sawyer.

"Don't make me strap your ass to this stretcher," Sawyer growled. "Quit giving the medics such a hard time, and let them check you out."

"Make sure Hutch is okay," she said groggily. "His hands were a mess."

"How 'bout you let me worry about Hutch, and you concentrate on patching your pretty little ass up, okay?" Sawyer said.

"I'm not going to the hospital," she huffed. "I'm fine. Want you to take me home."

Cam squeezed her hand, and Sawyer stroked the hair from her face.

"And where is home, Reggie darling?"

She frowned. "Wherever the hell you take me."

Sawyer chuckled. "Good answer, honey. Good answer."

"Where's Hutch?" she demanded again.

"I'm right here, baby," he said, and she turned her head to see him standing there beside her. Concern creased his brow as he stared down at her. "I wonder if you shouldn't go to the hospital and let them scan that noggin of yours. You seem a bit fuzzy."

She pushed Sawyer's hand away from her shoulder and sat straight up. "I don't need to go to the goddamn hospital. What I need is for everyone to back the fuck off so I can breathe. And then I want to go home." She was desperate for home. Their arms. Being with them.

The paramedic gave the guys a look of sympathy and then retreated with his jump bag. "She's all yours," he said.

She glanced over at Hutch and saw that he hadn't been tended to at all.

"Goddamn paramedics," she grumbled. "I told them to make sure Hutch was taken care of."

Cam's hand stole up her neck, and he massaged gently at the nape. She groaned in sheer bliss and leaned into his touch.

"Not to worry, love. Sawyer and I will take care of our baby brother as soon as we get the both of you home."

She looked gratefully up at Cam. He must have heard by now that it had been Hutch's brother behind the attacks. With his statement, he reemphasized that Hutch had two brothers who cared about him.

"Baby my ass," Hutch growled. "What are you, six months older than me?"

"Seven," Sawyer said with a grin. "*I'm* six months older. Cam is seven."

"And you wouldn't keep count, I suppose," Hutch said darkly.

"Can we go already?" she asked as she slid off the stretcher. Her feet hit the ground, and she went down like a rock, her knees buckling and the rest of her sliding to the ground like jelly.

Sawyer and Cam both made a grab for her and hauled her to her feet between them.

"Feet aren't working right," she mumbled.

Sawyer laughed. "Yeah, we can see that."

Cam frowned. "Are you sure we shouldn't take her to the hospital?" He wasn't even talking to her now. He was talking over her head to Sawyer. As if she wasn't even there.

She growled under her breath but was ignored by both men.

"If you could just give me a little help to the truck, I'll be fine."

Instead of help, she found herself lifted into the air, and she fell against Cam's chest with a plop. She turned to look behind her, to see Sawyer wrap his arm around Hutch's waist and help him along. She nodded her satisfaction that Hutch was taken care of and then wilted against Cam.

"You know I'm going to kick your ass over this stunt later," Cam said.

She nodded and closed her eyes. "Yeah, well, give me a few days first. Then I'll let you *try* and kick it." As long as he'd be there, she'd bend over and present her ass for him to kick all he wanted.

He chuckled and relaxed against her. He crawled into the backseat, still holding her, while Sawyer stuffed Hutch into the front and then walked around to the driver's side.

It hit her like a ton of bricks. More forcefully than any of the blows from Daniel. This was what she wanted. More than anything. The three of them. Cam, Sawyer and Hutch. With her always.

She hadn't trusted them. Hadn't trusted that they could deal with the relationship. But she couldn't be responsible for the way they handled it. All she could do was manage her own contribution.

Elation surged through her veins until she was nearly dizzy with it. It was on them. She had to trust them to do what they'd promised. That was all she had to do and all she *could* do.

If it worked, it worked, but she couldn't continue to try and manage every aspect, make herself crazy trying to be all things to everyone. She could only be herself and that's all they said they wanted. Her.

She wanted them. Loved them with every piece of her soul. And they loved her. Wasn't that all that was important?

She turned her face into Cam's stomach and wrapped her arms around his waist. Her knees dug into the back of the seat as she pressed herself tighter against him, but she couldn't let go.

She loved them all so damn much, and she was tired of running. Tired of being miserable without them.

She knew there'd be statements to give, reports to file. The chief would want the full story. But for now, all she wanted was to go home and sleep for about twenty-four hours. It was too important that she be at her best when she next talked to the guys. She couldn't afford to fuck it up.

When Jeremy stuck his head in the door, she mumbled appropriate responses to his questions and promised a full report later. She wasn't entirely sure what the hell he'd said, but he left, so she must have nodded in the right spots.

"What did I just promise to do?" she muttered when Jeremy had gone.

Cam chuckled. "Just that you'd be in as soon as you woke from your coma."

"Oh. Well then, let's go home so I can enter that coma."

And coma it was. She barely remembered being put to bed, only that she was snuggled up tight to a warm, male body. They couldn't be *too* angry with her if they were still hanging around. She held on to that knowledge, along with the hope that it wasn't too late to make things work between them.

She slept for an ungodly amount of time, only to wake up and have a painkiller shoved at her with breakfast in bed. By the time she'd finished eating, the world was fuzzy around her, and she was only too happy to let them tuck her back into bed.

There were vague memories. Light touches to her cheek. A hand smoothed through her hair. The more annoying wake-ups with fingers shoved into her face with a demand of how many. She batted them away and told them to go to hell.

The next time she woke there weren't actually any men in her face or next to her on the bed. She yawned big enough to crack her jaw and then looked at the time. Noon. But what day? She felt like she'd slept an entire week.

She lay there for a long while, staring up at the ceiling. She would have to face them with what she'd done. They'd have questions. She'd hurt them. A grimace worked over her face. She hadn't wanted to hurt them. That was the last thing she'd ever wanted to do. All she wanted to do was keep them safe, because she simply couldn't live without them.

She stretched and tested the limits of her body. To her satisfaction, she found that she was limber, not stiff, and that she could move with no pain.

Good damn thing, because she needed flexibility if she was going to pull off her grand plan of seducing all three men into taking her at the same time. If they weren't still pissed at her. Fear gripped her. She'd never seen them so angry . . . or so resigned. That resignation frightened her.

She got up and took a quick shower, hoping she could be dressed and ready to go before any of the guys swooped in with painkillers or demands to stay in bed. She needed to go into the station and tie up loose ends. And she needed to talk to her chief.

Ten minutes later, her hair still wet, she headed down the stairs, prepared for the inevitable confrontation.

All three guys were in the living room, and her hungry gaze found Hutch. Other than a bruise darkening the side of his face, he looked fine.

They all looked up when she walked over to where they sat.

"What the hell are you doing up?" Sawyer demanded.

She ignored him and went over to where Hutch was slouched on the sofa. For a moment she hesitated, afraid he'd reject her advances. Then she steeled herself and hooked her leg over his, straddling his lap. His arms came around her at the same time hers curved around his neck. She hugged him fiercely and kissed the side of his neck.

"Thank goodness you're all right," she whispered.

"I could say the same for you," he murmured as he stroked her hair. "And it's thanks to you that I'm okay. Even if I'm pissed as hell that you put yourself in front of me like that."

He pulled her away so he could look her in the face. His anger was building even as he fought with the relief he felt over her safety. He was as transparent as plastic wrap.

"I swear to God, if you ever pull a stunt like that again, baby, I'm going to lock you in a damn cage."

She raised one eyebrow then leaned forward and kissed him into silence. Then before he could react, she shoved off his lap. "Anyone seen my keys?"

Three sets of confused stares locked onto her.

"Why on earth do you need your keys?" Cam asked.

"I have to run to the station," she said calmly. "I need to talk to the chief. It's important. I won't be long."

"Reggie, we have to talk," Sawyer said firmly.

She softened just a bit as she stared into his blue eyes.

"I know we have to talk," she said quietly. "This is something I need to take care of. Then I'll be back."

"At least let one of us drive you in," Hutch protested.

She shook her head. "I'll be fine." She glanced over at Cam to judge his reaction, but his features were locked in stone. She had a feeling he was going to be the hardest sale when she came back to grovel.

She sighed and squared her shoulders. She wouldn't let herself dwell on her possible failure.

"I'll be back," she said firmly.

"Will you?" Cam asked in a distant voice. "Or have you already left?"

Her gaze swung back to his, met his dark, unreadable eyes. He was sewn up tight. No emotion. In total self-preservation mode. And the damndest thing about it was she couldn't even blame him. She'd hurt him. Hurt them all with her continued resistance, her stubbornness.

"I'll be back, Cam," she said softly. "The question will be whether you still want me."

Without waiting for his response, not that she expected one, she turned and walked toward the front door. Her keys were lying on the table in the hall, and she scooped them up and walked into the midday sun.

CHAPTER 37

Carl and David sat in on her statement, and she went over every single detail of her encounter with Daniel Bishop. Daniel remained in stable condition in the hospital despite suffering two gunshot wounds. One from her and one from Jeremy.

After two hours of the exhausting, painstaking rendering of details, Carl and David excused her with their thanks. She stumbled into the hallway and started toward the chief's office. When she rounded the corner, she nearly ran headlong into her father.

He caught her arms to steady her then held her out as he stared down at her. "Regina," he said stiffly. "I assume you're well?"

She was too tired and too impatient to get back home to stand around exchanging barbs with dear ole dad.

"I'm fine," she muttered. "If you'll excuse me, I need to see Chief Witherspoon."

He hesitated for a moment and then his lips drew in. "Your mother was worried," he said gruffly. Not *I was worried*. Your mother was worried. Regina sighed and shook her head.

"Tell Lydia I'm fine."

She stepped away, forcing him to release her arms, then walked around him and down the hall.

She tapped at the chief's open door. "May I come in, sir?"

The chief looked up from behind his desk. "Regina, of course. Come in."

She walked in and closed the door behind her. Taking a deep breath, she walked over to the chair in front of his desk and wiped her damp palms down the legs of her jeans.

She settled into the chair but sat forward on the edge, her posture stiff and tense.

The chief stared speculatively at her. "Is something wrong, Regina?"

"No," she said quietly. "I needed to speak to you about something. It's . . . personal."

"All right. I don't need to tell you that whatever is said here will remain strictly in confidence."

"I understand, sir, and I appreciate it."

Why was this so hard? But it had to start here. If she couldn't even tell the chief, how could she expect to be able to handle it when her relationship became public? And it would. No way she could continue to live with three men without small town talk making the rounds.

"Regina?" he prompted. "There was something you wanted to say?"

"Yeah, uh, there's something I think you should be made aware of. As my superior."

"Okay," he said patiently.

She took in a deep breath. "I'll be remaining with Cam Douglas, Hutch Bishop and Sawyer Pritchard on a permanent basis. That is I'm involved . . . romantically with them." Her cheeks tightened and heated as she stumbled over just how to explain such a relationship.

The chief obviously caught on, because his eyes widened despite his best attempt to remain impassive.

"I see."

"I know there'll be talk," she said quietly. "I don't want to ever do anything to bring dishonor to this department. I love my job, but if it ever comes down to me choosing between them and my job, it's a no-brainer. I'll choose them."

"Are you saying you want to quit?" the chief asked.

She shook her head. "No. I want very much to keep my job, but I also know things could get difficult. You might be pressured to let me go. I don't want to embroil the department in a public relations nightmare, nor do I want the people of this town to ever doubt the ability of their police department to keep them safe. As much as I want to keep my job, I won't allow my personal choices to jeopardize our department or its reputation."

The chief sat back in his chair and fiddled with the pen in his fingers. "As you well know, I try never to get involved with my officers' private lives. I operate on the principle that if it doesn't affect the job, it ain't none of my business."

She sensed an unspoken *but*.

"But in this case, I feel compelled to ask if you've thought this through, Regina. Are you sure this is what you want and what is best for you?"

"I know it's . . . different," she said for lack of a better word.

"That it is," the chief muttered. "You have obviously steeled yourself for the worst of the gossip and the possibility of losing your job, but have you thought longer term than that?"

"I just know I don't want a life without them," she said quietly. "I know it'll take sacrifices. I'm not fooling myself into thinking it'll be easy."

The chief studied her for a moment. "I can see you're serious about this. You've always fiercely defended those boys and they've always had a huge soft spot for you. I won't say that I don't think you're making a mistake, but as your chief, it's none of my business as long as it doesn't interfere with your job."

Hope rose in her chest. "Does this mean I still have a job?"

"Of course it does. I can't afford to lose good officers. Your sex life is none of my business and it sure as hell ain't the public's business. Not that they won't make it theirs, but you have to be prepared for that. I can't guarantee you what'll happen next week or next month, especially given the fact your father is the mayor, but as far as I'm concerned you're a good cop and unless you fuck up on the job, you're staying."

"Thank you, sir," she said around the knot in her throat. "I won't let you down."

"I know you won't, Regina." He glanced up at her with kind eyes. "This won't be easy for you. You know that."

She breathed in deep. "I know. I don't expect it to be. And maybe the important things shouldn't be easy." She stood. "Thank you. I really appreciate your understanding. If you don't mind, I'd like to get back home. I have three men pissed off because I've left them high and dry."

The chief chuckled. "I have a feeling you'll run circles around those boys. I almost feel sorry for them."

She grinned and turned to walk out of his office. She hadn't taken a full step when she looked up and saw her father leaning against the wall just outside the chief's door. His face was drawn into a tight mask, his eyes dark and angry.

He straightened and stood staring at her for a long moment. "If you persist in your line of behavior, I'll have no choice but to recommend your removal from the police department."

She laughed. It came out dry and cracked, but it was either laugh or give in to the fury racing like a tornado through her veins. The bastard had eavesdropped on her conversation with the chief, and now he was trying to blackmail her into compliance?

There was so much she wanted to say. She wanted to blast him with both barrels, but he wasn't worth it, and the men she loved were home waiting on her.

She walked forward, pressing close and angling her face until they were just inches apart.

"Since you quite obviously eavesdropped on my conversation you already damn well know that if I ever have to choose between them and my job, then I'll find a new profession. Now, if we're through, I have somewhere to be. Namely home."

She turned to walk away but cast one last scornful look in his direction. "You don't have the balls anyway."

She drove home feeling lighter than she had in ages. She was through worrying about outside forces. Her father, the chief, what the town would think if they knew. Those things were completely and utterly out of her control.

As she turned into the drive, nervousness scuttled up her chest.

Seduce then speak. It had a nice ring to it. Hopefully they'd cooperate. She was much better at showing them how she felt than at spilling her guts. There would be plenty of time to talk later. They were guys. Actions spoke a lot louder than words.

CHAPTER 38

*T*he house was quiet when she let herself in. The living room was deserted, not that she'd expected them to wait with bated breath for her return.

She dropped her keys on the coffee table and mulled over her options. Chances were, Cam was in his office and the other two were up in their rooms. Which made her plan to make them all take her a little difficult.

Would they come to her if they knew she was at home? Or were they tired of making all the moves? She couldn't blame them if they were. She hadn't made it easy for them.

She drifted up the stairs, not disguising the sounds of her homecoming in the least. But when she reached the top, no one walked into the hallway.

She stared at the bedroom door at the end. The room with the really big bed. She hadn't really understood its significance until now. A common room? She nearly giggled. They all had their own rooms and then there was the room. The sex room.

She rolled her eyes but walked toward the closed doorway. She threw it open and walked in, leaving it open behind her.

Sexual tease expert she wasn't. Like Sawyer, she'd been around the block a few times, but she wasn't that experienced at seduction. She much preferred that to be the guy's job.

Remembering the other night with Sawyer, when she'd been so provocative, told her that she could do it under the right circumstances. This being one of them.

Well, they knew she was home. They had to. They were too tuned in to what went on around them not to figure it out. Maybe when they realized she wasn't going to be beating down their doors, they'd come in search of her. And she'd be waiting. Boy, would she be waiting.

She slipped out of her clothes and tossed them toward the window. Then she walked naked to the bed and smoothed her hands over the plush down comforter. She crawled onto it, enjoying the softness on her bare skin.

She stretched out on her stomach and nuzzled her face into the pillows. It was tempting to sleep, but her plans didn't incorporate sleep for quite a long time.

Pushing herself up, she rolled until she was on her back. She slid her palms over her belly and then up to her breasts. She palmed both and fingered the nipples until they were taut and straining upward.

She imagined lips around each point. Hutch on one side. Cam on the other. Sawyer between her legs.

She closed her eyes and pulled harder at the tips, rolling them between her thumb and forefinger as an ache began between her legs.

Her left hand went seeking lower, smoothing down her belly and to her pelvis. In her mind, Sawyer was spreading her wider as he thrust deeper. Hutch had moved over her mouth, his knees on either side of her head. They both slid into her welcoming body.

She moaned at the force of the fantasy. There was only one thing missing. She wanted them all. At the same time. Filling her, loving her.

Her fingers slid through the tight little curls and between the two lips to her clitoris. It was tight and sensitive. As soon as she touched it, her entire lower half twitched in response.

She slid her hand up and down, allowing her finger to roll over her clit and then lower to the moist entrance that quivered in anticipation of having a cock. Her finger made a poor substitute.

Soon, very soon if she had her way.

She arched her hips and let out a dreamy sigh.

"I'd ask if you want any help, but it looks like you're doing fine on your own."

Cam's sexy voice washed over her, inciting prickly little goose bumps over her skin.

She opened her eyes and raised her head to see all three men standing in the doorway. There was no disguising the blatant lust in their expressions. She stared into Cam's eyes, searching for something beyond the arousal.

Slowly, she let her hand move back up her body, leaving a slightly damp trail up her middle. Then she raised her finger to her mouth and sucked it inside, removing the traces of her passion with her tongue.

Identical groans sounded from the doorway.

Not willing to let them disrupt *her* fantasy in any way, she crawled up to her knees and then slid over the edge of the bed. She sauntered over to Cam, grabbed a handful of his shirt and began dragging him toward the bed.

His eyes widened in surprise, but he made absolutely no effort to stop her. Smart man.

She turned her head to look at Sawyer and Hutch, who still stood there, their gazes inquisitive.

"I'll let you know when to join," she said huskily.

"Yes ma'am," Sawyer murmured.

She hauled Cam over to the bed. Her hand still full of his shirt, she yanked him downward until their lips met in a fiery clash. His hands gripped her waist then moved upward, skating over her skin on their way to her breasts. He palmed the soft mounds and rolled his thumbs over the tips.

"Strip," she said against his lips.

"I do love it when you get all bossy on me," he said.

He jerked at his jeans and shirt, and in short order he was standing naked in front of her. Unable to resist the temptation of his too perfect body, she put both hands flat against his chest.

In no hurry, she smoothed her palms down his firm abdomen and then lower to his distended cock. She wrapped her fingers around his length and pumped up and down, enjoying the feel of his hardness in her palm.

With her other hand, she pushed at his chest until the backs of his knees were touching the edge of the bed. Then she shoved more forcefully until he fell over, his back hitting the mattress with a thump.

She crawled up after him and gazed down at him, her eyes drinking him in like someone starved for water.

Placing both hands above his knees, she ran her fingers upward, tracing a line to his hips. When her head was level with his cock, she leaned over and kissed his stomach, allowing her lips and her tongue to linger in the shallow indention of his navel.

The muscles beneath her mouth jumped and quivered in reaction. She smiled, enjoying her power, her ability to make this gorgeous man squirm. Even better? Two equally gorgeous men waited at the door for her command.

His cock brushed her chin when she moved lower. Her tongue flicked out and licked at the tip, and he groaned as her mouth flirted with the crown of his penis.

It was an intoxicating sight. Cam lying there flat on his back, his sexy hair splayed out over the pillow. His powerful body rippled every time he tensed. His cock, thick and long, stood at attention, stretching upward from the dark hair at his groin.

It was a temptation she was unable to pass up. Her intention to torture him thoroughly, she placed the tip in her mouth and closed her lips around it. Then with infinitesimal slowness, she inched downward, sheathing him in the damp confines of her mouth.

His fingers tangled in her hair, almost rough as he arched his hips. She took him deep, letting his cock slide across her tongue and to the back of her throat. She loved the taste of him. Musky. Comfortable and warm. She felt safe, like she was surrounded by him. By his love.

She shivered as she sucked up and down. She wrapped her hand around the base and worked up and down in rhythm with her mouth.

His hands tightened in her hair then loosened and massaged gently as he coaxed her to take him harder, deeper.

Still gripping him with her hand, she allowed him to slide free from her mouth, and she looked up at him through passion-dimmed eyes.

"Are they watching, Cam?" she asked huskily. "Are they watching me suck your cock? Do they like it? Are they as turned on as you right now?"

His eyes glittered brightly against flushed cheeks. He turned to the side as she did, to look at Sawyer and Hutch. They stood in the doorway though Hutch had pushed his way farther in. Discernible bulges centered their groins, and their gazes were fastened on Regina and Cam.

Her eyes still on Hutch and Sawyer, she lowered her head and took Cam in her mouth again. She continued to watch out of the corner of her eye as she rolled down his cock. Her cheeks worked in and out as she sucked him deeper.

He was hard and throbbing on her tongue, and she couldn't wait any longer to have him inside her. She moved up his body, straddling his hips. Using one hand to hold his cock in place, she arched up and positioned him at her entrance.

A long hiss escaped him as she hovered over him, the head of his cock fitted to her rim. Then she sank down on him, sheathing him in one fluid motion.

Her pussy rippled and contracted as she welcomed him into her body. She closed her eyes and absorbed the moment, the feeling of him buried so deeply.

His hands curled around her hips, but his touch was gentle. Loving. His fingers caressed her skin as he coaxed her to ride him. She undulated her hips, rocking forward and then back.

She put her hands on his stomach and slid forward, aligning their bodies as her hands skated up his chest and around his neck. Her lips found his, smooching softly, the sound sweet in her ears.

He curved his hands over her ass, cupping, gently squeezing as he rocked his hips upward.

She sipped at his lips, tasting him, the flavor of the coffee he drank on her tongue. As she lay on his chest, their bodies undulating in perfect rhythm, she glanced over at Sawyer, locking gazes with him.

"Come to me," she whispered. "Take me."

Sawyer strode forward, ripping his clothes off with every step. He reached for the tube of lubricant lying on the nightstand and hurriedly squeezed a generous amount onto his fingers.

She lost sight of him as he moved behind her. And then she felt his warm lips against her shoulder as he bent over her back.

His hard chest pressed against her back, pushing her further into Cam's embrace.

Sawyer kissed a gentle line down her spine, ending at the small of her back. Then he kissed each cheek of her ass before he spread them.

The motion stretched her pussy around Cam's cock and both she and Cam gasped in pleasure at the sensation. Sawyer's fingers, slick with gel, rubbed over the seam of her ass. He delved one finger inside the tight ring, causing her to jerk forward against Cam.

Cam caught her in his arms, holding her in place as Sawyer fit his cock against her anus.

She shuddered and closed her eyes as the broad head pushed against her. Wider and wider she was stretched. It burned. Intense. Just when she thought her body wouldn't give way, she opened and accepted him, and he slipped inside her ass.

Her eyes flew open at the shock of having two huge cocks stuffed in her body at the same time. She couldn't move. She didn't dare. She wasn't sure her body could take the strain.

Sawyer groaned, a delicious sound, as he pressed forward. His hips came to rest against her ass and he paused, allowing her to absorb the wicked sensation of being so tightly stretched around both his and Cam's cocks.

"What does it look like?" she said with a moan. She wanted to see. What would it look like to see their cocks buried so deeply in her body?

"I've never seen anything so erotic," Hutch spoke up, surprising her.

She glanced over to see him watching, his eyes burning with unsated lust.

"You should see it, Reggie," he said huskily. "A cock in your ass, a cock in your pussy. You're stretched so tight around them that it looks impossible you could take them."

Sawyer slid back, dragging his cock across the distended ring of her ass. A hiss of pleasure escaped her, the sound harsh in the silence.

Then he slammed forward, rocking her hard against Cam.

The cry rising from her chest died in her throat and sounded garbled.

Cam's hands gripped her hips as he arched into her, working in rhythm with Sawyer's thrusts. They took turns fucking her, one in, one out.

It was an overwhelming sense of pain mixed with the most exquisite pleasure she'd ever experienced. She couldn't process it, wasn't sure what to do, how to react. So she let them dictate the pace, and she opened herself up to the barrage of sensations.

Finally, she looked back over at Hutch. She let all of her desire, her need, bleed into her expression. Her lips parted in invitation.

Hutch needed no urging, no coaching. He shed his clothing and closed in on her. He crawled up on the bed and levered himself up so that his cock was aimed directly at her mouth.

As Sawyer split her ass even wider apart, she opened her mouth to accept Hutch's cock. It slid between her lips, over her tongue, her taste buds abrading the silky soft foreskin as she sucked him to the back of her throat.

All three men were inside her body. She was connected in this moment to all of them. Her chest expanded. Her heart swelled with love for her guys. *Her guys.*

Cam and Sawyer rocked her between them as Hutch slid back and forth in her mouth. Hutch's hands dug into her hair, holding her head between his palms as he fucked in and out.

She lost her ability to concentrate. She knew nothing but the three cocks fucking her body. Giving her so much pleasure. Good. It felt so good. Nothing would ever feel so wonderful.

Sawyer bent her lower, causing Hutch's cock to slide even deeper. She swallowed convulsively as Hutch strained forward. Sawyer began to ride her hard.

The slap of flesh meeting flesh rose sharply, echoing across the room. Sawyer's thrusts moved her over Cam's cock, and Cam rose sharply to meet Sawyer's movements.

Sawyer's hands dug into her shoulders as he ground her ass down over his cock. She opened wider to him as he forced more of himself inside her.

Tears burned her eyelids, and her cheeks puffed out wider around Hutch's erection.

They were all connected through her. She was the glue holding them together. She was the center of all three men.

A tear slid down her cheek. She loved them so much. How could she have ever run from their love? Through it all, it had remained steady. Like them. Never wavering. She'd never felt so unworthy of something yet so grateful for it at the same time.

"Reggie!" Sawyer cried as he slammed into her once more. She felt the burst of power from him. He trembled against her ass, and then she felt the hot spurt of his release deep inside her.

Hutch withdrew, allowing her to catch her breath just before she screamed as her body caught fire. She sobbed endlessly as her orgasm crashed around her. Instead of a sharp rise and fall, there was just one swell after another. Rising, ever rising.

She was still quaking when Sawyer slipped from her body. His cum seeped from her ass and trickled down the back of her leg as her stretched-out opening quivered and spasmed to regain its shape.

Cam's gentle hands slid up her sides, touching and soothing her.

"I want you to turn around, Reggie darling," he whispered. "Turn around and face Sawyer. I want you to sit on my cock then lean back and let me hold you. Open yourself for Hutch."

Her legs shook uncontrollably as she tried to do his bidding. Finally Hutch picked her up and rotated her body. Cam scooted to the edge of the bed to let his legs dangle over the side then reached for her hips to guide her down over his cock. As Hutch held her arms, Cam held his erection in one hand and eased her down with the other.

He nudged at her ass and slid in easily. She gasped at the fullness the new position offered. She felt him in every nerve ending in her throbbing ass.

"Lean back," Cam murmured. "I've got you, love."

Hutch moved between her legs and spread them to match Cam's. Her pussy was open and accessible, and Hutch wasted no time fitting himself to her.

He plunged deep. Cam cupped his hands under her ass, offering her up to Hutch like a prize. They moved together, sensuously, fucking her ass and pussy with a finesse she would never have attributed to them.

"You're ours, Reggie," Cam panted. "Only ours. We won't let you go."

Her heart squeezed and fluttered at his words.

Hutch stared down at her, the same determination in his green eyes. There was tenderness in his expression, but at the same time, there was a ferocity that took her breath away.

Cam's fingers dug into her ass as he raised her and lowered her onto his cock. Hutch's hands curled around the underside of her knees and held her legs wide apart as he flexed his hips and thrust deeper inside her.

Sawyer appeared behind Hutch, his skin damp from a shower. His cock was already erect again, and he wrapped his hand around the base, pumping back and forth as his gaze connected with hers.

Hutch closed his eyes and pressed forward, forcing his way

deeper into her pussy. The sense of fullness was overwhelming to her. Sharp. Intense. Edgy and nearly painful.

As he withdrew, her pussy sucked at him, calling him back. He and Cam found their rhythm, alternating their thrusts. Hutch placed his palm over her pelvis and slid his thumb down into her folds and over her clit.

She slammed her eyes shut and clenched her jaw tight as he stroked her clit with every thrust forward. The taut nub was unbearably sensitive, and each touch unleashed a barrage of excruciating streaks of pleasure.

"I need to come," Hutch gritted out. "Are you close, baby? I can't hold out."

She expelled her breath in one long whoosh. "Just keep touching me. Please. Oh, God. Don't stop fucking me."

He increased the pressure on her clit and lunged forward, his cock sliding over engorged tissue.

She screamed. He shouted hoarsely and Cam bucked upward, forcing himself deeper into her ass. She convulsed around both cocks, her body wigging out in fourteen directions.

Gentle hands touched her. Surrounded her. Held her while she came apart.

She murmured her protest when Hutch slid from her body. Cam remained, tightly lodged. He stilled as though waiting. She stirred faintly, gathering her strength.

And then Sawyer stood between her legs, his big hands curving up the inside of her thighs. He gently opened her and with great care, he fit his erection to her quivering opening.

"Can you take me again, Reggie?" he whispered. "I don't think I'll ever get enough of you. I can't touch you without reacting like an adolescent."

She moaned and slumped against Cam's damp chest. Cam's

hands skated up her sides, lovingly, soothing her overwrought nerves.

Before she could muster a coherent response, Sawyer thrust forward. She took him. All of him. Shock ricocheted up her spine as another orgasm exploded through her pussy.

No preamble, no work up. Just a sudden and explosive burst.

"Ah Jesus, Reggie." Sawyer's groan filled the room, and he began rocking against her. Hard. There was no gentleness in his possession, and it was definitely a possession.

He owned her. Oh yeah, he did. Body and soul. He owned her heart.

He drove her hard into Cam, but Cam cradled her. Sheltered her with his body. Cam's movements stilled as Sawyer's became more fierce.

As suddenly as her own orgasm had flashed, Sawyer stiffened and let out a hoarse yell. He thrust his hips forward, locking them against her. He slumped over her for a long moment, his breathing harsh and erratic.

"Oh Christ, Reggie. Honey, I'm sorry. That was fast."

She managed a weak smile and kissed his shoulder. "Not as fast as I was."

He withdrew as Cam smoothed his hands down her arms. Cam kissed the back of her neck, and she shivered. Despite the fact she'd just come again, she couldn't control the rise of desire. Sweet, warm. Love could do that.

"Help her," Cam said.

Sawyer reached down and picked her up. Cam's cock slid free of her ass, and she moaned at the sensation. Before she could complain, Cam reclaimed her, taking her from Sawyer's arms.

If she thought he would treat her delicately, she was wrong.

He dropped her on the bed, turned her over and mounted her swiftly. His cock slid back into her ass in one powerful thrust.

She fell forward onto the mattress, her hands splaying out to catch herself. Cam came with her, molding her back to his chest as his hips pumped relentlessly.

All of his earlier restraint was gone. He took her with a frenzy she wasn't used to from him. Out of control. Wild and delicious. A hidden reserve that had sprung free.

His mouth brushed over her shoulder. She gasped when his teeth sank into her skin.

His legs tangled with hers, pushing outward to spread her even further.

And then she felt fingers twine with hers. On either side. The warm brush of a sensual touch. Comforting. Sawyer and Hutch.

They gripped her hands and held her as Cam arched over her body again and again. Soft words drifted through the air, but she was beyond hearing them.

She curled her fingers around theirs and held on as Cam bucked. Faster and faster. He rode her furiously, and then she felt his release. It rolled over his body like a tidal wave. Every muscle rippled and shuddered against her.

Heated spurts filled her. Hot and exotic. She tried to push her ass up higher, to take more of him, but she was completely and utterly spent. And so she lay there as his hips rocked against her ass.

Slower now. More gentle. Then he stopped, resting inside her body as though he hated the idea of pulling away. "This better damn well not be good-bye, Reggie. I won't let you go."

Her heart fluttered with hope. Emotion clogged her throat until breathing became hard.

"Get off her, Cam. Let her breathe."

Sawyer's voice, gentle and unaccusing, ended the silence.

Cam rolled away, but his hands found her, stroking and petting.

"Are you all right, love?" he murmured close to her ear.

She couldn't speak. Hell, she couldn't even open her eyes. She was wasted.

"Reggie, honey, you can't lay there like you're dead. Hutch will worry."

There was a thread of amusement in Sawyer's voice that almost made her grin. If she'd had the energy.

"Oh, I don't know. She doesn't have to be conscious for me to fuck her," Hutch said casually.

She lifted one hand and curled down all her fingers except her middle one. Even that took more effort than it was worth.

Three sets of chuckles filled the room, and despite her fatigue, she smiled into the sheets.

"I suppose we should let her sleep," Cam said magnanimously.

"Don't go," she mumbled.

"Not going anywhere, baby," Hutch said. "We're going to clean you up and then put you to bed."

She nodded, although she had no desire to move.

Sawyer leaned over to brush his lips across her ear. "But when you wake up, we're going to talk."

CHAPTER 39

egina woke to warm bodies surrounding her. Or maybe she was surrounding them. She was sprawled across Hutch's chest, her arm and leg locked possessively over him. His left hand rested on her shoulder, and she angled her head to see the raw wounds around his wrists. She frowned at the reminder of how close she came to losing him.

She turned her face so that she could kiss the red skin.

A stubbly jaw pressed to the center of her back and a hairy leg was laid over the back of hers. Cam.

Which meant Sawyer was probably gone. Disappointment edged her contentment for the moment, but when she looked down, she saw him propped up on his elbow, at the end of the bed, watching her.

Without a word, she pushed herself off of Hutch and crawled down to the end, reversing her position on the bed.

Sawyer opened his arms to her and she settled her head on his chest and stretched out her legs between Cam and Hutch.

"Are you okay?" Sawyer murmured against her hair.

Oh yeah, she was more than okay. Life didn't get any better than this. When she looked up, Hutch and Cam both stared back at her. Cam cupped his hand over her leg and rubbed up and down in a gentle motion.

"We weren't too hard on you?" Cam asked.

Heat bloomed in her cheeks. "You gave me exactly what I wanted," she whispered.

Sawyer ran his hand through her hair, and then kissed the top of her head. She turned so that she could see him as well.

"You didn't hurt me, Sawyer. I don't know what you're thinking right now, but I swear if you pull away from me again, I won't be responsible for the injuries you incur."

He chuckled and dropped another kiss on her forehead. His lips lingered for a long moment, and he stroked a finger lightly over her cheek.

"Whose job is it to feed me today?" she asked. "I need to talk to all of you, but I'm not going to do it naked or with you naked, because you distract me."

Hutch grinned. "I'll feed you, baby."

She quickly shook her head. "No. I'll cook. I don't want you hurting your wrists."

She could swear that Cam paled. Hutch placed his hand on her knee. "No offense, baby, but you and cooking don't exactly get along. Plus, I'm fine. Just a little raw, but it doesn't affect my fingers."

She gazed doubtfully at him.

"I'll go down and help him, Reggie," Cam offered. "Anything to keep you out of the kitchen."

She glared at him and nudged him in the chest with her foot. He grinned and captured her foot, pressing a kiss to her toes.

"Guess that means you get a shower with me," Sawyer said. "There are advantages to not being able to cook worth a shit."

Cam rolled his eyes and then crawled off the bed.

Despite the lightness of their moods, Regina could still sense the strain, their hesitancy. They were worried. Even after last night.

Suddenly she couldn't wait to talk to them, to tell them how much she loved them. Food could wait. This couldn't.

"I don't want breakfast, after all," she said.

Hutch lifted one brow in shock. Sawyer's hand froze on her shoulder, and Cam stopped on his way to pick up his clothing.

"Ah hell, I knew she had a head injury," Hutch muttered. "I never should have let her talk us out of taking her to the hospital."

She laughed and planted her foot in his chest. She pushed out of Sawyer's arms and rolled to the edge of the bed.

"You've got ten minutes to get dressed and meet me downstairs. Living room."

Without waiting for their reaction, she darted for the bathroom to take a quick shower. When she stepped out a few minutes later, the room was empty.

Nervous excitement ran circles through her chest as she pulled on her clothes. This was huge. This was the rest of her life.

A year ago, she would have never imagined that she'd be taking a step like this, but she felt completely at peace with her decision.

She loved Cam, Sawyer and Hutch. Always had. They'd been hers since they were children. Their friendship, their bond, had only strengthened over the years and had taken the next logical step from simple friendship to physical intimacy and deep love.

She all but flew down the steps, her muscles quivering with anticipation. When she rounded the stairs into the living room, all three men were there.

Cam was at the window, staring out the front, his hands shoved into his pockets. His posture was stiff, uneasy. Sawyer was sprawled on the couch, leaning back, his stance seemingly at ease, but his brow was creased in concentration. Hutch sat forward in the chair catty-corner to Sawyer. His elbows dug into his knees, and his expression was solemn.

Now that she was here, she had no idea how to go about telling them everything that was in her heart. How could she possibly put into words the depth of her love? There weren't enough words in the English language to get across just how much they meant to her.

"I love you," she blurted out.

Three heads turned in her direction. Warmth spread through their faces. Cam relaxed his stance, but still he waited, not moving. Her knees shook, and her hands were clammy. She'd never been so afraid in her life. But she forged ahead, determined to make them understand.

"I love you," she said again. "All of you. So much."

"We love you," Cam said simply.

She moved closer, into the living room, not comfortable sitting. She remained at a distance, needing it in order to keep her composure.

"I want to stay. If you'll still have me."

The three men tensed. Hutch's hands curled into fists.

"If we'll have you?" Hutch said in disbelief. "Baby, I'm not sure you're going to get a choice in the matter. I've even researched the penalty for kidnapping a police officer and tying her to a bed."

A grin twitched the corners of her mouth. Her legs were trembling, and so she slid onto the couch at the opposite end to where Sawyer sat.

"I've been unfair," she said in a low voice. When they would have protested, she held a hand up. "Let me finish please. I have so much to say. So much to apologize for."

She looked at all three as tears swam in her vision. "I don't know why you haven't given up on me. I've spent the last year running from you, from your love. I lied to you, to myself, pushed you away, and yet you still never gave up. Why?" she asked as she forced her gaze to them once more.

"Because we love you," Cam said. "I can't offer you a more complicated answer. It's just that simple."

Her chest swelled with emotion. It was all she could do to remain sitting, when she wanted to launch herself into his arms. Never let go of him.

"I know you think I only stayed because of the danger to all of you," she said in a low voice.

Three expressions suddenly became brooding.

"Why did you stay, Reggie?" Sawyer asked in a soft voice. Dangerously soft. Deceptive because of the steel thread lining his words.

She looked down at her hands. "At the time I told myself that I was staying to protect you, so I could keep an eye on you. I said all sorts of things to justify my reasons for wanting to be with you. I was afraid."

"Afraid of what, baby?" Hutch asked.

"Of it not working, and destroying me when it didn't," she said.

"And what about now?" Sawyer prompted.

She returned his gaze. "I realized that I didn't trust you." She flinched when he winced. "That didn't come out right. I do trust you. I've always trusted you. But when it came to believing that this could work between us, I just didn't trust that you could all deal with . . . sharing . . . me. I was so worked up over having to make sure each of you was satisfied. I was freaking out over the idea of being all things to all three of you, and it left me wondering if there would be anything left, if I would lose myself trying to be something I wasn't."

"Oh, baby," Hutch said, his breath forcefully exhaling in a rush. "We never meant for you to feel that way."

Cam crossed the room and knelt in front of her, taking her hands in his and squeezing gently.

"We only wanted you to be yourself, Reggie darling. We love you. Not your idea of perfection. You're stubborn, impossibly stubborn. Pigheaded, obstinate, can't cook worth a damn, but we wouldn't change a thing about you."

Her mouth crooked upward in a smile. "You know, you should really try to control yourself when listing my many attributes. All that praise could go to a girl's head."

Cam chuckled and cupped her face in his hand. "See? That's why we love you so damn much. You're an irreverent hoyden, and when you're old and gray, we still won't be able to keep up with you."

She softened all over and sagged into his hand. The idea of growing old and gray with them touched on every dream she'd ever imagined.

"I want to stay," she said. "I love you all so much, and I want this to work between us."

"We love you too," Cam said. He tugged her closer and touched his lips to hers in a sweet kiss.

She pulled away and glanced up at Hutch and Sawyer, who wore similar expressions of contentment. Then she stood, moving past Cam to pace the confines of the living room.

"I don't want to quit my job. I know you all hate it and that you worry. I spoke to my chief . . . about us. I was up-front in that if I ever had to choose between you and my job, that I'd choose you hands down."

Shock shone in the guys' expressions as they stared back at her.

"I'll be careful. I'm always careful, but my job is a big part of who I am, and I don't want that to change. I don't want to stay home and for you to take care of me. I don't like feeling helpless. I'd much rather come home after a long shift and have you take care of me," she added with a grin.

"And you have to promise to be patient with me." She quickly went on before they could respond. She twisted her hands in front of her then wiped them down her jeans. "I'm not used to unconditional love. It sort of freaks me out. I'm sure I'll piss you off on a regular basis, but know that I love you more than anything, and I'll do whatever it takes to make this work."

Her speech was over. Three men descended on her at once, their expressions ranging from fierce to loving and all parts in between.

"We don't want to change a damn thing about you," Sawyer said first, as he dragged her into his arms. Hutch and Cam hovered nearby, their warmth enfolding her in its embrace.

"Yeah, we hate your job because we worry about you, but we'd never ask you to quit, honey. We don't want to change you. We love you just the way you are. Beautiful. Insufferable. But you're also the air we breathe."

She stared up at him in shock. Sawyer getting mushy? But what she saw in his eyes stunned her. They glistened with unshed tears, and there was such love and devotion in his gaze that her knees threatened to buckle.

"You're such a damn liar," she whispered. "You said you didn't know anything about murmuring sweet things."

He grinned and slowly released her as Cam moved forward to take her in his arms.

Cam didn't say a word. He simply swept her against his chest and lowered his lips to hers, drinking deeply of her. Her hands tangled in his mussed hair as she melted against him.

"I need you, Reggie. I'll always need you," he said against her lips. "Stay. Be with me. Always."

"You'll never get rid of me now," she murmured.

His eyes glittered with satisfaction, and then she was pulled away as Hutch claimed her.

He wrapped his strong arms around her and held her tight. Squeezing. His body shook with emotion and his chest heaved in and out.

"I love you," he said in a choked voice. "I'll always love you, baby."

She closed her eyes as tears slipped down her cheeks. It was simply too much. All she could ever want was here for the taking. She gripped him, curling her arms around his waist. She inhaled his masculine scent, taking it deep inside her soul.

The path to happiness was a twisted road with more pitfalls and barriers than a minefield. So what if hers wasn't more conventional? All that mattered was that these men loved her, and she loved them. The rest of the world could go fuck themselves.

She could make them happy. For the first time, she didn't question that. And they could make her happy. They already did.

"Anyone want breakfast?" she asked. "I'm cooking."

She broke away from Hutch and started for the kitchen, an insane grin on her face. She mentally counted and before she hit three, the protests started.

Sawyer all but tackled her. His arms surrounded her, and he plucked her off her feet. He threw her over his shoulder and did a quick spin, chuckling the entire time.

"Quit torturing Cam and Hutch, honey."

She giggled as she flopped against his back like a rag doll.

Cam bent and nudged her chin up with his fingers. He kissed

her lightly. "Hutch and I will cook, love. You, however, are in charge of dessert."

Sawyer's hand tightened on her ass. She smiled back at Cam. "I think I can handle dessert, but I never realized you had such a sweet tooth," she teased.

"Only for you, Reggie darling. Only for you."